CW01551771

The Legend of the Teenage Sages

by

Jacob Cortez

Bloomington, IN

Milton Keynes, UK

AuthorHouse™
1663 Liberty Drive, Suite 200
Bloomington, IN 47403
www.authorhouse.com
Phone: 1-800-839-8640

AuthorHouse™ UK Ltd.
500 Avebury Boulevard
Central Milton Keynes, MK9 2BE
www.authorhouse.co.uk
Phone: 08001974150

First published by AuthorHouse 9/11/2006

ISBN: 1-4259-4955-X (sc)
ISBN: 1-4259-4954-1 (dj)

Library of Congress Control Number: 2006906177

Printed in the United States of America
Bloomington, IndianaThis book is printed on acid-free paper.

I would like to dedicate this book to Mrs. Edith Lentz—
my teacher and more importantly my friend.
Thank you for all your support and hard work.
You have made my dream come true.

I would like to give a special thanks to my Mom's best friend, Deborah Briese. Thank your for all your editing and ideas on making my story come to life.
I would also like to thank my parents and friends for their encouragement and help with this long process.

Thank you…

The Legend Begins

Long ago, before dinosaurs roamed the Earth; before sea creatures existed— before life itself arose, the Gods had a plan to create a world of Magic and Wonder. They sent fourteen Angels from the Heavens to construct Their dream:

The Angels of Fire and Magma created volcanoes.
The Angels of Water and Ice created oceans and glaciers.
The Angels of Wind and Lightning created oxygen and electricity.
The Angels of Earth and Nature created earth and vegetation.
The Angels of Telekinesis and Telepathy
created knowledge and people.
The Angels of Mythical Creatures and Magic
created myth, animals, and sorcery.
The Angels of Darkness and Light created Hatred and Good.

These Angels created the world known as *Earth.*

The Gods wanted Earth to be a place of Peace and Serenity; a place without Evil. So They sent the Angels to Earth once again to spread Knowledge through the Peoples and Beings, and to teach them the Way of Life. But the Gods' greatest enemy, Satan, created his own Evil beings of Hatred and terror and sent them to Earth under the command of his apprentice, Apocalypse. These horrible Beings wanted to rule all through Pain and Misery while destroying Good.

The Angels of the Heavens knew they had to stop Evil from polluting their peaceful creation, but they also knew that they were not powerful enough to defeat him individually. So, they traveled to the highest point on Earth, Mount Everest in Nepal. The Angels soared to the peak, and began chanting an ancient Prayer of their kind. Their Powers combined, and two became one so their was only seven:

The Sage of Fire and Magma
The Sage of Water and Ice
The Sage of Weather
The Sage of Earth
The Sage of Telekinesis and Telepathy
The Sage of Myth
The Sage of Darkness and Light.

The Sages set out to protect the Earth from Hatred and Tyranny. They fought many battles to spread the Knowledge and Power of Good. The Sages sent a Mythical mist through the air that changed the nature of the beings who breathed it. These Mutants had the power to stop Evil, but only when in contact with the Sages. Satan took advantage of this weakness by attacking the Heavens and forcing the Sages to come to its defense, since control of the Heavens meant control of many other Worlds besides Earth. During their absences from Earth, the Mutants could easily be swayed by Apocalypse to join the forces of Evil.

In order to thwart Apocalypse, the Sages created twenty-one artifacts, known as their Treasure, to hold and restore their Power while they were away from the Earth. Because the Treasure also held part of their Spirits, it had to be entrusted to worthy living Beings who would ensure its safety, and use it only for the Good of all Beings. The Sages already knew who would be Chosen to receive the Treasure in order to begin reclaiming the Peace and Serenity of the Earth. They also appointed certain special Beings to spread the Treasure throughout the Earth, hoping that at least some of it would not fall into the hands of Evil, until the time it could be claimed by the Chosen. These Beings could be trusted implicitly to recognize and aid the Chosen on their way to becoming the new Sages. However, once the Chosen obtain the Treasure, they would have trouble protecting it and keeping it for their own. Locating the Treasure would be a test to see if those Chosen were ready to claim their Final Power and fulfill their

Destiny as the New Sages; to keep that Power for eternity and be willing to work together on their quest to protect the Heavens, Earth, and other Worlds in the universe.

In order for the Chosen to finally claim their Destiny as the New Sages, they would have to complete yet another test; the test that would allow them to unlock their Final Power. The Ancient Sages protected the Final Powers by hiding them in places outside the reach of Evil. The separate Keys to unlocking the Powers could be found only by each Chosen upon the completion of certain tasks. In the first parts of the Testing, much Power would be gained, yet was easily controllable. In order to unleash the Truth of the Final Power, the Chosen would have to look within themselves, which would be far more difficult than the Future Sages would be used to. Each Chosen would have to express their acceptance of and desire for becoming their true Inner Self. The desire to become whomever they really are inside would be the most important step towards becoming a New Sage. For one can 'accept' that their nature is to be Evil, but not choose to actively follow that path, just as one can be Good yet not 'desire' to actively do that which is Good. The way to Final Power would be very different from the previously bestowed Powers, for the acceptance of their Destiny would also take some getting used to. But that is only the beginning of what would be in store for them.

The Earth and Worlds have undergone extensive growth and change in the many eons since the Earth began, and the words of the Ancient Sages have long since faded into legend. The Way of Evil is again threatening the Knowledge of the Way of Good. Now is the time for the legendary Ancient Sages to reveal the identities of the Chosen. The Future Sages don't know who they are inside because they are teenagers; ordinary teenagers with an extraordinary Destiny they are totally unaware of. They will have to find their Powers and use them to prevent Evil by becoming part of the Spirits of the legendary Fourteen Angels known as the Seven Ancient Sages.

But First—they will have to find the Beginning…

Chapter 1—The Best of Teenage Friends

A cold drenching rain, pulsating its way with the wind, pounded along the busy streets of Flagstaff, Arizona. The rain was hammering like wrestlers throwing each other to the ground. A foggy mist hovered over and circled around cars waiting impatiently for the signal lights to change. People were running along the sidewalks; scampering between the awnings of the Old-fashioned storefronts like mice scurrying around trying to find food, shielding their heads from the cold driving rain with plastic bags, newspapers, or simply their crossed arms. Even the lucky few who had managed to bring umbrellas were trying their best to find shelter from the gusting wind and pounding rain.

In the shelter of an awning-covered alleyway were four wet teenagers, nestled close together. During a seeming lull in the buffeting rain, they ran to the nearest indoor shelter they could find—a coffee shop.

It was a small cafe, like the ones in the old days. There were red comfortable-looking booths under the windows hung with dusty lace curtains. The polished floor was a checkerboard of black and white tiles, and small vases of silk wildflowers were on each white table. At the back, a plump waitress with long curly blonde hair in a pink uniform dress and a grubby white apron was washing the shiny top of the counter with what looked like a very old, dirty rag. She disappeared through a swinging door behind the counter while the four sodden teenagers were making their way towards a booth in the corner under a window. The two teenage guys and two teenage girls knew each other very well. In fact, you could say they had known each other their entire lives, having lived within blocks of each other in the same small neighborhood in Flagstaff since birth. The had been inseparable since their first meeting at the local preschool, and their friendship had only grown along with them through the years.

Sitting at the far side of the table were the two teenage boys. The one on the left was Jake, who was very tall for his age. At school, he often felt like a giraffe walking around amongst tiny ants. He was fourteen years old and about six feet tall. He had short, thick brown hair, light brown eyes, and a small pair of silvery-rimmed glasses. Ever since he was little, Jake had always tried his best to make the right choices: he would never try to climb on top of the refrigerator to get to the cookie jar, because he truly believed that it *would* spoil his dinner. However, that doesn't mean that Jake can't think for himself. He was a natural born leader, who could easily inspire others with his confident, thoughtful manner and wry sense of humor. He doesn't like to see anyone picked on or left behind, and he would never give up once he decided to tackle something, be it homework or tree climbing. No matter how many times he crashed his bike when he was little, or took a tumble rollerblading, he would always get back up and try again, even if he already had a ton of bruises. Jake also made a point to help everyone out the best he can, and was the one everyone came to with problems, because they knew he would help find a solution, no matter what.

The teenage boy who was sitting next to Jake was also tall, but not as tall as Jake. Mike was also fourteen years old, and had sea blue eyes and long black hair down to his shoulders that he mostly kept in a ponytail. He always wore dark clothing, preferably black. Mike had a muscular build, which all the girls at school loved, and he wore a gold halo earring in his left ear. But mostly what made Mike, *Mike,* was that he liked to take chances: whether it was coming up with a wild answer on a homework question or riding his bike up and over the biggest ramp on the block. Any time a wild opportunity presented itself to Mike, he would do it. He loved to do crazy things, but that is what his three best friends loved about him. He would never back down from a challenge, whether it was a game, a bet, or a dare. Unfortunately, that also included fights, which made his friends upset, and sometimes a little nervous. Mike would never get into a physical fight with any of his three friends, but at school some kids wanted to fight him just because they thought it made them look cool, and he would just go right ahead and do it without thinking about the consequences. The good thing is that Mike never starts the fight, so he never gets into much trouble. But lately, Mike didn't want everyone at school to be scared of him, so he had been laying low on the whole fighting thing, and his friends had been helping him do so. He listens to his friends most of the time, because he cares about their opinions.

The teenage girl who sat across from Mike was Toni. Like the others, she was fourteen. Toni had long, curly black hair which, like Mike, she kept in a ponytail. She always said that she doesn't like her curly hair, but the others always disagree. She was half African-American, and had an olive complexion with dark brown almond-shaped eyes. Toni was short for her age and, some would say, a little on the plump side. She always liked to dress stylishly, like everyone else at her middle school, so that people wouldn't make fun of her and would like her. Toni was the funny one of the group. She always made the others laugh even when they were feeling down. She always has a joke or funny comment to cheer them up. The only thing is, when a serious matter occurred, she often joked about it. But her friends always forgive her, because they know she is only trying to make them feel better, which all four friends loved.

Sitting across from Jake, beside Toni, was the oldest of the four. Her name was Rebecca, but Toni, Jake, and Mike all called her Becca, for short. She was also fourteen, but was a few days older than the rest. Strangely, all four of the teens were born in the same month—December. Becca was a very kind and caring person. She had long, light blonde, silky hair and blue eyes behind thick glasses. Her skin was smooth and fair, and she had a thin, but muscular build. Becca was the smart one in the group. In fact, she's probably the smartest one at her middle school. She was fluent in four different languages: Spanish, French, German, and of course English. She also had taught herself how to read ancient Egyptian hieroglyphics as well as several other pictographic languages. This was definitely a talent Becca had, but the other three said it was a gift, mainly because she helped them a lot on their Spanish homework. Becca doesn't get offended when people make fun of her intelligence. She enjoyed being knowledgeable on many different topics, and wasn't afraid to prove people wrong, but never in a way that would hurt anyone's feelings.

Once the four had settled in and were looking over the laminated menu, they looked up when the impatient tapping of a high-heeled shoe echoed in the nearly empty coffee shop. They looked towards the back of the shop to see the waitress leaning against the front of the counter, arms crossed and toe tapping impatiently. "Well, are you going to order something to drink or are you just taking up table space?" asked the waitress sarcastically, one penciled-in eyebrow raised.

"Ah… yes. Of course," said Jake, politely. "I'll take a cappuccino."

Toni gave the waitress a dirty look in reply, but luckily the waitress had already turned back to the counter to pick up a tattered, little spiral notebook. "That sounds great. I'll take one for me, too," Becca agreed while the waitress stalked over to the table. She looked at the others, and they nodded in agreement.

"Same for us, too, please," said Mike, gesturing between Toni and himself.

"Okay, then," said the waitress, as she wrote the order down in her torn-up notebook. "Would you like anything in your cappuccino?" she said sarcastically. "Flavored syrup or sugar, perhaps?" She came across very rudely.

"We would each like extra cream in our cappuccino, but no flavoring, thank you," said Becca kindly. Becca knew the waitress was being rude, but firing sarcasm back at her wasn't going to solve anything.

"All right, then." The waitress stomped off, her footsteps echoing on the tile throughout the entire coffee shop.

"What was *that* all about?" asked Toni, puzzled. She stared off after the waitress with narrow eyes.

Mike laughed as a grin appeared on his face. "My opinion is that she was back in the kitchen enjoying her time flirting with the chef until some loud, obnoxious, wet kids walked in just because they needed shelter to get out of the rain." The others laughed.

"She's a waitress, for crying out loud! We're only expecting her to do her job. Why would she act like that?" asked Jake. He wasn't use to being treated rudely by an adult, so he was slightly taken aback.

"Well, I guess that means no tip for her," laughed Becca, as she looked past the counter where the unattended cappuccino maker stood.

"That's funny, I don't see the waitress anywhere, and the cappuccino maker is right behind the counter." She looked around. "Where is she?"

"I don't know," said Jake getting up from the booth. "I'll go see what the hold up is." He walked over to the counter and rang the silver bell next to the cash register. Nobody responded. Nothing happened. Jake looked back at the other three and saw them shrug. He turned around and rang the bell once more while trying to see through the little window in the kitchen door. Still nothing happened, and no one showed. "Hello?" Jake called. "Are our drinks going to be ready soon?" Jake could hear giggling from the kitchen. He wasn't in the mood to put up with this. He turned to the others. "Let's get out of here, guys. I don't think we'll be seeing those drinks anytime soon." The others got up from the booth and followed Jake out the door.

Toni gave the string of hanging bells an extra hard shake as she passed through. "*Some servi*—hey, the rain stopped!" she said, peering up at the gray sky.

"Good," said Becca excitedly. "I want to get back to the tree house and read comic books. Today's Sunday and school's tomorrow, so I want to finish up the comic book I'm on—I'm at a really good part!" The others nodded in agreement. One thing they all had in common was a love of reading comic books. They thought it was cool that the characters in them could have superpowers, so they found the comics they read entertaining and interesting.

The teens were walking along the wet, dirty sidewalk, huddled together for warmth. "Hey, I forgot!" yelled Mike suddenly. "There's a fair after school Friday night at the fairgrounds, and it's only about five minutes away from the school. There's supposed to be awesome rides!"

"I'm surprised you forgot about something like that," laughed Toni. Mike wasn't the type to forget exciting events.

Becca and Jake laughed, nodding in agreement. "You got a point there Toni," said Jake grinning.

Mike looked at them with pleading eyes. "So, do you guys want to go?"

Jake laughed, looking at the others. "It sounds fun to me."

Toni nodded. "Yeah, it will be something to do around here—it would be a good break from school."

"What about all of Friday's *homework*?" Becca asked, eyebrows raised. "I want to get that done..."

"Come on, Becca!" Mike pleaded. He couldn't believe she was even thinking about turning something like this down. "The fair only comes once a year, and if we miss this one, we'll have to wait a whole other year until the next one!" Mike stopped and made puppy eyes at Becca. "*Please*?" he begged, rolling his lower lip into a pout.

Becca said nothing and then sighed, "Alright—stop nagging me."

Mike laughed as he put his arm around Becca. "I knew you would come through." Becca looked up at him and rolled her eyes. Toni and Jake laughed. After a ten-minute walk, the teens finally arrived at the tree house in Becca's two-acre backyard. Her yard had white horse fence all around it, and beyond that was the National Forest where the teens could look out the tree house windows to watch elk and deer walk gracefully out of the woods to nibble the shrubs along the fence.

Becca's parents had built the tree house for her and her friends, because she was an only child. It was an *okay*-looking tree house made out of logs that they had all helped her dad haul back from the forest. It was square with windows on all four sides that could be opened and two big skylights in the ceiling. It had a rough, cedar-shingled roof and was tall enough for someone to stand up inside without hitting their head. (Only Jake, once in while, had trouble remembering that part, since he was the only one that had to crouch down an inch.) The entrance to the tree house was a trap door in the center floor that was reached by a rope ladder about fifteen feet long. The floor space inside, with the trapdoor closed, could easily fit five or six people laying down, so there was plenty of room for the four teens and all of their belongings.

They climbed up through the trap door and found the corner where their sleeping bags and pillows were kept. Sunday night was 'Comic Book Night' for the four. They had worked very hard the previous school year in order to earn the privilege from their parents. So, every Sunday night, rain or shine, Jake, Mike, and Toni would all spend the night at the tree house. A large blue cooler on wheels also sat in one corner in the back. Becca's mom usually packed them dinner, snacks, and cold drinks since she knew how much they hated to miss even a moment of Comic Book Night to come in for dinner. She usually left the cooler on the back porch, but Becca's dad must have hauled the cooler up into the tree house for them using the pulley system Jake had rigged up. Each teen took a sleeping bag and pillow from the pile and spread it out under their favorite window, returning to the cooler to stock up on munchies before plopping down to get started on some serious comic book reading. After the initial jockeying for position with book bags, pillows, drinks, and snacks, they all fell silent, reading until it was too dark to see the words.

"You know the rules, guys," said Becca. Her eyes were already halfway shut. "Once it gets dark, it's time for bed."

"Yeah, we know," said Toni grumpily. She closed her comic book, stretched both her arms out in front of her, and groaned loudly as she returned the comic to the huge pile next to the cooler, which she had been using as a backrest. She then slumped down on her sleeping bag. "I really don't want to go to school tomorrow."

"Summer's almost here though," said Jake as he climbed into his sleeping bag and fluffed the pillow behind his head with both hands. "Hopefully, the rest of the school year will go by quickly— but you would never know with the amount of homework that these teachers give us." The others sighed and they all gazed out the skylights up into the velvety black starry sky. Mike grumbled sleepily and turned toward the wall. "They are *so* beautiful, aren't they?" A smile lit up Becca's face and her eyes twinkled with reflected starlight.

Jake laughed. "You sure love the stars, don't you Becca." He propped his head up on his elbow and turned to looked at her.

She looked back across the trapdoor at him and smiled. "Goodnight everybody," said Becca, snuggling into her pillow.

"Goodnight," they all echoed, settling in for the night. Silence crept through the room, broken only by the occasional snore from Toni and the rustle of sleeping bags from the teens. Outside, a concert of crickets and night birds chirruped peacefully in the clear night.

Chapter 2—Back To School

Becca was woken up by a loud, snorting snore from Toni. She shut her eyes tightly and stretched. "I can't believe I've learned to sleep through that," she said while yawning hugely. Becca abruptly raised her arm and checked her watch. Her eyes went wide and she shrieked in dismay. The other three woke with pounding hearts.

"What's the matter?" asked Jake worriedly, his eyes only half open.

"Are they here?" asked Mike still half-asleep. The others turned to stare at him, puzzled.

"You guys!" yelled Becca, panic in her voice. "We have five minutes to get to school before the bell rings, and it takes ten minutes to walk there!" Becca had never been late in the whole time she had attended school. Being late for school, for Becca, was like getting a failing grade on your report card.

"Well, it only takes five minutes to run there," said Toni grinning. She immediately regretted saying this once she saw the look on Becca's face.

"Then let's quit chatting and move!" shouted Becca. All four teens squirmed rapidly out of their sleeping bags. In all the commotion to grab the correct shoes and book bags, there was a loud bang and a cry of pain.

Mike looked over at Jake. "Are you okay, man?"

Jake laughed, gingerly rubbing the lump on his head with eyes squinted shut. "I'm okay, but I don't think the roof is..." He peered cautiously sideways up at the ceiling.

"We'll have to fix it when we get back," said Mike, looking at the new crack in the board ceiling. "We don't have time right now to worry about it. We have to go or 'you know who' will ring our necks!" he said slyly nodding his head towards Becca who was grabbing her backpack and plunging through the trapdoor and down the ladder. The others did the same and followed her down hurriedly. Becca was running across the yard with the others following closely behind as if she were in a relay race.

"Wait up!" Toni called after her. Toni wasn't the best runner, but she was doing a fairly good job keeping up with Jake and Mike who were right on Becca's heels.

Becca looked like a prisoner trying to run away from three cops. They dodged traffic haphazardly as they went across the street. There was another group of kids also running hard up the sidewalk in front of the school, but Becca pushed through them like a bowling ball knocking down pins.

The other three teens were panting heavily, frantically trying to keep up with her. About the time Becca barreled through the double doors, Jake and the others were just passing the group of kids that she had plowed through the middle of. "Sorry about that," Jake called to the kids as the teens flew past them in their frantic attempt to get in the front door before the final bell rang.

"We have forty seconds to get to class before the bell rings!" screeched Becca from the doorway. "If we're late, my mom won't let you guys stay over on Sunday nights anymore. So, you better get a move on!" Her watch was programmed to precisely the same time as the school's clocks. Of course, that didn't surprise the others.

The teens jogged up the cement stairs past the pine trees, through the open doors, and ran down the hall where all the lockers were. "Guys, I just realized something," said Toni out of breath, grasping her backpack tightly so it wouldn't slip down her shoulders. "I think those kids we knocked into back there were—"

"Toni, we have no time!" shouted Becca, still running as fast as her legs could carry her. "We have exactly ten seconds until the bell rings." The classroom was five paces in front of them. They ran inside their 'Skills for Success' class, and fell into their desks with five seconds to spare. "Yessss! We made it!" cried Becca happily.

Mike, Jake, and Toni looked like they had been underwater for hours and were finally able to gasp for air. Becca, however, looked perfectly normal; as if nothing happened—she wasn't even breathing heavily.

"I don't know how you do it, Becca," wheezed Mike, out of breath. He looked at the others leaning back in their chairs, breathless. "We're totally beat! I don't know why we decided to be a madman like you—we would have been better off walking and being late!"

"You guys, I have been trying to tell you—" Toni was cut off by the bell, followed almost immediately by a group of kids dressed in black that ran into the classroom.

"You're *late*," said Mr. Zolvitch sternly to the kids in black as they were passing his desk. "One more time and it's a week's detention for the four of you." The kids turned toward Jake, Toni, Mike, and Becca, and gave them an evil glare. All the teens, except Toni, looked around, bewildered.

"Those were the kids we shoved out of the way?" Becca asked. She glanced briefly over her shoulder at the kids who had sat down at their desks in the back row. The kids glared back at her.

"I've been trying to tell you that," replied Toni, shaking her head. "It's your fault that you don't listen."

"I didn't even notice it was them," said Jake, turning to the others. "I was running so fast trying to keep up with *you*," he scowled at Becca.

"You four!" yelled Mr. Zolvitch, turning from the whiteboard and facing the teens. "No talking while I'm talking!" The four teens immediately faced the front where Mr. Zolvitch was lecturing. "Today," he said, "we'll have a free day. Only a couple of days until summer break, so I'll let you work on your homework in groups if you talk *quietly* amongst yourselves." Chaos broke out instantly, but soon calmed while the class pawed through their backpacks pulling out textbooks, notebooks, and pencils. Mr. Zolvitch was a weird teacher. He joked around a lot, pretending that students had gotten into trouble—but those times when he really did yell they had a hard time figuring out if he really meant it or not. Mr. Zolvitch had a beer belly and always wore long pants and long-sleeved shirts. He had a black beard striped with gray down the middle and wore thick plastic-framed glasses.

Becca leaned over toward the other three. "I already finished my homework," she whispered.

"Good!" said Mike quietly. "Then you can finish my Spanish homework, I still have to finish my math."

Becca stared at him, mouth slightly open.

"Same here," said Jake, suddenly reaching for Toni's homework. He handed both papers to Becca with a sweet smile.

Becca stared at the three of them, eyebrows lowered. "All right," she said dully, "but you guys really have to learn to do your own homework."

"I do!" said Jake, pulling out his math homework. "I just didn't want to do it over the weekend…" Jake looked expectantly at Toni.

"Oh—same here," she said quickly, grinning.

Becca shook her head and immediately started to work. She was an extremely fast writer and worker. As she was zipping through their homework, Toni and Jake busily stared at the ceiling, counting in their heads. Mike was whistling tunelessly through his teeth as he worked on his math. Mr. Zolvitch turned to the whiteboard and started writing words with a black marker copying from a piece of paper he held in his left hand. While his back was turned, one of the four kids dressed in black threw a crumpled piece of paper across the whispering room, which landed with a soft thud on Becca's desk. Becca immediately stopped writing and focused on the ball of paper. The other three teens looked over at her. She took the paper, opened it up, and read it quickly. Her eyes got wider and she rolled them in circles.

Toni stared at Becca, curiosity evident on her face. "So…*what does it say?*" she asked.

"See for yourself," replied Becca as she handed Toni the note. Mike and Jake leant over Toni's desk as she unfolded the paper. They began to read the note silently:

We'll get you back eventually—you will pay. We suggest that you watch your backs!

–GOTHS

The four teens dressed in all black were a group known as the "Goths". They were the bullies of the school, and everyone was afraid of them; everyone except Mike, Jake, Toni, and Becca, that is. The Goths usually wore black shirts that had skulls or leering faces on them and long chains hanging from their belts connected to their baggy, sagging pants. Lots of kids wore baggy pants, but what made the Goths really strange was the black makeup and the spiked dog collars they wore on their wrists and around their necks. The two guys had jet-black hair that was spiked up in Mohawks with gel, and both the girls had long, straight, greasy black hair all the way to their waists. Felix was the taller guy and the leader of the Goths. John was the shorter guy, but had a mouth to make up for his height. Courtney was the taller girl, and definitely the rudest girl at the school. And Jenna, the smallest one, always found a way to get into trouble.

Toni chuckled and rolled her eyes. "Oh—I'm *scared...*" she said sarcastically.

"What a bunch of jerks!" exclaimed Jake, crumpling up the piece of paper.

"That's probably what they think about us," Becca moaned, "since we're the ones that pounded into them by accident." Although the teens disliked the Goths, they still never wanted to start anything up with them. And besides, the teens were never rude unless they were defending themselves.

Mike's eyes narrowed and his teeth clenched. "I say we go and kick their—"

"That'll only attract attention Mike!" said Jake, cutting him off. "Besides, I don't want to get grounded before the fair Friday night!" He looked at Mike with raised eyebrows, hoping that he was convinced.

"Good point," said Mike, shutting his eyes and shaking his head. It was as though he were in a trance. "I don't want to get grounded either—I want to go to that fair!" He pounded his desk with his fist.

Mr. Zolvitch turned from the board and looked fiercely into Mike's eyes. Mike frowned and looked back down at his homework. Mr. Zolvitch turned back around and continued writing.

Toni raised her head from her work and glared at the others. "So let's keep it cool until at least after the fair on Friday night, all right guys?" she whispered.

The others nodded in agreement and got straight back to work.

Jake looked over at Felix and gave him an unpleasant smile, which Felix did right back at him. The two had been enemies since they arrived at the middle school. Whenever either of them got a chance, they'd start mouthing off at each other, making rude or snide comments. Jake wasn't even sure exactly why they disliked each other.

"Done!" said Becca to the other three as she tossed down her pencil in relief.

"Done? Already?" asked Mike in disbelief. "How could you be *done*? I've only done...1...2...3...4...*four* problems on my math homework!"

"You're forgetting, Mike," said Becca, with a smirk on her face, "that I can speak four different languages fluently."

Mike moaned. "Yeah, I did forget about that, I don't even know how you've managed to learn them so quickly—it's not normal!" Becca rolled her eyes.

"Here," said Jake handing Mike his own math homework. "I'm finished. You can copy mine." Jake sighed, relieved.

Mike grinned. "Thanks." He rapidly started copying down Jake's answers.

Several minutes later, the bell rang. Everyone packed up their books and papers into their backpacks and waited to be dismissed.

"Don't forget," said Mr. Zolvitch. "The Fair Committee is selling tickets in the library. I think its twenty dollars for unlimited rides, and you can play one game at each booth, for one dollar. But remember the number of unlimited wristbands is limited—you guys have fun."

Everyone except for Mike, Jake, Toni and Becca left their seats. They were always the last ones out, so they wouldn't be shoved out the door by the other students trying to get to their next classes.

"Don't forget!" said Mike, before the other three got up. "We have to get the tickets today. We're *ALL* getting the wristbands for unlimited rides." He glared pointedly at Becca.

Becca fell silent. "*Alright*! Stop pressuring me!"

"You all brought twenty bucks to school today, right?" asked Jake.

"Surprisingly," laughed Toni. "I managed to remember mine."

Jake looked questioningly over at Mike. Mike laughed. "Seriously, do you think that I would forget? The question is do you have *yours*?"

Jake laughed. "Yeah I have mine. I was just messing with you." He looked at Becca. "What about you? Did you remember to bring twenty bucks?"

Becca's eyes suddenly went wide—wider than normal. "Darn it! I *forgot*!" she exclaimed.

"Nice try, Drama Queen!" said Mike, shaking his head. He knew she was going to pull something like this. "I brought an extra twenty just in case anyone *forgot*." He reached into his pocket, pulled out a twenty-dollar bill and showed it to Becca with a smirk on his face. "You can pay me back when you get a chance."

"Oh—thanks, Mike," said Becca sarcastically, snatching the bill out of his hand. "*I'll pay you back tomorrow...*"

Mike and Jake were walking next to each other ahead of Becca and Toni. "That was a good one," said Jake, thumping his fist into Mike's fist.

Mike laughed. "Yeah, I know! I'm not stupid. I had a feeling she would pull something like that."

The four stood outside their math class waiting to be let in. Mrs. Coalgian, opened the door from the inside and walked out into the hall, and stood facing all the waiting students. Mrs. Coalgian was a short teacher with short, curly, blonde hair who wore lots of makeup. She always wore sweatshirts and sweatpants, even on the hottest, most humid, days. "Students," she said, "go in the room and find your seats, but don't get out anything because we're about to have a fire drill." Mike, Jake, Becca, and Toni were the first ones to walk in. All their teachers, except for Mr. Zolvitch, let them choose whatever desks they wanted as long as they behaved. The teens always sat in a group at the front next to the window, which they were at now, waiting for the drill.

"I love fire drills!" said Jake to the others with a grin on his face.

"Who doesn't?" asked Toni. "We'll get to do our math homework until the end of the period, and then there will be no new homework since the fire drill is about to—"

She was cut off by the wailing of a loud ear-splitting high-pitched siren that echoed through the hallway. All the students, and Mrs. Coalgian, put their hands over their ears and walked out the classroom toward the door that led down to the school's sports fields. They walked across the basketball courts and lined up on the damp, yellowed grass of the ball field. The teens took their hands off their ears and waited for the principal, Dr. Mac, to come down to let them know when it was okay to go back inside.

"That's weird," said Toni, gazing around her as though looking for something.

Becca looked at Toni, puzzled. "What's weird?"

"Well," said Toni, now standing on her toes in an attempt to see above the crowd of other students, although she wasn't having much success. "I don't see the Goths anywhere—they're usually pretty easy to pinpoint. They are in this class this period, you know."

Jake started looked around for them also, towering over the others. "Yeah, that is weird—I don't see them either."

"I'll bet you anything they decided to ditch the fire drill and stay in the hall or something," said Mike. "Knowing them, I wouldn't be surprised."

Becca glanced at Mrs. Coalgian and realized she was getting out her attendance sheet. "Well, I'll bet you anything they'll get caught," she said.

Eventually, Mrs. Coalgian started to read off the names from the attendance sheet. She called almost everyone off, including the four teens, until she reached Felix's. "*Felix?*" she said loudly. There was no answer. She looked around at the group of kids staring at her. "Has anyone seen *Felix*—in fact, I don't see him or any of the friends he hangs out with. That's strange. I saw them walk into the classroom."

Mike pointed toward the basketball courts and laughed. Mrs. Coalgian turned around at once, her face turning red with anger. The principal, was walking down the field toward Mrs. Coalgian followed by the Goths. Dr. Mac was a short, fat, bald man who always wore suits and oddly splotched ties. They all seemed to be very upset. However, their anger fell far short of Mrs. Coalgian's fury. "*WHERE HAVE YOU BEEN*?" she inquired tersely, the irritation obvious in her voice.

Dr. Mac gave the Goths a nasty glare. "They were hiding in a hallway corner where they thought no one would see them." He scowled at the Goths. "But obviously they were *wrong*!"

Toni, Mike, Jake, and Becca all exchanged glances and laughed along with some of their other classmates. Mrs. Coalgian turned around and held up her index finger to her students. They all immediately fell silent. "I apologize, Dr. Mac," said Mrs. Coalgian, giving the Goths an annoyed look. "I'll give them a week's detention, and I'll be having a little *chat* with each of their parents."

"No!" yelled Felix, his voice fearful. "You can't do that!"

"Please Mrs. Coalgian!" pleaded Courtney. "We don't want to be grounded from the fair!"

Mrs. Coalgian smiled darkly. "Well you should have thought of that before you decided to ditch the fire drill!"

"But—" said John, cut off by Mrs. Coalgian's gritted teeth.

"And if you argue," she said, "it'll be another week!"

John instantly shut his mouth and looked at his friends. They each had a frustrated expression as though they wanted to hurt somebody.

"Now get in line and no more talk!" said Dr. Mac. He walked away and held up his thumb, giving the okay to all of the teachers to head back to class.

The teens followed the other students back to the classroom and returned to their seats. Mrs. Coalgian went straight to her middle desk drawer where she took out a flowery-covered notebook. She then turned to the phone on the wall next to the whiteboard and started calling the Goths' parents. Jake, Mike, Toni, and Becca all leaned their chairs toward Mrs. Coalgian hoping they could overhear the conversation. Unfortunately, she was covering up her mouth so no one could hear.

"Darn!" said Toni, "I sure would like to know what punishment they'll be getting so I can rub it in their faces!"

"Oh, well!" said Becca. "At least we know they're getting a detention…that's horrible enough!"

"Yeah, you're right," said Jake. "But honestly, Becca, you've never even *been* to detention. How do you know it's so horrible?"

The bell rang and the teens left their math class. Next, they had history, which went very slowly—it was their least favorite class. After what seemed like hours, it was finally over. Lunch was next on the agenda, but first they wanted to buy their fair tickets in the library.

"I hope there's not a long line," said Toni, rolling her eyes. Toni was the impatient type and she got bored easily if she had to wait around for very long. Waiting for something she really wanted to do ticked her off.

Sure enough, when they got to the library, there was a very long line.

"You jinxed it!" said Jake, glaring at Toni as if he were about to hurt her.

Mike glanced ahead of the line and began cracking his knuckles—he was getting very apprehensive. "I hope they don't run out of wristbands."

The teens waited in line for fifteen minutes and were three fourths of the way there. Suddenly, four kids in black cut in front of them.

Mike jumped from the sudden intrusion. "What the heck is your problem?!!" he yelled at Felix.

Felix turned around and squinted his eyes. "Do you want to *make something of it*?"

"Don't do it, Mike!" said Jake, as he and the other two held a flailing Mike back. "He isn't worth getting in trouble for."

Mike stopped struggling and sighed heavily. "Yeah, you're right," said Mike smirking. "I don't want to waste my time fighting trash like them, but I still wouldn't mind *taking out the garbage*."

Felix and the others leered at Mike as they stepped up to the table where the tickets were being sold. Becca looked to her right and saw Mrs. Coalgian looking at them from the nearest aisle of shelves with a book lying open in her hands. She caught Becca's eye then went back to reading.

"Why are you guys getting tickets anyway?" Toni called after the Goths. "When you get home your parents are just going to say you can't go to the fair."

"That's what you think," said Jenna, walking up to Toni. "We'll just tell them we're not going and go anyway." The Goths laughed and walked away with their wristbands.

Mike went up to the booth. "We would each like a wristband, please."

The lady in the booth frowned. "I'm sorry, but we just sold our last wristbands," she said.

"You have to be kidding?" said Mike. He held out his cash as though certain he would get what he came for.

The lady gently pushed his hand away. "No, I'm sorry," she replied. "You could try the supermarket, but they might be sold out, too."

Mike forlornly stuffed his money back into his pocket and walked away.

Becca felt worse than ever for trying to get out of going to the fair. She looked helplessly at the others and ran up to Mike. She hugged him, "Mike, I'm so sorry—truly I am."

"Thanks," he said, trying to smile. "There's always next year."

Jake, Toni, and Becca felt horrible; seeing their best friend hurt made them feel bad as well. Not only didn't they get tickets, but time ran out for lunch as well. They had science class until the final bell rang. The teens left the building after going to their lockers and started to walk home, another school day gone by.

Mike turned toward the others and waved goodbye. "I'll see you guys tomorrow morning at the bike rack." The teens all lived in the same block, but lived on different streets parallel to each other. They met each morning at the bike rack next to the teacher's parking lot.

"Well, I'll see you two girls tomorrow," said Jake, waving goodbye to Toni and Becca.

Toni and Becca tried to smile brightly as they waved back. Becca sighed. "I feel really bad for Mike," she said sadly.

Toni nodded. "Yeah, me too, but it'll all be over by the end of the week."

"Yeah, I hope so," replied Becca.

The two girls hugged and waved goodbye as they each went different directions to go home for the night. They had each experienced difficulties such as this at one time or another in the past and had always worked through them as a group. They were sure that time would heal Mike's disappointment. They would just have to be as supportive as possible until Mike's dark cloud blew over.

Chapter 3—A Fair Fight?

The four teens made an early start to school the next morning. When they all met up at the bike racks it was light outside, but the air was slow to warm because the sun was still hidden somewhere in the gray overcast sky. The sun's warmth was slowly cracking in, yet it was still cold for an early summer morning.

Jake shivered as he rubbed his hands together. "It's freezing out this morning."

Becca exhaled deeply, expelling a large cloud into the air that they all watched slowly dissipate into the clear mountain air. "Yeah, a bit."

The four teens were at school a half hour early. Toni shivered, making her whole body shake. "Do you guys want to go inside? I'm really freezing my butt off!" She began jumping up and down trying to stay warm.

Jake laughed. "That would make sense."

They walked inside and sat on the benches near the office. The others noticed that Mike wasn't being his usual cheerful and talkative self. Obviously, he was still feeling down. They weren't sure how long it would be before he was back to normal. They all sat in silence for several long moments, thinking about the fair and the coming school day.

"Come on, Mike!" said Toni, making everyone jump. "Cheer up!"

Mike looked at Toni and sighed. "I am cheered up, it's just that I'm still disappointed…" He shut his eyes and shook his head. "Never mind."

"*I know,*" said Toni thoughtfully. "But you—"

"Hey, guys!" said a familiar voice. The teens looked up and saw Mrs. Coalgian gazing down on them. "I think I have something that might cheer you all up." She held out her left hand, which had four wristbands looped around it. "Ta da!"

Mike jumped up with excitement—his face lit up with a super-size grin that nearly reached his ears. "Where did you get those?" he asked, stunned.

Mrs. Coalgian chuckled, but then got serious. "From Felix, John, Jenna, and Courtney's parents."

"But they told us—" Toni was cut off again.

"They were making plans to sneak off to the fair and use these wristbands. Their parents found out, and returned them to me this morning," she said, a smile in her eyes. "I was going to return them to the ticket booth, but I remembered that yesterday afternoon you guys ran into a little *problem* that I happened to *see* and *overhear*." She raised one eyebrow and looked directly at Becca. "So I'll sell them to you, if you still want them." The other three jumped in the air and yipped with excitement. Becca looked at the floor. They each gave Mrs. Coalgian their twenty dollars and took a wristband.

"Thank you so much, Mrs. Coalgian," said Mike, staring at his wristband as though it were a thousand-dollar bill.

"Yeah," said Becca, staring at Mike. "Thanks *a lot*."

Mrs. Coalgian smiled and gave Becca a sly wink. "See you guys second period and at the fair Friday night." She walked down to her classroom and unlocked the door with a key attached to a string of at least a half-dozen assorted, jingling and clanking, key chains.

Mike jumped in the air, pumping his fist. "*YES*!"

"So, Mike," said Becca grinning, "everything worked out perfectly in the end, didn't it?"

Mike nodded. "Yup, it sure did," he replied. "Thank you guys for sticking by me, and I apologize for being such a downer."

"No problem," said Jake. He patted Mike roughly on the back. "It's good to have your old obnoxious self back."

"Isn't it weird how he gets so apologetic when things go his way?" asked Toni kneeling close to Becca.

Becca shook her head and laughed, "Knowing him, not really..."

The rest of the school week before the fair went by quickly for the teens. They were so excited about going that they concentrated even harder on getting their work done quickly. The only school day that seemed to drag on forever was Friday. Throughout the day, the teens kept noticing the Goths huddled together, talking and looking at them. The teens just shrugged and ignored them, then went about their normal routines.

Mike was looking at his watch, counting down the seconds until the final bell rang. "Three—two—one!" he chanted, pointing at the clock with one finger on each count until he was cut off by the bell. He looked at the others and beamed. "Are you guys ready to go?"

"Whenever you are," said Toni. "You're the thrill master!"

Mike laughed as he pitched his voice deeper. "Then put your wristbands on and get ready to *rumble*!" he said announcer-style.

They jumped up from their seats and ran out the classroom door, down the hall, and out of the school. They raced across the street as fast as they could, barely giving the crossing guard a glance and a wave.

After a few blocks of non-stop running, the teens finally arrived at the fairgrounds. The music coming from inside the entrance seemed to be calling their names, like siren song, to lure them inside for some fun. The flashing lights of the rides and the loud sirens and buzzers from the game booths, both served to increase the level of excitement. After showing their wristbands at the gate, they entered the fair. The teens stopped and gazed around at every entrancing detail—listening and breathing as though they were part of the fair themselves. The sweet scent of cotton candy and the salty smell of popcorn made their stomachs growl. Screams and laughter from the rides made them antsy to join the fun. It seemed like a hundred different vendors lined the midway trying to sell unusual or intriguing items to the crowds of people who walked by.

Suddenly, Becca and Toni were knocked down from behind, dragging Mike and Jake with them. They all got to their feet and brushed off their clothes, looking around to see what had happened. An enormous clown towered over them with a red painted smile on his white painted face. The teens jumped back in fright. The clown slowly smiled and bowed with outspread arms, like a courtier. He pulled his yellow and green polka-dotted pants up over his huge tattooed stomach and trotted off into the crowd like a penguin; if penguins had rainbow clouds of balloons, that is.

Becca laughed when she saw the dumbfounded looks on the others' faces. "Nothing like a warm welcome from a huge dorky clown, knocking you down to the nice dirty ground." The others stared at Becca for a few silent moments, and then burst out laughing at her unintentional rhyme.

Mike turned around and around trying to see everything at once. He then shut his eyes and took several deep breathes. "I am now finally ready to go on some rides!" he announced to the others.

Toni reached up and put her arm around him. "Don't worry, Mike, we'll get to them all in good time—but if we go on all of them at once—well—the chunks from the inside will win the battle." Mike looked down at Toni with the most skeptical expression on his face. Toni frowned as she backed away toward the others. "I should have known that was never a problem for Mike—the more *chunks* the better!"

Becca and Jake studied the scowl on Toni's face, and then saw a grin appear on Mike's. They pushed Toni ahead of them to follow Mike down a dirt pathway leading through many vendors' tents. A glowing, glistening object on a small table inside a tent caught their eyes. A strange looking woman was seated on a spindly chair outside the grubby tent, which seemed to be painted all over with odd symbols. They walked over to the lady who was wearing a long purple gown. She had many glittering bracelets and wore gigantic hoop earrings. The teens were somewhat startled by the heavy black eye makeup she wore.

"She looks like either a crazy gypsy or, possibly, a rabid raccoon," thought Toni and she began to giggle hysterically, but a sharp pain in her side caused by Jake's elbow shut her up almost immediately.

Becca stepped forward to the woman and gave her a friendly smile. "Hi, um—are you a fortune teller?"

The gypsy stood up suddenly and raised her hands—the teens took a couple of steps back from the sudden interaction. The gypsy smiled brightly. "I am not a mere fortune teller—I can tell you the *future*!"

Toni bent close to Jake. "Doesn't a fortune teller always tell you your future?" Jake shook his head and chuckled.

"I can tell you about warnings, your destiny, and things to come..." the gypsy said mysteriously. She shut her eyes and whispered, "I tell you what Spirits are near you or what Darkness will bring." The gypsy opened her eyes and looked at the teens. "I will charge five dollars for all of you!"

The teens looked at one another and nodded assent.

They followed the gypsy inside the tent and circled around a table that held a large brilliant crystal ball on an ornate gold stand in its center. The gypsy shut the tent flap and plunged the crowded space into darkness. The only light was coming through the seams of the tent and the glow from the crystal ball. "Take a seat," she said kindly. The teens pulled out beat-up wooden chairs from under the table and sat down quickly, staring at the glowing, swirling fog that seemed to be moving inside the crystal ball.

The gypsy came gliding over and sat down across from them in the large cushioned chair. She began to move her hands lightly just above the surface of the crystal ball, humming at the same time. The glow from the crystal ball was reflected brightly in her eyes—an intense white glow, but the teens were too mesmerized by hazy movements inside the crystal ball to notice. The gypsy began to speak in a whisper. "*Exciting things shall come your way...an adventure shall ignite...but a mystery shall infuse...a mystery to tell all and show all—all but the true Darkness beneath. A loss will come, far greater than any before, sadness and sorrow shall spread...but at the same time a powerful gain will come to you, to help show you the way to those who are close to you...and truly apart...*"

Becca began to blink and she shook her head. It was as though she couldn't take her eyes off the crystal ball, but she finally managed to drag her gaze away. She looked around at the others and realized their eyes were out of focus as they continued staring into the crystal ball. Becca looked up at the gypsy and noticed the frightening white glow coming from her eyes. Becca gasped loudly, making the others lose focus, and looked at her. Becca pointed at the gypsy. They all looked at one another in fright, but said nothing.

The gypsy suddenly began to shake and frantically toss her head back and forth, rattling her many bracelets against the table. "*LOOK INTO THE CRYSTAL BALL!*" she commanded.. "*SHE IS WATCHING EACH OF YOU CLOSELY. SHE IS HERE AT THIS MOMENT—THE DARKNESS SHALL NOT LEAVE—SHALL NOT LEAVE UNTIL THE POWER SHALL BE IGNITED—A FIGHT SHALL BREW TO*

SHOW ALL AND TELL ALL AND TOGETHER THY SHALL... DEFEAT! DEFEAT! DEFEAT!"

The teens peered more intently into the crystal, examining it more closely. The gray fog churning inside the ball grew darker, obscuring the already faint images until they could see nothing but darkness. Two red glowing shapes began to slowly burn through the featureless gloom, as the outline of a pale face lit by gleaming red eyes emerged. The face opened its mouth in an inaudible scream, showing many sharp fangs—then the face began to scream—a shrill, awful, heart-chilling scream that could only be heard from inside the tent; only inside their heads. The crystal ball seemed to visibly shrink then exploded outward. It shattered into a thousand shimmering shards that flared briefly and dimmed, disappearing as they fell to earth. The teens flew back out of their chairs, knocking them over backwards or sideways in their haste. They got quickly to their feet and ran as fast as they could out of the tent, stumbling over chair legs and each other, not bothering to look back.

Jake took the lead as he sprinted ahead of the others and led them into the crowded ride section. He stopped, hunched over, hands on his knees and gasping for breath. The others stopped beside him also breathing heavily, Toni collapsing in a heap onto a nearby bench. After several moments, Jake suddenly stood up and began laughing very hard and shaking his head slowly from side to side. The others looked at each other and then at Jake, puzzled.

Mike walked forward, grabbed the still laughing Jake by both shoulders and shook him. "WHAT IS THE MATTER WITH YOU!?!"

Jake just kept laughing. "That," he said standing up, "was the *best* prank someone *ever* pulled on us!" The others silently stared. Grins crept slowly across their faces, as Jakes words set in.

Toni looked up at Jake, shook her head and laughed. "You really think that gypsy thing was meant to get people scared?" She looked questioningly at Becca.

Becca nodded in agreement. "Jake's right—it was more than likely a prank!" Becca's eyes narrowed and her face grew tense with anger. "It was a cruel prank! That glass could have cut us!"

"Becca, calm down!" said Mike soothingly. "It was just a harmless prank—we're not hurt—and it gave us a good laugh. Now, let's do what we really came here for and go on some rides!"

Becca nodded and sighed deeply. "You're right—it was very weird though—and that face was so *scary*—but we're all fine. No harm done, I suppose." Becca sounded as though she were trying to convince herself. "Okay, so where to first?"

Toni stood up, eyes wide as she pointed ahead of her. "Over there, guys. Let's do that one first! There's a chair lift circling over the entire fair." The others followed her finger and looked toward the lift. "From there we can get a better look at all the rides and games, and then choose the best ones!"

It was only mid-afternoon and the fair didn't close until midnight, but the teens had to be at Becca's house by dark, because her parents were making them dinner. So, they had to hurry if they wanted to be sure to hit all their favorite rides and booths. The others agreed as they ran to get in line at the chair lift, flashing their wristbands at the lady attendant. It only took two people per car, so Jake and Mike took one and Becca and Toni took the next one right behind them.

Drifting silently over the heads of the crowds, hearing only the myriad voices and laughter, the clank of the rides, and the smell of popcorn, cotton candy, funnel cakes and hotdogs, the teens soon forgot about what had happened. The exciting goings-on below seemed to drain the memories, making it fainter and, somehow, less scary. The fair was divided into four main sections: a section for animals, arts and crafts, food, games, and a huge section full of exciting, thrilling rides.

"Wow, look at it all!" yelled Mike over his shoulder to the girls. His mouth was slightly open and his eyes lit up. "I want to go on the *Gravitron* first!" yelled Mike, pointing toward a black flying saucer-shaped ride farther along the midway.

Jake looked down to where Mike was pointing and listened to the screams coming from the riders. "Yeah—judging by those screams, it sure sounds good!"

The teens hopped off at the end of the chair lift and jogged over to get in line at the Gravitron. There were many people waiting in line, but the ride took many people at a time, so it made the crowd disappear quickly.

A tall, gaunt, unshaven man in a filthy t-shirt was going around taking tickets and checking wristbands. The teens showed him theirs and ran inside the circular room. Other people were standing leaning on long red pads all against the walls so the teens found four pads next to each other, and did the same.

The man sitting in a chair in the center of the ride began to speak. "We will start in ten seconds." He pushed a button and loud, ear-piercing rap music came on through speakers over their heads.

"I hate this song!" yelled Mike, shouting over the loud music.

"It's *alright…*" said Jake, looking next to him at Toni, who was snapping her fingers and nodding in time to the music, "but looks like little '*Toni the Tiger*' is enjoying it more then any of us."

The ride started to move with a lurch. Everyone began to turn slowly along with the ride, except for the man in the middle who was lying back, relaxing in his chair. The ride spun faster and faster pinning everyone to the pads on the walls. The pads began to rise to the top of the wall as the floor opened. Everyone was looking at the ground whirling beneath them. Many people were screaming in fear, afraid of falling out.

"This is amazing!" screamed Jake. He tried to lift himself up to turn towards the others, but he was slammed back by the overpowering force of gravity.

Becca moaned. "I can't move at all." She shut her eyes.

Toni had her hands behind her head, letting everyone know she was enjoying the ride. The music was still pounding when the ride began to slow and the floor gradually slid closed again. All the pads began to slide back when Mike accidentally did a front-flip from several feet off the floor by abruptly trying to throw his body away from the wall. He hit the floor of the ride with a loud thud and lay stunned, laughing, until the other's feet touched down.

"Are you okay?" chuckled Jake. Toni and Becca were laughing hysterically.

"Yeah, I'm fine," said Mike, pushing himself up and shaking his head several times to clear the fuzziness. "That was awesome!"

The ride and blasting music finally came to a stop, and the four teens walked dizzily off the ride, lurching along until their heads caught up with the motion of their bodies. "Hey, guys, the Ferris wheel is right over there," said Becca, pointing. "Let's go on it to get our eyes back into our heads."

"Good idea," said Toni, trying to keep her balance.

The Ferris wheel carried box carts, which could fit six people at a time. The teens got on the ride, sat down three to a side, and tiredly rested their heads on the open window ledge

Toni shook her head. "I think I'm almost back to normal, but that ride was about to make me sick," she said.

The others said nothing. They didn't want to think about the possibilities of Toni's statement.

Jake looked out the window. "So, where do you guys want to go next?"

"I was thinking we could go to the game booths and try to win some prizes," said Toni. "I saw a little girl walking around with a huge teddy bear twice her size."

"Hey, Toni, I'm pretty good at the booths", Jake said lazily from across the aisle. "Do you want me to try to win you something? I mean, you can do it if you want, but if you want some *extra* help…"

Toni looked at Jake as though she was offended by the question. She sighed deeply and said, "*fine*, you can do the baseball throw. I suppose I'd have a better chance to get that gigantic stuffed animal with your help than without." Toni looked directly at Mike. "You should play for Becca."

Mike glanced at Becca. "Is it alright with you?" Becca looked hurt for a moment then smiled and nodded.

Jake, along with Mike, had played on the school baseball team. Jake was the pitcher and Mike the catcher. Out of all the games their team had played, they had only lost one. Mike was good at aiming and throwing far, but he couldn't throw as hard and fast as Jake. The ride ended and they all walked toward the game booth section and stopped in front of a basketball-throw booth to watch some other kids finish playing.

"Let's try this one as a warm-up to the main event," said Mike to the others.

A tall man with short brush-cut hair wearing a basketball jersey was running the booth. "You guys know the rules," he said to Mike when the other group had moved away to play darts next-door. "Three shots for a dollar. Do you want to try it?"

"Yeah," said Mike, eyes gleaming, handing over his money.

"Well, start whenever you're ready", the man said, lining the balls up on the counter.

Mike aimed carefully with one eye closed, hefting the ball thoughtfully in one hand until he shot it high toward the hoop. It swished through the net without hitting the rim.

"Awesome, Mike!" said Jake, wide eyed. He looked at Becca. "Someone's getting a prize!"

Becca giggled and pumped one fist in the air, the other pressed to her mouth. "Don't feel nervous that all of the pressure is on you", laughed Toni, squeezing his shoulder encouragingly.

"Thanks," said Mike, sarcastically, the next ball balanced on one palm. "You always know what to say to make me feel a whole lot better!" Mike took the basketball and aimed it toward the hoop again. He tossed the ball, what seemed to be, straight up. This time it circled around the rim several heart-stopping times but still went in.

"Yeah!!" exclaimed Jake, pounding Mike on the back. Becca was clapping and bouncing up and down.

"That was a bit close," said Toni. She talked leant over Mike's shoulder so he could hear her. "*TOO CLOSE!*"

"Toni!" snarled Jake, giving her a warning look by tilting his head and raising one eyebrow.

Toni smirked at him and stuck out her tongue. "Sorry".

"Alright!" said Becca. "One more shot—you can do it!" She was getting jumpy, and she put her hands together as though praying, but still bouncing on the balls of both feet.

Toni looked at Becca as though she were crazy. "Calm down!"

Mike picked up the last ball as if it weighed two tons. He aimed quickly and shot. The ball hit the top of the backboard, and fell straight down into the hoop. "BOOYAH!" he shouted, slapping both palms against the counter.

"Okay..." said the man dully. "You can choose one of the large ones." He pointed to a small group of bedraggled-looking stuffed animals.

Becca grabbed the biggest teddy bear of the lot. It was lavender-colored with a purple satiny bow around its neck. "Thank you *sooo* much Mike!" she said hugging him and the bear at the same time.

"No problem," he laughed. "It was fun—really tense with this *thing* irritating me," he said flicking Toni on the shoulder. Toni squealed and rubbed her arm.

The four teens strolled away towards the baseball throw. The object was to knock down the three foot-high, heavy, plastic bottles stacked in a pyramid. This time, a lady was standing in front encouraging people to play.

"I'm going to play this one for me and then my friend," said Jake, approaching the booth and laying his money on the counter.

"Sure," she said folding the dollar bills and tucking them into her blue canvas apron. "You have one try to knock all of the bottles off the table to win the big prize." Jake turned to the side lifting his left leg up and putting it sharply back down as he threw the ball with his right arm with great power. The ball struck the pyramid of bottles at its base. Not only did the bottles fly off the table, the bottom two broke into several pieces. Toni squeaked and jumped in the air.

"That was incredible!" the lady said, wide-eyed. She looked at the broken bottles. "I can't afford anymore broken bottles. You can have two prizes and say you won the second."

"Really?—sure—okay…" Jake couldn't believe it. He didn't realize he could throw that hard. Toni immediately seized a huge light blue fluffy bunny with a bright blue ribbon and Jake took the large stuffed white gorilla with a tan felt face and feet.

While the teens were busy looking over each other's prizes, they overheard a little girl wailing and pleading. "Look at that, Daddy, a gorilla! I want one!" A little girl in a pink frilly dress was walking along holding tightly to her father's hand and pointing at the gorilla Jake was holding.

"Maybe later," said her father, smiling down at her. He got down on his knees in the dirt and said to her, "Why don't we spend the money Granny gave us on some cotton candy? Daddy's not real good at those kinds of games." He looked up at Jake who returned his smile.

The little girl looked gloomy for a moment, but then she sighed and nodded as she looked wistfully at the gorilla. "Okay, Daddy."

Jake walked over to the little girl and bent down so he was eye level with her. "Hey, I found this lonely gorilla and I've been trying to find someone to give him a good home. Do you think you could do that?"

The little girl's face lit up and she turned to took at her dad. "Is it okay to take him?" she asked. The man nodded, and she gleefully took the gorilla from Jake. "Thank you! Thank you! Thank you!" She looked between her father and Jake as she hugged the gorilla close and petted its smooth snowy fur.

"Thank you," said the dad. "That was very thoughtful."

Jake just smiled and nodded, then gave a small wave to the pair as he walked over to the other teens. "Let's go." The others exchanged grins and followed Jake along the midway to the next section of rides.

Several rides later, breathless from screaming and drenched from the log ride, the teens collapsed on a bench to take a short break. Toni was beaming and shaking her wet curly hair like a dog after a bath. "God, I love the water!"

"You guys, we don't have much time left," said Becca, looking at her watch. "It's going to get dark pretty soon, and my parents are expecting us for dinner."

"Well, then let's get a move on," said Toni, as she and the others made there way along the midway toward the exit—inhaling the gloriously sweet scent of kettle corn and cotton candy.

"Boy, I'm hungry!" said Jake, rubbing his stomach with both hands. He looked back at the lighted fair entrance. "That kettle corn really got to me." The others breathed deeply, smelling all the wonderful food they were leaving behind.

"*Finally*!" said a quiet voice from the shadows between some dumpsters.

"Who said that?" asked Mike, looking around to try and locate where the voice came from.

"Isn't it obvious, Mike", said Toni, squinting at the shadows. "It's *Felix*. I wondered if that ugly bunch was going to show up."

"Very good, chubs!" said Felix, stalking out of the shadows with his gang. "You guys stole our bands!" he accused, poking Jake in the chest with one finger.

"We did not!" said Becca hotly. "You *lost* them because of your own stupid behavior."

"You guys are going to pay right now for what you did," said John, moving up next to Felix. Courtney and Jenna stepped from the shadows, revealing their pale sneering faces as well as the short wooden bats each held.

"You guys are going to try to fight us?" asked Jake incredulously, not trying to keep the laughter out of his voice. "Like Mike explained to you earlier, we don't fight *trash*."

Felix's face flushed with anger. He jumped suddenly at Jake, knocking him to the ground, and punched him swiftly several times in the side of the head. John, taking the opportunity while the others were too stunned to react, tried to fly tackle Mike. Jenna leaped at Toni, bat held high, while Courtney advanced slowly on Becca, slapping the bat menacingly into her open palm with each step.

Felix tried to punch Jake in the throat, but missed when Jake turned his head to avoid the blow. Instead, Felix slammed his fist into the gravel just above Jake's right shoulder. Jake immediately heaved his shoulder up and over onto Felix's extended arm. He then rolled over, pinning Felix's arm underneath his shoulder, forcing him over onto his back. Jake then sat up, one arm across Felix's throat and one knee across Felix's stomach.

"Had enough or should we continue?" said Jake angrily, flashing eyes only inches from Felix's pain-contorted face. Felix nodded meekly, and turned away.

John was unsuccessfully trying to punch Mike in the stomach, but Mike was easily holding him back with one arm. Mike winced in pain when one out of the ten or so John had attempted connected with his ribs. Mike suddenly grabbed John's neck with his free hand and punched him hard in the face, knocking him down. He lay whimpering on the ground, cowering when Mike stepped around him to slide one foot gently against John's ribs.

With their adversaries apparently down for the count, Mike and Jake turned to check on Toni and Becca. Toni had Jenna's arm holding the bat pulled up between her shoulder blades. Unfortunately, Jenna's long hair was wrapped around the part of the bat gripped in Toni's hand, so her head was wrenched awkwardly over against her shoulder. Toni seemed to be alternately tugging on Jenna's hair and harshly whispering in her ear each time Jenna squeaked in pain. Becca backed away from

Courtney's wildly swinging bat until her back was against one of the smaller green dumpsters. Courtney's bat swiped Becca's glasses off and sent them flying into the side of a dumpster They snapped in half on impact and one lens went skittering across the gravel. Ignoring the next swing, Becca reached back to hook both arms over the top of the dumpster and swung both legs up to connect squarely with Courtney's stomach. Courtney folded up with a groan, ending up on her knees with both arms wrapped around her stomach. She moaned again softly, leaning over until the top of her head rested in the gravel and her dark hair flowed down around it hiding her face.

A loud angry shout made them all jump. The teens heard a sudden voice of anger. "STOP THIS AT ONCE!!!" Mrs. Coalgian stood watching them, holding her small daughter's hand and surrounded by a group of curious people. She dug in her purse and pulled out her cell phone. Flipping it open, she punched in a short number and waited.

Toni immediately let go of Jenna's arm, but kept the bat twisted in her hair. From a distance, it looked like she was holding Jenna up. Mike and Jake helped the Goth guys up from the ground. Jake kept a firm grip on Felix's shoulder, afraid that if he ran the rest of the gang would too. Mike pulled John up from the ground by the front of his t-shirt, and pretended to help dust him off. Becca slid abruptly to the ground when she pulled one bruised arm from over the top edge of the dumpster.

Toni finally released the bat twisted in Jenna's hair and went over to help Becca up. "They…they attacked us", Becca said to Mrs. Coalgian, her voice trembling as she looked over at Courtney, horrified at what she had done.

"Don't worry", said Mrs. Coalgian, walking over to hug both Toni and Becca. "An ambulance is coming, and the police will sort out the rest. Hopefully, once and for all".

"That hurt!" said Toni rubbing her side. She looked over at Jake and Mike who had released the Goth guys into the care of some bystanders, and were now busily comparing bruises.

"That was an awesome fight. But painful!" said Mike, coming over to sit down next to Becca. He clenched his stomach and coughed.

"*Is nut antyfwing to be pwowd of,*" Jake said, holding a bloody nose. His hands were red and his shirt was badly stained.

John rubbed the back of his head. "Ow, that big guy hurt my *head*!" he was overheard complaining to the paramedic.

Mike snickered. "That's what you get for jumping on me, butthead!" he yelled. Mrs. Coalgian shushed him and he gave an apologetic grin.

Flashing lights and sirens marked the arrival of an ambulance and a police car approached and stopped. Two cops got out of the car but not before turning off the siren. Three paramedics hopped out of the back of the ambulance with big gray boxes and immediately started toward the injured teens. A moment later, that siren went off also.

"We've been expecting one of these gang fights to break out at the fair," one of the police officers said to Mrs. Coalgian, pulling out a notebook. The other policeman walked around talking to people in the crowd and checking on the other kids.

Mrs. Coalgian sighed. "This wasn't gang activity; just a normal teenage fight between some kids from school." She looked shrewdly at all the teens.

The officer asked each of them to briefly describe what had happened while he made a few more notes in his book. He finished the interviews by writing down all of their names, addresses and phone numbers, as well as their parents' names.

"No broken bones, just cuts and bruises," reported one of the female paramedics to the officer. "The boy with the bruise on his head will be coming with us overnight to make sure he doesn't have a concussion. The rest are good to go as soon as I get their parents names and addresses," she said indicating the clipboard she carried in one rubber-gloved hand.

"I'll be calling their parents right now," said the officer walking to his car with Mrs. Coalgian and the paramedic following him through the still flashing beams of red, white, and blue.

Toni, Becca, Mike, and Jake were standing together silently in a group. The Goths were doing the same, not bothering to glance over at the teens.

"I knew they were planning something at school, but I didn't think it would be this," said Becca quietly. She shut her eyes tiredly. "I just want to go home—first a horrid prank, and now a bloody fight! *I just want to go home...*"

The second police officer walked over to the Goths carrying a metal clipboard. People leaving the fair glanced curiously at the scene as they passed. Dusk was falling rapidly, the sun still glowing orange in the west. The officer with the notebook returned from his car with a flashlight.

"Well," the officer said, "Becca's parents are picking the four of you up. You are to stay there until your parents contact you. All of them were upset, but are glad that you aren't badly hurt. We won't be pressing any charges against you, but a report will be filed regarding the fight. I suggest you stay out of trouble or the next time the law won't be so lenient." He nodded seriously to them all and walked back toward his car, meeting up with the other police officer along the way. They got into their car and turned off the rotating lights before they pulled away.

When the paramedics finished loading John into the ambulance and had stowed away their gear, the big rear doors closed and they drove away without flashers also. Mrs. Coalgian walked back over to the four teens from where she had been talking to the police officers. "I agreed to wait with you until your parents arrive, okay?"

"Sure," the teens agreed. She walked over to the remaining three Goths and could be heard telling them the same thing. Two minutes later a black Hummer and a black Jeep approached from different directions. The Goths jogged over to the black Jeep and climbed clumsily inside. It drove quickly off, spitting gravel, even though Mrs. Coalgian was frantically gesturing to the driver to lower the window. The Hummer belonged to Becca's parents. Her mom, Trudy, jumped out the passenger side door almost before the big SUV had come to a stop. Trudy had blue eyes with long, smooth brown hair and a thin muscular build like Becca. She grabbed Becca in a gigantic hug, rocking her back and forth and smoothing her hair. Her dad, Bill, strode over soon after. He was a tall balding man with thick glasses, who looked amazingly like his only daughter. Seeing the arrival of the parents, Mrs. Coalgian waved goodbye and left toward the parking lot with her daughter in her arms."

"Are the rest of you guys okay?" he asked, worryingly hugging each of them in turn. He finished by firmly hugging his wife and daughter, leaving his left arm gently around their shoulders as he turned to the others. "We're fine," said Jake, smiling slightly. "We're just glad it's over, and nobody got badly hurt."

"That's good," said Bill sighing. "However, you're all still grounded for the weekend. But that shouldn't interfere with the plans. You three…." he said pointing to Toni, Mike, and Jake, "are going to be staying with us for a while. Your parents had to go to New York on business." All of the teens' parents were good friends. They had met in elementary school and had maintained their friendship throughout the years. In fact, that was how the teens had first met.

"Really? No kidding?" asked Jake, with an astonished look on his face. "Yup," said Trudy, smiling brightly.

"That is so cool!" said Mike. "I hope it's alright with you guys, of course?"

"Michael!" said Trudy, taken aback. "You have always been like family, why would you even ask that?"

Mike laughed, but felt slightly embarrassed.

Toni sighed. "Gosh, I would have loved to have gone to New York with my parents." Toni was dismally. She was very close to her parents and didn't like to be away from them for very long.

"Well, that's the surprise," said Trudy, putting her other arm around Toni.

"What's the surprise?" asked Becca curiously. "I don't get it." She looked at her dad who winked back at her.

"We'll tell you all about it in the car," said Trudy. "But first, how did this all happen?" Her voice suddenly got serious.

"Well…" said Becca, eyeing the others, "as we were leaving the fair, the Goths sort of ambushed us. They got in trouble at school Monday and their parents weren't allowing them to go to the fair. But for some reason, they blamed us. We all had to defend ourselves…they had weapons!"

Bill looked pointedly at Trudy. They were well aware of the continuous problems the school had with the Goths.

"Hey…where are your glasses?" Bill asked Becca. He gently touched the bruise on the bridge of Becca's nose. "You'll be lucky if you don't end up with a black eye too, Champ."

Becca reached into her pocket and pulled out her broken pair of glasses, still missing one lens.

"Well, it certainly looks like you're going to have to wear your contacts, even if they hurt, until we get you a new pair," said Trudy.

"Alright," said Becca dissatisfied. She put her broken glasses back into her pocket and sighed heavily.

"Alright. Now for the rules," said Trudy holding up one finger at a time as she ticked them off her list: "No sleeping in the tree house, no comic books, and no staying up late. You'll be staying in Becca's room upstairs."

"Fair enough," Toni agreed. "A good night's sleep inside won't do us any harm."

"Well, then let's head home and we'll tell you what's going on," said Bill herding them toward the Hummer with widespread arms. They all got in and buckled their seat belts.

"So what's going on?" asked Jake, still looking at Becca. Becca just shrugged.

Bill laughed. "We bought an R.V!"

"Alright!" said Becca astounded. Her excitement soon turned to confusion. "What does that have to do with anything?" she asked puzzled.

Trudy smiled indulgently. "We're all going to take a road trip to Florida. After a week there, we'll be heading to New York to meet up with your parents." She grinned even wider.

The four teens were speechless.

"Are you serious?" asked Mike trying to contain his excitement. "I don't think I can handle another practical joke."

"Yes," said Bill, "no joke." The Hummer was suddenly filled with screams of delight and the slapping of high fives all around.

"This is going to be awesome!" screamed Becca, excitingly bouncing in her seat.

"When are we leaving?" asked Jake.

"Sunday morning," replied Trudy. "We know you have school next week, but since there are only a few days left, we decided to take you out early for the summer!"

Again, the Hummer was filled with shrieks of excitement. The teens talked gleefully amongst themselves all the way back to Becca's house busily making plans.

When Becca's three-story house came into view, it was tough to miss the enormous silver R.V. the size of a bus stretching the entire length of the driveway. Becca's dad had to park the Hummer in the street. The four teens scrambled out of the vehicle in a hurry and ran toward the R.V. to look inside. As Mike reached for the handle, Bill yelled at them. "Stop right there! No peeking!"

The teens stopped dead in their tracks then turned slowly around to face Becca's dad. "Why not?" asked Becca, pouting.

"Because..." said Trudy. "You guys are grounded. You can see it Sunday morning when we leave." Her reply was met by groans all around.

"I forgot to ask," said Mike. "What about packing all our clothes and stuff?"

"You'll see when you get inside," said Trudy, tapping in a code on a number pad next to the garage door. After the door slowly opened, they all walked through and into the house and stopped in the mudroom to take off their shoes. Downstairs was a spacious family room, two spare bedrooms that shared a bath, and an enormous recreation room with a pool table and a big screen TV. French doors at the bottom of the stairs opened out onto the pool area.

They walked up several steps to the main floor, containing the kitchen and dining rooms, a living room, a guest bedroom and bath, and the master bedroom where Becca's parents slept.

"We thought we'd order pizza," said Bill picking up the phone. "Pepperoni and extra cheese, right?" The teens all nodded in agreement. "When you get upstairs you'll find all the stuff your parents packed for you in the bunkhouse. They dropped it off this morning while you were at school. They had to catch the first early afternoon flight to New York from Phoenix, so they didn't have time to see you before they left, but you can call them later tonight."

The teens went upstairs to the third floor. Since Becca was an only child, she had the whole floor to herself. It had her room, a giant playroom, a guest room with several sets of bunk beds known as the 'bunkhouse' and a huge bathroom. They looked in the bunkhouse on their way to Becca's bedroom and saw a row of labeled suitcases pushed up against a bottom bunk, which was full of sleeping bags and pillows.

Mike, Toni, and Jake pawed over the bags looking for their own. There seemed to be one large one and one small one for each person.

"It looks like we're all packed," said Jake thoroughly checking through his belongings. The smaller bags contained nightclothes, comic books, and other special personal items that they would need for the trip. "Let's take these to Becca's room since we'll need this stuff later." Jake carried the three small bags while Toni and Mike grabbed the sleeping bags and pillows.

Becca's room was a palace. It had a king-size waterbed, a walk-in closet, a television, a mini fridge and a microwave, and plenty of room for four teenagers to spread out on the floor. It didn't take them long to unroll the sleeping bags and stash their luggage around the room.

Mike grabbed a comic book from his bag and flipped through the pages while he flopped down on the nearest pillow. Jake sat down in front of the television to look through the many video games lined neatly up on a shelf under it.

"What are we going to do tomorrow?" asked Toni, sitting down on the corner of Becca's bed. "We're basically grounded from anything we *like* to do."

"I know!" exclaimed Becca, thinking aloud. "Mom and Dad said we couldn't sleep in the tree house, but they didn't say we were grounded to the house. How about we go and explore in the forest and see what interesting things we can find? Kind of like a nature walk."

The others looked at her as though that were the worst idea ever. "Sounds kind of cheesy, don't you think Becca?" asked Jake, a smirk on his face.

"Well, it's better than doing nothing," she replied. "I don't see you guys coming up with anything more exciting."

"Okay," conceded Jake, "you have a point. I guess we'll be allowed to do that since we don't usually explore in the forest."

"I'll go down and ask my parents just to make sure," said Becca, walking out of her bedroom and trotting down the stairs.

"Wouldn't it be cool if we saw a mountain lion or a bear?" asked Mike, unrolling his sleeping bag with a snap.

"I doubt we'll see one," said Jake. "When has anybody ever seen one around here?"

"Well, if either of those things comes after us," said Toni, wrapping herself in a purple fleece blanket that had been lying folded on the end of the bed. "I'll trip both of you while we're running. I only need to run faster than the person that falls down first. That way it'll get you guys and not me."

"You are one cruel person," laughed Mike. "But knowing you, you won't be able to catch up to me to trip me."

Before Toni could say another word, Becca walked in the room. "The pizza's here and my Mom and Dad said we could go exploring as long as we take a flashlight and the G.P.S system."

"What's a G.P.S system?" asked Toni, slithering off the bed onto the floor.

"You've never heard of one?" asked Becca. Toni shook her head. "It's about the size of a walkie-talkie and has a screen that shows you a map of where you are and where you need to go, and then tells you how to get there. It also lets you know how far away you are from that spot. That way, you know where you are all the time. Dad has already programmed ours with the location of the house, so if we get lost, there is only one button to push to tell you how to get home."

"How does it do that?" asked Toni.

"Satellites," said Jake. "It's pretty advanced technology."

Becca laughed. "Exactly, now let's go down for pizza."

The four teens left Becca's room and ran down the stairs to the kitchen where the pizzas were laid out on the green granite counter alongside plates and cans of soda. They stood around the counter eating and talking until Becca's parents made them all go up to bed.

Once upstairs, they got ready for bed and arranged the sleeping bags in a circle just like in the tree house. Becca even got one out of her closest for herself, since it would be more fun to sleep on the floor with everyone else. Once the light was off and they were all comfortable, they talked about how nice it was that Mrs. Coalgian gave them a second chance to go to the fair, and how bad they felt about getting into the fight. Mike and Jake gave the girls a blow-by-blow report on their part of the fight, since Toni and Becca didn't see it. They still couldn't believe the Goths actually attacked them. No one mentioned the gypsy woman or the weird things that had happened in her tent. They also speculated about wild beasts they would meet in the woods, and the great times they would have on the road trip.

Little did they know that tomorrow would be the beginning of a journey that would change their lives forever.

Chapter 4— The Sages' Treasure

Mike was first to wake up early the next morning with a muffled yawn and a big stretch. Amazingly, the sleeping bag had blocked out Toni's snoring. A loud jaw-cracking yawn from Becca woke up Jake. They glanced suspiciously at each other.

Becca smiled hugely. "Tomorrow is the road trip! I can't wait."

Jake yawned in reply and unzipped his sleeping bag. "This is going to be a great trip!" He winced as he carefully put his hand over the bruises on his face. "I just wish this would go away! Maybe I should have taken some aspirin last night."

Mike got up and stretched as he walked over to look out Becca's window. He yawned again and scratched his head. "It looks like it will be a nice day, so why don't we go exploring now?"

"Sure," said Becca, getting up from the floor and delicately touching her sore nose. "I'll go get the G.P.S and leave a note to let my parents know we've gone. They're probably still asleep. Meet me in the kitchen when you're ready to go." She left the room and disappeared down the stairwell.

Mike and Jake met up with her later when they went to find something in the fridge for breakfast. Becca was busy filling a backpack with snacks, flashlights, and bottles of water. The others looked at her with a weird expression on their faces. "This stuff is just in case of an emergency. Are you guys ready?" She looked at Jake and Mike who were both peeling oranges. "Where's Toni?" she asked when she had finished stuffing things in and zipped the backpack. "She couldn't possibly still be asleep, could she?"

"I'll get her," said Jake stuffing the last piece of orange in his mouth and heading for the stairs. He couldn't help but laugh when he saw Toni all the way in her sleeping bag, the drawstring pulled tight. "Let's go," he said as he gently prodded her inert form with his toe.

Toni moaned and yawned somewhere in the depths of the sleeping bag. When Jake opened the drawstring to look inside, a pillow came hurtling out just missing hitting him in the face. "No!" Toni said sternly. "Go away!"

Jake laughed as he picked up the bottom end of the sleeping bag and hauled it up over his head. Toni spilled out in a heap, grabbing the pillow by Jake's feet and clutching it over her head. "*Come on sleepy head...*" he said, gently wrestling the pillow out of her grasp. Jake finally managed to pull her bodily to her feet where she stood leaning against him limp as a rag doll. "Everyone is waiting on you, so get a move on," said Jake, pushing her towards her suitcase. "See you downstairs in five," he said sternly, closing the door behind him.

When Toni arrived five minutes later, the teens walked out Becca's back door and hopped over the rail fence onto a game trail that paralleled the fence for a ways then led to the forest. It was cooler under the trees and there was moisture in the gentle breeze. A thick layer of pine needles underfoot muffled their footsteps. The early morning sun streamed through occasional gaps overhead and made everything glow with an ethereal light. They could hear the wind whispering through the towering pine trees.

"Isn't it amazing?" asked Toni, looking up at the trees dreamily. She breathed in deeply, then shut her eyes and exhaled.

Mike put his hands on the back of his head. "It's so relaxing out here. I could find a place to lie down and fall asleep instantly."

"That would be amazing since you just got up fifteen minutes ago, but I agree. It's more peaceful than anything," said Jake.

They began to walk up a steep hill strewn with many rocks and small boulders. Becca's house soon fell from view as she led the others up through the thick woods. When she reached the top of the hill, she held out her hand to let the others know to stop and be quiet. Jake, Toni, and Mike moved in closer and gasped in surprise. There was a herd of nine full-grown elk and four calves grazing in a meadow a bit further up the trail.

"That is so incredible," whispered Toni, intently watching the elk. One of them raised its head and looked up at them still chewing. It stared at them for several seconds, then turned and ran into the trees to their left.

"Cool," said Becca, as the rest of the herd followed the first elk at a jog.

During the next fifteen minutes, all they saw crossing the meadow were many different kinds of birds and several nervous rabbits who bounded off into the long grass at their approach. Once across the meadow, they climbed steadily upward until they arrived at a huge, flat, sloping rock where they all sat down for a well-deserved rest.

Mike climbed up the high end of the rock and looked down through a gap in the thinning trees toward another large open area dominated by what seemed to be a mountainous outcropping of bare rock with many steep cliffs. "We've never been this far out," he said. "I would remember that incredible heap of rocks over there. It looks like it would be cool to climb!" he said enthusiastically.

Becca clambered up next to him. She looked around and sighed. "Yeah, I've never been out this—*hey*! Did you feel that?" She held her hand out as a raindrop fell into it. The four teens looked searchingly into the sky. There were gray thunderclouds gathering back the way they had come, as if preparing for a huge storm.

"That's funny," said Jake, eyes narrowed. "It wasn't cloudy at all when we left. Just blue sky." He looked at the others bemused.

"Same here," said Mike. He looked back down the slope in the direction they had come. "Should we try and head back to Becca's house?"

As if in reply, the rain began to pour down harder and quickly turned to hail.

"I don't think we'll make it," said Becca sliding back down the inclined boulder and grabbing the backpack to hold over her head as protection from the pea-sized hail. She looked over at Jake, who was helping Toni untie a knot that kept her from pulling up the hood of her sweatshirt.

"Come on," said Mike, leaping down and dog-trotting off, hunched over, down through the trees toward the mountain of rock. "Let's go by the boulders down there at the base of those cliffs. Maybe we can get between them out of the wind. We need to find some kind of shelter in case it gets any worse." The wind had been steadily rising and now was gusting furiously around them tugging at their clothes.

"Good idea," Toni agreed, finally getting her hood in place.

The four teens ran, the wind at their backs, shielding their faces with their arms. They zigzagged their way down over the rough ground and around several huge stones that must have tumbled from somewhere above. As they struggled up the short rocky slope at the base of the cliff, they realized that the boulders they had seen from the hill were actually two enormous slabs of the cliff face that had broken off and slipped down. The two pieces had come to rest with one slab supporting the end of the other, creating a roughly triangular opening between them.

"Hey, look! A cave!" cried Mike loudly to be heard over the echoing crack of thunder. He was pointing toward the large gap between the two gigantic wedges of rock. The opening was twice the size of a normal doorway and seemed to lead right into the side of the mountain. They scrambled underneath the archway and sat down against either side, looking out the cave's entrance. The remaining light dimmed as black clouds swirled menacingly over the little valley. Lightning flashed nearby and hail and rain began to come down even harder.

"Perfect timing," said Jake grinning. He pulled a flashlight out of Becca's backpack and turned it on. He glanced around the cave entrance, shining the light all around.

"Let's check out how far back this cave goes and make sure no animals are in here with us," said Toni, sounding a bit frightened. Armed with flashlights from the pack, they took only about five steps deeper into the cave before they came to the back wall.

"Well, that's it," Mike said resting his palm against the cool, smooth surface. "I don't see anything alive or even interesting," he said sounding rather disappointed. He turned his light upward as if checking for bats or insects on the ceiling.

"I do," said Becca, obvious delight in her voice. They all focused their flashlights where Becca had hers pointed. Their lights illuminated a smooth stretch of wall covered with different kinds of markings.

"Do you know what this is?" asked Becca excitedly. She turned around and looked at the others, her face lit eerily by the flashlights.

Jake squinted his eyes, and leaned closer to the surface. "It looks like some kind of hieroglyphics!" he said, becoming just as excited as Becca. "But that's impossible."

Toni edged closer to the wall and inspected the markings also. "What does it say, Becca? Can you read it?"

"Well," said Becca, "I'll do my best." She trailed one hand lightly over the wall, side-stepping along until she came to the beginning of a line. She then slid one finger along, pausing briefly at each symbol, and mumbling under her breath.

"Read it out loud," said Mike, crouching down and aiming the flashlight at Becca's moving finger.

Becca nodded as she translated: "*Ancient powerful Sages from the Heavens had spread Knowledge and Serenity throughout the Earth. Each of these Sages had a Power far different from one another's that they used to create Earth and prevent Evil. They had Power far beyond Mortal thinking. These Sages wanted to have their Power and Knowledge on Earth for the rest of Eternity, so it would not fall into the hands of Evil. Here may be found part of that Power, which is one of the Keys for the Future Sages. Hope for the Future lies beyond this wall.*"

"It doesn't make any sense!" said Mike, now getting to his feet. "Beyond this wall?"

"I don't know," said Becca, looking amazed and then suddenly confused. "Maybe I translated some of it wrong. It's not quite like what I've studied in my books. But there's more: *In order to save their power from great evil, the Sages had to hide it where none would ever see, except for the Chosen Ones.*"

"The Chosen Ones?" asked Toni. "But then why did they hide it here? This place wasn't exactly tough to find."

"Maybe it means that only the Chosen Ones could see it," said Jake. He looked at Becca and raised his eyebrows.

"We don't even know if any of this is true. It's all highly unlikely," said Becca skeptically. She looked at the others and then back at the wall. "But it also says: *Whomsoever can read the ancient Saying of these Ancient Sages will open the door to beyond this wall. They will gain the Power of the Ancient Sages who have lived as the Fourteen Angels before Time itself.*

But only the Chosen Ones can read the saying and have the gateway opened before them. They who have written this Knowledge were the Partners of the Ancient Sages. They who have written this Knowledge will be the Partners of the Future Sages to help them on their quest for Eternity more. -Thor - Merlin - Misty - Granite - Juhani - Flairen – Ororo."

"I guess those are the names of the people who helped the Legendary Sages on their quest," said Becca. She stepped back and observed the wall from a few paces away.

"But how could they still be alive looking for these Future Sages?" asked Jake bewildered. "If this is as old I think it is, they were seriously out of *luck*..."

Becca's eyebrows lowered in thought as she placed her hand on her chin and pursed her lips. "I don't know..." she said slowly, shaking her head.

"Th—There," said Toni, pointing toward the wall. "LOOK!"

Below the final row of hieroglyphics more symbols were forming like footprints in wet sand. Becca's eyes went wider as she followed every line and curve. She began to shake, tossing her head. "This—this can't be *possible*..." She rubbed her eyes with the back of both hands, confused. She looked like she didn't know whether to cry or laugh.

Jake looked at Becca with concern. "What—what does it say Becca?"

Becca stared hard at the wall, then turned completely around to face the others. Her face was sweating and pale. "It says: *Welcome Chosen Ones, thy Saying shall appear."* The others could only stare at her, open-mouthed.

With a flash of golden light, all the hieroglyphics disappeared and larger ones appeared in their place. Toni nervously took a step back. She held a fist to her mouth to keep herself from screaming. "*Becca*?" she said, pointing.

Becca swung around to face the wall. She carefully traced the four symbols imprinted there several times before she said slowly, *"Aru Conoha Ra Nicto."*

The cave suddenly shook violently and an avalanche of small rocks fell from the ceiling. The teens dropped immediately to the floor and tried to shield themselves from the stinging rocks and choking dust. The shaking ended with an echoing crash. When the dust cleared, they could see, in the dim glow of the remaining flashlights, that one of the great slabs of rock had slipped down and was now blocking the entrance.

At the back of the cave, another doorway had opened. The entryway had four bright lights streaming through it to form pools of color on the dusty floor: yellow, blue, purple, and silver.

The teens got up and brushed themselves off.

"Is it over?" asked Toni quietly.

The others stared first at the brilliantly colored spots of light then at the doorway itself.

Recognizing another chance for a wild adventure, Mike suggested they go in, and boldly stepped toward the doorway.

"Well, we really have no other choice," said Toni sarcastically, gesturing back toward the blocked entrance.

Jake placed a hand on Mike's shoulder, "I'll go first." He got ahead of Mike and cautiously passed through the brightly lit entrance. The others exchanged looks and quickly followed.

The chamber had to be almost forty yards across and just as deep. It was circular, flaring out somewhat near the doorway. It had a high curved ceiling of the same gray stone as the walls. The floor seemed to be made of squares of white marble. The room was illuminated only by the colored lights radiating from objects held by statues along the walls. A wide opening between the two nearest statues allowed the teens to see that the center contained a table-sized rectangular stone tablet supported by a wide, waist-high stone platform.

Around the perimeter of the room were fourteen spectacular angels carved of pure white marble, even whiter than the floor. Each was nearly seven feet tall and had a pair of graceful feathery-seeming wings spread behind it. Every other angel was joined to the angel on its right by their raised hands. Each pair held an arm out in front and slightly toward the other, palm upward. The right-hand angel of each pair used its left palm to support the up-raised palm of the angel on its left. Four pairs of angels held a radiant glittering object in their joined hands.

The four teens gathered apprehensively around the tablet still gazing around wondrously.

"Well, what does it say, Becca?" asked Mike anxiously. He looked across at Becca, who had already begun to study the hieroglyphics printed on its smooth, white surface.

"*The amethyst gem contains the Power of the Psychic Sage.*" All of the teens, except Becca, looked over at a pair of angels to their right who were holding something that pulsated with a shimmering purple light. "*With this power, you will have the ability to use telekinesis and other types of telepathy.*

"The white diamond contains the Power of the Weather Sage. You will have the ability to control, manipulate, and create any aspect of the weather, such as wind, lightning, and rain.

'The sapphire gem contains the Power of the Ice and Water Sage. With this power, you will have the ability to control, manipulate, and create any type of water or ice.

'The yellow amber contains the Power of the Nature and Earth Sage. With this power, you will have the ability to control, manipulate, and create anything found in nature. You can also control, manipulate, or create anything involving the earth itself such as boulders, soil, or earthquakes.

*'The ruby gem contains the Power of the Fire and Magma Sage...*That's funny," said Becca, looking up at the others. "There's no description for the Fire and Magma Sage."

"It's probably because there's no ruby gem," said Jake, looking around the room again.

Becca looked herself and discovered that three pairs of angels had empty hands. "There are two more that don't have descriptions: *The emerald contains the Power of the Myth Sage. The black opal contains the Power of the Light and Dark Sage...*But why are they missing?" She looked at the others, lost in thought, and returned to studying the remaining lines of symbols.

"That's the million dollar question," said Jake. "Like you said, Becca, how can any of this be true?"

"Yeah!" said Mike, walking over to stand in front of the amethyst gem. "How is it possible?"

"I don't know," said Toni. "But if it's true, it would be awesome!" Toni gave Mike a warning glare. "Don't touch anything! You don't know what could happen!"

Mike laughed. "Sorry, *Mom*," he replied sarcastically.

"Wait. There's more," said Becca. "*Chosen Ones, you will know which to choose from within. For you are the Chosen Ones of the Sages and it is your destiny.*"

"Are they referring to *us* as the Chosen Ones?" asked Toni, incredulously. The others looked at her like she had three heads. Toni shrugged, "Well, what if they are? The wall outside said only the Chosen Ones would be able to make the saying appear to open the wall, and that much sure happened just like they said."

"Well, there's only one way to find out," said Mike, walking toward the angels holding the yellow amber and stopping in front of it. He couldn't take his eyes off it. It was the most beautiful thing he had ever seen. "I choose the Sage of Earth. Earthquakes? Now that's my thing!" Mike was just about to touch the amber.

"MIKE! NO!" shouted Toni. Her voice echoed.

"Why?" Mike asked, taking his hand slowly away from the amber. "You already warned me, and I chose to ignore you. What do you have to say different this time?"

"Well," said Toni calmly, "let's all choose one and then we'll touch them at the same time, just as a precaution."

"Good idea," said Jake in agreement. "We don't want to advance too far without knowing what we are doing. And if nothing happens then we can all look foolish together."

"Alright," said Toni, walking over to the angels holding the glowing sapphire gem. "You know me. I love the water. I choose the powers of water and ice." She looked at Becca and Jake waiting for them to choose theirs.

"Okay," said Becca, "being able to control things with your mind… that's definitely my thing!" She walked over to the angels holding the glowing amethyst gem.

"Well, I guess I only have one choice—*thanks, guys,*" Jake smirked. "But, luckily for me, it's the one I wanted. Imagine controlling the weather, lightning, and wind at will. Definitely awesome!" He walked over to the angels holding the glowing diamond and looked at the others. "On three?"

The others slowly nodded. "Okay then," said Jake, taking a deep breath. "*One—two—three*!"

The teens grabbed the gems, which dissolved into glittering colored sparkles that rushed around their bodies like comets until plunging into their chests. The four delirious teens floated gently up into the air. A powerful wind made their hair blow madly, but didn't disturb their positions several feet off the floor. Their faces remained expressionless, eyes wide open. Mike's eyes and body were glowing yellow. Jake's eyes and body were glowing silver. Toni's eyes and body were glowing blue. Becca's eyes and body were glowing purple. A ball of intense golden light rose up out of the tablet like a small sun, slowly expanding to fill the entire chamber. Once it had encompassed and obscured the light from the four teens, it winked out. The glow from the teens' bodies faded quickly as they crumbled to the ground, unconscious. The darkness was total.

Chapter 5— A Road Trip With Strange Powers

The four teens awoke suddenly in Becca's bedroom with their hearts pounding. Their heads felt about to explode. Becca reached over to look at her alarm clock and realized it was early Sunday morning and the sun had not yet risen. She sighed and plopped back down into her pillow.

Jake moaned and rubbed his head. He got up and started pacing around the room. "I had the strangest dream about all of us…"

Becca nodded as she looked at the others. "Same here, and mine was really strange—it almost felt as if it were *real*."

"Yeah," said Toni, "my dream started in a cave. We were all there because it had started raining." She looked over at Jake and Becca. "We had to get away from the hail because it was hurting…"

"And," said Mike, "we found weird hieroglyphics on the wall…" He looked at Jake.

Jake's eyebrows lowered as if he were deep in thought. The others were telling the same dream that he had had. "A door opened, leading to a room with statues of angels holding—"

Becca cut him off. "The Ancient Sages' treasure which held their power. We each chose a power and then I woke up!" She started to sit up, but then realized her head hurt too much, so she laid right back down again. "I read *real* hieroglyphics for the first time—at least in my dream…"

"Wait a minute," said Mike, looking back and forth at Jake and Becca, "your bruises are gone!" Toni stared at Mike and then at Jake and Becca. Her eyes went wide as she put her hand over her mouth. Jake and Becca looked at each other then felt their own faces.

"They are!" said Jake stunned. "It doesn't hurt anymore!" He smiled widely, looking over at Becca.

"Same here," said Becca. She hit herself in the face with a stuffed animal from her bed. "Okay, *that hurt* but the point is, it didn't hurt more than it should have." The others stared at Becca, puzzled, then laughed.

Toni raised her shirt and looked at her side. "The bruises are gone from my hip!" She stared at Mike. "What about you?"

"I don't feel a thing," said Mike. "But how could that be?" He looked at the others, stunned, as they all fell silent for several seconds.

Jake reached for his glasses and put them on. He squinted and looked around the room, then took them off to clean on his shirt. The others stared at him, unsure of what he was doing. Jake put his glasses on and then took them off. His eyes got wide.

"What's up?" asked Mike.

A grin swept over Jake's face. "I can see perfectly without my glasses!" He stared at them then reached over to his suitcase, and tucked them into one of the pockets, acting as if it were perfectly natural to wake up one morning not needing them anymore.

"I can see well too!" said Becca. Her eyebrows suddenly lowered. "Oh wait, I still have my contacts in." She touched her eye to make sure, and then her expression grew scared. "Their not there! But I didn't do anything with them! Though I don't remember taking them out last night."

The teens said nothing, staring back and forth at each other. Jake's face lit up. "We're all somehow—healed...But how?"

Becca shut her eyes as she slowly spoke. "Maybe our dreams weren't dreams after *all*..."

Toni stared at Becca, confused, but then her brows lowered in thought. "How could the dreams be real... it was only a dream no matter how real it appeared to be. But it did seem real. I could feel the things happening to me...But how could that be? Of course it wasn't real. If it was real then I would still be in that cave." But the question that was on all the teens' minds was if it was a dream, then what did they do all day yesterday and where had they been?

Mike stood up quickly and went over to the door, but then he tripped over Toni's backpack and fell. The whole house shook violently; Becca's belongings falling off shelves. When the shaking stopped, Mike slowly got up and looked at the others.

"What did you do Mike?" asked Toni looking around, clutching her pillow for dear life. "But the real question is... what just happened?"

Mike said nothing and then looked at his hands. Suddenly, they began to glow a bright yellow. The others stared at him, too stunned to move. "The dreams…" said Mike slowly. He looked up at the others—his eyes were glowing a bright yellow also. "They were real!" As Mike raised his hands, the house shook again. The others grasped Becca's bed for support. Mike lowered his arms, and when he stopped glowing, the house stopped shaking. "We all have the power we chose," he said calmly.

The teens were all shaken up. How could any of this be real? Were they still dreaming? But they knew they weren't, so what was going on? They all heard the sound of footsteps pounding up the stairs from below. Becca's bedroom door opened so quickly, it slammed into the wall. The teens shot up to their feet at lightning speed.

"Did you kids feel that?" asked Bill, looking at them nervously. Trudy noticed the dent in the wall from the door and rolled her eyes. The four teens glanced at each other and shook their heads. They still looked frightened, including Mike, but they didn't want to say anything they weren't sure of. It did sound totally outrageous.

Trudy sighed. "Well, I guess you guys slept through it. It was probably a tremor," she said. She looked at Bill and laughed awkwardly. "You guys really must have been tired when you came home last night. I can't believe you went straight to bed." The teens exchanged looks. Now they knew that what they thought was the impossible, was really unbelievably true. "Anyway," said Bill, "let's get everything ready because today's the road trip." They smiled at the teens and walked out of Becca's room, shutting the door behind them.

Becca looked at the others, smiling brightly. "I forgot all about the road trip!"

Jake yawned. "But what about everything that is going on—what's going to happen?"

Becca sighed. "I don't know, but to make sure…I want to try something." Her eyes began to glow purple. She held up her right hand towards the sleeping bags. The sleeping bags flew sluggishly into the air as though being dragged by an invisible force, then rolled themselves up neatly and tied themselves together. Becca lowered her hand as her eyes went back to normal. "All you have to do is think what you want. Wow! It's so amazing!"

"Becca, what's that on your right shoulder," said Jake suddenly, pointing towards Becca's arm. Becca pulled up her sleeve. A small amethyst was somehow attached to the skin on her upper arm just below the shoulder. Below it was a tattoo of hieroglyphics in black. Becca tried fruitlessly to rub them off, then moved to examine them in the mirror above her dresser. They all gathered around.

Toni stared at Becca's arm. "What does it say?" Toni squinted her eyes. "Wait—I can read it! It says what your powers are: '*telekinesis and telepathy*'. We all probably have one too!" said Toni excitedly, pulling up her right sleeve and looking at her reflection in the mirror. Mike and Jake did the same. Sure enough, there were the markings in black along with their own special gems: Mike's was amber, Toni had blue sapphire, and Jake had a white diamond.

Mike cupped his hand over the amber as though he was making sure it was real. "I guess it's just a little reminder." He tried to pull the amber off his arm, but he ended up pulling his skin along with it—it was no use.

Toni suddenly held her hand above her head. The others looked at her as though she were crazy. "I want to try my power," she said, judging by the others questionable expressions. Her eyes began to glow blue. Light particles began to emerge from her hand followed by a huge wave of water. The water splashed over Becca's room, soaking everyone and everything, except herself. Her eyes went back to normal as she lowered her arm. The others gave her an unpleasant look as they shook the water out of their hair.

"Thanks, Toni!" said Mike, a bit angrily, wringing water from his t-shirt. "Now I won't need to shower the traditional way."

Toni frowned and blushed. "I'm *so* sorry. That wasn't quite what I thought was going to happen. I guess we need to think things through before we do anything, so we don't end up actually doing something stupid."

"Then I'll clear up this mess," said Jake. His eyes went white and a soft breeze filled the room. The others looked over to Becca's window and realized that it wasn't open. The breeze began grow stronger, drying out everything, but knocking more of Becca's belongings about the room. He raised his hand as a mini-cyclone appeared. He lowered his arm and the wind died down. Jake's eyes went back to normal. He looked around at the others and couldn't help but laugh at their tangled hair. "Gosh, guys," he laughed. "Nice look. Glad I could help."

"Thanks for the blow dry," said Becca, looking around her disastrously messy room.

"This is incredible," said Jake, the widest grin upon his face. "I bet you anything that this is only a small fraction of what we can *really* unleash if we put our minds to it."

"Well, let's not do anything stupid. I don't think our powers are meant for people to know about right now," said Becca. "Let's talk about it in the R.V. We'll have plenty of time on the trip to Florida to figure out what we're supposed to do."

Jake looked at the others and nodded. "Good point, Becca. We'll stick with your plan."

"Well, we're all ready, thanks to Becca," said Toni, looking at the rolled up sleeping bags. "Let's take our stuff out to the R.V."

The teens struggled down the stairs, their heavy suitcases thumping along behind. They walked out of the garage and saw Bill attaching the Hummer to the back of the R.V. He looked up at the teens and smiled.

"May we go in the R.V. now, Dad?" asked Becca. "We have our stuff ready—unless you've decided to make us stay here?"

"Well, that's an idea," laughed Bill. Becca scowled at him. "Alright, I guess you all can go on in. Make sure you have everything, because if you're ready, we're going to be heading out any second." The teens smiled and nodded. "Go on ahead inside. Your mother is cooking breakfast."

They stepped up inside and gazed excitedly around—the R.V. was huge! The inside felt twice as wide as a regular bus because sections of both the living area and dining area could slide out. There was a kitchen where Trudy was cooking breakfast, along with a dining room table, and a large refrigerator. There was a couch with a television in front of it, and in back, beyond the couch, were two bedrooms. "This is awesome!" exclaimed Becca, dropping her suitcase abruptly on Jake's foot. She beamed and studied every tiny detail of the R.V.

"Isn't it fantastic?" said Trudy, stirring the eggs on the pan she was holding. "Take your stuff through to the bedroom in the back and unpack your suitcases. We'll store them under the bed in our room. We designed that bedroom back there especially for you guys when we ordered the R.V. at the dealer. I hope you like it."

The others nodded and made their way back to the rear bedroom. The door to the first bedroom was open allowing them to see what looked like a queen-sized waterbed, a vanity table and chair, and a combination wardrobe and entertainment center. The next door was a large bathroom with a sink, toilet, shower and bathtub. Behind a folding door across the hall from the bath was a linen closet with several shelves of towels and a rod for hanging clothes at the bottom.

The door at the end of the hall was only half-open, so Becca pushed it the rest of the way with her suitcase. She gasped, "This is so awesome!" The second bedroom had a twin-size bed along each wall, with a window on either side and an enormous picture window on the back wall. In the ceiling was a big skylight that could be opened to let in air. "It's just like the tree house, only with a hatch in the ceiling instead of the floor!" On the front wall, next to the door, was a small desk with a row of four cabinets above it. Each bed had two deep drawers under it for their clothes. They each chose their usual place, and then all began emptying their suitcases into the drawers under their beds. When the bags were empty, Becca put them on her parent's bed, while the others unrolled the sleeping bags and passed out the pillows. But before they could sit down to talk, Becca's mom called to them to come eat breakfast.

Becca exchanged looks with the others. "Let's wait until after breakfast to talk about what's happening…"

"Good idea," said Mike, pulling out his comic books from his backpack and piling them on the desk. The teens left their room and went to sit down at the table. Trudy put eggs and sausage on everyone's plates and poured glasses of milk for the four teens. They hadn't eaten since yesterday morning, and hadn't realized how starving they were; there was lots of eating and very little talking. Trudy walked back over to the stove, wiping her hands with a towel. She checked that all the cabinets were closed, and that the drawers and refrigerator were firmly latched.

It was still dark when Bill finished checking the house, turning off all of the lights, and making sure everything was locked up. He came out of the house locking the front door behind him and turning on the burglar alarm. He then crossed the driveway and made sure all the storage bins under the R.V. were locked up tight. Finally, he climbed in the driver's side door of the R.V. and buckled his seatbelt. "Do you kids love it or what?!" he shouted from the front, turning the key to start the vehicle.

"Are you kidding?" laughed Jake. "What more could you ask for?!"

Bill chuckled. "Everything secured back there, Trudy? Then let's get ready to ride!" He pulled carefully out of the driveway, and they were on their way.

"You guys were hungry!" said Trudy, returning from putting away the suitcases. She took away their empty plates, looking at each of them expectantly. The teens looked at each other curiously. "Well…how is the room? Do you like it?" asked Trudy.

"It's really wonderful, Mom!" said Becca enthusiastically. "I wouldn't change a thing. It's perfect!" The other teens echoed her praise.

"Great! We hoped it would seem like a home away from home. We're headed to New Smyrna Beach, Florida where we will be camping by the beach for a couple of days to go swimming and such. From there, we'll take you to *Islands of Adventure*: It's a theme park based on your favorite extracurricular reading materials—comic books." The teens looked at each other with excitement. "Then from *there*, we'll make our way to New York *City!*—Sound like fun?"

Mike hiccupped loudly and covered his mouth with his fist. "Oh, yeah—it sounds great!" Becca giggled.

Toni sighed dreamily. "I love the beach even though I've never been there! I sooo love the water…"

"Is that why you chose the—" Mike was cut off by a sharp pain in his side and an accompanying glare from Becca.

"Chose what, dear?" asked Trudy, eyeing Mike thoughtfully.

"Um...chose to do a project about the ocean," he said quickly.

Trudy nodded and shrugged. "Oh, then I guess you'll get to see it for real, and we'll all get to enjoy it with you."

The others exchanged looks. "Thank you for the breakfast Trudy," said Jake suddenly, getting up from his chair.

"Yeah, thank you," the others said, also getting up.

They followed Jake back to their room and shut the door. "Good job, Mike," said Toni sarcastically. "You almost blew it back there."

"Sorry," said Mike sheepishly, sitting down on his bed. A bright yellow flash from under the edge of the pillow caught his eye. He looked around at the others with wide eyes before tossing the pillow aside to reveal a small stone tablet with hieroglyphics written on it. "Look!" he exclaimed.

"That's weird," said Toni, looking over toward her own sleeping bag. She looked at Mike's and then at everyone else's sleeping bags. "We all have one."

Becca went to her bed and read the stone tablet to herself. She grunted. "Oh! It's being more specific about what our powers can do."

Toni gave Becca an expectant look. "Okay," she said, "let's hear it."

"Okay," said Becca, picking up her own stone tablet. "Umm...mine says: *You have the ability to move almost any object with your mind. The bigger the object, the more difficult it is to move. You can make certain things appear and change the appearance of certain things. You have the ability to enter a person's mind, if it is not blocked against you carefully. You have the ability to see and know what is happening around you. You may also mentally communicate with anyone from a reasonable distance.*"

Mike was awed and his mouth was slightly open. "That's incredible!"

"Oh, and listen!" said Becca suddenly after reading further. "*If you wish to combine your abilities or use a greater amount of power, repeat the Ancient Sage's saying...*" The tablet abruptly vanished before their eyes, leaving a few iridescent sparkles on her hands. Becca looked up in surprise and grinned at the others. "I can definitely get used to this."

Jake touched Becca's right arm gently. "Look at your arm, Becca," he said. "It looks like there are more symbols there than before." The line of symbols now continued up around the right side of the stone.

Becca shrugged. "I guess it's so we don't forget." She looked up at Toni. "Well, what does yours say?" she asked.

Toni picked up her tablet and began to read aloud. "*You have the ability to control, manipulate, or create any type of water and ice. You have the ability to freeze almost anything. You can walk on water, create water, and ice cyclones. You can even breathe underwater and turn yourself into any form of water at will. You will be able to survive freezing temperatures.*" Toni smiled and squeaked with excitement.

"That's pretty neat!" said Mike. The tablet disappeared from Toni hands with a sound like seagulls crying as several more black markings appeared on her arm as if written by some unseen hand.

Mike picked up his tablet and Jake did the same. Mike began to read aloud. "*You have the ability to control, manipulate and create any type of earth or nature. You can make any plant, tree or flower grow at any time or of any size. You can also move any type of earth, whether rock, dirt, sand or mud. You can make boulders soar into the air at will and create unimaginable earthquakes. You can call blocks of earth from the ground and make volcanoes erupt.*"

Mike had a look of astonishment on his face. "That's unbelievable! How can I do that?" The tablet disintegrated into a small pile of sand as the markings appeared on Mike's upper right arm. "But the real question is...what is the purpose of our extraordinary powers?

"And finally mine," said Jake, examining his tablet closely. "*You have the ability to control, manipulate, and create anything dealing with the forces of the sky. You can create and control the powerful winds of tornadoes and hurricanes of any size or shape. You can create electricity and control lightning and thunder. You can make rain, snow, or hail. You can walk on clouds and command their movements. You can make your body flow like the wind and soar through the air.*" Jake paused for a moment and looked further down the tablet. "It looks like there's a warning here for all of us." He continued reading more slowly being careful of his translation. "*Be warned, Sages. Your newfound abilities will be hard to control. In the near future, you will gain more experience, allowing you to become more powerful. Your destiny will soon reveal itself. Remember that you are the Chosen Ones. Good luck."* The tablet evaporated into a tiny cloud of mist as the markings appeared on Jake's upper right arm. "This is almost too overwhelming. I never thought of our abilities as being 'power'. That's a lot of responsibility." Jake sighed.

"We all must have an astonishing amount of power, if what the tablets said is true," said Toni looking at her own arm then back to the others. "We just have to concentrate on learning how to control it."

"Well, then we should test it," said Mike. His hands began to glow as he looked around at the others. "Let's see what we can really do, and then we'll know exactly what it is we're up against."

"Okay," said Becca, smiling broadly, "but we obviously can't do it in the R.V. We'll have to wait until we stop for the night." She checked her watch. "And, we're not going to be stopping for a good long while yet."

Mike rolled his eyes at her. "Well it's obvious we can't do it in the R.V. Becca," he said. "But we don't have to wait for the R.V. to stop." He nodded his head toward the skylight. "We can all use our powers to fly—*right?*"

Toni looked scared. They hadn't even really tested their powers, so what made him so sure that they could fly? "But what if our powers don't work?" she asked. She looked at the others nervously.

Mike laughed. "Then we'll all fall to the ground and get run over by speeding semis." Toni stared at Mike in horror. She started shaking and wringing her hands.

"Cut it out, Mike," Jake warned, giving him a threatening look. "She's scared enough." He looked at Toni. "You saw us each use a simple amount, so why, all of a sudden, would we lose it all?" he asked her gently.

Toni sighed, still unsure of herself. "I guess you guys are right…"

Jake looked around at the others. "What if we get lost? How are we going to know where to find the R.V?"

"I'll know where to locate it," said Becca standing up. "By using my telepathy, I'll be able to find it with no problem."

Mike laughed. "Then it's settled. Let's go!" He was too excited, still very optimistic. He would try the unimaginable in a heartbeat, if he felt there was half a chance he would succeed.

"Shouldn't we find out what that says though?" asked Toni, pointing towards the back of the bedroom door. The others followed her gaze to where more hieroglyphics were written in glittery red letters.

"It's another warning," said Becca, walking toward the door. She began to read aloud: *"Be warned—now that you hold this power, great Evil will try to destroy you in order to steal this power. You must fulfill your Destiny without being destroyed, and then you shall help the Heavens penetrate this great Evil. For if you, Chosen Ones, are destroyed, the world will fall into the hands of Apocalypse."* Chills ran down their spines. The hieroglyphics vanished in a swirl, like water down a drain.

"Well that's just great!" exclaimed Toni. "Now we have some ancient evil thing at our backs trying to destroy us in order to take our powers. If you ask me, we were better off without all this power stuff. This sounds like an awful lot to handle for a bunch of teenagers. I wonder if there's any more surprises that we need to know about!?"

"You worry too much, Toni," said Jake, grinning confidently at her. "This so called *'evil'* will never find us. Who would ever imagine that a bunch of teenagers are the Chosen Ones?" He pulled the desk chair in the middle of the room so he could open the skylight. "Besides, Toni—what's the worst that can happen?" He handed down the screen then hoisted himself up through the opening followed by Mike and Becca. Toni thought about what he said, and in her opinion—with all this going on—anything could happen. She hesitantly followed the others up through the skylight.

The teens struggled to stand up on top of the R.V., the wind blowing violently against them. The only one having trouble staying afoot was Toni because she was still on her hands and knees. "Wait a minute!" said Mike, looking nervous. "People are watching!" It was true. People inside other vehicles were staring at the four and pointing. Some even honked their horns and tried to flag down Bill to let him know that something wasn't right.

"I think I can take care of it," said Becca, holding her arms to keep her balance. Her eyes flashed purple and the four teens were enveloped in a glowing purple bubble of light. "There!" The people who were staring at the teens began to squint, and turned their heads around trying to see where they had gone. It was almost like they had become invisible, but the teens could still see each other.

Toni was still shaking nervously but she managed to smile at Becca and compliment her on her quick thinking. "Cool move!" Becca's eyes and body glowed purple as she rose up in the air off of the roof of the R.V., hovering right above it as it was moving.

She grinned and looked around. "Whoa, this is remarkable! It feels very weird though…like I'm swimming or something."

Jake's eyes and body began to glow white. He closed his eyes and imagined the wind lifting him into the air like a kite. He felt himself soaring into the air, becoming one with it. He stopped to one side of Becca. He slowly opened his eyes and looked cautiously down at the others. "Come on, guys, let's go. You have to feel what it's like!"

Mike grinned as his eyes started to glow yellow. He turned his head back toward a rugged boulder they had just passed right off the highway. The boulder, that was as big as he was, began to glow a bright yellow also. It lifted off the ground and spun lazily up into the air. When it came zooming up along side them, Mike jumped off the fast-moving R.V. and landed squarely on top of it. It lifted him up to Jake and Becca. His body still glowed softly as he waited with the others for Toni.

"Come on, Toni!" yelled Becca impatiently. She tried not to laugh when she saw her struggle to stand up.

"I'm too scared!" she yelled. "I don't think I can do this!"

"Come on, if anything happens we all have your back," said Jake warmly.

Toni looked up to him and stared into his eyes fondly. "You promise?"

Jake smiled. "Of course, we're your best friends. We wouldn't let anything happen to you, '*wink, wink*'!" He and the others laughed, including a rather reluctant Toni.

Toni's right hand began to glow an intense blue. She twirled her fingers around until a thin round disk of ice formed beneath her. It slowly rose, lifting her up. "Hey, I can keep my balance pretty easily. This isn't so tough to control after all!" She suddenly did a flip in the air and laughed madly. "This is so amazing!"

"Let's go then!" laughed Mike, soaring high and fast up into the air. The others quickly followed. They were flying as though they had been doing it their entire lives. Even though the wind buffeted them, they still enjoyed the beautiful view of the cities and roads down below them. They soared up further, dipping into the undersides of the white puffy cotton-ball clouds and came out damp on the other side. They held their arms out at their sides and closed their eyes, zooming along letting the sky totally relax them.

"This is so peaceful!" said Becca, the wind blowing gently through her hair. She twirled in circles and laughed, closing her eyes. She placed her hand on her hip and mumbled. "I think we're in New Mexico…"

"How do you know?" asked Mike, now on his knees grasping the boulder with his hands too. He was moving very fast. If anything were hit by his boulder—they were in for a painful crash.

"Because a clear picture keeps appearing in my head, showing me New Mexico!" stated Becca confidently.

"Oh…" Mike slowed to a stop in midair. He got to his feet and stood up, pulling the elastic hair tie off of his ponytail and shaking his head. The others stopped in midair to wait for him. "Now it's time to see what I can really do!" He twitched his fingers mysteriously, making a handful of black seeds appear. Satisfied with the outcome, Mike punched the boulder he was riding with his free hand which smashed into hundreds of small pieces. Before he could plummet to the ground, he threw the seeds which hurriedly sprouted and grew into giant green, floating leaves, half his size. He landed on one, which amazingly, held his weight perfectly. Dozens more giant leaves began to appear throughout the sky. Mike began to hop from leaf to leaf as though walking on the moon. He was now leaping extremely high and far. He began to get further and further away by the second. The others laughed and rapidly swooped away to follow him.

They caught up to him and continued to watch him with curiosity. He twitched his fingers yet again and a brown seed the size of a baseball appeared in his hand. He tossed it down below him and a giant cushioned hairy, green leaf, twice his size, appeared. It looked sort of like a green mattress. He hopped off the smaller leaf, landing smoothly on the bigger one. The other leaves slowly vanished. The new leaf began to glow yellow as he zoomed off again. Tiny yellow stars as bright as the sun trailed behind him like the tail of a comet.

Mike glided down then jumped off the leaf, descending quickly to the rocky desert. The others gasped. Mounds of earth and rock rose from the desert floor, carrying him up into the air. The mounds rose higher and higher carrying him right back up to the rest of the teens. A boulder flew out from the column of earth under him and he jumped onto it, soaring back up high in the air. He threw another seed out in front of him and did a rather flashy flip onto the newly appearing giant leaf. He looked defiantly at the others, breathing rather heavily. A large grin spread on his face. "Let's see you all do that!"

Toni laughed. "Wow, that was pretty amazing, but if you insist—I'll beat that!" She flew closer to Mike until she was hovering right in front of him. "Except my performance will be better and more enjoyable. For someone who likes *exciting rides,* this will be even more exquisite." She turned around sharply, scowling at the others. "Stay behind me and do what *I do...*"

The others glanced curiously at each other then followed. Toni waved her hand and the puddle she was standing on vaporized. Wisps of fog crept up her legs and around her body like snakes. Her glowing form was just visible through the mist, which seemed to enable her to fly through the air more quickly. She threw both arms out in front of her and sent a bolt of ice shooting out of each hand to create a narrow pathway of ice in midair. She hopped onto it and began to slide, creating more of a path as she went along. She laughed with excitement as she slid along faster and faster.

"Awesome!" yelled Mike, flying over to the start of the frozen pathway. He hopped off his leaf and landed on the pathway, also sliding down the slope. His eyes and body stopped glowing. Jake and Becca glanced at each other and smiled, then eagerly followed right behind him. The teens were hundreds of feet up in the air, sliding down a delicate path of ice—this was definitely something out of the ordinary—yet they were having the time of their lives! They were catching up to Toni until only a couple of feet separated each of them.

"OH, YEAH!" screamed Becca, her back on the ice and arms up in the air. All of the teens' backs, except for Toni's, were getting wetter and colder by the minute from the quickly melting ice. They ignored the piercing cold—they were having too much fun. Becca laughed out loud. "This definitely beats Mike!"

"Hey!" yelled Mike offended. "I wouldn't say so." He rolled over to his stomach, so he was sliding along headfirst. "This is just as exciting as any other ride!" The ice slide ended, and the teens slid off into a free fall. They used their powers to catch themselves, and flew even higher into the air.

Jake turned to stare at Mike, "You're kidding, right? I mean—we're only hundreds of feet in the air sliding down ice, and you're bored?" Jake laughed and shook his head. "Mike—I would pay someone who could figure you out." Jake grinned and yelled to Toni, giving a thumbs up. "I give it a ten!" Toni laughed and bowed.

Becca snorted. "Okay guys, you want a performance, I'll show you a performance. Your eyes will now be treated to a most spectacular performance by *me*. It's my turn now—just stay here and be astonished!"

"Yeah—okay—whatever," said Jake laughing.

Becca gave him a nasty glare as she soared off a little way ahead of them. She put her hands out wide apart as if holding something invisible. She shut her eyes and a moment later, a glittery substance appeared between her hands. She suddenly opened her eyes and they brightly flashed purple. She threw her arms straight up and made the glittery stuff fly into the air. It was like tiny stars of all colors. They exploded into miraculous fireworks, forming a picture of the four teens, and then it slowly began to fall. Becca raised one hand toward the stars and they began to soar around her, as if spinning in an invisible cyclone. The glitter flew into a ball up into the air, which exploded with a loud *crack*. From the explosion, a great sword appeared. It had a shiny, silver, thick blade with a large amethyst gem attached to the golden handle. It slowly and gracefully fell into Becca's hand. She swung it around experimentally, and then pointed it at Jake. "Beat that!"

The others were awestruck by Becca's display of her abilities. Toni and Mike turned as one to look at Jake. Surprisingly, he was *smirking*.

"Well, Jake," said Mike. "That certainly beats mine and Toni's. Still think you can beat it?" His eyes squinted and he snickered.

Becca's eyebrows arched. "I don't think he'll be able to—the look he's giving us seems *questionable*."

"Okay," said Jake, nodding his head and grimacing. "Just you watch—I'll beat it—and more importantly, I'll beat it with style!" He soared over to the cloud where Becca had been floating. He looked over at the others and grinned mischievously. His eyes changed suddenly to a shade of fog white. He tilted his head slowly to one side as his hair began to blow wildly with the gradually increasing wind.

"I have a feeling we're going to need this," said Becca, raising her glowing hand. A purple force field of light appeared around them like an iridescent soap bubble.

With his head still, Jake blinked and looked up into the sky. The others did too. Wavy white and gray clouds began to form blocky shapes in the distance. Jake snapped the fingers on his left hand causing stronger winds to blow. One after another, funnel clouds began to form, descending to the wide desert plain. Bushes, shrubs, and dust were flying about forming massive tornadoes. More and more tornadoes kept appearing as if replicating themselves. The tornadoes approached and began to circle around the four teens. Soon, all that was visible was a wall of gray circling clouds.

Mike, Toni, and Becca looked amazed, but then became frightened when Jake clapped his hands as a huge bang of thunder shook the sky. Suddenly, lightning struck through and around the circling tornadoes. Jake wasn't affected at all by the powerful force of nature, but his hair was still blowing crazily. It was as though he had become nature itself. He blinked again, making rain begin to pour hard and fast. The rain then turned to huge pieces of hail—the hail then turned into graceful falling snow before it reached the ground. Jake held up his hand and the snow soared up to form a giant snowflake right above him. Jake did a back flip right up into the air and landed confidently on the delicate platform. He began to spin around and around, faster and faster, until he became a human cyclone himself. Another loud crack of thunder shook the violently churning sky. The tornadoes circling around the teens began to slow, and then died out leaving behind odd piles of sand and debris. The clouds slowly dissipated, revealing only the clear turquoise blue of the sky. Jake's spinning slowed also, then stopped abruptly. The snowflake was gone.

Becca raised her hand and the force field around her and the others winked out. The three stared at Jake wide-eyed—he was grinning at them. "Well, to be honest, I had no idea what I was doing and I don't even know how I did it. I just...suddenly feel so—so—*weak*..." He stopped glowing and fainted, falling through the now clear sky, unconscious and limp.

"Oh, no!" Becca screamed. She clasped her hands over her mouth as she watched Mike soar down after Jake.

"I've got him," said Mike calmly, throwing a seed toward Jake. A giant leaf appeared and skyrocketed downwards overtaking Jake, who landed gracefully on it. The leaf flew back up to Mike with its unmoving passenger.

"Why is he so weak?" asked Toni, picking up Jake's wrist then suddenly dropping it.

"I think he's asleep," said Becca leaning over to watch Jake's slowly rising and falling chest. "He does seem to be breathing." Becca sighed. "He must be exhausted because he used a great deal of power all at once," she said faintly. "He has to be more careful. He isn't used to it yet—none of us are. To unlock something that powerful—it's dangerous. It could hurt us or somebody else—and even worse—he could have lost control!"

"Do you think he'll be all right?" asked Mike, looking at Jake worriedly. "He looks like he needs to go to the hospital." He slapped Jake rather hard in the face to make sure he was knocked out. Jake only grunted.

"And just how are they suppose to treat him?" asked Toni, staring at Mike strangely for slapping Jake. "And, how are we going to explain what happened!?"

"He'll be alright," said Becca. "I'm sure of it, but I suggest we take him back to the R.V. straight away!"

"Right," said Mike. He gazed quizzically at the leaf holding Jake. "Umm—*follow*?" The leaf flew directly behind Mike, so close that it almost touched him. Becca and Toni looked at each other and laughed.

"You know Mike," said Becca, a smirk lighting up her face. "I could gladly take Jake off your hands. It will be a lot simpler for me."

Mike lowered his eyebrows. "Well, you know what, Becca? It's just as easy for me to carry him as it is you!" Becca looked taken aback, but then looked at Toni and laughed.

Toni looked down far below them searching for the highway. She squinted her eyes and peered down as far as she could. Once she spotted the highway, her eyes lit up and she turned to Becca. "The highway is right down there, but how do we find the R.V.?"

"Just follow me," Becca said, soaring diagonally downward, banking gracefully like a giant swallow. Toni and Mike followed her, as did the leaf that Jake was on. Mike looked behind him at Jake, who seemed to be on the verge of sliding off the leaf. He waved a glowing hand and vines sprouted out of the edge of the leaf and tied themselves around Jake's wrists and ankles. The teens continued to soar.

"We're close!" yelled Becca suddenly. It was mid-afternoon and the teens were beginning to catch sight of the highway. Becca soared down until she was only about five feet above the street, dodging cars and trucks of all sizes. The invisible force faded from them, but luckily, they were all going too fast for anyone to see.

"There!" said Becca, pointing ahead of her to the R.V. She landed on top of it, followed by the others and the obedient leaf holding Jake. Becca snapped her fingers and the skylight door opened. She jumped down inside to stead the ladder for the others. Toni came climbing down, her glow fading away. Mike made the boulder he was soaring on shrink to the size of a pebble and fly inside his pocket. He climbed down the ladder followed by the floating leaf with Jake still tightly secured to it. Mike was still glowing as he waved his hand for the leaf to disappear. Jake dropped abruptly but gently onto his bed. Mike stopped glowing as he and the others circled around, watching Jake sleep.

Chapter 6— The Teenage Sages

Jake's eyes slowly fluttered opened. He gazed up at his three best friends who were looking down at him. He slowly sat up and rubbed his eyes.

"You won the performance award," said Becca coldly. "Now I hope you feel horrible enough to think twice about doing something stupid like that again!"

"What do I win?" asked Jake, smirking innocently. But the look on Becca's face made him regret even asking the question.

"Our *respect*!" said Becca through gritted teeth.

"That was incredible!" yelled Mike. "I didn't think anybody could have beaten my performance—but gosh—that was amazing!"

"Yeah," said Toni in agreement. "It really was awesome!"

"But it was also risky and dangerous," said Becca coldly. "You could have hurt yourself, not to mention us. We obviously need to get accustomed to our powers before trying to use a great amount."

"You're right," said Jake. "I apologize—but I think it was the spinning into a cyclone that pooped me out. It sure looks easy on TV." The others laughed.

"We all can do some pretty amazing things," said Mike. "These powers are unbelievable! I've never even dreamed of being able to do some of the extreme stuff that I can do now."

"Yeah, and I bet this can all be put to good use," said Toni. "We must have our powers for a reason, and now it's time to put them to *proper* use: fighting crime and evil, just like in the comics!"

"I don't know," said Mike. "That sounds kind of corny. I was thinking more along the lines of solving problems as they come along, not going around looking for trouble. That can only cause more trouble, as I am well aware from personal experience."

"But we don't want to attract too much attention," said Becca. "People have never seen anybody with our abilities before. Not for real, anyways. Besides, we don't want people knowing who we really are. I feel like we are supposed to use our powers anonymously for good, not plaster our faces all over the newspapers."

"But think of the fame!" Mike yelled excitedly. "Everyone would know who we are! We'd be like movie stars!"

"You and your fantasies, Mike!" said Toni annoyed. "You *would* be the one who would do this only for the attention. If everyone knew who we were, they would all try to decide what things we should do. We have to think of ways to do things for the betterment of humankind, not just for personal glory. And the only way not to be overwhelmed by suggestions is to not let anyone know."

"Toni's right," said Jake. "What we need are disguises. How about costumes that suit our abilities?"

"That sounds like a good idea. We'll also need fake names to protect our identities," said Toni. "And the comic book heroes have cool aliases that tell something about their abilities. We can do the same thing! If people can't call us by our real names they'll have to call us by something else."

A blinding bluish flash suddenly lit the room, and the teens squinted around their fingers to shield themselves from the brightness. Becca stared at the back of the bedroom door and began to read aloud the new hieroglyphics that had appeared in brilliant fiery orange. "It says, *Now that you are aware of your amazing Power; know that other humans have been gaining Power as well. But remember, you are the nobler and stronger ones for you are the Chosen Ones and Holders of the Powers of the Ancient Sages. There are Others who have become mutated because of the Mythical Mist. Be warned, yet again, these Others may be very powerful. They can upset the balance of Good and Evil by using their Powers for or against you.*

There is no way of knowing which they will choose." The hieroglyphics vanished in a wisp of flowery-scented smoke.

Toni sighed as she sat down on the bed next to Jake. "That has to be the weirdest one yet," she said calmly.

"So, what this means is that we aren't the only ones out there who are gaining weird powers. But our powers are better, since we are Chosen Ones who have power of the Sages, whoever they are," said Mike. He looked at the others confused, still not sure of everything going on. "I hope these messages get clearer as we go along, cause this one sure wasn't much help."

"It's like the world is turning into a comic book," said Jake. "But is that a good thing—or are we in *danger*? In the comics, being a hero always has its down side."

"Well, that doesn't change the fact that we've been destined to use these powers to help destroy evil," said Becca. "So let's get started with the first step—we each need a code name."

Toni's eyes lit up and a sly smile crossed her face as she looked sideways at Mike. Mike looked expectantly in her direction as though he knew what was coming. "You could be *Mother Nature*, Mike," she said grinning sardonically.

Mike scowled back at her. "Ha, ha, very funny. I thought a name like Quake would suit me best." He closed his eyes and tilted his head to one side as though picturing going around every day with the name Quake.

"That's pretty cool," said Jake. "I want to be called Cyclone since I control the weather and the weather depends mostly on the winds."

"Cyclone is alright," said Toni approvingly. "It suits you."

Becca considered Toni's tone; she could tell that Toni was also thinking of a name for herself. "What are you going to be Toni?" she asked.

"I was thinking something like Arctic Cat," she said smiling.

"Awkward," said Mike. "First of all, it's two names; second of all, you're not feisty like a cat!" Mike suddenly broke off, shut his eyes and grinned. "On second thought you might *be*. But besides, that one's already a brand name." Toni scowled at him.

"He's right," said Jake. "It needs to be shorter—more elaborate—something that will suit you AND be easy for people to remember." Jake looked at Becca for support.

Becca stood in silence, one finger tapping her pursed lips. After a few moments, she said, "It has to be something related to water right?"

"Yeah," said Toni, starting to follow where Becca was coming from.

Becca smiled, proud of herself. "Then what suits you well—is Aquarius. It's the zodiac symbol for a water bearer."

"Yeah," said Jake. "Aquarius sounds perfect."

"Okay, I like it," said Toni nodding slowly in agreement. She looked over at Becca again. "And *you*?"

Becca answered without hesitation, "Star. I believe the stars contain the answers to what happened in the past as well as what is coming in the future. They represent wisdom and psychic happenings that are far more expansive and important than the mind can ever imagine."

The others stared silently at Becca, looking at her as though she pulled another smart one on them again. It was just like Becca to have a long, but reasonable, explanation for her answer.

"Cool," said Jake, breaking the awkward silence. "So…it's Quake, Cyclone, Aquarius, and Star."

"And we should be known as 'The Teenage Sages, Saviors of the Earth'," said Becca, smiling at the others. "If we're going to work as a team, then we should also be identified as a team."

"Teenage Sages," the other three said together approvingly. Their bodies began to glow as they floated a foot above the floor. Then just as quickly, went back to normal and floated back down. The teens stared at one another, unsure of what had just happened.

"So now we have our names," said Toni. "But what about our costumes? How are we going to get those?"

"I'm sure I can create them pretty easily," said Becca. "I just need an idea of what to make. Once I have a visual image in my mind, it should be simple."

"I can draw them," said Jake. He jumped up and began to go through the outside pockets of his suitcase. He came out with four sheets of white paper and a pencil. He then turned the suitcase flat to use as a desk and immediately started to sketch, his pencil going in every direction.

"Hey, I was thinking guys..." said Becca, "what if we had the power to make our costumes immediately appear on us but also make us look a few years older?"

"You can do that?" asked Mike, taken aback. "But why would we want to look older?"

"Well, some people out there might not take us seriously because we're younger. But, if we could seem to be more mature teenagers, around seventeen or eighteen, they couldn't dismiss us so easily."

"Would we be able to go back to our normal selves?" asked Toni concerned. She glanced over Jake's shoulder to see how the drawings were coming along. He scowled and put his arm defensively over the page.

"Definitely," said Becca. "I mean, it would be tough to explain at school why we all suddenly look so much older. Besides, I'm enjoying my young teenage years."

"Fine with me," said Jake, his pencil scratching the paper wildly, but still listening intently to the conversation. Jake was very capable at multitasking and could easily do many things at once.

"Then it's settled," said Becca.

"Becca!" said Toni suddenly, bolting up from the bed.

"What?" Becca snapped.

"How did your parents not know we were gone, or do they?" Toni asked, fearfully, grabbing Becca's arm. "What if they found out? What if they know what's been going on? How could we possibly explain when we don't even understand ourselves?" said Toni quickly, panic making her voice shrill.

"Oh, I covered that already," Becca said while gently prying Toni's fingers from around her forearm. "Right before we left, I did something to the room so that if my parents had walked in or called us, we would have answered or appeared to have been doing something that we would normally do, like watch television."

Jake looked up from his drawings and laughed. "Good one."

The others settled in and watch television while Jake continued madly scribbling and erasing. It wasn't until late afternoon, while the

R.V. was still crossing the deserts of New Mexico, that curiosity finally got the better of them.

"Are you almost done there, Jake?" asked Mike despairingly. He brusquely grabbed the remote and began switching through the channels for what seemed like the five hundredth time, his pupils dilating from the flashing of the television screen.

"I'm just finishing up Toni's costume." Toni was paying no attention to the television. She was lying on her back, legs crossed, engrossed in a comic book.

"You have to remember," said Jake, looking at Mike, "these costumes have to be designed to not interfere with using our powers. If they don't suit us, then we'll have a hard time in them."

"Got it," said Mike.

"Done!" said Jake, standing up suddenly while grabbing the papers and holding them firmly in his left hand.

Toni's eyes reluctantly left her comic book as she sat up. "Really?"

Jake grinned smugly, obviously proud of the work he had done. "Yup!"

Toni got up from the bed and reached for the papers. "Let me see! Let me see!" she said excitedly.

Jake snatched the papers quickly away and held them up above his head to keep them out of Toni's determined reach. "Nope, you'll see your costume when Becca gives it to you."

Toni's eyes narrowed. "Fine then," she said coldly and flounced back over to throw herself back onto her bed.

Becca walked over to Jake "Okay, let me—" Becca was cut off by her mom's voice.

"Your dinner is ready!" her mom said joyfully.

"Okay!" yelled Becca. Mike immediately jumped off the bed and walked out the door leaving the other three behind. Becca looked over at Jake. "I guess I'll see the costumes after dinner," she said as she brushed past him and out the door. Jake nodded and quickly followed Toni from the room.

Not surprisingly, Mike was first to finish his plate and willingly accepted a second serving. "I was hungry! You can't blame me!" The others laughed, including Trudy.

"Well, Becca," said Trudy, wiping her hands on a towel. "I'm going up to drive the evening shift. I put the leftover macaroni and cheese in the fridge for later; just heat it up if you want more. Please stack the dishes in the sink when you're finished." She and the others glanced pointedly at Mike.

"Well, I'm full now!" They all laughed again.

The teens went back to their room, and Toni shut the door carefully behind them. She yelped in surprise when she saw yet more hieroglyphics written on the door in a vivid shimmering red. The others spun sharply and crowded around to get a closer look.

Becca began to read aloud. "It says—*One more thing: The longer you hold the Power of the Sages, the more it becomes part of you, and the more you'll need this Power for eternity's sake.*

"Is it just me or does it seem like someone is actually talking to us?" asked Mike. He stalked around the room, peering under the beds and behind the curtains as if expecting to catch someone or something spying on them.

"Yeah, I was thinking the same thing." Toni agreed. "Like when it said *one more thing*. That's very *weird*."

"So, not only are we Sages, but sort of mutants, too, in a way." said Becca. "The Power is starting to become part of us, as if we have to have it to survive…"

"Well, isn't that a good thing?" asked Jake, although his tone sounded uncertain.

"*I*—I guess so," said Becca. She watched the hieroglyphics pulse eerily before unraveling like a sweater and disappearing.

"Well," said Toni pushing through the others to reach the center of the room. "Moving on…I want to see what my costume looks like!"

"Oh, that's right! I almost forgot." said Becca. "Let me see the drawings, Jake."

"Okay," he said sternly, "but if you don't like it, that's just too bad," Jake said to Toni as he walked over to the desk to grab the four sheets of paper he had been working on earlier. He handed them ceremoniously to Becca. She bowed in thanks and carefully looked over each page.

"Okay!" she said with a smile. "Not bad. I'm sure they'll look better once we're in them. Let's give it a shot!" Becca lined them up across the room, giving each one an appraising look. She began to glow and then snapped her fingers at each of them in turn. The teens looked each other up and down with amazement as they began to morph slowly into older forms of themselves.

Jake studied the expressions on the others' faces. "I guess you like them then?"

"Oh, yeah!" The others all agreed enthusiastically.

Mike was now taller and more muscular than before, with a short black beard. He was wearing a shiny black, armored breastplate with many designs embossed on it in gold. A short black cape hung smoothly from his shoulders to his waist. Mike's long dark hair hung down just past his muscular shoulders, allowing his tattoo and amber stone to still be visible. The baggy, black leather pants he wore had a wide black belt that matched the boots on his feet and the half-gloves on his hands. "I look awesome!" crowed Mike, stepping in front of the mirror and tucking his long hair back behind one ear to reveal the same golden halo earring as always.

Becca pushed him gently to one side so she could see herself, too. She was also a lot taller, and her hair was longer and a brighter gold. She wore a short, blue skirt made from a strangely patterned leathery material with a golden belt. She had a tight, short, purple belly shirt with a four-pointed star cut out over the chest. Tall, purple leather high-heeled boots reached just to mid-thigh. Bracelets made of linked golden plates were on each wrist, and a brown leather scabbard draped across her body from over one shoulder. The sword she had made appear earlier was hanging at her side. Her tattoo and amethyst gem sparkled on her right arm. "Hmm…not too shabby," she said softly as she turned from side to side.

Toni was taller too, but not as tall as the others. Her baby fat had finally turned to sleek, strong muscle. She had darker, longer hair, and wore a long, royal blue silk hooded cloak that brushed the ground. Under the cloak, she wore a shiny black bodysuit of form-fitting leather. It had a narrow bright blue belt that matched her tall high-heeled boots. Dark blue lipstick made her lips seem as though they were made of ice. She also wore long black gloves that made her fingers and hands look strong and lethal as she flexed them. When she pushed the others out of the way to twirl in front of the mirror, six glittering white-jeweled snowflakes were visible on the cloak and one on the hood. "See, I always said I would grow out of the awkward puppy stage! Too cool, Becca!" she said, laughing.

Jake was now taller than ever and had longer brown hair down to his shoulders. He was just as muscular as Mike and had a short beard in dark brown flecked with blond. He wore a tight, black leather, sleeveless shirt with two silver ribbons hanging from each shoulder. A lightning bolt was cut out of the chest of the shirt revealing part of his chest. A heavy silver belt was at the waist of the baggy, black leather pants, and each pant leg was embossed with a shining silver tornado on the thigh. He could see that the diamond in his tattoo shone as brightly and magnificently as the silver plates at his wrists when the others moved aside to allow him to look in the mirror. "Wow! You did a great job, Becca!"

The rest of the teens beamed at Becca, and she blushed. They couldn't believe how different they looked or how real their costumes appeared.

"These costumes couldn't have suited us any better, Jake," said Becca approvingly. She took out her sword and looked at it approvingly, even making a few experimental feints.

"It's truly amazing, Jake," said Mike. "Perfect." He opened and closed one fist, enjoying the feel of the soft, strong texture of his new glove.

"I love mine," said Toni. She pulled her hood and threw the sides of her cloak back, letting it land like a cape. She stretched out her arms, flexing her hands to feel the tight leather gloves.

"So," said Becca, "when you go into your Power form, this is what you'll look like."

"Does this mean we're protectors now?" asked Mike beaming.

"Not yet," said Becca. "We might have amazing powers, but we haven't helped anyone yet!"

"Well, how are we going to know if someone needs our help?" asked Jake.

"I guess I'll get a message of some kind in my head if something dangerous is near. Actually, we all probably have the ability to sense danger," said Becca, holding her hand up to her head.

"Well," said Mike, "there's no point in staying in costume all day, no matter how great I look." A golden glow flared briefly as he changed into his normal self. The others agreed and did the same.

"Well," said Toni, "I'm going to go read." She was about to sit down on her sleeping bag, when the R.V. began to accelerate up a steep hill then abruptly stopped with a squeal of brakes. Mike and Becca lurched to the floor and Jake banged his head on a cabinet door that flew open, showering him with extra blankets and pillows. Toni slid on the slick material of sleeping bag to end upside-down in a heap against the wall.

Becca shot up quickly, pulling Mike up with her. "Didn't see that one coming," she laughed. "I wonder what happened?" she asked opening the bedroom door and sticking her head into the hall.

"Sorry, kids!" yelled Bill. "Everybody okay back there? There was unexpected traffic at the top of this hill. It looks like there's a major accident up ahead."

The teens looked up and out the bedroom windows at the sound of sirens as several police cars and ambulances quickly went by driving on the shoulder of the road. The teens glanced at each other and nodded. They changed quickly into their Power forms and flew out the skylight like before. They passed over the R.V. and raced up the mountain over the line of stopped cars toward the flashing lights in the distance. As they approached, they could see policeman keeping a group of people near the road while a bunch of fireman tried to secure a van and a car that were hanging over the edge of the steep cliff. An ambulance sped past the teens to reveal two men on the opposite rocky slope exchanging gunfire from behind some huge boulders with another group of policeman who were sheltering behind their open car doors. Just as the teens arrived, one of the police cars peeled away from the rest to chase after another vehicle that was speeding away.

"Aquarius and I will take care of the bad guys, you two help the people stuck over the cliff," said Jake quickly. They immediately soared off in different directions.

"Quake!" yelled Becca. Keep the cars from falling. I'll help the people trapped inside." She soared out over the edge and swooped down out of sight.

"Righteo!" yelled Mike. He raced to the bottom of the cliff and looked up to study the cars. They were both precariously hung up by their front tires on twisted tree limbs and scrub growing from the side of the cliff. Two giant, glowing yellow seeds appeared in Mike's hands and he threw them into a gap in the rocks. Two trees sprouted out of the hole and their massive trunks grew rapidly up to support the vehicles in a sturdier position. He then flew up to assist the people in the car.

Becca was trying in vain to open the double doors on the back of the van, but they were jammed shut. The parents and children were crying for help and pounding on the door from the inside. Becca could hear their fear echo in their voices. "Okay," she said calmly. "Move back! The doors are going to come flying up." The people in the car did as they were told and carefully moved back without delay, though they were wondering how Becca could be staying in midair. Becca jerked her arms upwards in front of the doors causing them to be pulled from their hinges. "It's okay," she said, holding her hands out towards the family. They began to float weightlessly toward her out of the van. They were in shock with all that had already happened, and the mother fainted when she found herself bobbing through the air like a balloon. Mike had already gotten the other people out from the car and had them floating on leaves beside the van. They weren't moving at all, and Mike and Becca quickly ascended the cliff to the medical vehicles, the victims trailing behind them.

Meanwhile, Jake had flown around the mountain on the other side of the road and silently landed behind the two men who had been shooting at the police. "YO!" yelled Jake. The men were startled and jumped back, nearly tumbling down the slope. They had stringy, greasy black hair and were unshaven and rumpled, and by the looks of it, they were twins. "Come quietly or I'll take you by force, which I really prefer doing, but I'm going to be nice and let you choose." The men looked at each other and grinned, and then pointed their guns at Jake and fired. Jake moved his arms quickly in front of him. As the bullets ricocheted off the silver wrist plates he said, "I guess you've chosen my preference." Jake gave a violent wave of his left arm and a strong gust of wind blew the pistols out of the shooters' hands.

They looked at Jake without fright. "I see," said one of the men, "that we're not the only mutants on the top of this mountain." They held one arm out toward Jake. Their hands swelled and split open as their skin peeled off and blood spewed everywhere. They clenched their teeth against the unbearable pain. Their arms began to mutate into metal, forming machine guns. Jake's eyes got wide in fear, and he shuddered as revulsion spread through him. "That's really *disgusting*," he exclaimed, backing away slightly.

The men started to shoot, but Jake flipped up into the air, dodging the bullets. "Gosh, I never thought I'd run into anything like this*!*" he told himself. Jake's eyes glowed bright white as he used his power to make the men spin faster and faster. So fast, that soon they were spinning up off the ground, in twin mini-cyclones. "How *dare* you put others' lives in *danger*. Because of *you*, people have been hurt. Now it's your time to pay!" Jake heard a loud explosion coming from the cyclone, as he saw a small rocket heading right toward him. Suddenly, Becca appeared right in front of Jake, her fingertips pressed to either side of her head just like she did in math class when she was stumped and thinking hard. The rocket stopped in midair, spun several times, and flew off in the opposite direction.

Jake exhaled deeply, putting one hand on his chest. "Thanks, Becca," he said.

Becca sighed heavily. "No problem, I just really don't want to think what could have happened…"

Another loud explosion occurred, bringing their attention back to the spinning men who had apparently been struck by their own rocket. Smoke billowed up everywhere, and nothing could be seen. Jake wiggled his fingers to blow the smoke away and put out the flames. Once the smoke cleared, Jake and Becca landed on the ground, and walked toward the two men where they lay on the ground with burns and bloody faces. They scanned the horizon when they heard the rotors of an approaching helicopter.

"Let's go," said Becca, looking around, trying to find the helicopter. She took Jake's hand and pulled him into the air with her. "We don't want to attract too much attention."

Further down the road, Toni was following the police chase. The cops were trying to shoot out the tires, but kept missing because the driver of the other car kept swerving off the road. The bullets ricocheted off the pavement, but didn't slow the vehicle down any. Toni was cruising about twenty feet above the police car, her hood over her head, when the police car spun off the road in a cloud of dust.

Toni smiled as she looked back at the cops and then ahead at the obviously stolen vehicle. She imagined she looked like a giant black bird about to swoop down on its unsuspecting prey. "Aren't you cops supposed to say *freeze*?" she asked deviously. Ice beams pelted out of her palms and hit the tires of the escaping car, freezing them solid. The car began to slide then somersaulted onto its roof and gradually came to a grinding halt. "*Literally*," she laughed. Amazingly, two men leaped out of the overturned vehicle and began to run down the highway, shooting behind them at the pursuing policemen.

Toni smiled as she slowly floated down to land next to the flipped car. She stood up straight, wrapped her cloak around her and shivered. She bent down to the road. "It's getting cold. You should watch your step!" she hollered at the running men. She touched the road gently with her index finger. A sheet of delicate white frost appeared slowly on the road and begin to rapidly spread. Soon the entire roadway ahead of her was covered in a thick layer of shimmering ice, slowly receding from behind like a wave on the beach. The tide of ice overtaking the two crooks sent them tumbling and spinning recklessly forwards until their heads crashed together and they slid painfully to a stop.

The cops stopped and stared in disbelief at both Toni and the crooks. Toni didn't realize they were standing right behind her until they leaped forward suddenly to handcuff the criminals. Toni jumped in surprise and quickly soared up into the air away from the police while their backs were turned, pulling the crooks up from the ground. She met the others up overhead where they were cruising around making sure the situation was under control. "Is everyone all right?" she asked.

Jake nodded. "For now."

"Let's get going," said Becca, looking around her frantically. "We don't want anyone knowing what happened!"

"But why not bask in the glory?" asked Mike, raising his arms and flexing his biceps.

The others looked at each other and rolled their eyes. However, they weren't surprised that Mike had said something like that.

Toni pushed her hood down and, rolling over on her back, let her cloak stream out behind her. "We did pretty well for the first time; at least, I think so." She closed her eyes and shivered again, flakes of ice trailing from her cloak as they flew along.

"We certainly did," said Mike. "And it was amazing. But I have a feeling that this was just a taste of what's coming."

"Come on, we need to go," said Becca, looking at the others." Dusk was creeping across the desert, illuminated in the west by a beautiful sunset. The air was cooler, soothing the teens and reminding them how tired they were from their first day as Sages. When they arrived at the R.V., they flew back in through the skylight, being extra careful not to attract the attention of onlookers in other vehicles. The teens quickly resumed their normal forms and crawled into their sleeping bags, exhausted. They fell asleep instantly, with images of the day replaying in their heads.

Chapter 7— A Very Windy Beach

It took three more uneventful days to arrive in Florida. During that time, nothing else exciting happened to the teens, for which they were grateful. At night, they would fly along above the R.V. just to get out. They spent most of their time in their room reading comic books, playing board games (Becca always winning), or watching movies.

Early one morning, Becca was flipping through the channels on the television when she suddenly stopped on a national news channel. "Look, we're on the news!" she cried. A helicopter news crew had filmed some of what had happened in New Mexico. It showed flashbacks of what the teens had done that day. They weren't aware that had been caught on tape, but at least they were spotted doing something good. Trudy must have been watching up front, because she came back to ask them if they had seen the story and to say how it was hard to believe that they were on the very same road where everything happened, but didn't see a thing. The teens had somehow managed to hold back their laughter.

Becca turned off the television. "We didn't do *too* badly."

"It was fun," said Toni, "but I want to get to the beach. The beach is my life!"

"You haven't even been to any beach, ever, Toni," said Jake, closing his comic book and placing it beside him on the bed.

"I know, but with my Power I can be the 'Goddess of the Water'. I'll be in complete control of my surroundings. I want to see how well I can manipulate such a huge volume of water." Toni shut her eyes as though picturing exactly what she would do. "I want to know what it feels like to live down deep," she took a deep breath. "Then actually feel what it's like to breathe underwater," she sighed as she mimed paddling.

The others stared at her. "Well," said Mike, "you can go in the bathtub right now and try to breathe there." The others laughed, but Toni's face grew red with anger as she made a pout face at him in annoyance.

Bill's voice suddenly filled the room, making the teens jump. "Hey, kids!"

Becca walked over to her bedroom door and opened it. "Yeah Dad?"

Bill looked back from the driver's seat and smiled back at her. "We're finally in Florida and we'll arrive at New Smyrna Beach in four to six hours."

Becca nodded. "Thanks, Dad! That's great news." She shut the door and walked back to the others. "So, do you guys want to watch another movie until we get there?"

"Might as well," said Jake. "There's nothing else to do."

"Yeah," said Toni, "I'm certainly never playing a board game with you again, Becca." Becca simply smiled.

It was a long five hours for the teens. They had just put in the third movie when Trudy announced that they had arrived, but needed to stop at the office to find out where their campsite was located. She hoped it wouldn't be crowded since school was still in session. The R.V. slowed to a stop, and the teens heard Bill get out and slam his door. A few minutes later, he came back and they pulled out onto the beach.

"Alright!" said Toni, leaping abruptly off her bed. "Finally! I'm going to go get my swimsuit on."

"Allow me," said Becca, as she stood up and snapped her fingers. Their swimsuits went on them as their clothes disappeared and reappeared folded on their sleeping bags. Jake and Mike were wearing swim trunks and muscle shirts while Toni and Becca wore bikinis with t-shirts over them.

"Umm…" snorted Mike. "That was kind of awkward."

"I have to agree," said Jake. "I am totally capable of changing on my own." The others laughed and joked as they left the bedroom and went to sit on the couch. Becca opened the door and looked out. They were parked right on the sand, about ten yards away from the water. "We can park right on the beach?"

"It's an R.V. camping beach, honey," said Trudy. "Anyway, you kids can have your beach day today, since Bill and I are going to New Smyrna in the Hummer to look around and then head up the coast to get the tickets for Islands of Adventure. Have fun and be safe! Please don't drown until we get back." She eyed each of the teens seriously, a threatening look on her face. Bill and Trudy walked out the door laughing as the teens waved and said good-bye.

"This is going to be a blast!" said Mike, a large grin appearing on his face.

The others got up from the couch and ran out of the R.V. They ran screeching towards the ocean where the waves were an incredible luminescent green. Jake and Mike threw off their shirts and flew into the air over the water and then did massive cannonballs into the waves.

Toni, on the other hand, did it in a more graceful style. She jumped out over the water as a huge jet of salty spray pushed her high into the air. She held her arms out gracefully then somersaulted quickly downward. The water circled around her making a tidy vortex. She did one last flip ending with a perfect dive.

Becca soared out over the water, pushing the water from her on both sides like walls. She caught a wave, surfed on her feet and then turned just in time to crash spectacularly into the next oncoming wave.

"That looked like it hurt," said Mike, doing backstrokes in the water and smiling over at Becca as she pulled a large strand of seaweed from her hair.

Jake took control of the wind and created a mini whirlpool around himself, making him go in circles. "You all right Becca?" he asked, concerned.

"I just swallowed a lot of salty, gritty water." Becca spat and rubbed her mouth. "I'm think I'm going to take a little break."

"Are you sure?" asked Toni hopping on the surface of the water, jumping the waves.

"Yeah. Don't worry," said Becca watching Toni nimbly skipping over waves with a grin on her face. "I'll be back." She jogged over to the R.V. and waved her hand to make towels and sun umbrellas appear on the sand.

"Having fun, Toni?" laughed Mike. Toni was dancing on top of the water as though there were music all around her. Surprisingly, the water was flowing in weird formations as though dancing with her.

Toni giggled and her face grew red with embarrassment. "A blast! Watch this." She flew over to a large wave coming their way. She hopped on the wave as it began to crest over her head.

"I can do that!" said Jake, diving under the waves. He made a powerful jet of air circle around him and propel him through the water at high speed. From above, it looked as if he were traveling in an underwater waterspout. He popped out of the water and landed on another passing wave, out of breath. He stood up and surfed it into the beach, laughing the whole time. He then waded over to where Mike and Toni were standing looking up the beach.

Mike grinned at the two of them and pointed over to Becca who looked very much like she was sleeping. "She looks like she's enjoying herself—I can change that." His eyes began to glow yellow as he whispered to himself '*whoosh*!' A wave of sand formed at their feet and crept stealthily up the beach until it crested up to hover over Becca.

"Who's blocking my sun?!" she asked sleepily, still laying back enjoying herself. Mike snapped his fingers and the pile of sand dropped right on her. She leaped up, sand streaming around her, and screamed loudly in frustration. She began to jump up and down trying to get the sand out of her swimsuit. Mike and Jake were laughing so hard that they sat heavily down in the water and were having trouble keeping the waves from breaking over their heads. Toni was laughing behind her hand. Becca suddenly snapped her head over at Mike, giving him the most evil leer possible. The three stopped laughing at once.

"So, you thought that was *funny*, huh, Mike?" Becca closed her eyes and shut her lips tightly. "Well, let me tell you something..." She opened her eyes, which were now a bright, pulsating purple. "Do you know what it *feels* like to get hit by a ball of *kinetic energy*?" A round object appeared in her clenched right hand, pulsing in time with her eyes and emitting a purplish smoke. "It's really *funny*! WATCH!" She rocketed like a bullet straight at Mike. A large rock rose up out from under the water with Mike guiding it up into the air so he could get fast and far away from Becca.

But she was hot on his tail. "I'm going to get you good!" she screamed angrily, but she was also laughing.

Toni and Jake looked at each other and laughed even harder. "Do you think she'll get him?" asked Jake. His eyes were focused on Mike who was turning sharply back and forth through the air, Becca following his every move.

Toni shook her head. "No doubt!" she laughed.

Mike stopped suddenly, trying to throw Becca off track, but she was too quick for him. She threw the ball of energy and hit him squarely in the back. He was knocked hard off his rock from the powerful impact of the nearly invisible force and crashed face first into the water with a resounding smack. Becca winced dramatically, then turned to look over at Toni and Jake who were all but drowning themselves with laughter.

"Quit laughing or you two are next," she said grinning and tossing a new ball of smoking energy from hand to hand. Toni and Jake had to go underwater to keep from laughing.

Mike's head poked out from the water and he gasped for air. After a few deep breaths, he started to laugh, too. "You got me good!" he sputtered.

"Well, next time don't go throwing sand on me!" She did a cannonball into the water splashing the others. She swam over to join the others in the shallows and turned to Toni. "So, how does it feel to breathe underwater?"

Toni smiled as she raised her legs above the water, letting herself float. "It's just like breathing air. I can also see clearly, almost like I have a pair of goggles on." She sighed heavily and smiled widely. "This is definitely the *life*!"

"Well, you're lucky," said Mike. "That means you can go anywhere in the water and find and see awesome things! It's a whole new world out there; a completely new adventure where many have never been. Imagine all the things you could see!"

"Well, then maybe we should all go exploring!" said Toni, eyebrows raised.

Mike shook his head and squinted his eyes. "How?"

Becca snapped her fingers and Mike and Jake flashed purple. "This will let us breathe underwater. You have an invisible air supply around you. It's kind of like a bubble that lets you breathe underwater."

"Well, let's go," said Jake, diving under a wave. The others followed. They swam deeper and deeper. It was very beautiful: there were splendid coral reefs and glorious plants of many different colors, but best of all were the myriad of jewel-like fishes that swam under, over, around and through the reef. The teens swam down still deeper, examining closely everything they could see.

Suddenly, Becca's voice echoed loudly in their heads. "*By the way, if you want to make contact with each other, just think out loud in your head.*" Jake gave Becca the thumbs up that he understood.

They were about thirty-five feet down when Jake felt a swirling rush of water behind him. He turned to look back and saw five dolphins swimming towards him, then dashing away. He looked at the others and could see the excitement in their smiles. The dolphins began to circle all of them, making enthusiastic squeaking noises and nodding their heads up and down.

"*I think they want us to go with them!*" said Toni eagerly to the others.

"*Well, then let's go,*" said Mike, swimming over to a dolphin and grabbing its dorsal fin. The dolphin immediately took off toward deeper water. The others each grabbed a dolphin and zoomed off after Mike.

They were going surprisingly fast and it was hard for the teens to hang on. The dolphins dodged plants, rocks, reefs, and even the occasional shipwreck. Suddenly, they came to a clear area containing what must have been an underwater mountain. The agile dolphins swam into a hole at the base and through a short tunnel where it seemed that the surface was visible only a small distance above through the shimmering blue water. The dolphins splashed gleefully around them as they climbed out onto a broad, flat area at the entrance to an enormous cave. The cave was lit from within by many blue, glittering crystals embedded in the walls and ceiling.

"This is so wonderful!" said Toni, looking around at all of the shimmering points of light that illuminated the cave. A cool, gray mist traveled in patches through the damp air. It was amazing. There were tiny plants growing in the dirt floor among the small puddles formed by water dripping from the rough stone ceiling.

"It must be one of those underwater caves with air trapped inside!" said Jake, glancing at the others excitedly.

"They're supposedly very rare." said Becca in disbelief, also highly amazed.

"How does the air stay in here?" asked Mike, crouching down next to a large boulder to touch one of the many blue crystals attached to it.

"I think it's because of the plants in here," said Becca. She knelt down and gently ruffled the leaves of a plant. "The crystals must provide enough light to allow these plants to make oxygen, letting us breathe."

Jake glanced around the cave at the low ceiling. "This cave doesn't look that big."

"Oh, look!" said Toni, pointing further down the passage to where brighter lights danced along the gray stone through a gap in the wall. "There's more light coming from down there around that corner." She quickly walked over and stepped into the patch of dappled light.

The room she astonishingly gazed into had many more blue crystals attached to the rock of the walls and ceiling. Her gasp brought the others immediately to her side. At the far end of the room was a large milky white stone carved into a life-size female angel grasping a glowing blue crystal in her outstretched hands. Just to the right of the statue was a teenage girl with violently blue hair. She was wearing blue boots, a sparkling blue mini-skirt and a blue leather halter top. She had her back to them and seemed to be studying a tablet on the wall that was carved with hieroglyphics.

They heard a voice from the far end of the room where the girl stood. "This is my special place. I come here to think or just to relax. It's good for me to meet new friends." She turned around and faced the teens. She had beautiful deep blue eyes, silver glitter that glistened on her face, and silver lipstick that seemed to brighten up the room even further when she smiled. "Hi, I'm Crystal."

"Well—hi," said Becca. "I'm Becca, and this is Mike, Jake, and Toni." The others smiled as Becca introduced them. Toni gave a little wave.

"So, how did you get down here?" asked Becca, her eyes focused on the carved angel holding the crystal.

Crystal laughed. "I should be asking you the same thing, but I'll be polite and answer your question first." She walked over to a boulder with no crystals attached to it and sat down gracefully. "I really like the water. Some say I'm a mutant, others say I have a gift. They all call me 'Beast Girl'." She paused and smiled. "I can change into any type of animal at will, letting me communicate with other animals."

"That's really amazing!" said Toni, very interested.

"Well, I love who I am. I've had this gift ever since I was born. My parents were scared at first, but then they learned to appreciate it like I did." Crystal sighed deeply and then smiled brightly.

"So that's how you got down here," asked Jake, "by changing into a water animal?"

"Yep. I love the water; it's my very favorite habitat." Crystal looked searchingly at each of the teens. " So—now that I've revealed my little secret, what about you four?"

"We're like you," said Toni. "Except—we just recently acquired our powers. You probably won't believe us, but we're the Chosen Ones, here to protect the Earth."

The girl stared at them in disbelief. She raised her eyebrows in surprise. "I do believe you. A lot of strange things are happening, so I would be crazy not to. So you have special abilities, too?"

"Yes," said Jake, "I can control the weather. Mike can control the ground and nature, and Becca can do many things with her mind. It was thanks to her that Mike and I were able to get down here. Toni on the other hand..." he said pointedly.

"Well..." said Toni, trying not to gloat, "I can control water and ice, making me able to travel and breathe underwater without any help."

"That's extraordinary!" Crystal shouted. "Do you have a codename like me?"

"Yeah, we do," said Toni. She pointed to the others in turn and said their codenames. "This is Star, Cyclone, and Quake. I'm Aquarius."

Crystal jolted her head in surprise at Toni and squinted her eyes. "What did you call yourself?"

"Aquarius," Toni repeated. She gave Crystal a questioning look.

Crystal looked up at the hieroglyphics and then at the blue crystal in the rock. "Those hieroglyphics up there say something about *The Ancient Aquarius*." Becca stared at the hieroglyphics. "I've been trying to get that crystal out for weeks. It glows brighter than the others. I don't even understand why their glowing because there's no source of light or electricity. It seems as though that big crystal powers the others. It looks as if you can pull it out of her hands easily, but I'll tell you—it isn't easy at all. I turned myself into an elephant to try to get it out, but it wouldn't even budge! I think only the Chosen One can take it." She looked back at Toni. "And, I think you're the C*hosen One*."

"Me!?" asked Toni, highly disbelieving what Crystal just said. She looked at the others and then again at Crystal.

"Yes," said Crystal sternly.

"Try to pull it out, Toni," said Mike grinning. "It could be worth a lot."

Toni hesitated then walked over to the statue. She grasped it firmly in both hands, bracing herself, and pulled with all her might. She flew backward and landed on her butt on the ground. "OWW!" she howled, rubbing her backside with one hand while cradling the crystal with the other.

"You've got it!" shouted Crystal with joy.

Toni looked at the glowing crystal that rested in the palms of her hands. "Hey, well look at that! I did it!" She stood up and held it out to Crystal. "Here, it's yours. This seemed really important to you."

"No, you should keep it," she said pushing it away. "It rightfully belongs to you. There was a reason why I couldn't pull it out and you could, so you better keep it."

"Wow," said Toni. The crystal was now glowing even more intensely. She held it up and stared at it with awe. The crystal began to evaporate into tiny glowing blue stars that streamed around over her head until splashing into the middle of Toni's forehead. The dark blue crystal, along with the sapphire gem on Toni's right arm, glowed still brighter, almost white. The cave lit up in a blinding flash—the others were astounded! As the last of the blue stars quickly faded, everything went back to normal. All that remained of the crystal on Toni's forehead was a faint bluish outline.

"I've never seen anything so spectacular!" said Crystal, stunned.

"You wouldn't believe all the strange stuff that has been happening to us," laughed Jake. "Speaking of strange stuff, how did those dolphins know where to bring us?"

Crystal laughed. "Those five dolphins are the creatures that I've known the longest in the ocean. They always come here with me. They told me that you were swimming by the coral reefs, deeper than any divers usually go, so I told them to bring you here. That's how I knew you were coming. Come on, I'll take you back to the surface. Pick a dolphin and let's go." She walked out of the cave, followed by the others. She jumped into the air, turned into a beautiful blue dolphin with a sparkling stripe down its sides, and dove into the pool where the four teens had entered.

The teens jumped into the water and grabbed on to the waiting dolphins. Becca quickly snapped her fingers. Right before the dolphins carried them underwater, a purple light flashed restoring their ability to breathe underwater. The dolphins swam quickly through the tunnel and out after the bright blue dolphin.

Soon enough, they were swimming up to the surface to the beach where the R.V. was parked. Crystal morphed back into her normal self as she swam ashore and waited on the beach. The teens didn't let go of the dolphins until the reached the shallows and could stand up. There was a tremendously strong wind howling and the surf was crashing hard against their legs.

"What's going on, Becca?" asked Jake, horrified, hurrying from swirling waters while shielding his eyes from the blowing sand.

Becca's eyes began to glow. "There's a very powerful hurricane approaching."

The others looked shocked at the news, and started heading up the sand to the R.V. when they heard a loud moaning from the ocean. They turned in time to see humpback whales leaping out and crashing back into the water, sending sheets of water flying high into the air.

"The hurricane isn't the worst part," said Crystal. "The whales told me there's a tidal wave approaching that could flood New Smyrna Beach! What can we do?"

The four teens began to glow as their costumes appeared and they changed into their older forms. The dark blue crystal Toni had received was now visible on her forehead, appearing with her alternate form. Becca looked up at Crystal. "We must prevent the disaster!"

"Becca," said Jake quickly. "Search the city with Crystal to make sure everyone's okay. Have everybody stay inside. We'll patrol the beach in case the tidal wave comes this way." Becca took to the air as Crystal morphed into a lithe blue cheetah and began running quickly up the dunes and into the downtown area. Becca searched from above while Crystal searched from below. Something caught Becca's eye: a small girl, who looked about ten years old, was walking up the street against the wind, her arms over her face. She was struggling hard and moaning.

Suddenly, a loud crack filled the air. Becca looked toward the sound in time to see several palm trees, that had snapped at their roots, on a collision course with the girl. Because she was covering her face, she was totally unaware of the danger racing violently toward her.

"WATCH OUT!!" Becca screamed. The girl looked up and screamed. Becca quickly swooped down in front of the girl, unsheathing her sword. POW! Becca had swung her glowing sword viciously, splitting the palm trees in half down the middle, making them soar on each side of them. A blue cheetah ran up to Becca and the little girl. Crystal morphed into her normal self.

"Are you guys okay?" she yelled through the screaming wind.

"We're fine," yelled Becca. "But we have to get her home."

"Where's your house?" shouted Crystal. The girl pointed to a two story house five doors down.

"I'll take her home," said Crystal looking down at the little girl. "Becca, keep looking around to make sure everyone else is okay. I'll meet you back at the beach." "Okay!" Becca leapt into the air, fighting her way through the powerful wind and torrential rain. Crystal morphed into a gorilla with blue fur, picked up the girl, and ran her to her house. Crystal pounded on the door with a blue fist until someone opened the door. The girl ran inside where she was greeted by her mom and dad who hugged her as tears poured down their faces. "Thank you!" they shouted hesitantly, slowly realizing they were talking to a Gorilla. Crystal turned around to lumber away towards the center of town.

Becca and Crystal searched the rest of the city thoroughly, fighting the wind and blinding rain every inch of the way. All seemed in order until they arrived at a violently swinging bridge where people were trapped in their cars. Becca gasped in horror and immediately flew over to the beach to find the others while Crystal went to see what she could do.

The other teens had been busy placing large boulders all around the R.V., keeping the punishing waves from hitting it. "Good news and bad news," said Jake. "The bad news is that the hurricane is passing through extremely slowly. The good news is that the tidal wave is heading over towards the highway suspension bridge, so it will miss the city!"

"WHAT?" yelled Becca, not believing what she was hearing.

"Is that a happy *what* or a bad *what*?" asked Mike, examining Becca with confusion.

Becca began to breathe heavier. "There are lots of people on that bridge trapped in their cars!"

"Holy crap!" yelled Jake. "Please tell me you're joking."

"No!" screamed Becca. "We have to go and prevent the tidal wave from reaching that bridge!" She soared into the air followed closely by the others. They landed on the bridge and noticed many people staring at them. It began to rain even harder and the wind was blowing fiercely. It was painful to the teens, as it swept needle-like across their faces.

Crystal looked out over the ocean and then at the others. "Do you have any ideas how to stop the wave?" she asked.

"Sorry, I don't," said Toni, peering off to the distance, searching for the giant mass of water. Suddenly, her eyes got wide.

"Well, we better think of something quick because the tidal wave is almost here," said Jake, following Toni's gaze. The others looked out on the horizon and gasped. Many people in their cars began to scream. Some even got out of their cars to run frantically along the madly swinging bridge. The wave was still in the distance, but it was growing larger and closer by the second.

"*Wave…wave…* that's it!" said Becca. "We have to create our own wave to go against the force of the other. Once the waves meet, the energy will be gone and it will fall back into the water."

"Will it work?" asked Mike, with a look of hope on his face.

"It should," said Becca. She shut her eyes. "If the wave we create is powerful enough and big enough."

"Well let's do it!" said Jake, soaring off the bridge. They all lined up in the air facing the wave about a hundred feet away from one another.

"*Ready?*" Becca asked mentally.

"*On three*!" replied Toni. "*One—two—three!*"

Crystal flew up in the air as a small blue bird and dove diagonally down toward the water. She suddenly morphed into a fantastically huge blue whale. She hit the water powerfully, creating a magnificent, toweringly gigantic wave that rolled majestically out toward the horizon.

Toni's hands were glowing brilliant blue as the water around her began to form into a wave of deep translucent blue as if gravity had gained control of it. The wave was massive and continued to build as it moved out into the ocean toward the approaching tidal wave.

Mike's glowing yellow hands began to vibrate as he created a small but powerful earthquake under the ocean several miles from the beach. This sent giant boulders the size of small trailers crashing down from the submerged mountain forming an immense wave.

Jake's hands were blazed an intense white as he pointed them in the direction the wind was blowing, and then suddenly at the ocean beneath him. The wind from the hurricane changed direction as it forcefully struck the ocean, making another monstrous wave than soon joined up with Mike's wave creating an even more powerful wave.

Becca's eyes were shut and her hands rested upon her head, which was glowing a gloriously bright royal purple. The water beneath her began to fly up into the air, roiling and rolling as it gained more and more molecules, growing larger and stronger by the second. She suddenly swung her right hand out over the water sending the giant wave traveling violently out across the water.

The four enormous waves combined into one colossal one as they headed out to meet the oncoming tidal wave. The teens watched the waves, along with the people on the bridge, to see if their spectacular once-in-a-lifetime bid would be successful.

"Oh, no!" yelled Mike. "I don't think it's big enough!" The waves collided brutally, making a sound like thunder. The tidal wave overpowered the one formed by the teens, smashing it like a bug. It was still coming.

"What do we do now?" asked Crystal, panicked.

"I'll try something," said Becca. She soared about a hundred meters away from the bridge then turned around to face it. Her body began to glow brightly as stars appeared around her. She closed her eyes and waited. The others felt helpless as they watched. The wave was approaching Becca. It was twenty feet away—fifteen feet—ten feet. Becca opened her eyes as the purple glow from them became so bright, it would blind anyone who stared directly into them. When Becca heard the roar of the wave behind her, she turned around sharply and threw her arm out as if casting a giant, translucent purple net. She spread her psychic force field out so that it stretched the length of the bridge. She tried to use her telekinesis to repel the wave, but it was too powerful for her.

Her teeth clench tightly and she squinted her eyes shut holding her arms stiffly straight out in front of her. Becca's voice echoed so loudly the others could hear her over the rumbling roar of the wave. "I CAN'T HOLD IT MUCH LONGER. IT'S TOO POWERFUL FOR ME!"

"Then it's my turn," whispered Toni. "I'm the Sage of Water. This is my job, not hers!" Toni suddenly soared up five feet off the bridge and her body began to glow blue.

"Be careful!" warned Jake worryingly. He hated seeing any of his best friends in danger.

"*Do not worry, for I am with her and guiding her,*" said Toni. Except it wasn't her voice; it came from her mouth, but it sounded calm and almost heavenly. Toni waited for the approaching wave. Suddenly, the crystal glowed from her forehead. Its intensity grew brighter and brighter as the wave got closer and closer, until it almost reached Toni. She yelled in a booming voice as if she had two voices: "*SERPENT'S LIGHT*!" The crystal hidden on her forehead emitted a flash so dazzling that no one could see Toni or the wave. Slowly the light began to fade, letting everyone see her once more. Toni's arms were glowing blue and the wave was slowly flipping back out into the ocean. It looked as though a monstrous water serpent of some kind was slithering back and forth across the face of the wave as it began to slide back out to sea. The others were dumbstruck. "We have to get rid of this wind," said Toni through clenched teeth. "It's hard for me to keep this up! You have to do something, Jake."

Jake's eyes fogged over as if clouds were swimming inside of them. Fog began to circle his white glowing body. "Becca, help Toni keep the wave steady." Jake soared into the sky and into the hurricane. The winds were more furious and powerful than ever. Sparks of electricity began to jump across Jake's body and between his outstretched hands. The white electricity traveled through and out of his body. He screamed, "*CYCLONE'S RAGE*!" Beams of intensely blue-white light struck out from his arms and legs. Jake was absorbing the energy from the storm through the beams of light and was shaking from the pain it was causing. Suddenly, a bolt of lightning leapt out of the center of the storm and stuck Jake in the chest. He screamed higher and louder, but still managed to continue absorbing the ferocity of the storm around him. The black leather of his costume gradually lost its color and turned pure white. After a time, his hair also began to change from brown to shocking white.

The hurricane abruptly vanished, and the beams of light shooting from Jake's arms and legs slowly dissipated. He had absorbed the whole hurricane. One final lighting bolt struck him from a small gray storm cloud that had managed to escape. The electricity coursed through his body and out of him. He was immediately unconscious and falling rapidly toward the ocean.

A blue pterodactyl plunged down, screeching, and grabbed Jake carefully by the shoulders with its talons. Crystal flew him down to the others waiting on the bridge. The wind was gone and Toni had eliminated the remnants of the tidal wave. Crystal laid Jake gently down on the road and then morphed into her human form.

"Is he okay? What's with the white hair and costume?" asked Toni with concern in her voice.

"From what we saw," said Mike, "he was struck by two bolts of lightning while neutralizing the hurricane." Jake was still in his white costume and older form along with the others, even though unconscious.

"Wow, he took a huge beating!" said Becca. She bent down to Jake and placed her hand upon his forehead. Her fingertips began to glow as Jake suddenly awoke, gasping in a huge breath.

"It's okay, man!" said Mike, bending down. "You took a beating, but you managed to stop the hurricane.

"Did you guys stop the wave?" he asked, still breathing rather heavily.

"All thanks to Toni!" said Becca beaming.

"It seems everything's back to normal," said Crystal.

Jake turned toward her and took her hand. "Thanks for all that you've done. Come with us. We could use someone like you to help us on our journey."

Crystal blushed, pulling away. "I would love to come with you, but my home is here in the ocean. But I promise I'll do my best to keep things safe around here. Maybe I'm not the only one with gifts. I should probably spend more time trying to make new friends, hopefully as nice as you four."

"Okay then," said Becca, touched by what Crystal had said. "I'm sure we'll see you around sometime. I guess we should head back to the R.V. It's getting pretty late. And we need to check to see if my parents are okay." The people in their vehicles began to move along the highway again. The sun was beginning to set, and the sky grew rose pink like the inside of a seashell.

"Well, I'll see you later then," said Crystal. The others waved goodbye as she jumped off the bridge, morphing into the blue dolphin before she hit the water. The teens jumped off the bridge too and flew back to the beach. Mike waved his hand and all the boulders protecting the R.V. turned into piles of sand. They all landed on the roof of the R.V. and went inside. There was water damage everywhere, and most of the objects and furniture in the R.V. were soaking wet. Luckily, Becca's parents weren't back yet.

"Great!" moaned Jake, looking at all the drenched stuff. He picked a wayward crab out from under a couch cushion and held it up for everyone to see.

"Mike, open the window for me," said Toni. Mike knelt on the soggy couch and slid the window open. Toni waved her hands and a torrent of water gushed out the window and back into the ocean. Jake tossed the crab out onto the sand then spread his fingers to bring wind gusting through the window to blow through the R.V. and dried everything out.

Everyone flashed brightly, turning into their normal selves.

"Mike," whispered Toni. "Jake still has his white hair. Do you think he'll even notice?"

"Probably not," he laughed, "and it's a good thing that your crystal only appears on your forehead in your alternate form, otherwise you would have a lot of tough explaining to do."

"I know," she said, rubbing her fingers along her forehead. "I can kind of feel it now. Mike caught Becca's eye and tipped his head towards Jake who was closing the window.

Becca mouthed silently, "*He still has it*?!" The three began to snicker. Jake turned around and looked at them suspiciously.

"What's so funny?" he asked smirking, hoping to catch what the others were saying.

"Well," said Becca sternly, "not only did you take a beating, so did your hair."

Jake squinted his eyes in confusion. "What are you talking about?"

"See for yourself," laughed Toni.

Jake hurriedly walked into the bathroom. He shouted and ran out, slamming the door behind him. He said calmly to Becca. "Change it."

"Are you sure?" she asked, eyebrows raised coyly.

"Yeah," said Toni, "I kind of like it."

"I said, change it." Jake grasped his hair with both hands as if to pull it out by the roots.

"Okay, okay—keep your pants on." Becca raised her glowing hand and touched Jake's head. She lowered her hand and then put her fist in her mouth to keep herself from laughing.

"What did you do Becca?" he asked angrily.

"Well, that's the point," said Becca trying to look serious around her fist. "I couldn't do anything. I mean I tried, but it didn't work."

"Look's like your stuck with the *fro*, man," said Mike patting Jake's shoulder.

"I'll just buy hair dye," said Jake calmly settling down on the couch.

"Jake, I hate to tell you this," said Toni, "but if Becca can't change it, I don't think hair dye will." She giggled.

"Don't worry about it, Jake," said Mike. "We weren't laughing because it looks bad…we were laughing because we knew you'd be angry."

"Whatever." Jake put his feet up on the couch and shut his eyes. "I'm beat."

"Becca, do you think your parents are all right?" asked Toni.

"Yeah, they're fine." Becca's eyes flashed purple. "They're almost here, actually."

The teens were resting in their bedroom watching television when they heard Becca's parents pull up. Jake was the only one exhausted, and was lying on the couch tiredly, trying to sleep. Becca shut off the television and they all went to greet Bill and Trudy.

"Hey, guys!" said Trudy cheerfully through the open door of the R.V. She climbed up inside with Bill close behind with several shopping bags. "How was your day? Did you enjoy the water?" It seemed they had no idea what took place while they were gone.

"Fun!" said Becca enthusiastically. "We did a lot, believe it or not."

"Well, that's good," said Bill. "Because tomorrow we're going to Islands of Adventure. We have your tickets."

The teens laughed excitedly until Bill broke the moment. "What did you do to your hair, Jake?" he asked abruptly.

Jake hesitated then looked at the others for support. He finally managed to say, "It always bleaches out in the sun, so I thought I would try a new look."

"It's certainly new," laughed Bill.

Mike leaned close to Jake. "Good cover up," he whispered.

"So how did you guys make it through the st—" Mike said loudly, but was cut off by a sharp elbow to the ribs from Toni. "—through the night?" Becca decided to erase the memory of the storm from her parents' minds so they wouldn't ask too many questions.

"It was good," said Bill blankly for a moment. "Trudy and I had a very lovely dinner and we brought pizza for you guys. It's still in the truck." Both Mike and Jake dashed out of the R.V., leaving the door open behind them.

"I know how much you were looking forward to spending some time in the water, Toni. Did you do a lot of swimming and tanning?" asked Trudy, a friendly smile lighting up her face.

"Basically," said Toni. Mike and Jake stumbled back up the steps carrying the pizzas and set them on the table. The teens sat down and ate hungrily, shoving food in their mouths as though they hadn't eaten for days. After a quick clean up, they went back to their room and changed into pajamas. They got into their sleeping bags and stared up at the dark ceiling, listening to the waves.

"You know," said Becca. "I was watching the Discovery Channel, and they say that scientists are afraid of an earthquake that will eventually occur in the middle of the Atlantic Ocean."

"Why is that?" asked Toni curiously.

"Because," said Becca, "it'll create a tidal wave ten times bigger than the one we faced today, meaning it could flood the entire state of Florida."

"Whoa, let's hope that never happens. It was hard enough preventing the one today," laughed Mike.

The calm, cool breeze soon sent the teens drifting off to sleep. They seemed to sway in their beds to the rhythm of the waves on the shore. They could almost still feel the waves pushing against them, like they were being rocked gently by the ocean.

Chapter 8— Islands of Adventure, Alright!

Mike, Jake and Toni woke up in a panic when a loud rumbling shook the R.V. The whole bedroom was shaking and their personal belongings were floating around in the air. "What's going on?" asked Jake, quickly looking around him.

"It's Becca!" said Mike, going to stand at her bedside. She was moaning and shaking like crazy. Mike began to shake her. "Becca! Becca, wake up!"

"*Let them go*!" she screamed into his face. Toni walked over to Becca as a jet of water soared out from her palm, splashing Becca in the face. Becca immediately jolted upright clutching her pillow. The objects that had been orbiting the room fell with a crash to the ground, and the room stopped shaking. Becca was still breathing very hard as she wiped the sweat and water from her face with her pillow.

"It's all right, Becca," said Toni, sitting on the bed and grabbing her hand.

"What happened?" asked Becca, looking frantically at each of the others.

"The room was shaking," said Jake, frowning and looking very worried. "Things were flying about. What's wrong?"

"It could have been Mike!" protested Becca.

"It wasn't me," said Mike. "Stuff was floating all around you, and you were acting as though you were having a bad dream."

"You're burning up, Becca!" said Toni, placing the back of her hand on Becca's cheek. Toni twirled her hand lazily until a giant snowflake appeared above Becca's head, releasing a breeze of cool air.

"Thanks," said Becca, flopping back down on her damp pillow.

"So, what did you dream about?" asked Jake, now sitting down next to Toni on the edge of the bed.

Becca hesitated. She put one hand up to her head and rubbed it. "I dreamed that all your parents were captured and taken hostage."

Jake squinted his eyes confused. "All our parents?"

"Yeah," said Becca, "including two other people I've never seen before."

"But who would take our parents and why?" Mike asked, looking as though he were very unsure of what Becca was saying.

"Why—I don't know—who—a lady with black hair that looked like an Egyptian goddess, like at the natural history museum. Or maybe it was a pharaoh." Becca sighed heavily and closed her eyes. Her eyes suddenly shot open. "Do you remember at the fair when we saw the face in the crystal ball?" The teens stared at Becca and nodded. "Well—she looked like that!"

The others stared at her skeptically. They thought silently for several seconds about what Becca had said.

"Weird dream," laughed Mike. "I never get dreams like that."

"I don't either," said Becca. She sounded unsure of herself, almost frightened.

"Then why did you dream about it?" Jake asked, eyebrows raised.

Becca opened her eyes and stared intently at Jake. "That's the point." The teens looked at each other then at her. Fear had come over them.

Jake gave Becca a questioning look. "What do you mean *that's the point*?"

"Well, it seemed so clear, and my dreams are never clear. It might have been a vision." Terror now showed momentarily on the other teens' faces. They couldn't believe it—they wouldn't believe it was possible. They were convinced that their parents were in New York City, laughing joyfully with one another. No evil pharaoh could have taken their parents, especially one that they saw in a crystal ball.

"I guess we have nothing to worry about," said Becca, trying to convince herself. "I mean, it's probably that my dreams are clearer now that I have these new—*abilities*. Not because anything actually happened."

"Let's hope," said Mike. "Hey, look! We've been driving all this time!" He was looking out the window, gazing at the passing trees and buildings.

"Toni, I'm kind of cold now," laughed Becca, crossing her arms in front of her and snuggling into the sleeping bag to shield her face from the cold breeze of the snowflake.

"Oh, sorry!" laughed Toni. She touched the snowflake and it evaporated in a puff of cool mist.

Becca got up and left the room. She walked through the living area to the cab where her parents sat in the front seats of the R.V. "So we're heading to Islands of Adventure now?"

"Yeah!" said Bill. "We'll be their in five or ten minutes, so get ready! Your mother and I are going to Universal Studios, which is right next to the Adventure Park."

"I thought Universal Studios *was* Islands of Adventure?" said Becca, confused.

"No, honey," said Trudy. "They're separate parks. Trust me, you'll enjoy the one your going to by far, and a section of the theme park is devoted entirely to something that the four of you all love." Becca walked back through to the bedroom and shared the information from her parents with the others. The teens changed into comfortable clothing since they planned on going for most of the day.

The R.V. slowly got dark as they entered the four-story parking garage set aside for R.V.s and buses. They left their room and followed Trudy and Bill outside. While Bill locked up the R.V., Trudy called the teens over. "Come on kids, I have your tickets and money for souvenirs and food," said Trudy, digging in her purse and pulling out the four brightly colored tickets. She then took four fifty-dollar bills out of an envelope and handed one to each of the teens. "Use this for whatever you need." She zipped up her purse and glanced up at her husband. "So, where do we go now?

"Follow me," said Bill excitedly. They followed Bill inside an elevator that took them up to the fourth floor of the parking garage. The doors opened up into a large room where two young women and a young man in white uniforms were answering peoples' questions. Bill walked up to one of the ladies behind the desk. "May I help you with anything, sir?" she asked politely, with a bright white smile on her tanned face.

"Yes," said Bill. "Where is the park entrance?"

The lady smiled and pointed to a very wide hallway at the other end of the room, which had a moving walkway. It was very obvious that it was the entrance because there was a large sign that said *Islands of Adventure* and *Universal Studios* hanging on the wall right above the doorway. Bill laughed. "Well, that couldn't have been more obvious, could it?"

There were several lines of people standing under the huge signs for Islands of Adventure and Universal Studios. More people in white uniforms were handing out tickets from booths in front of both theme park entrances, while a little ways further past the gate other staff members took the tickets back and stamped the back of each person's hand.

"Well," said Trudy. "You kids have a blast! We'll all meet here when both parks close." She bent down and hugged Becca tightly. "And remember—do not split up! If any of you get lost…well, I don't even want to think of what will happen." She walked away with Bill toward the Universal Studios entrance and waved a last goodbye.

The teens walked down to the entrance to Islands of Adventure where they handed in their tickets and received their hand stamps. They then pushed their way through the metal turnstile to enter the park. The teens gasped in awe. It was extraordinary! A huge plaza opened in front of them lined with benches and shops. There were fantastic fountains and huge beds of colorful flowers. Vendors strolled around selling cold drinks, ice cream, and balloons from pushcarts with striped umbrellas. But even more amazing, the area of the park that they were in now was based on comic books! It had stores, shops, booths, restaurants, and rides named after comic book heroes such as the Incredible Hulk, Spiderman, X-men, and Captain America.

"This is a dream come true!" laughed Jake, gazing around him, with his mouth slightly opened.

"This is any kid's dream!" said Mike, looking as stunned as Jake.

"Well," said Becca, her eyes focused on the towering green roller coaster at the end of the plaza when she heard the screams of fear and excitement from the people on the ride. "Which ride first?"

Mike laughed as he looked up toward the same roller coaster as Becca. "It's called the 'Incredible Hulk'—how about it?"

"Well, let's go then!" yelled Toni excitedly, running up to the arched entrance to the ride. They jogged down a short sidewalk and through a little building where they passed through a room with many red-flashing lights and walked across a wide railroad bridge staircase with steam filling the air. A loud hiss filled the room as a surge of steam came puffing up in front of Toni, causing her to scream and freeze it out of self-defense. The frozen cloud of steam hung momentarily in mid-air then shattered like a mirror on the ground. The others stopped in their tracks and turned to stare at her. Toni gave a slight, embarrassed sort of laugh as she pushed through the others, making her way to the ride.

There were gates separating the lines for each of the small carts. Each cart was big enough for four—two in front and two in back. Jake and Mike teamed up for the front of the cart and Becca and Toni teamed up for the back. They stood together waiting patiently for their turn. Since it was still early, the lines weren't very long. Getting into the cart at the head of line in front of Becca were two girls with bubblegum pink hair. She wondered briefly if they were mutants or just liked pink. About two minutes later an empty cart arrived, and the teens hopped in and waiting tensely until the curved metal safety bars moved down over their shoulders and locked into place. Slowly the roller coaster moved out of the covered area and began to ascend a long slope. Then, suddenly, it skyrocketed upwards into a tunnel and out into the bright sunshine. The teens held on tightly as the ride proceeded through a series of loops, curves, and hills. Everyone was screaming and whooping in delight. Several minutes later, the ride came to a stop back in the original building. They left the building full of exhilaration. Judging by their hair, the roller coaster was a major thriller.

"That was an awesome ride!" laughed Mike. The others agreed. "I mean, that was probably the *best* ride I've been on yet!"

"It's the only ride you've been on," joked Toni, who was walking beside Jake.

"No, I mean, ever!" Mike looked as though he couldn't be happier.

"So where to now?" asked Becca, looking all around her in amazement. Jake walked over to a ride called 'The Storm Accelerator'. It had a picture of a comic book hero from the X-men called Storm soaring through the clouds shooting lightning bolts out of her hands. It was a ride that spun you in circles, making you dizzier by the second. There were only about ten people in line so the teens got on right away. By the time the ride was over, they were so dizzy that Toni had fallen down on the grass next to a bench. Mike went over to help, but zigzagged into a trashcan and fell down next to her. Becca and Jake sat down on the bench with their hands on their heads and their heads between their knees to wait for the dizziness to pass. After a couple minutes, Jake and Becca helped Mike and Toni up from where they were sprawled on the grass.

After more than an hour of excitement and thrills, the teens decided to leave the comic book section and head over to see the cartoon section of the park. There, they went on several elaborate water rides. Next, they explored the Jurassic theme, full of replicas of dinosaurs and snack bars offering turkeys' legs and shish kabob. (Both of which Mike declared delicious.) After that, the teens moved on to the mythical theme, which was based on knights, wizards and dragons. This section had two roller coasters. One was much bigger than the one they had previously ridden and the other was for little kids. The larger rollercoaster was called 'Twin Dragons' and featured carts on two parallel tracks that could race each other. The four teens couldn't keep their eyes off the ride, especially when their ears were echoing with the thrilling screams and the roar of the wheels on the metal tracks.

"We are definitely going on that ride!" laughed Mike. The teens were walking over to the ride when someone tapped Becca sharply on her right shoulder. She turned around while the others walked on without her. Becca found herself face to face with a tall old man in long purple robes with a long, puffy, cloud-like white beard. In his right hand, he held a gnarled wooden staff with a shiny glass ball containing a sparkling crystal of deep amethyst on the end.

His eyes focused on Becca's, and he smiled brightly, revealing a set of unusually white teeth. "This, my Lady Star, belongs to you." He held the staff out to Becca with his right hand while waving his left hand over the glass ball. The ball vanished with a faint 'pop'. Becca's eyes went wide as she examined the staff and then looked quizzically at the old man. He leaned in to whisper to her. "Take a look!" He touched a bony finger to her forehead. Becca rushed to look at her reflection in the pool of a nearby fountain. The purple crystal appeared to be embedded in the skin in the middle of her forehead just like Toni's! Becca placed her fingers on it, examining it gently. Suddenly, it began to glow a radiant violet. Becca was momentarily blinded, but when the light dimmed, the old man was nowhere to be found. She looked to where the old man had been standing, but he wasn't there! She gazed all around her, but he was nowhere in sight. He had simply vanished!

Becca heard the others coming her way calling her name. She turned around to find Toni, Jake, and Mike approaching and glaring unhappily at her. "What are you doing? We're going to be last in line now!" yelled Mike angrily.

Toni noticed the faint outline of the purple crystal on Becca's forehead. "Becca, what is that on your forehead?" Becca sighed and told the others what happened.

"That is really strange!" said Jake, eyebrows down, lost in thought. "I mean, he said it belonged to you?"

"Yeah, I mean, he said "my Lady, Star" and that's certainly my codename!" said Becca in confusion.

"But how, and why, would he know that?" asked Toni.

Becca shrugged, but then suddenly searched Toni's forehead to find the faint blue outline of her sapphire-colored crystal. "You don't think mine could unlock special things like yours, do you?" They paused, and then heard a familiar voice ahead of them.

"Well, look who it is!" The teens turned around and were surprised to be face-to-face with the Goths. Felix began to speak again, "I see we're not the only ones who decided to take a little—trip."

"Beat it, Felix!" yelled Jake. "Like you, we want an enjoyable vacation."

"You know," said Felix, "I have to agree with you on that one. In order to *enjoy* the vacation, we would have to make things a little more real." He snickered with his gang. "Come on guys, you know what to do." He then ran off into the Cat in the Hat theme area with the other three Goths trailing behind him.

"What do you think they're up to?" asked Toni, squinting off in the direction Felix and his gang had gone.

"All that I can sense is that there's something different about them—something *new*," said Becca, her eyes glowing.

"Let's follow them, just to make sure they don't do anything stupid that will cause trouble, and then we'll come back here," said Jake, walking off in the direction the Goths had gone. The others agreed and followed him down a cement path lined with trees with striped trunks and bushy cotton candy-like tops. Mike laughed at all the unusual rides and costumed characters in the theme area. Becca's eyes began to glow again.

"What is it, Becca?" asked Toni.

"They're not in this theme," she said. "They're back at the comic book theme."

The teens went quickly through the exit of the Cat in the Hat theme that led right to the comic book area. Toni walked beside Becca. "What do you think that whole crystal thing was about?"

Becca sighed again, deeply, and focused on the sidewalk passing under her feet. "I'm honestly not sure, but I have a weird feeling that there's a crystal for all of us. What is the crystal for, and how did that old man know that it belonged to me?"

Toni looked at Becca as though she had just read her mind. Becca smiled. "It's okay. There are a lot of things that are happening that still need to be explained." The two caught up to Mike and Jake who had stopped to look for the Goths.

"There!" whispered Jake to the others, pointing toward the comic book store where the Goths were examining the life-size posters of superhero comics that stood on the sidewalk in front of the shop. The girl Goths noticed Jake and the others and elbowed Felix to get his attention.

"Finally!" said Felix relieved. "Now it's time to spice things up a bit and finish the beating we started at the fairgrounds."

"We're not going to fight you again!" said Becca, annoyed. She and the others couldn't believe that the Goths were up for another fight after their humiliation the last time.

"Yeah!" yelled Toni. "You guys already got a good enough beating!"

Felix laughed. "Oh, but *we* aren't going fight you!"

Mike looked at Felix, confused. "What are you talking about?"

Suddenly, Felix's hands began to glow a brilliant orange, bright as the sun. Jenna, John, and Courtney's hands were also glowing. They turned to face the superhero posters, and each placed their hands flat against the picture until it also began to glow orange. The posters rippled and stretched, gaining thickness and form until a final flare revealed real superheroes standing in place of the paper ones! They had become real! On the right was a lady called Storm from the X-Men, as well as Cyclops and Wolverine. To the left stood Spiderman. They were living, breathing beings, not cardboard cutouts! The four teens were shocked at what the Goths had done. It was unimaginable, and thought to be impossible. Many of the people walking along the sidewalk came up to look at the superheroes. They must have thought they were ordinary people dressed up as comic book characters.

Becca gasped, "You're mutants!"

Felix laughed, "Yeah, and with powers like this, no one can stop us. Now we can really do whatever we please."

Fear spread through the four. How had the Goths become mutants? The only mutant they met besides themselves was Crystal, and she was born with her power. Could they have been born with powers too? These questions rang through the teens' minds.

"Do you know what we're going to do now?" asked Jenna, a wicked grin on her pale face.

"Hopefully nothing stupid," said Jake, through clenched teeth.

"We don't find it stupid!" yelled Felix. "But rather *fun*! And now to share the fun, we'll let these guys take care of 'entertaining' you. You four will be the first to *suffer* at this theme park!" Felix tuned his glowing orange eyes toward the superheroes who were staring straight ahead like robots. "*Torture them!*" The superheroes began to walk slowly and stiffly towards Becca, Mike, Toni, and Jake. Jake looked over to Felix, who smiled evilly back at him. "Come on, guys!" Felix yelled to the others. "Let's go to the control room where we can help people *enjoy* the rides." The others followed him off toward a tall building by the edge of the mythical theme.

The teens looked at each other in mild confusion. What was going on? It was all happening so fast. "You don't think they have their *real* superhero powers—do you?" asked Jake. But once these words were spoken, a powerful gust of wind struck Jake hard against his chest, sending him sliding five feet across the pavement and knocking him to the ground.

Becca, Mike, and Toni looked over at Jake lying on his back, squeezing his eyes shut against the pain then up at the superheroes who continued walking down the sidewalk toward them. "Well, that certainly answers his question!" said Becca, eyes wide. Becca and Toni looked quickly at Mike who was suddenly in costumed Power form. He was gleaming a very bright lustrous yellow-orange, like a tiger's eyes. They looked around behind them at Jake who was now standing up, also in his Power form. Becca and Toni glanced at each other through glowing eyes and nodded as they both suddenly flew up high allowing Jake and Mike to charge the approaching superheroes.

Jake waved his hand as a wall of wind slammed into the superheroes, forcing them to the ground. "Becca, take Cyclops. Mike, you handle Wolverine. Toni, you tackle *Spidey*, and I get Storm."

Becca and Toni morphed into their Power forms and their costumes appeared. Cyclops immediately shot a red laser beam at Becca through the golden visor around his head. She dodged it gracefully, the beam missing her by a hair.

Wolverine's fingers shot out four deadly looking metal claws as he began to strike at the boulders Mike made shoot out of the earth through the cement. Spiderman threw web balls at Toni, but she made a thick icicle appear in her hands and hit them as though she were swinging a bat.

The sky darkened as it filled with black thunderclouds. Storm flew up in the air and held her hands up to direct dazzling blue lightning bolts to strike the ground at Jake's feet. He was running and swerving, trying to dodge each one. One bolt hit a tree causing it to burst into flames. Toni quickly waved her hand and a fountain of water spouted out from the ground, soaking the tree and putting out the fire.

The four began to move away from each other as they fought in their own directions. Many onlookers were quite amazed at what they thought was a staged fight performance. Some began to question the special abilities they were performing. Kids were screaming in delight and cheering. Unfortunately, they were cheering for the superheroes, not for the teens.

Mike turned to face a bunch of the kids who were cheering for the superheroes and gave them a dirty look. While his back was turned, Wolverine used one of the flying boulders like a springboard and plummeted down towards Mike, striking him in the chest and cutting through his armored breastplate with his razor-sharp claws. Mike was thrown back through the fence surrounding the Incredible Hulk roller coaster and crashed agonizingly into one of the huge metal upright beams that supported the track. When Mike screamed in pain, a giant block of earth and cement lurched up from the ground under Wolverine, catapulting him high in the air. He landed in a jumbled heap at the other end of the plaza. It was as though the earth had heard Mike's cry of pain, protecting him. Mike fell to his knees, as he placed his hands painfully onto his bleeding wound. When he pulled himself up on the metal support posts, he could feel it vibrating and shaking violently. Mike looked up, clutching his side, and saw that the rollercoaster was going much faster than normal. It didn't even stop to pick up more people. It just kept going at a frantic lightning speed, bouncing on the tracks. Many people were screaming, but it was different—they weren't screams of excitement. They sounded more like shrieks of fright and pain. Something wasn't right.

Suddenly, a familiar voice echoed through the teen's heads, "*You guys, something isn't right. The rides are out of control! The Goths must be in the control room! We have to get rid of these 'things' to help those people!*" Becca lost her concentration as Cyclops shot a beam at her, hitting her directly in the chest. She flew back fifty feet and smashed through the plate glass display window of the comic book store. She tumbled to the ground, cutting her arms and legs. Becca screeched in fury and pain. "That's it! Now it's time to stop trying to defend myself and kick some superhero butt!!"

She leaped up into the air and flew like a bullet, punching her fists alternately into Cyclops' stomach like a flying jackhammer, knocking him to the ground. He tried to get back up, but Becca waved her arms violently as he flew away from the invisible telekinetic force. Cyclops went airborne, zooming straight up. Glowing purple balls of energy appeared in Becca's hands, but before she could throw them, she was hit with another laser beam. This time it hit her directly in the face, and she was thrown brutally to the cement by the force.

Mike looked over to where Becca was lying unconscious. "Becca!" Right when he shouted these words, Wolverine came out of nowhere and slashed Mike's back, leaving a bloody wound. He screamed as the burn whipped through his insides. The cement cracked and roared beneath Mike, cradling him and lifting him into the air. Mike twitched his glowing hands as rippling green vines writhed up through cracks in the pavement below. The wrist-thick vines wound around Wolverine, wrapping his arms and legs like snakes around a tree trunk, preventing him from moving. Mike looked over to the duck pond under the coaster where a giant boulder rested. He lifted his hands as the boulder rose into the air and darted towards Wolverine. A giant shadow appeared above Wolverine as he gazed quizzically up at the floating boulder. He squinted his eyes in fear at Mike as though begging him not to do what he was about to do. Mike grinned as he lowered his glowing hand, causing the boulder to slam Wolverine into the ground.

Jake stopped dodging the lightning bolts. One had struck him, and the electrical current painfully echoed throughout his body. Jake's shouts of agony echoed through the park. People, who saw what had happened, screamed in terror and began to run blindly toward the park entrance. Storm spoke to Jake for the first time. "Continue fighting me and you will feel what Mother Nature truly thinks of *man*."

Jake painfully drug himself up from the ground and stood, shakily. He smiled. "If you don't leave *me* alone, I'm going to show you what I think of *you*." A sudden whip of wind passed through him as he formed the bolts of electricity from inside his body into spheres with his hands, like luminous static snowballs. They expanded rapidly to twice the size of his hands as he stacked them in a pyramid on the ground. "Do you know what it feels like to get hit with a ball of electricity? Well, I'll show you, but first I'll give you a hint—it doesn't feel *good*!"

Electrical spheres flew at her like meteors as he threw violently with his immensely strong pitching arm. Storm screamed as she was pushed back against a streetlight, snapping it in half. Her body glowed and throbbed with static as the electricity traveled through her and into the streetlight, exploding the lantern in a shower of sparks and tiny shards of glass. Storm dropped to the ground amidst the debris and didn't move.

"Yo, Spidey!" yelled Toni annoyed. "What's up with the web balls?" She moved a shield of ice rapidly up and down, blocking every one of the sticky web balls that showered her like hailstones. Suddenly, Spiderman shot his hands out at her, sending out rope-like webs that wrapped around her and her shield, making them incapable of moving. He shot another web at her, but this time he held onto the other end. He used all his might to swing Toni back and forth over his head like a ball on a string. She hit the ground repeatedly, like a hammer, swearing more profusely every time she knew she was going to hit the ground.

Spiderman suddenly swung her around over his head like a helicopter blade and let go. She landed awkwardly and painfully on her side across the tracks of the roller coaster. She could feel the track begin to shake violently as the roller coaster approached. It was coming her way! Trapped in the net of webs, Toni squinted her eyes in fear, afraid of what might happen next. The cries of people in the coaster grew louder and more shrill. She closed her eyes. The crystal on Toni's forehead appeared and began to glow.

The coaster miraculously lifted and traveled over her as it followed a track of ice. She opened her eyes and gazed up at the coaster soaring over the solid ice above her. She smiled, relieved. She struggled, trying desperately to get out of the net that restrained her, but it was no use. She closed her eyes again as her body began to turn blue. Flakes of ice appeared on her skin and glittered in the sunlight. They began to expand, creating a solid cocoon of ice around her. The ice thickened then became covered in fine cracks. Toni burst out of the shell of ice, breaking the web as she shot out of it.

Toni floated in the air and shook her head, letting her hood fall down around her shoulders. Snowflakes fell from her hair. She looked down at the kneeling Spiderman on top of the comic book store. He shook his masked head as he leered up at Toni in disbelief. Toni smiled and began to sing, "*The itsy bitsy spider went up the water spout, down came the rain and WASHED THE SPIDER OUT!*" With these words, a thick jet of water, like out of a fire hose, came churning out at bullet speed from her hands, hitting Spiderman head on. But suddenly, as he was falling, he shot Toni in the mouth with a web, keeping her from speaking. Spiderman flew backwards over a fence and into a pond with a loud echoing splash.

Toni peeled the web off her mouth as she soared down to Becca who was still lying on the ground, unconscious. Toni bent down to place her hand on Becca's head just as she moaned, rolling over on her back. "Are you all right, Becca?"

Becca put one hand up to gingerly touch her bruised forehead. The stone glowed once more, and the bruise disappeared. "I'm okay, but my head really hurts."

Toni looked at Becca, bewildered. "But you just healed yourself!"

"No," said Becca getting up, "I healed the outside, but not the inside. I can only heal from the outside. If I tried to heal from the inside, it would take too much out of me."

Toni shut her eyes and shook her head. "You *are* one complex person." Becca smiled up at her. Toni looked around for the others until she spied Mike resting on top of an enormous rock at the end of the plaza. Jake was leaning on it, talking to Mike from the ground. Toni flew over to see what was wrong, since Mike was taking off his black armor. As he placed his hand over the bloody wound on his side, Toni hopped up next to him to take a look. "Are you okay?" she asked.

"I'm wounded pretty badly," he glowed briefly and his costume disappeared. Mike lifted up his shirt, revealing his muscular chest and stomach. There were purple bruises across his ribs and stomach, and blood was dripping from the gash in his side. "I mean, it doesn't hurt as much as it's suppose to. Now we know —we're invulnerable to a lot of pain, but we obviously can still feel it."

Toni sighed and held her hand out as ice crystals began to appear. They swirled around for a moment and formed a crystal clear bowl in her hands. She touched the base of the bowl with her glowing blue index finger and water filled it to the brim. "This will help." She handed Mike the bowl. He waved his hand and a spongy leaf, the size of a small towel, appeared in his palm.

Mike dipped the leaf in the water and placed it on his wound. "OWW! WHAT'S THE MATTER WITH YOU, WOMAN?!" He threw the leaf off his wound and down onto the ground, drenching Jake when he dropped the bowl, which shattered, then melted away. "WHAT DID YOU DO? THAT BLOODY WELL HURTS!"

Toni laughed. "Well, what did you expect, apple juice? Its salt water and it will help heal the wound and prevent it from bleeding." She pointed her index finger lethally at Mike. "Now stop being a little girl and put that leaf on your chest!"

"No, I will not!" he yelled.

"Fine with me," said Toni shrugging. "Go ahead, bleed to death!"

Jake laughed. "Mike, just put it on. She's just trying to help." Mike said nothing. However, the leaf on the ground suddenly sprang up and wrapped tightly around his chest and back. Mike yelled in pain as he tried to tear the leaf off, but it was no use. Becca strolled over, her glowing purple hand raised. Mike's black armor suddenly appeared and repaired itself as it soared over to cling on Mike. The rest of his costume appeared when he changed into his older form.

He shut his eyes tightly, grimacing from the pain. "Becca, what are you doing?" he asked, exasperated.

Becca lowered her glowing hand. "You need to be healed, and that's THAT!"

"Guys, not to ruin your 'War of Big Mouths' or anything, but I don't think we're quite done yet." The boulder Mike was standing on shivered and rocked, then flew up into the air with him on it. He dove recklessly off toward the other teens and ended up knocking Jake, Becca, and Toni to the ground. Wolverine stood up straight and flexed his muscles so that his lethal metal claws glistened in the sunlight.

Across the plaza, Storm got up slowly, brushed the broken glass from her costume, and looked menacingly over at the teens. Streams of electricity began to travel up and down her body, giving her a glowing aura of lethal blue static.

Cyclops, who had been knocked to the ground after being hit hard enough to dent his metal helmet, also pushed himself to his feet. He shook his head as if to clear it from the pain, and then began stalking across the plaza toward the teens.

Spiderman climbed out of the water, shook himself like a dog, and began to crawl toward the teens like a giant red and blue insect. The teens got to their feet and circled around, back-to-back, ready to fight. The rest of superheroes met in the middle of the plaza and stalked side-by-side toward the teens. They laughed as they got closer.

A commotion on the left side of the plaza caught Mike's eye. He squinted his eyes and took a better look. "Guys, please tell me those are dress-up characters over there?"

The other teens turned to look where Mike was pointing and saw *Captain America*, the *Incredible Hulk*, and *Batman* moving toward them from between a store that sold fudge and one that sold souvenirs. It was hard for the others to tell at that distance if they were people in costumes or not.

Becca whispered in horror, "No, they were sent by the Goths."

"Are you sure?" asked Jake. But as soon as he said the words, all the comic book heroes began to charge straight at them.

A booming voice echoed through the air, "*RICOCHET!*" A bright green light appeared around the teens like a soap bubble. The superheroes ran into the bubble and ricocheted back twenty feet in the air. A force field had appeared around the teens!

"Was that you Becca?" asked Toni, fear on her face.

Becca shook her head. The voice boomed out again, "*FLAMES OF FURY!*" Two fireballs blasted past the falling superheroes. The fireballs touched down among the heroes then exploded like powerful grenades two seconds later. The superheroes flew back another twenty feet and landed in a tangled pile.

The green force field evaporated from around the teens. They looked up curiously into the clear blue sky and spotted two people winging towards them with a magnificent Pegasus. A glowing green teenage boy was riding the beautiful, blindingly white winged horse while a glowing red girl flew next to him with a ball of fire in either hand.

The girl wore black leather pants and a short black leather top with red flames stitched all over. She also had on long black, elbow-length leather gloves with a flame embossed in gold on the back of each hand. She had thick, silky curly brown hair. Her eyes were an intensely luminous shade of red, like glowing coals. And on her right arm was a red ruby encircled by a black hieroglyphic tattoo!

The boy on the Pegasus had short blonde hair and radiant green eyes. He wore a tight black shirt with long, baggy brown leather pants. An emerald silk robe fluttered behind him and down over the hind end of the Pegasus. He looked like some kind of mythical sorcerer from medieval times. Around his wrists, he wore golden wrist plates that looked exactly like Becca's. He smiled and laughed a lot, showing straight white teeth.

"That was awesome!" shrieked the girl with the brown hair, pumping one fist in the air.

The boy on the Pegasus laughed and called down to the teens, "Ya'll need any help?"

The teens were still a bit shaken up and surprised, but were relieved at the same time. "Thanks!" said Jake, truly grateful.

"The name's Flare!" yelled the girl. "Both for my style and my ability. And this is my brother, Myth." Myth jumped off the Pegasus from thirty feet above, which had just disintegrated into a swirl of opalescent stars, and landed on his feet rather remarkably. He bowed theatrically, and Jake stepped forward to introduce himself and the others.

"Nice to meet you," said Myth cheerily, giving each of them a brief, but dazzling, smile.

"Same here," said Toni blushing. "We owe you one."

Myth laughed. "I guess you do. I'll take your word on it."

Flare floated down and delicately landed next to her brother. "You don't owe us anything. But I suggest we get a move on." She inclined her head toward the superheroes who were now hesitantly getting up from the ground, glaring at the teens with hatred.

"So, do you guys want to split up?" asked Flare.

Becca nodded. "Good idea."

"Alright." said Jake. "Flare, you can take Captain America. Myth, how about you dealing with Wolverine. Quake, why don't you handle the Hulk and Batman. Star, Aquarius and I will take up where we left off." They flew like bullets to where the superheroes were still recovering from the grenade blast. Amazingly, there were still quite a few people crossing the plaza and shopping in the stores. Some of them even sat down on the benches with their ice cream and drinks to watch, what they thought, was the show.

Flare began to throw fireballs at Captain America, but he kept blocking them with his round shield. She swore as she spun furiously in place, gaining thermal energy. Fire began to expand around her, making her look like a small blazing tornado. She slowed to a stop and swung her arms out to sling the fire tornado at Captain America. He leaped aside, barely dodging the tornado. Jumping agilely to his feet, he threw his round shield like a Frisbee. It hit Flare in the stomach and sent her flying backwards to crash into a pair of trash bins.

Her eyes glowed even brighter and flames seemed to flicker eerily within them. The ground began to shake and a huge crack opened up, revealing a reddish orange glow. The crack spread across the plaza to where Captain America was waiting. Sulfur-smelling smoke billowed out of the gap followed by a slow-moving ooze of molten lava. Flare raised her hand upwards and spouts of lava came shooting out of the ground. One came from below Captain America, pushing him high into the air. Flare leaped up to intercept him and began to pummel every inch of his body at incredible speed. She then kicked one leg out and struck him with a powerful blow to the chest, sending them both flying in opposite directions.

Flare grinned as she held out her glowing red index finger and began to draw with it in the air with fire. It was a picture of a giant flaming bird. The bird came to life and soared directly at Captain America, continuing right through his body like a fiery arrow. He shrieked once as his body glowed black then flared white-hot and disintegrated into nothing more than cardboard ash. Flare glanced over to look at Mike who was dodging the combined attacks of Batman and the Hulk by jumping from boulder to boulder as they rose out of the ground. Mike rode a rising boulder up to Flare.

Mike smiled. "Hey, hot stuff! I'll take care of the Hulk if you can give this to Batman." He flicked his fingers and a black rose appeared. He tossed it at Flare who caught it in one gloved hand. "Throw it at the bat!" Flare smiled and winked at him.

Flare tossed the black rose at Batman like a dart. Batman saw it coming and positioned his cape in front of him so the rose hit the cape and fell to the ground. He lowered his cape and picked up the rose. He looked up at Flare with a puzzled look on his face, and Flare smiled and waved. The rose suddenly exploded like a bomb sending Batman flying back with tiny black seeds all over him. Black thorny vines sprouted from the seeds and wrapped themselves tightly around his body. The vines were squeezing the life out of him. Batman began to glow a ghastly shade of black until abruptly blazing white hot and melting into ash. The spectators on the benches applauded and whistled.

A tremendous crash got everyone's attention as the Hulk jumped out from the souvenir shop and landed on Mike, flattening him hard against the cement. Mike sunk down through the cement into the ground then popped out in front of the Hulk, kicking him hard in the face. Hulk was sitting up holding his jaw when Mike threw two tiny pebbles at him. As they passed his shoulders, the pebbles expanded until they were big enough to suspend him between them in mid-air. The pebbles continued growing until they clashed together, crushing the Hulk between them. His legs kicked feebly a few times before a white flash left him nothing but cardboard ash.

Spiderman came flying past Mike at great speed. He landed with a splash like a wet Nerf ball. Mike looked down at Spidey and then back at Toni, who had her arms raised, mist glowing around her. "Something wrong?"

Toni sighed in annoyance. "He just keeps on getting back up!" she said to Mike in exasperation. "Why won't you just *die*!?" she pleaded, hitting Spiderman with another fire hose-like water jet.

Mike laughed again. "Take it easy. Just try something different—look—here's a head start." Mike raised his glowing yellow hand as the earth beneath Spiderman humped up and sent him spinning into the air like a little kid on a trampoline. Spiderman shot a web across to the rollercoaster track. It not only slowed him down, but acted like a bungee cord to whip him past Mike and Toni. Spiderman now clung to one of the huge metal uprights and made a rude hand gesture at them. Toni raced after him, screaming in frustration.

Flare laughed as she walked over to join Mike. "She is certainly one impatient woman for, I'm guessing—an eighteen year old."

Mike laughed, too. "You got that right, but she's not eighteen. If fact, none of us are as old as we look! Our costumes just let us look older."

Flare looked at Mike in stunned confusion, but said nothing. They watched Toni and Spiderman for a few more moments before she asked, "So, how old are you guys really?"

"We're all fourteen—you?"

"Same as my brother and me—we're twins—but we turn fifteen in December."

Mike turned to her, shocked. "That's really weird. Our birthdays are all in December, too."

Flare stared at Mike for several seconds in disbelief, and then looked back over at Toni, who was now pelting Spiderman with balls of ice. "Does she need help?"

"No—" laughed Mike, taken aback. "Of course not. She's... different. She likes doing things herself. Besides, if we try to help her, she'll just get mad. Or should I say mad*der*." Flare giggled.

Toni screamed again. Spiderman was still dodging everything she threw at him while occasionally sticking out his tongue at her and blowing raspberries "I'm annoyed, tired, and bored with fighting you," yelled Toni, hands on her hips.

Spiderman grinned at her in an evil way. Toni grinned right back at him. She raised the back of her hand against her chin and wiggled her fingers at him. She blew onto her hand as big frozen flakes flew off of it, hitting Spiderman. He stiffened and then froze solid. "Finally!" shouted Toni. With her eyes still fixed upon Spiderman, Toni stretched her arms wide creating a long, blue rod of ice between her hands.

The frozen Spiderman slowly started to twitch, squirming his way out of the frozen shell. He sprang at Toni, but she saw him coming. She pointed the ice spear at him, and it shot out of her hand without her using any physical strength to throw it. It stabbed deep into his stomach, but no blood came out. He clutched the spear as he began to glow black. Toni took a deep breath and slowly exhaled after Spidey flared white-hot then turned into ash. She turned away when she heard a loud crack behind her. She turned to find Myth fighting Wolverine who had him backed up against one of the fountains.

"*FLAMES OF THE PHOENIX!*"

A glowing red bird appeared behind Wolverine. Its enraged screech echoed across the nearly empty plaza. (The spectators 'oohed and ahhed'.) It sent a blazing fireball at Wolverine through its large hooked beak when it screeched a second time. Wolverine exploded backwards toward Myth. Myth snapped his fingers and a metal cage appeared. Wolverine landed in the cage and the door locked shut. Myth walked over to him and smirked, dusting off his hands. Wolverine stepped over to the side of the cage and agilely slipped between the bars. The smirk slid off Myth's face. "Oops, didn't think about that!"

Myth jumped backwards, dodging Wolverine's lethal slash. He shouted, "*WARLOCK'S DUST!*" Green sparkling sand appeared in his hands and he threw it in Wolverine's face. Wolverine immediately keeled over, fast asleep. Myth chanted to the sky again. "*FAIRIE'S WAND*!" A wooden wand appeared in his hand. He waved it experimentally a few times then touched it to the ground. Electric bolts shot through the tip of the wand striking Wolverine.

Wolverine shook wildly for several moments causing him to wake up. He got slowly to his feet and began to laugh wickedly. "I heal myself every time I sleep, kid. Thanks, but you're done for!"

Myth sighed, and then leered directly into Wolverine's eyes. "Then I guess we need something that will kill you in one hit. *HALLUCINATION BEAM!*" Myth shouted into Wolverine's face. Three purple glowing boomerang-shaped beams slashed completely through Wolverine. He dropped at Myth's feet and began to glow black. His body shivered and flared white-hot. The flash faded to reveal Myth standing ankle deep in ash.

Myth shook off his boots. "Messy." He then ran over to Becca who was being helped to her feet by Toni and Flare. Cyclops kept shooting beams of red light at them. They were coming so fast that the teens didn't have time to fight back or dodge, and were forced to take cover behind a statue of Superman. Myth shouted, "*RED WATER!*" The beams of light turned into reddish gold water that splashed onto the teens, giving them nothing more than a good soaking. Becca laughed and shook her wet hair. She rubbed her palms together then opened her hands wide to reveal a pile of glittery purple and silver stars. She threw them at Cyclops where they exploded into fireworks, sending him flying through the air yet again.

Becca unsheathed her sword and held it tightly up over her head. "I'm *sooo* tired of you!" The shimmering silver-bladed sword blazed a bright amethyst. The light coming off Becca's sword seemed to grow thicker and more powerful. With a final pulse, a heavy beam of violet light streamed away from Becca's sword and towards Cyclops. It split the red beam and drove deep into his helmet. He fell over backwards, hitting the pavement with a metallic clang. His still form glowed briefly black then shone white-hot leaving behind a drift of ash. Becca re-sheathed her sword and turned to face the others.

They all jumped and cowered at an amazingly loud clash of thunder. The sky grew dark as inky black storm clouds formed overhead. Mike walked up behind the others who were now watching Jake. "What's going on?" Becca pointed to the sky. A girl in a uniform carrying a broom and a dustpan with a long handle brushed past them to sweep up the pile of Cyclops' ashes. Toni gave her a ridiculous look as she crossed the plaza to empty them in a nearby trash can. Toni shrugged and turned her attention back to the sky.

"Fool!" yelled Storm from above. "Do you really have the nerve to mess with Mother Nature?"

Jake laughed as he tossed a lightning ball up and down in one hand. "If you're Mother Nature, what does that make me? Father Nature?" He suddenly threw the lightning ball at Storm as though throwing a fastball. Storm waved her hand and a lightning bolt appeared. She gripped it with both hands and swung it like a bat. It connected with the ball with a loud crack and flew right back at Jake's head. Jake summoned his own lightning bolt and volleyed it right back at her.

"I see how it is!" laughed Jake. "A game of tennis!"

"Fool!" yelled Storm. "You joke too much." She caught the ball, turned in a quick circle, and threw it back at him with all her might. Jake was able to deflect it one-handed with his bolt before it struck him, and then caught it with his free hand. The lightning ball was gradually expanding as it gained power each time it was hit back and forth.

"I'm not one for games," said Jake, tossing the lightning ball up and hitting it with his bolt bat as it got more difficult to throw. "I like to play by my rules, in other words—*cheat*!" He glanced up into the dark sky and it grew increasingly windier. A flash of green lit the sky as a tornado dropped down out of the churning clouds and hit Storm directly from above. She was trapped in the middle of the spinning vortex, unable to get out.

The lightning ball came whizzing back toward Jake from the tornado. He swung his hands up over his head guiding the ball upward. It hovered right over his head as if resting in mid-air. It now sparked so brightly that it lit up the entire pitch-black sky like a tiny sun. Suddenly, Jake plunged his hands forcefully towards Storm as the lightning ball arrowed toward her with great speed. It hit her, sending gigantic lightning bolts racing to the ground. The tornado vanished back into the black clouds, revealing only Storm. She was hanging limp in the air, glowing dark lethal-looking black that quickly blazed white-hot. The ashes wafted away on the wind. The storm clouds vanished, revealing the clear blue sky and a sparkling yellow sun that lit everything in its path.

Jake looked down in time to see a purple force field wink out of existence from around the rest of the teens. Luckily, the people standing nearby were smart enough to run for cover. Though many stepped out of shops and gave the teens a hearty round of applause.

Jake flew down to the others. "We have to find the Goths and stop them! We have to help the rest of those people before they get hurt."

"Flare and I took care of this roller coaster before we joined up with you," said Myth as he made another beautiful Pegasus appear.

"Let's go after them at the control room!" yelled Mike, flying off on one of his many boulders. The others soon followed. Mike—in the lead—turned his head back toward the others. "Where *is* the control room anyway?"

Becca shut her eyes for three seconds. "It's in the tall building that looks like a castle tower in the mythical theme area. There's an elevator and an emergency stairway that leads to the top, but I think we can make a bit of a better *entrance*."

The teens flew quickly over the cartoon and Jurassic sections of the park and made their way to the five-story building housing the ride control rooms. It wasn't difficult to pick out considering what was orbiting around the top of the tower. It was almost far too difficult and unimaginable to be believed.

Chapter 9— A Force Again Unleashed

"What *is* that?" asked Toni, in a harsh whisper.

"Look's like they came up with a final trick," said Myth, soaring down to the base of the building on his winged steed. They both glared up at the half-blue, half-red beast. "It's an Ancient Chinese Dragon," said Josh wisely.

Becca looked over at the Twin Dragons rollercoaster. The carts were not there. She looked up at the dragon. "They've used the coaster to create the dragon!"

The others looked over at the roller coaster, too. "But what about the people that were on them?" asked Jake incredulously.

Becca squinted her eyes shut. "They're inside the dragon—trapped."

Flare screamed, "How are we supposed to get them out?"

Becca sighed. "We can't—they've become part of it."

"What if we accidentally hurt them trying to get in the tower?" asked Toni.

Becca closed her eyes and shook her head. "It's the only way."

A monstrous roar echoed through the air sounding a lot like a train whistle. The teens covered their ears, and then gazed above them to discover that the snake-like dragon had noticed them. The upper surface of its scaled body was red and its elongated underbelly was blue. The scales twinkled in the sunlight as it looped and writhed its way through the air, somehow managing to fly without any wings. It was at least fifteen or twenty feet in length. The dragon lunged down at them with its two silvery horns framing its glassy green eyes giving it an even fiercer look. It howled again as it plummeted towards them, as red and orange flames were emerging from between its glittering teeth. Suddenly, a large fireball shot out of its mouth right at the teens.

"Go!" yelled Jake. They all leapt up and soared back into the air toward the dragon. The fireball hit the street easily missing the teens. Toni shot beams of ice out of her fingers. Jake threw lightning bolt after lightning bolt. Becca fired a purple beam at its eyes. Mike threw boulders. Myth sent out a green beam, and Flare shot a beam of magma.

The beams all hit the dragon, but with little effect. Its hard scales protected it, giving it nothing more than a slight bit of a punch. The dragon turned its head towards Toni and shot a ball of fire directly at her. Toni raised her arms and a thick ice-shield formed in front of her. The fireball was deflected by the shield but the force of it sent Toni exploding through the windows. She slowly stood up. She was brushing away the broken glass as she watched the dragon attack the other teens.

She turned from the window to find the Goths sitting in front of a long row of computer consoles, surprise evident of their faces.

"Put everything back to normal! NOW!" Toni demanded.

"I don't think so," said Felix, getting up and walking toward her. "You're the one that needs to leave. You aren't wanted here," he said menacingly. Toni lunged at him in an attempt to grab the front of his shirt, but Felix rolled an empty desk chair between them. When she angrily flung the chair aside, he quickly added, "and if you get rid of us, you won't know how to get everything back on *track*. We already put our own codes in the system and changed all the passwords." Felix's voice got stronger as his fear went away. "You have no choice, so get out!"

"Don't I?" asked Toni sarcastically. She pulled her hood up over her head, and wrapped her cloak around her. "Tell me, have you ever been in a snow storm in Antarctica?" Felix and his gang looked at each other, puzzled, but said nothing. "Let me give you a hint—the cold will make you go so numb that you won't feel your body parts freezing solid and dropping off."

"You don't scare us!" yelled Felix bravely. The other Goths gathered around him, nodding and gesturing rudely.

Toni smiled and held her hands out in front of her. "*Winds of the Arctic, snow of the Antarctic, I call upon you to blow your wrath into this room!*" Wind began to howl and gust, knocking over the chairs and sending stacks of papers on the control consoles swirling around the room. Blowing snow felt like needles piercing their faces. All that was visible through the raging blizzard was the intense sapphire glow of Toni's eyes. The Goths dropped to the floor and wrapped their arms around their heads. They were shivering violently and gasping for breath as they tried to huddle together against the frigid winds.

Toni cocked her head to one side. "Do I scare you *now*!?"

"*Y—you—w-w-w—win! We'll f-f-fix—it!! J-j-just s-stop bef-f-ore we f-f-freeze!*" yelled Felix, through chattering teeth and blue lips.

The wind and snow stopped. The Goths got up immediately and went to retrieve the frosty chairs so they could sit down at the control consoles. Toni heard a faint whimper coming from behind the row of computer banks to her left. There were five men tied up with tape across their mouths. Snow had drifted over them, so they were shivering and struggling to get free. Toni walked over and cut their bonds with an icicle.

A large eruption shook the building as Becca suddenly smashed violently through another window, landing painfully on the ground next to Toni. Noticing Felix, she stood up quickly and walked over to him enraged.

"We're finished," said Felix through clenched teeth, voice raging. "Now what?"

"Get rid of the dragon!" said Becca fiercely.

"W—we can't!" said Jenna stepping forward. "Once we create something, it has to be destroyed in order for it to go away!"

"It's the truth!" yelled Felix when Becca grabbed the collar of his black t-shirt in her gloved fist.

Becca looked at them in disgust and pushed Felix away. Some ropes in the corner of the room caught her eye as she used her telekinesis to raise them into the air. They violently shot at the Goths, wrapping around them tightly so they couldn't move. "Hey!" screamed Felix madly. Becca walked next to Toni ignoring the Goths pleas for freedom.

A series of small explosions, like firecrackers, drew their attention outside. Toni and Becca flew through the broken windows to see the dragon still circling the tower, screeching and howling in fury. Boulders and colored beams of light pelted it, and it suddenly changed course to fly shrieking and flaming down toward the other teens outside.

"Let me try something!" said Myth. Spreading his hands about shoulder width apart, he closed his glowing eyes and sang: "*Twin birds of the sun, do hear my call: Use your power sublime, to defeat the dragon above!*"

A pair of magnificent Phoenixes exploded out of a flaming circular doorway that had opened in mid-air. One was vivid orange and the other the color of blood. Flare flew up to join them, her whole body blazing like pure fire! Every part of her was flame! The dragon howled again as it shot a yellow fireball at the three. Flare and the Phoenixes responded by throwing there own scarlet fireballs. The three red fireballs merged into one huge globe of flame. It barreled right through the dragon's yellow fireball, demolishing it, and hitting the dragon head on between its silvery horns. A deafening explosion rang through the park, cloaking the top of the tower in black, billowing smoke.

Flare cheered, swooping around the Phoenixes in celebration. But when the haze cleared, she couldn't believe her eyes: The dragon was unscathed! The fireball had had no effect on it whatsoever! The teens looked at each other with dismay.

Something caught Becca's eyes farther below. Near the locked door of the tower stood a familiar figure in purple robes with a snow-white beard. It could only be the man who had given Becca her crystal. His voice suddenly reverberated inside her head. "*You can only defeat it through the Power of the Crystal. You must look deep inside yourself to call upon the Angel of Telekinesis!*" The wizard waved his staff and disappeared. Becca shut her eyes and let a cool sense of serenity seep through her body like mist.

"*Everyone get behind me!*" said Becca forcefully. It sounded as if another person was speaking the same words along with her.

Jake looked questioningly at her, confused and rather surprised by her intensity. "*Becca*?"

Becca's voice became louder. "*Do as I say—please!*"

The teens got behind her without further question. Becca waved her glowing right hand in a large circle in front of her body. Thousands of miniature stars twinkled and swirled in front of her like a small nebula. She suddenly straightened both arms through the center of the whorl of stars, palms forward, and shouted, "*FORCE OF THE PSYCHIC!*" The crystal on Becca's forehead began to shine with a dazzling azure light. A beam of tiny sparks shot from her shaking palms, making everything blurred. It hit the dragon with amazing force, propelling it away from the tower and sending red and blue scales raining to the ground. The dragon flew screaming and thrashing over the park with its bellows of rage causing the buildings and rides to shake. More scales slid from its body, like tiles off a roof as it flew. The dragon screamed in pain, trying to fly back toward the roller coaster enclosure.

"*Now is your chance!*" yelled Becca, with the same strange double voice. She flew after the dragon with her fists extended out in front of her sending out a stream of exploding stars at the dragon. The others quickly followed her, sending their own beams of energy hurtling into the dragon's now unprotected hide. The shimmering beam of ice, opalescent beam of wind, jet of molten lava, translucent yellow beam of sunlight, and crackling stream of electricity all struck the dragon simultaneously driving it to the ground. A wave of blackness spread out from where the beams collided, changing to brilliant white. What was left of the dragon collapsed in a drift of grey ash.

About thirty people, liberally dusted with ash, lay on the ground where the dragon had been. The teens quickly flew down to them. Becca inspected the two nearest ones. "I think they'll be okay! I think they're just asleep!" said Becca, her voice back to normal. Becca, Jake, Mike, and Toni glowed briefly as they changed back into their normal selves. Myth and Flare followed their lead and changed back also. Myth was now a handsome teen with bright, emerald-green eyes, and Flare was a very pretty girl with brown eyes the color of caramel.

"So?" said Jake. "Thanks for all help! What else should we know about you guys besides that you're great fighters?"

"Well," said Flare, "first off, you should know our real names: I'm Rachel and this is—"

"Josh—I can speak for myself, Rachel!" he snapped. "I don't know if Rachel told you, but we're twins."

"Rachel mentioned something about that to me," said Mike.

"I've never met twins," said Jake. "That's pretty neat!"

Rachel and Josh looked at each other and laughed. "Not really, at least most of the time!" they replied in unison.

"And not to mention," said Mike mysteriously, "that they were born the same month we were—December!" The others stared at Josh and Rachel.

Jake chuckled. "That's really—"

"*Strange*," said Becca, cutting him off. "I mean, what are the odds of meeting someone like you guys AND being born in the same month as the four of us?"

"I have to agree with you there," said Josh, looking a bit puzzled. "That does seem to be statistically unlikely." Becca's face lit up with interest at Josh's intelligent reply, certain she had found a new friend in Josh.

Toni rolled her eyes and changed the subject. "So, where are you guys from?" she asked, smiling brightly.

"Flagstaff, Arizona," said Josh.

"No way!" said Becca, taken aback. "That's impossible! That's where we're from!"

"You're kidding!" laughed Rachel in disbelief. She looked at her brother and beamed. "They come from the same place and were born in the same month as us…"

Mike was the one that looked the most excited. "So, how did you guys manage to run into us *here when we haven't even seen each other in Arizona*?"

"We'll have to tell you later," said Josh. "There're too many people looking interested in us at the moment." All the teens looked around and noticed that several groups of people were milling about near the tower talking to park security and pointing in their direction. "I know this is probably a lot to ask, but could we stay with you guys?"

Becca looked at the others and nodded. "Sure! No problem!" she said. "But why?"

"We're— sort of…I guess you could say—orphans, at the moment." Josh sighed. "Our dad died when we were little and our mom was kidnapped about a month ago. We heard her scream, but when we tried to get to her, a lady with black hair used some sort of magic, or something, and they just—vanished! We went to the police but—"

"They didn't believe us," finished Rachel. "They were suspicious about her leaving us in the middle of the night, and figured that she had just abandoned us. But our mom was so loving to us, more than any mom we could ever imagine—she would never have done something to hurt us!" Josh put his arm around her. "We had to go to a community group home while they tried to locate a relative willing to take us in. We escaped from there just before school let out for the summer," she said, her voice trembling. The other four teens looked at them sympathetically.

"So, we need a place to live, temporarily, while we're looking for our mom," said Josh.

"Well, we better get back to the gate to meet my parents," said Becca. Her eyes glowed briefly. "All kinds of police and medical people are on their way—they would have been here sooner, but they were having trouble getting through."

Rachel and Josh looked at Becca as though she were crazy.

"She's psychic," laughed Toni. Josh and Rachel nodded, now looking less frightened. The teens began to head back to the exit of the park. On the way, they saw many people getting off the rides, looking very sick—some even puking.

"I don't think that even I could be on a ride that long!" said Mike. The others grinned.

"Will it be alright with your parents if we stay with you for awhile?" asked Josh hesitantly.

"I'll handle it," said Becca. "No worries."

They exited the park to find a very worried-looking Trudy and Bill waiting anxiously for them in the crowded entrance hall. They immediately ran over and hugged the teens while Rachel and Josh stood off to one side. "Are you alright?" said Trudy, nearly in tears. "When they made the announcement that everyone had to leave both parks because the rides were malfunctioning, we were a little concerned. But when some folks who came out of Islands of Adventure told us it was because someone had taken over the main control center, and people were trapped on the rides, we really started to worry."

"They wouldn't let us in to search for you, even when we told them we were both doctors! Thank God you're all okay!" exclaimed Bill, grabbing them all in a group hug.

Trudy glanced over at Rachel and Josh. "Who are you two?" she asked, very kindly. "Do you need some help?"

Becca's eyes flashed purple. "*They've always been our friends. They're on the road trip with us.*"

Becca's parents stared at the unknown teens, their eyes unblinking. They smiled suddenly when Becca's mom broke the silence. "I know that dear! It's not polite to joke around and make your mother look like a moron!"

Becca laughed, sheepishly. "Sorry, mom."

Josh leaned over to whisper to Jake. "Shouldn't we just tell them the truth?"

"We will," said Jake, "just not yet."

They all got on the moving walkway since it seemed the easiest way to move through the throngs of people. One of the uniformed ticket-takers walked over to them, her bright smile looking pasted on. "We're sorry for the inconvenience and would like you to accept this gift from us." She handed Bill a shiny blue card. "This card entitles you to two weeks in a hotel suite of your choice."

"Wow!" said Trudy. "Thank you, miss!" The lady nodded and smiled, hurrying over to the group of people who had gotten off the walkway.

"We can use this in New York!" said Bill excitedly, studying the tiny print on the back of the card. He looked up at the teens and smiled. "Let's hit the road!" he said happily, shooing them into the elevator.

When they arrived back at the R.V., all six teens went directly to their room in back. They all sat down on cushions on the floor and eyed each other. The R.V. suddenly started moving, and after several seconds, it stopped into an outside parking lot.

"Well," said Becca, yawning, "you guys don't have to tell us everything tonight since we've all had a long day. Let me get you a sleeping bag." She snapped her fingers and a green sleeping bag appeared at Josh's feet and a red one at Rachel's. "Oh, and since your traveling with us, I'll make it so you automatically go into your older form when you fight—if that's okay with you?" Josh and Rachel looked at each other and nodded back at Becca, who dropped a single tiny golden star on both their heads.

Becca's stomach suddenly growled expressively and quite loudly. The others laughed. "I don't know about you guys, but I'm starving! We were supposed to have gotten something to eat at the park, but we were a little too busy to remember!" She then waved her hands and a stack of six pizza boxes appeared on the floor in front of the television. "I took it from the restaurant at Islands of Adventure, but we deserve it for what we did, so I don't consider it stealing."

"You worry too much, Becca!" said Mike, through a fully stuffed mouth. Becca rolled her eyes as she picked up her pizza. Becca left and soon came back with sodas for all of them.

After about fifteen minutes of nonstop eating, all six pizzas were gone, and Becca waved her hand again to get rid of all the empty boxes and cans.

When everyone else began to get ready for bed, Becca looked at Josh and Rachel with a confused look upon her face. "Do you guys have any of your belongings?"

Josh smiled and waved his hand. Two suitcases suddenly appeared and stacked themselves neatly in the corner.

"You're good!" laughed Becca. The teens quickly changed into their pajamas and snuggled down into their sleeping bags. The R.V. stopped not long after and they heard Becca's parents say goodnight and walk into their bedroom.

"Well, good night guys," said Mike, rustling around in his sleeping bag getting comfortable. The others replied sleepily, including Rachel and Josh who were happy to be somewhere safe and comfortable.

"That was one amazing thing you did back there, Becca," whispered Toni, yawning and punching her pillow to fluff it.

"It wasn't me. I think it was the crystal," said Becca, sounding fully awake. "Remember what you did with the tidal wave?"

"Uh-hmm" replied Toni.

"I think these crystals are related to the increase in our abilities. Like they magnify the power somehow." Becca turned her head to see Toni's reaction, but realized her eyes were closed.

"Do you think so?" asked Jake from across the room.

"It kind of makes sense," said Mike.

"You controlled a huge amount of power, Becca!" said Rachel. "I've never seen anything so spectacular!"

"What's this about a tidal wave?" asked Josh curiously.

"Toni saved New Smyrna Beach from a tidal wave using the same sort of incredible power that Becca did," said Mike. He laughed at the look on Josh's face.

Rachel gasped in awe. "That's fantastic!"

"We all stopped it!" said Toni suddenly. "I didn't do anything you guys couldn't have done." She yawned until her jaw cracked. "Lets go to sleep, guys. We have another big day ahead of us." Everyone tossed and turned for a few moments, then Toni sat up and tried to push her window open, pounding on the window seal to try and free it.

"Try sliding it open, genius," said Mike rolling over.

She made a face, and then slid the window smoothly open. "Great. There's no breeze and I'm boiling!" Her face was glowing in the moonlight. A bright white flash came from behind her and soon she could feel a cool refreshing breeze coming in through the screen. Toni untied her hair, letting it blow in the breeze. She sighed and turned around to smile at Jake. Flopping back down, she was almost instantly snoring.

The room filled with sounds of chirping crickets and the gentle wind comforted them. But what was more comforting to the teens, was they were all together and safe.

Chapter 10— The Sages' Temple of Destiny

The teens were awoken the next morning by the rumble of the R.V. engine starting up. They were on their way to New York at last. It was wet outside and there was the fresh scent of rain. The teens were warm in their sleeping bags and they didn't want to get out into the cold room. Rachel sat up rubbing her eyes. "Don't mind me guys," she whispered. She waved her hand as a smokeless flame appeared in the air in the center of the room. Becca waved her hand as the window magically shut. The teens yawned and stretched in their sleeping bags, slowly waking up.

"So!" said Josh, eyes wide open, "do you want to hear the rest of our story?"

Toni spoke up immediately. "Definitely. Why don't you start with where you got your powers and gems?" Becca eyed Rachel intently.

Rachel sighed and pulled her sleeping bag up around her shoulders. "I'll try to make it short." As she spoke, she poured sparkling embers from hand to hand like sand in an hourglass. "We were exploring in the forest when it started to rain. A group of us from school was having a picnic in the national park, and we went on a hike with some other kids. The storm got worse so quickly that we had to search frantically for a place to take shelter from the hail, lightning and high winds. It was so strange because there hadn't been a cloud in the sky when we left. Anyway, my brother and I got separated from the rest of the group and stumbled upon a cave. I noticed hieroglyphics carved on the walls, and somehow I was able to read it. When I spoke the words aloud, the cave began to shake. A doorway opened in the wall where the writing had been. Glowing lights of six different colors were shining magnificently, lighting up the whole cave. Josh and I went through and realized that they were glowing jewels. I picked up the ruby and Josh picked up the emerald." She tilted her head at Josh. The four teens looked expectantly at him.

"There were more jewels," said Josh, "but we blacked out before we could look at any of them. When we woke, we were back home, and soon noticed we had strange powers." Josh pulled up his right sleeve and revealed a beautiful dark green emerald with black writing encircling it. The teens eyed the emerald in awe. "So what about you guys? How did you get your powers?"

Toni, Becca, Jake, and Mike, looked at each other, still stunned. "Believe it or not, our story is only slightly different," said Jake. "We were exploring in the forest behind Becca's house when a terrible storm came out of nowhere. We found a cave to take shelter in, but a huge boulder fell and blocked the entrance so we couldn't get out. Becca read the hieroglyphics and opened the door. We all went through and chose our jewel, but not before wondering who had taken the other three—but now we know. Well…at least where two of them went."

"We never saw a boulder," said Josh, eyes on the ceiling and deep in thought.

"That's weird. How could you have missed something so huge hanging right over the entrance," said Mike.

"Actually, it's not that weird," said Becca.

Toni eyed Becca curiously. "What makes you so sure?"

"It makes total sense!" said Becca philosophically. "There were only four jewels left when the four of us arrived—"

"So…when we took the remaining gems, there was no longer any reason for the cave to stay open," said Jake, picking up on Becca's train of thought. "The entrance had to be blocked so no one else would find the cave," he finished, mesmerized by the patterns the dancing flame made on the ceiling.

"When did you say your mom was kidnapped?" asked Toni, glancing over at Rachel.

"About two days after we got our powers," said Rachel, looking at Toni, confused. "Why do you ask?"

"Well—" said Toni, eyes now focused on Becca's. "As you know, Becca is a psychic. Last night, she had a dream that all of our parents, as well as two people that she didn't know, were kidnapped by an Egyptian-looking lady with black hair." Josh and Rachel gasped. Toni sat up suddenly. "Do you think it's true then, since their mom was actually kidnapped?" Toni clapped her hands over her mouth. She took a deep breath and paused, tears starting to flow down her cheeks and over her fingers.

"If it's true, it means our parents were kidnapped right after we got our powers!" said Mike angrily. "That mystery lady with the black hair obviously wants something from us."

"It has to be the Sages' treasure!" said Jake, moving over onto Toni's bed and putting his arm across her shoulders.

Rachel looked very confused. "But why would she want that?"

"I don't know," said Jake. "But it's probably very important to her if she has the *damn nerve* to take our parents!"

"How will we get them back?" asked Toni, tears now rolling freely down her cheeks. She turned her face into Jake's shoulder so the others couldn't see how upset she was.

"Don't worry," said Becca comfortingly. "We'll get them back. She obviously wants our power for some reason. But she wouldn't have taken your parents, unless she wanted the treasure as a ransom. That means she'll have to leave us clues in order for us to be able to find her to give her the treasure."

Toni smiled weakly and wiped her eyes with the back of her hand. She frowned. "Well then, why didn't she take *your* parents?"

Becca paused, shaken, for several seconds staring into Toni's eyes. "I—*I don't know*," she sighed. "And that's the truth." Becca turned to Rachel and Josh, eyes narrowed. She had just realized something. "You said your dad died when you were young?"

"Yeah," nodded Rachel, "I think we were three or four."

That didn't make any sense to Becca. She had remembered another adult in her dream—a man. "What did your father do for a living?" She didn't know why she asked—it seemed to have just spilled out.

"He was an astrologer," said Josh confused. "Why?"

"I—I don't know…I just wondered," said Becca, and that was the truth. *"It's as though I had to know for a reason…"* she whispered to herself.

"What was that?" asked Josh.

Becca smiled. "Oh—nothing…just thinking out loud."

Tiny wisps of fog gathered into a small gray cloud above the flame floating in the center of the room. It gave a small, tinny rumble of thunder, then drizzled briefly on the flame, putting it out, before fading away. The teens were lost in thought, pondering everything they had just heard. Jake gave Toni a final gentle squeeze before walking over to his own bed and lying down. He lay quietly for several minutes, just gazing up at the sky. The weather had cleared, and the sun-filled sky was adrift with bright, fluffy, white clouds.

"They're gorgeous aren't they?" whispered Jake, eyeing the clouds. "Everything about the sky makes me happy. It's like my mood changes with the weather." He looked up at the skylight and sighed heavily, eyes glowing white. "I'll be back guys. I just want to go out for a little while by myself." The skylight opened and Jake flew out. He felt a sudden rush of wind beside him, and found Becca there next to him. The others had stayed behind. Jake and Becca cruised up above the clouds and sprawled out on the downy mass as though lying on a feathery mattress.

Jake turned to at Becca. "Why did you ask Josh and Rachel about their dad earlier?"

Becca sighed. "Because I saw him in my vision…but… it doesn't make any sense if he's dead—how could I see him?"

Jake said nothing but thought about what Becca had said. "Do you believe in God?" he asked abruptly, breaking the silence.

"Yes," said Becca, turning on her side to look at Jake, one hand holding up her head. "Do you?"

"Yes, and I also believe in angels. I believe they guide us through difficulties and lead us out of danger." Jake held his hand out above him as a large cloud took the shape of an angel with her wings spread out and her hands together in prayer. The cloud angel twirled as a halo of stars twinkled around her head. She then unfolded her hands and pointed off to the right. Jake and Becca both sat up and looked at each other before following where she was pointing. They saw a golden bridge leading up to a golden gate in one of the clouds.

"What did you do, Becca?" asked Jake, stunned.

"I—*I didn't!*" Becca's eyes were wide, but not glowing.

Jake laughed in disbelief. "Should we go through?"

"Yes! Of course!" said Becca excitedly. "But let's get the others first." She squinted her eyes then opened them.

A minute later, the others appeared. Jake soared to the gates with the others following close behind. Each panel of the gate was about twenty feet tall and twenty feet wide, and glistened magnificently in the sun. The gate had the same fancy sort of scrollwork as the kind in front of the observatory back in Flagstaff, only much larger and made of gold. They peered expectantly between the glittering bars… and saw only sky.

Jake smiled. "Let's go," he exclaimed, pushing experimentally on the right-hand panel of the gate. The others followed him without any hesitation when it began to open smoothly inward. But the gate didn't open up onto just another part of the sky as it had seemed when they peeked through the bars. It revealed an entire city in the clouds! The immense beauty mesmerized them and rendered them completely speechless and motionless.

They stood at the top of a short stairway that looked down over the wide courtyard paved with cobblestones that looked to be made of cloud. A large, white marble fountain, created entirely of angels carved in white stone, stood majestically in the center surrounded by a large oval reflecting pool. Jets of pure water arced and sparkled as they fell back splashing into the pool. The buildings to either side of the courtyard seemed to be made of blocks of milky white marble, and each was crowned with a spectacular roof of lustrous opalescent tiles. The vista beyond them was of fantastic mountains, valleys, streams, and waterfalls, all made entirely of luminous white clouds!

Even more astounding and breathtaking were the hundreds of angels walking and floating between and above the magnificent city. There were female and male angels everywhere! All of them had long, beautiful, tapering, white wings like doves, and wore golden glowing halos as bright as the sun. They were all smiling and laughing through snow-white teeth and talking joyfully amongst themselves as they rested on the clouds above or walked through the courtyard around the fountain.

Beyond the courtyard full of angels, rose a wide, elegant staircase of polished marble. At the top of what seemed to be hundreds of steps, were a pair of gigantic red doors gleaming with silver fittings. The enormous doors led into a stunning white castle whose towers rose higher than any of the surrounding cloud mountains! Flocks of white doves flew gracefully around the castle, their snowy feathers glinting silver in the sunlight. All around them, the teens could hear the soft sound of a choir singing, more enchantingly beautiful than anything they had ever heard before. The lovely music seemed to be coming from the many open windows of the castle.

The teens were so astonished they couldn't move. They stood quietly taking it all in; afraid it would vanish the moment they spoke. The singing soon ceased, and the glossy doors to the castle slowly opened. A pair of exquisite angels came soaring through the doors on wings with long trailing ends. They were glowing white and leaving a trail of white glittery stars. One wore a long, gauzy, white dress and the other wore a long white robe with a golden sash tied around the waist. The lady in the white dress had long, curly, black hair, lustrous as a raven's wing. It was held away from her face by a golden comb, shaped like a dove, just above each ear. Her eyes were the color of violets. The man in the robe had short golden blonde hair and striking blue eyes that seemed far more beautiful and mighty than the other angels. They glided down to the teens on outstretched wings and landed gently in front of them, their feet bare.

"Hello, I am Jennifer," said the angel in the bright white dress, bowing slightly. "The Queen of All Guardians is aware of your presence. She bids you welcome and wishes to see you now." The six teens just gaped at her, as if she had spoken a completely foreign language. She turned toward the blonde angel.

"I am Ivan," he said, also bowing. "Please follow us and we will lead you to her. We are all delighted to finally witness the arrival of the Chosen Ones." Ivan and Jennifer spread their extraordinary wings and lifted effortlessly into the air. When the angels turned toward the castle, the teens glanced at each other in amazement then shook off their paralysis and leaped into the air to follow. Mike nudged Jake and pointed out the narrow silver swords sheathed between the wings of their guides. The angels on the clouds waved and smiled dreamily at the teens as they flew by.

The teens followed Jennifer and Ivan as they flew over the fountain in the courtyard and up the staircase. They flew through the glossy red doors, which silently closed behind them as they paused to land in the spacious entry hall. A long carpet of sunset red clouds led away from them across the polished white floor. The sun was shining through the many stained glass windows and brilliant streams of color danced across the gleaming expanse of floor.

Ivan and Jennifer led them along the red carpet toward a wide, red-carpeted stairway with silver and gold railings at the other end of the entry hall. As they walked along the carpet, they passed elaborate silver chandeliers hung with numerous crystals that glittered in the light from at least a hundred white flickering candles on each. From halfway across the room, the teens could see that there was an arched doorway on either side of the stairs. As they approached the massive staircase, they could see that about halfway up a smaller stairway branched off from either side. These side staircases each led to a golden-railed balcony lined with red doors, but on opposite sides of the room. The center stairway was at least twenty feet wide and continued all the way up to a single red door at the top.

Ivan and Jennifer stopped at the foot of the stairs and faced the teens, who were still busily examining every detail of the splendid entry hall. Jennifer began to speak, "Go up the wide staircase and knock three times on the door. We may speak no more, for now that is Queen Jasmine's place." She bowed and took one step to the side. Ivan now spoke soothingly to the six teens. "Let God guide you in every step you take." Ivan closed his eyes and spread his arms and wings wide. "This sanctuary is the home of all Guardian Angels. Welcome to the 'Clouds of Heaven'." He smiled brightly and stepped aside, folding his wings and gesturing for them to begin climbing the staircase.

"Thank you!" said Jake to the angels. The others followed him slowly up the wide staircase and up to the glossy red doors. The door didn't have markings of any kind or even a knob! Jake knocked three times on the shiny surface. The door swung silently open. The teens stepped through the doorway to find angels lined up on either side of the room, bowing and singing in front of long oak benches inlaid with silver and gold markings. At the end of the room was the most exquisite angel of all seated on a throne of silver carved with twining vines. Her halo was bright upon her long, straight, white silky hair. Her smile outshone even the brightest sun. Her lips could make roses bloom. She held a spiraling white staff with a glowing crystal on the end. A diamond tiara graced her head, and she wore a regal white velvet gown with a white fur cape. She was barefoot and the toenails on her delicate feet were painted garnet red.

The angels stopped singing as the teens approached the Queen and watched them curiously. The lovely angel smiled as six chairs appeared below the five steps that led up to her throne. "I am Queen Jasmine. Young Sages, please sit, for I have much to explain." Her voice could calm any harmful spirit, quiet a crying baby, or bring comfort to those in need. The teens sat down in the chairs and felt as though they could never be happier. "Kindly leave us," she said to the other angels. They glided by, shutting the door quietly behind them. "Are there any questions you wish to ask me before I begin?"

"Your majesty, what is the purpose of this place? Is this Heaven?" asked Jake wistfully.

Queen Jasmine smiled. "This is the home of all Guardian Angels. This is the place where we rest. Here we watch over every human being and try to guide and protect them every step they take through life. We also guide their spirits once they have left their bodies. We show them around our home and comfort them before they take the Stairway to Heaven."

"Stairway to Heaven? Isn't this Heaven?" asked Toni curiously. The tall golden candelabra on either side of the throne threw flickering light across her face.

"The stairway is the means by which the freed spirits reach Heaven. This is only a resting place. Heaven is a sanctuary far more beautiful than this. Far more beautiful than anyone Earthly could imagine." The teens were silent, thinking about what she had just said.

"Wait a minute," said Mike, reminded of something. "How come we're allowed in here? We're not dead are we?"

Queen Jasmine smiled very wide. "I think it is time to fulfill the promise that I made to the Sages so long ago. Follow me." She stood up and led the teens down the long room and through the red door. They went down the stairs and stopped where Jennifer and Ivan stood waiting. They both bowed low before Jasmine. "We are going to the temple," she said in her almost musical voice. Ivan and Jennifer nodded and led the way to the arched doorway to the right of the staircase. Ivan unlocked the red door with a silver key and opened it to reveal yet another courtyard. He then stepped aside and bowed to let the Queen and the six teens pass through the doorway.

This courtyard was much smaller than the one in front of the castle, but was surrounded by high walls. The entire space was filled with trees and flowers of all kinds. The walls were almost completely hidden by climbing vines with many kinds of sweet-smelling flowers. Jewel-toned butterflies and hummingbirds flitted overhead or zipped across the paths of white gravel in search of nectar. The pathways meandered through the garden, stopping at wooden benches near small bubbling ponds or white polished statues. A lawn of brilliant green cloud lead to a diamond shaped area in the center of the courtyard. This area was devoted entirely to roses of every size, color, and scent. Magnificent roses the size of dinner plates and the color of the sunsets competed with tiny white ones no bigger than thimbles. There was no elaborate fountain in the center of this courtyard—only a serene statue of an angel with furled wings and outspread arms carved of the purest, most luminescent white marble.

The teens were, again, speechless as they crossed the garden on the perfect green lawn. They knew they would never again find a place so peaceful and beautiful. "This is my private garden where I come to think and pray for the spirits who have gone on to the Stairway. I hope you have found it restful," said Jasmine as they made their way toward an arched doorway in the opposite wall. "Get ready to soar," she said, opening the shiny red door and pushing it wide.

The six teens followed the Queen out the door and found themselves looking out over another amazing view of the Clouds of Heaven from the top of a rugged slope of cloud boulders. They could see another huge building in the distance that looked like an elaborate white cathedral with numerous bell towers. Jasmine spread her wings and gently floated up into the air. She didn't even flap her wings, she just—*glided.* The teens took flight also and pointed out to each other the many amazing things they saw passing below. They flew over many buildings like those around the main courtyard of the castle, but also passed over parks with silver or gold leaved trees and more gardens of colorful flowers. Many of the parks contained herds of white deer grazing peacefully in green cloud meadows among white rabbits and silvery-colored squirrels.

As they got closer to the cathedral, they could see that an enormous round window of stained glass nearly filled the peak of the building above the massive front door. Jasmine landed in front of the building on the white stone steps. She walked up the last few steps until she reached the door, and then turned to face the teens who were lagging behind goggling at the sights. "What is this place?" asked Rachel, wonderingly, staring up at the roof hundreds of feet above her.

"This is the Sages 'Temple of Destiny'," said Jasmine. "In a moment I shall tell all, and you will gain the Knowledge of the Ancient Sages." She turned to face the enormous door, which was at least twenty-five feet tall and nearly as wide. A raised line ran down the middle of the door that divided it into two halves. The halves seemed to be fused together along this line, and there didn't seem to be anyway to open them. Jasmine turned once again to face the door and held out her magnificent white staff. She rapped it suddenly three times on the marble floor under their feet, the sound ringing and echoing in the teens' ears. A wind began to swirl around them; lashing at Jasmine's cape and making her hair ripple out behind her like a silken flag. "*God of the Sages, hear my call, for I bring forth the souls of the New Sages.*" Her voice echoed and the crystal grew extremely bright, shining with a golden light. With a sound like the clash of thunder, the door to the Temple split down the center. The teens jumped back and watched in amazement as the now separated doors glided slowly apart. Through the opening came the powerful humming and chanting of angels, which made the teens shake with astonishment. It sounded like God.

The teens looked at each other with their hair blowing in their faces. "Please enter first," said Jasmine respectfully. "You are the *Chosen Ones*," she said bowing and stepping out of the way. Toni walked through without hesitation with Jake following right behind her. Becca stepped forward, rubbing her forearms to try to get rid of the goose bumps. She stopped for a moment.

"I'm sensing amazing things in there," she said, tentatively, before entering the Temple. Josh, Rachel and Mike followed, all gazing around in wonder. To their surprise, the Temple was completely empty. The polished floor gleamed in the light streaming through hundreds of stained glass windows both overhead and along the walls. The walls, ceiling and floor were covered with unusual designs in gold, silver, onyx, and mother of pearl. In the center of the room was a raised platform on which rested a golden pedestal holding a tilted slab of white marble swirled with silver. At the far end of the room, beyond the platform, was a large pair of silver doors, though not as monstrous as the entry doors.

There was another rumble of thunder as the doors began to close behind them. Jasmine guided them toward the platform in the center of the room. The teens moved slowly in her wake gasping and gaping in awe at the beauty and grandeur surrounding them. Sunlight was shining brightly through the stained glass windows in the ceiling sending ripples of color dancing along the shimmering inlaid metallic designs on floors and walls. "The Ancient Sages built this temple so they wouldn't be forgotten, no matter how much time had passed," said Jasmine climbing the two steps up to a platform. She led them over to the marble table. They could now see that Ancient Egyptian hieroglyphics were carved into every square inch of it. The designs on the floor seemed to flow out from the base of the slab and move outward across the room, the pattern moving, uninterrupted, up the walls and partially over the ceiling.

"But that wasn't the only reason," she said gesturing toward the stone tablet. The teens gathered around. Fourteen diamonds were deeply carved into the white marble in the center of the slab surrounded by hieroglyphics. Each diamond overlapped the next making a ring of connected shapes. "They dedicated this temple to honor the Fourteen Angels of the Heavens whose Power you now share. Each of you shall have the power that the Fourteen Angels created. You have part of it now, but not all of it. The rest has to be earned by completing several tests to prove the worthiness of your intentions. And this, my Young Sages, is where your quest now begins."

She pointed to the doors at the far end of the room. "Those doors are meant for you to go through and obtain the Power that the Sages have been keeping safe for so long. Only their chosen descendants may pass through the portals, so that the rest of their Power can become part of you. All of you now hold one third of their power. However, Aquarius and Star have two thirds." She pointed to the crystals that were again visible on their foreheads.

"In order to get through these doors, you will have to find all three Sources of Power. Aquarius and Star only have to look for one more Source. The rest of you will have to find two."

"I knew this crystal meant something when the old man made it appear on my forehead," said Becca happily, knowing she was on the right track.

"What did you say?" asked Jasmine. "A *man* made it appear? Was he old?"

"Actually," laughed Becca, "he was *very* old. He wore a long purple robe and had a fluffy white beard."

"But it can't be, could it?" puzzled Jasmine. "Unless…the Guardians of the Crystals know of your arrival—they must be coming to find you and help you on your quest!" she exclaimed. "It is time!" she cried, waving her staff. "Let me show you the story that the Fourteen Angels of the Heavens have passed down to us." Six white mats appeared on the polished floor. "Lay down and look to the stars. They shall show you the way to your destiny." The temple suddenly went dark as glowing white stars appeared on the ceiling.

Jasmine smiled. "A long, long, time ago, fourteen of the most powerful angels in the Heavens were sent by the Gods to create a wondrous place full of mystery, myth, and magic. The teens watched as fourteen spots of color appeared amongst the stars: opal, silver, purple, pink, blue, turquoise, gold, yellow, dark green, light green, red, orange, black, and white. "These are the colors of the Angels," she informed them.

The colors floated into a circle which began to spin. A gray sphere formed within the whirling colors. A red and an orange star flew out of the circle and into the gray sphere, turning it red. "The Angel of Fire and the Angel of Magma created volcanoes," said Jasmine. A volcano spewing lava appeared on the sphere like a miniature movie. A gold and a yellow star disappeared into the red sphere. "The Angel of Earth and the Angel of Nature created land and growing things." Earth encased the red sphere and vines quickly covered it, changing it to green. Next, a dark green and a light green star went into the green sphere. "The Angel of Mythical creatures and the Angel of Magic created Mythology." The teens saw unicorns and dragons and all sorts of other creatures appearing on the sphere, turning it a glittering green. A dark blue and a light blue star now plunged into the gleaming green sphere. "The Angel of Water and the Angel of Ice created oceans." Patches of blue spread across the sparkling green sphere. Next, an opal star and a silver one dove into the green and blue marbled sphere. "The Angel of Wind and the Angel of Lightning created weather." Puffy white shapes appeared on the blotchy surface of the sphere.

"That looks like the Earth from space!" said Becca, astounded. Jasmine smiled.

"Shhhh!" said Toni harshly as a pink and a purple star vanished into the partially hidden sphere.

"The Angel of Telepathy and Telekinesis created humanity," continued Jasmine. Pictures of people now flashed across the surface of the sphere. Abruptly, the two remaining stars of black and white disappeared into the sphere. "And finally, the Angel of Darkness and the Angel of Light created night and day upon all the lands." A slideshow of the sun and many different kinds of buildings appeared then faded. The sphere now pulsed with golden light. "This is how the Fourteen Angels of the Heavens created the Earth and all life upon it."

"But, how are the Fourteen Angels related to the Sages?" asked Rachel, confused.

"Because they *are* the Sages—look," explained Jasmine kindly, waving her staff once more. The sphere disappeared and fourteen colored angels appeared in a circle. Jasmine waved her staff once more. The fourteen colors appeared next to each other in the shape of Angels. They were high on a mountain of greenery. "Each of these Angels had related powers to the others, such as fire and magma. The Angels agreed that they needed a way to stay on Earth, and teach people the Way of Life without drawing too much attention. But at the same time, they had to combine their knowledge.

"So they combined their powers," said Becca.

"Exactly!" exclaimed Jasmine. "By doing that, they formed into their own creations known as the Ancient Seven Sages, guardians of the Earth." Two colors teamed up and blended together. "Angels teamed up with another whose power was related in someway, for they knew by doing this their power and knowledge would be by far at its maximum. They taught one another, including themselves, their knowledge, showing beings the proper Way of Life. They have been on Earth for many millennia."

Jasmine waved her hand and the images above vanished. The darkness faded and the Temple became filled with light once again. When the teens got to their feet and stretched, the white mats vanished also. Jasmine gestured that they should continue walking towards the silver doors. "Many millennia after the Sages taught the Beings on Earth the Way of Life, the Evil known as Satan, an Angel outcast by the Gods, sent his Dark Minions to attack the Earth. In order to better protect it from the coming Darkness, the Sages created a fog that altered any Being who breathed it. The fog enabled these Mutants to fight Evil directly without the Sages being right there with them. This let the Sages fight many battles without having to be physically present at each one. Unfortunately, their control of the mutants decreased with their distance from them, allowing many of them to be enticed to follow the Paths of Evil and Wrong. Satan took advantage of this fault, by launching a direct attack on the Heavens, knowing that the Sages would be obligated to leave the Earth to protect Heaven. He hoped that as that battle raged, Earth would quickly fall completely into his hands."

"How did Satan know that the Sages would leave the Earth to defend Heaven, since their whole purpose was to protect the Earth?" asked Josh.

"Because Heaven was far more important than the Earth: Without the Heavens, the Earth, and many other worlds, could not exist. Therefore, it had to be protected at any cost," Jasmine replied, stopping in front of the immense silver doors. The teens could see now that the panels of the doors were covered with carved spirals of many different sizes.

Jasmine continued speaking as the teens gathered around her in front of the doors. "Even though the Sages were obligated to aid in the defense of Heaven, neither could they leave the Earth unprotected or it would be corrupted by the Darkness that Satan would create. During their time on Earth, the Sages had grown in Power and Knowledge of the Way of Life. So, they decided that they would select seven very special Beings to receive part of their Powers. These Chosen Ones would be the new Protectors of the Earth, and in the future, of other worlds and perhaps even the Heavens themselves. The Sages gazed into the future, as told in the stars, and studied the possibilities closely. And there…they found *you*." Jasmine smiled as she looked at each one of the six teens in turn. "To keep their Powers safe from Darkness until the Chosen could claim it, they split it into three parts. They hid these parts containing their Spirits in three different locations and in three different forms, known as Elements."

"The gems and crystals!" cried Becca, now understanding.

"Right again, Star! The Ancient Sages had created one Element for themselves and one Element for each of the Angel Spirits that formed together to form the Sage. All Elements together are known as the Treasure. The Ancient Sages hid the Elements of the Treasure in different locations all over the Earth, hoping that they would remain untouched until the coming of the Chosen. The Sages built this Temple to store and protect their Final Power; one that could not be lost to the Darkness under any circumstances. This Power is that which will help the Future Sages destroy the Evil and Darkness forever. Once this Power is obtained, you cannot die of any sickness or even old age. Only the complete destruction of your physical body can end your life. But remember, the many Minions of Satan do not know of this Final Power in which the Sages have created—this could be at your advantage. That Power lies beyond these doors."

Mike stepped up and tried to lift the ornate handle to open the silver door. It didn't budge no matter how hard he tried. "How do we open the door?" he asked, frustration in his voice.

"First, you must find the three Elements that belonged to your Sage. These are part of your keys that you must obtain that will help unlock the Door to your full Power," replied Jasmine. "You all already have the first part of the Treasure, the gemstone on your arm. Young Star and Young Aquarius already have the second Element, the crystal on their foreheads. Each of you will need to find the two crystals that belonged to the Angels before they were Sages, which they hid. You will also need to present the Sages' Weapons. These weapons are also keys to unlocking the door, because the weapons are to help you fight evil when you receive your Final Power. When you have collected all three Elements and each of your weapons, you must then locate the Chosen Ocarina and learn the Song of each of your Sages' Angels. Once you have accepted your destinies and played the Angels' Songs on the Ocarinas in front of this stoned arch door with all the Sages present, then and only then, will you be able to open the door."

Jasmine suddenly turned to look at Becca. "I sense that you have the weapon of the Psychic Sage!" Becca held out her hands as the sword she created a few days ago appeared in them. Jasmine took the sword from her and swung it mightily. She then handed it back to Becca. "I am guessing that you used your power to create it?" Becca nodded, eyes wide in amazement. "That is how the Psychic Sage wished for you to obtain it." Becca gripped the sword tightly as it disappeared in a flash of purple light, still puzzled on how she was able to obtain the weapon of the Psychic Sage and not even realize it.

"What do you mean by 'accepting' your destiny? I thought your destiny was the same as fate?" asked Jake. "I didn't think you had a choice to accept it or not."

"Destiny and fate *are* two different things, Jake. If you are fated to do something, it means that no matter what happens, you will end up doing that one thing no matter what choices you make along the way. In other words, all paths lead to that one moment. A destiny, on the other hand, is something that you have to knowingly choose. The possibility is there, but that doesn't mean you have to choose that path if you are going to be uncomfortable with the outcome. Everyone has to make these kinds of important choices. This is your chance to prove who you *really* are deep down inside."

"Where do we find these weapons and ocarinas?" asked Toni.

Jasmine smiled. "You will find out soon enough, for the ones who were the Sages' mythical partners still remain on Earth. They are, even now, searching for you. Allow them to guide you and help you on your quest."

"Who are they?" asked Josh, curious of what kind of beings were searching for them.

"Be patient. They will find you soon enough. Just keep following the direction that you're heading in and you will find clues." Jasmine looked intently at each of the teens.

"Wait a second…" said Rachel. "You mentioned a seventh Sage, but there are only six of us?"

Jasmine frowned. "Cleopatra, apprentice of Apocalypse, who is the son of Satan, holds Raven, the Sage of Darkness and Light. She has brainwashed her into aiding her every wish. You must bring the *Light* back to Raven and then bring her here in order to obtain the Final Power."

"You said that the Evil wants our Power," said Toni. "Then what Evil took our parents?"

Jasmine frowned again, darkening her lovely features. She walked over to Toni and placed a hand upon her cheek. "Cleopatra has taken your parents. I believe that her hope is that you will give up your Powers to free them."

"Where do we find her?" asked Jake.

Jasmine looked up at the glorious stained glass ceiling for several moments. "I don't know," she said at last.

"But that means the longer it takes for us to find them, the longer our parents have to live in torture," said Rachel angrily.

"Cleopatra needs your parents alive and healthy in order to get what she wants. Trust me on this and follow the steps that I have given you. You will receive more Knowledge on your journey. You must go now. I'll be watching over you closely and I'll be with you, whether you realize it or not." Jasmine closed her eyes briefly as if to bask in the colored light streaming from above. She opened them again before saying quietly, "Blessings upon you and your quest."

Mike smiled. "Thank you. We'll find the Elements and the Weapons, and we'll bring Raven back into the Light."

"I have one last question," asked Rachel, looking back at the silver door as they passed the platform holding the marble slab on its golden pedestal. "Why didn't the Sages use the Final Power themselves?"

Jasmine smiled. "I was waiting for someone to ask that question. The Sages created the Final Power as they were preparing to leave the Earth after several millennia as Guardians. They couldn't use it on themselves because they were too old, and they had to reserve what Power they had left to defend the Heavens. Even angels age eventually, so they needed someone younger that could adapt and learn more quickly and easily." By now they had reached the colossal, red entry doors which slid silently open as they approached. "Now, I have kept my promise to the Sages and told you all of the things you need to know. You may leave the Temple now, and I shall stay and pray for you." She turned around and waved her staff and a beautiful silver prayer bench with white embroidered cushions appeared. She knelt down upon the seat and closed her eyes, hands held together. She looked exactly like the Angel that was formed in the clouds earlier.

"Our quest begins now, guys," said Mike. "Our questions are finally answered and we know what we need to do. Let's get back to the R.V." He walked briskly out the door followed by the others. The teens suddenly stopped in astonishment. Hundreds of angels covered the steps of the Temple and spilled into the courtyard in front of it. Jennifer and Ivan were in front of the crowd smiling brightly at them.

"Sages," said Jennifer, "we will be watching out for you. Do not fail in your quest. It is as important for you as it is also for us. We want the Earth to be safe and peaceful as it once was." She paused and turned to Ivan. "We have something that will help you on your quest, Cyclone." She smiled at Ivan who gracefully waved his left hand in a circle. What looked like a hollow, white rock with a line of holes in it appeared in his outstretched palm.

"This is an ocarina," Ivan said, holding it delicately in his hands. "It is one of the Instruments of the Sages. I knew the Angel of Lightning very well. He gave me this ocarina and taught me his Song. This Song has a name that was well known by the Humans on the Earth. You will memorize how to play it instantly. The Song is called 'Fantasia on the Dargason'." Ivan held the Instrument to his mouth and began to blow through it, moving his fingers over the holes. He played a mythical, heavenly song. The angels on the steps, along with Jennifer, began to hum along with the melody.

Jake's eyes glowed white. After about thirty seconds of playing, Ivan stopped, but Jake's eyes still glowed. Jake waved his hand and the ocarina disappeared from Ivan's hand and reappeared in his own. Jake began to play the same song, but this time it sounded as though the Heavens were singing with him.

The teens looked at each other in astonishment. Jake's eyes returned to normal. He waved his hand, and the ocarina disappeared. The teens walked down the temple steps and took off into the air, waving goodbye to the Angels behind them. After passing over the parks, they came again to castle grounds. They flew around the fantastic towers and over the courtyard with the fountain made of angels. Eventually, they reached the golden gate where they had entered the Clouds of Heaven. The six teens looked back one last time to witness the glory of the incredible city before passing through the gates. When they turned around again, the magnificent gates were gone.

The teens were floating silently in the air, thinking of the extraordinary experience they had just had. They were beginning an extraordinary journey—an adventure—to save not only their parents, but all of mankind. Their quest had now begun.

Chapter 11— A Prayer Not to Be Forgotten

Jake turned his head to look at Becca. "Where are we?"

Becca looked down at all the skyscrapers that seemed not too far below them. "It looks like we're in New York. But something isn't right. Its summer time and its—"

"*Snowing*!" yelled Toni excitedly. "This is awesome!" Snow was falling heavily on the city of New York, leaving the grimy streets covered in a clean blanket of white. It was cold and the wind was blowing harder than usual.

"I'm sure the people down there are pretty confused as to what's going on," said Mike, gathering some snow in the palms of his hands. "Then again—I'm pretty confused too."

Jake suddenly looked above him and gazed at the clouds. "This isn't natural weather. Something or someone is controlling it."

"Maybe it's a sign that we're going in the right direction," said Josh. "It's probably giving us a clue or something—are you okay Rachel?"

Rachel was shivering madly and she looked rather ill. "*I'm—n-n-nott—one—for the—c-colddd*," she whimpered through bluish lips.

Becca went over to Rachel and took her hand. "Hang in there. Let's try to find the R.V. and my parents." Rachel nodded and followed Becca and the others down toward the skyscrapers. The snow was steadily falling, and many cars and people filled the streets.

"There!" yelled Becca, pointing toward the R.V., which was pulling into the parking lot of a large hotel. The teens soared down to the R.V.

and entered through the skylight. Right then, Becca's door opened and Trudy walked in. "Remember what happened at Islands of Adventure?" she asked.

"Umm… yeah? How could we forget?" replied Becca, heart racing from the sudden surprise of their very close call.

"Well, with the free hotel tickets they gave us,' said Trudy, "we decided to stay in a five-star hotel! Get your things packed up so we can register, and then we'll meet up with your parents."

The teens looked at Becca in horror. Trudy and Bill couldn't meet their parents, because Cleopatra had them! Becca's eyes flashed purple, as she looked deep into her mother's eyes. "*We're waiting for them to come to the hotel,*" she chanted. "*They might not come for several days.*" Trudy was motionless with her eyes out of focus. Becca stepped back as her eyes went back to normal.

Trudy suddenly said, "Won't it be exciting? The rooms are supposed to be huge and I hear they have wonderful room service!" The teens smiled. Trudy looked over at Rachel who was still shivering heavily. "Becca, get this poor girl a sweater! She's freezing! What crazy weather!" Rachel forced a smile. Trudy left the room, shutting the door quietly behind her. "Pack your things kids! And be sure to bring your sleeping bags. The hotel has a special room reserved just for us," she yelled from the hallway.

A cabinet door opened and a sweater flew into Rachel's arms. She quickly put it on. "Thanks."

The teens packed up their belongings and lugged them outside where Becca's parents were waiting for them. They followed Trudy and Bill into the hotel. It was difficult because of the heavy falling snow and the slick pavement in the parking lot.

There were two men in black uniforms opening doors for the people entering and exiting the hotel. There was also a man in a red uniform with a baggage cart. Trudy and Bill walked over and put their suitcases on it and the teens quickly did the same, thankful they didn't have to carry them through the hotel. The doors opened and they walked inside feeling a rush of warm air.

They were in a very large, luxurious lobby. There was red carpet everywhere, and glass elevators along either side. Decorative furniture and potted plants created little islands throughout the room. A hallway to their left had signs for fast food restaurants. Trudy and Bill walked up to the massive mahogany check-in desk. A man behind the counter in a white uniform took their tickets and gave them an electronic key card. The teens followed Becca's parents while another man dressed in red rolled the luggage cart close behind them. They entered one of the glass-sided elevators—it was huge! There was enough room for all of them to spread out. They rode up to the fifteenth floor and down the hall to room 1599.

When Bill opened the door, they entered and gasped. It was astonishing! The room was about ten times as big as the R.V.! There was a large screen television, a beautiful stone fireplace, leather couches and chairs, a master bedroom with its own glass and marble bath, another bathroom just for guests, and a whole kitchen with all of the usual appliances. In front of the big screen television was a giant air mattress that was built into the floor. It looked as though it could hold ten people. The whole wall facing the entrance of the hotel was a bank of windows where you could see the snow continuing to come down hard.

The teens walked over to the air mattress and put their sleeping bags on it. Trudy and Bill ordered Mexican food from room service, and the teens ate as though they had not eaten in a month. They had spent almost an entire day in Heaven and their brains were filled to the max with information. They were beat to the bone and mentally exhausted, so they got ready for bed, turned out the lights, and crawled into their sleeping bags. Even though Rachel's sleeping bag was closest to the fire, she still began to sneeze and cough. Becca made a cup appear and Toni filled it with water. Josh waved his hand and the water turned greenish in color.

"This is an ancient drink that the elves used to clear colds and to help them sleep better." Josh handed the cup to Rachel and she sat up to take a sip. She choked and spit it out into the fire with a look of disgust on her face. "Well, what did you expect? Apple juice?" he asked with some irritation. Rachel punched him in the arm and then pinched her nose. She drank what was left in the cup in two large gulps, looking as though she were ready to puke. She threw the cup into the fire then slid back down in her sleeping bag.

"That bad, huh?" asked Mike grinning. Rachel moaned.

"Well, goodnight, guys," said Jake, fluffing his pillow and zipping up his sleeping bag. The others bid him goodnight as they all bundled up in their sleeping bags and relaxed in the warmth of the fire.

"I want to thank you four for letting my brother and I stay with you guys," said Rachel suddenly. "It means a lot to us. I've never felt more at home, even with all the strange stuff going on."

"We're glad to have you," said Toni into her pillow. She lifted her head out of it. "Did you expect that we would leave you with no place to go? Besides, we should be thanking you for being a part of our lives. All six of us are the best of friends now!" The others agreed. They quickly dozed off to sleep, able to relax the first time in many hours. Toni had fallen asleep with a smile of joy on her face because of all the snow. Somewhere out there, Cleopatra and her minions were laughing and waiting for them. The seventh Sage was waiting for the teens also—confused—but inside, searching for hope.

A bright white light appeared to hover outside the oversized window, waking Becca up from a sound sleep. She walked quietly over to the window without disturbing the others. But when she got there, the only lights she saw were the ones on the surrounding buildings. She sighed and walked back to her sleeping bag, and was soon fast asleep. The light appeared again, but this time the teens stayed asleep. The light passed through the glass and went to hover over the sleeping teens. Jasmine appeared and smiled as she watched them dream.

"*Sleep well, my Future Sages knowing that I am always watching over you. It is my duty, as a Sage, to keep watch over you. It is my duty to make sure you succeed, and most of all… keep you safe. For this, I shall pray. When the time comes, I shall defend you and help you lead the Darkness into the Light. As I am the one who knows the most of Darkness and Light, I will make sure that you aid us in leading the Worlds into the Light of Love. But remember, it is up to you to bring Light to a special girl once again…before it is too late.*"

Jasmine looked out into the stars and a tear rolled down her face. "*The other Ancients shall soon be with you. Be careful, Chosens. Every decision you make now will count in the future. You will soon unlock your true destiny and find your true selves.*" She looked fondly at the teens' peaceful faces. "*You will know what I have said in your dreams, but you will not remember until the time is right, and once it is—you must look deep inside your hearts to discover its true meaning. There is always more than meets the eye. Remember also these words...it is the most important thing that I have said.*" Jasmine closed her eyes, but a faint white glow could still be seen through her pale eyelids. "*Each of you has turned out beautifully—just like we had hoped.*" Jasmine raised her glowing staff and disappeared again into the bright light, which whisked out through the window and disappeared into the falling snow. It grew colder outside in the darkness as the fire inside slowly dimmed.

Chapter 12—The First Clue

Jake was first to wake up early the next morning. He heard a faint laugh behind him. He walked over to the couch facing the giant window to join Mike who was there bundled inside his sleeping bag and staring out the window. "It's still dark out, and it's still snowing. I'm not really one for snow, but I do want to explore New York City. I've always dreamed of coming here. Do you want to go today? I know Toni will."

"Nah, that's alright," said Mike. "I think I'm going to stay inside and sleep." Toni suddenly pushed her head in between Jake and Mike from behind the couch, making them both jump.

"Don't do that Toni!" yelled Mike angrily, hand over his chest. Toni was laughing so hard that she had to clutch the couch.

"Well, I want to go out now," said Toni, finally managing to find her breath. "Who else is coming?"

"I'll go. Mike wants to stay inside and sleep," Jake replied.

Toni scowled at Mike. "I'll go ask Becca and Josh—I know Rachel won't come, but at least she has a *reason*!"

"Ask us what?" asked Becca, yawning. She and Josh plopped down on the other end of the leather couch.

"To go have some fun in the snow!" said Toni grinning.

"Sounds fun to me," Becca replied.

"I would love to go," said Josh, "but I better stay with my sis." The teens glanced over at Rachel who was all the way zipped in her sleeping bag and snoring loudly through her mouth.

"Do you want us to stay with you?" asked Becca, now feeling guilty.

"Nah!" said Josh. "She'll be fine. She just needs to stay inside—ever since she got her power as the new Sage of Fire and Magma, she gets feeling somewhat weak in the cold. Mike and I will be here for her and so will your parents. Rachel sneezed and her sleeping bag suddenly illuminating in.flames. A flash from Rachel's eyes put the fire out as though it was never there.

"Well, we'll try not to be gone too long," said Toni, eyeing Rachel wearily. "If we're not back by lunch then you know something's wrong."

They quickly dressed in warm clothes. "Oh—and Mike?" asked Becca, pulling on a coat. "Make sure my parents know that we went out."

Mike nodded. "No problem!"

Toni, Becca, and Jake left the room, all bundled up except for Toni, and headed for the elevators. It was early morning but the hotel was nice and warm even in the hallways. The three walked into the lobby where they grabbed some donuts and juice from a table in the breakfast room. After gobbling them down, they headed out the automatic doors and onto the sidewalk. The doorman wished them a nice day. The sidewalk had been shoveled and carefully salted in front of the hotel, but other parts of the sidewalk were still snowy. As they walked, they watched the heavy traffic go by.

"Do you guys want to get a better view from above?" asked Jake, throwing his juice container in a garbage can. He leaped into the air and soared up into the sky with Toni and Becca quickly following. It was an extraordinary view of the city and skyscrapers seemed to be everywhere.

"Wow!" said Jake flabbergasted.

"We're only missing one thing," said Toni, holding her hand out to the snowflakes.

"And what is that?" asked Becca. Toni grinned at her. Two snowballs came swishing through the air at Becca and Jake from below, hitting them both directly in the face. Toni laughed and flew off fast, Becca and Jake right on her tail. Toni dodged buildings and, at the same time, created more snowballs to let fly at them.

"Here are the rules!" yelled Jake, irritably wiping the snow from his face. "Becca and I against you since this is your *natural habitat*!"

Toni grinned. "That sounds like fun. Prepare to enter a world of hurt!"

They landed in an open area near a pond in Central Park. Toni moved quickly away from the two of them to work on her strategy. Becca suddenly shot her glowing hands forward. The snow began to gather in front of her and Jake, creating a solid wall of protection about six inches thick. She leaned close to Jake and whispered, "Okay—create a *little bit* of wind, if you know what I mean, to distract her. I'll build a few snowballs to get ready to throw at her. She's about to get nailed at her own game!"

Jake nodded and raised his head so he could peek over the wall. "Giant snowball coming your way!" He jumped into the air to float above the wall then waved his arms sending two mini blizzard tornados on their way toward Toni. Toni launched a snowball the size of a boulder over at Becca just before she was snatched up by one of the tornadoes. Toni laughed as she was spinning.

"I wouldn't be laughing yet!" yelled Becca grinning. Hundreds of tiny snowballs sped like bullets through the air at Toni. She shouted in pain as she crouched down covering her face with her arms. An igloo suddenly appeared around her, shielding her from the snowballs.

"Alright Becca!" yelled Jake grinning. "When you said you were going to make a few snowballs, I really thought you meant a *few*."

Becca laughed triumphantly. "Give up yet, Toni?"

"Not yet!" Toni yelled back, appearing from out of the igloo. She puckered her lips like she was going to whistle, and a misty gust of icicle wind came shooting from her mouth, circling rapidly around Jake and Becca. The two were encased in a sheet of ice in moments, unable to move an inch.

"I win!" yelled Toni. Becca and Jake slowly began to unfreeze. As they moved parts of their bodies, the thin layer of ice cracked apart and fell away.

"*You ch…cheated*!" yelled Jake, through jittery teeth.

"No, I didn't!" Toni laughed and crossed her arms. "Since I won, I get to choose what we do next!"

"*That will be my decision…*" The teens looked over toward the unfamiliar voice. It sounded dark, deep, and cold. Standing in the snow with its head down and shadows circling it, was a small hooded figure. It was wearing the same kind of silky hooded cloak as Toni except longer, and very black.

"Who are you?" Jake asked, stepping forward.

"Do not come any closer!" It whispered lethally. It raised its hooded head with one frail-looking white hand. It was clearly a girl, but her skin was a pale white and she had black hair and glowing black eyes. The teens stepped back, startled. "I am Raven, apprentice of the great Dark Pharaoh. I know you are on a journey now and I know some of the tasks that you must complete. Your first clue to unlocking a certain riddle lies at the tallest point in New York. There you will find—" her voice broke and she fell to the snow with Becca standing directly over her. Becca's eyes were glowing purple. She was furious.

"There won't be any chasing of clues or solving riddles. You're going to tell us right now where their parents are. You aren't any more powerful than we are—the Darkness will never win—you should know that, Raven."

Raven's eyes began to glow an oily-looking black. She showed no emotion whatsoever. "Silly child, the Darkness is very powerful, and IT always wins. GOTHIC'S MORTAL SIN!" she said forcefully.

A wall of some black shiny substance, outlined in white, flew at the teens. The weird thing was that they could see right through it! Becca was knocked back violently, followed by Toni and Jake. They each hit a tree and were pinned by the sheet of blackness. Raven hovered like a shadow over Becca, sending a chill up her spine. "The Sages of Light are no match for the Sage of Darkness. If you are wise, you will follow my clues."

"Do you really think that Power is the Dark Side?" Jake asked in disgust. "Because you're wrong. Strength and power come from the inside."

Raven's eyes slowly met Jake's. She looked like some kind of wraith or spirit of death. "If you really think that, then let's see how good you are—'THE RAVEN OF RAVEN'!" A giant black, shadow-like bird with four red eyes in the middle of its forehead appeared. It formed under Raven and she sunk into the bird as though it were a liquid hole.

Becca, Jake, and Toni broke free of the sheet of blackness as their eyes began to glow. The bird took a deep breath and blew huge black and gray flames from its smoke-colored beak. The teens flew up and dodged the flames. Becca made a tree pull out of the ground from its roots. She grabbed it by the trunk and swung it at the bird like a baseball bat. It went right through the bird, not affecting it whatsoever!

"My turn!" yelled Jake. He threw a lightning ball at the shadow bird. A rippling black force field appeared in front of the bird, causing the ball to bounce right back at Jake who narrowly dodged it.

The bird flew at Toni, knocking her to the ground, cawing in a gravelly voice. Toni got up and threw a handful of powdery snow from the ground into its eyes, making it partially blind. The bird flew up, shaking its head. Toni's hand turned into a dagger of ice as she jumped up after the bird and stabbed it in the stomach. The bird began to glow a dark, shiny, purplish-black. A loud crack echoed across the park. Where the bird had been, were now three smaller birds, opening there beaks and exhaling black and gray flames. Suddenly, a heavenly tune filled the air. It seemed to come from all around the teens at once. The birds froze exactly where they were. The flames froze too, and hung in mid-air like dirty rags.

The teens looked quickly around for the source of the fantastic song. Behind them, perched in a tree, was a male elf in violet clothing, playing a lavender ocarina. The Song was very high and sweet. The elf stopped playing and raised his head. His long white hair fell back, revealing a long pair of pointed ears. His eyes focused on Becca's. "Young Star, the Ravens are still. By this melody, you are the only one who can destroy them. Use the Weapon of the Ancients."

Becca nodded, still shocked at what she was seeing. The sword appeared on her back as she unsheathed it and held it tightly with both hands. Purplish lightning struck the sword from the gray sky above causing it to glow a blindingly bright outline of luminous purple. She swung it across her body, purple sparks falling from the silver blade, and it hit the birds with a sound like shattering glass. The birds screeched once into the snowy sky and disappeared in a blur of shadows. Becca sheathed her sword and gracefully walked over to the elf. She smiled brightly. "Who are you?"

The elf smiled back. "As you can see, I'm an elf. My name is Elestar. I have come to find Star and teach her this melody—with this ocarina." He held the ocarina up in front of him, letting Becca observe it. "Listen carefully again to this melody, that when I play it, you shall not forget. The Song is called 'Peace Within'." He began to play the heavenly Song again, watching Becca's eyes as they began to glow. She waved her hand once and the ocarina disappeared from the elf's hand and reappeared in her own. Becca began to play the Song perfectly and it echoed through the park. She waved her hand again and the ocarina disappeared.

"Wow," said Jake. "So you're an elf?"

"Yes," said Elestar, pulling his bright purple robes around himself and hopping lightly down from the tree. "There are many mythical creatures, such as myself, throughout the entire Earth. Humans can't see us, but you and the mutants can. I understand that you are fulfilling a quest. The Angel of Telepathy gave me that ocarina long ago so that I could teach you her Song. I knew you would come here, but let me tell you this: The Evil Ones, like Raven, do not know why you are gathering the Treasure. They only know that the Seven Sages had scattered these items throughout the land. The Dark Ones do not know their purpose. They do not know the true reason that you seek the Elements. Never let them know this! For this is to your advantage! They hope to manipulate you in order to obtain your Power for themselves! You may let them think they are succeeding, but maintain control of your Powers! You must be able to fight them!"

Becca, Jake, and Toni stood still, stunned by the elf's passionate outburst.

"I am sorry that I did not show myself before—Raven would have killed me."

"What do you mean, kill you? Why?" asked Jake in confusion.

Elestar shut his eyes and sighed deeply. "Because the Dark Side doesn't want you to gain control of any items, such as the ocarinas, before they do. They may not know what they are for, but know they must be of great importance for the Sages to have hidden them so well. The Dark Ones also suspect that Raven is one of the Seven Chosen, though they believe that she was chosen by fate and nothing more. You know the true reason—or at least, *you will find out*. The Dark Side doesn't want to take any chances of letting you become more Powerful than they are. They would have destroyed me because I sought to help you gain more Knowledge and Power."

Toni gazed at Becca then looked at Elestar. "If you know Cleopatra, then do you know about our parents?"

Elestar sighed. "I have heard about them."

"Do you know anything that could help us out?" asked Becca.

"Follow the clues Raven has given you. Go to the tallest building in the city. Only the One of Lightning can obtain this item. It was well hidden so the Evil could neither recognize nor reach it. But be warned, Darkness will be near. Once you obtain this Element, it will point you toward your next destination. This is all the Knowledge I have. I am sorry I do not know more."

"Thank you," said Jake. "We need all the help we can get. Any information helps us."

Elestar smiled. "Good luck. My race relies on you—we can only hope this Ancient Evil will not spread to our lands." He knelt down on the ground in front of them. "Good luck, Chosen ones. Blessings upon you. If you succeed, then you will truly become the New Sages." He looked down at his hand, which had begun to glow purple. A black seed, the size of a pellet, appeared in it. He looked upon Becca, Jake, and Toni. "Continue protecting us—*it is your Destiny!"* He threw the seed to the ground and a blinding light appeared with a *pop*. The light was gone in a second, and so was Elestar.

The three looked around wondering where he had gone. Becca waved her hand and her ocarina appeared. "It's our *destiny*. It's our job to protect."

"It's our choice," said Toni, remembering the words of Queen Jasmine. "We are who we will become. We have a responsibility to fulfill and a journey to complete. Without us, his people will have no hope. We shall fulfill their hope and give them unfailing faith in us." Toni sighed. "I feel different now. Not just because of my Power, but in the way I feel about everything. I want to protect and I want to become who I have been chosen to be."

"I think we all feel the same," said Jake. "So, let's do what we have to do. Should we get the others now?"

"They've already been informed," said Becca, her eyes glowing. "They'll be meeting us at the Empire State Building."

"There!" yelled Jake, soaring up into the sky while pointing out a very large building at the other end of Central Park.

The rest of the teens, including Rachel, reached the top of the Empire State Building about the same time as Becca, Toni, and Jake. The sides of the building curved inward to create the roof, and on the central peak of the roof was a tall metal spire. The teens spread out, searching intently for the clue. A stone platform suddenly appeared perfectly, but impossibly, balanced on the spire. More amazingly, it was wide enough for a hundred people to stand on at once. The six of them landed warily on the platform, knowing that the clue had to be there. In the center of the slab was a stone tablet with a picture of two diamonds connected to each other. One diamond was pearly white and the other was silver.

"What does it mean?" asked Jake, getting down to his knees and rubbing his hand over the tablet.

"Isn't it obvious?" asked Toni, smirking. "I think I have an idea what you need to do."

"I don't get it!" said Jake, frustrated.

"Well," said Becca, "Elestar said only the One of the Lightning can obtain the Weapon.

"Who's Elestar?" asked Mike.

Becca sighed as she began to explain to the others everything that had happened. She then looked over at Jake, who held his ocarina in his hand. "Are you ready Jake?"

"Yeah—I understand now." Jake placed the ocarina to his lips and played. The Song filled the sky and echoed between the buildings. It began to get darker as gray thunderclouds appeared. Jake stopped playing. Thunder pealed crazily and white bolts of lightning struck everywhere. Suddenly, a bolt was streaking right for their heads! It stopped about a foot above their heads and formed into a glowing ball of pure white light. When the light faded, an ivory bow and a silver arrow appeared. Next, the arrow floated around and set itself into the bow. The bow pulled back its string and aimed out into the harbor at the Stature of Liberty. The arrow began to glow as it whistled through the air toward the Statue of Liberty. The teens followed its progress until it hit the torch in the Lady's raised hand, transforming it into white fire.

The bow floated down to Jake. He grabbed it and, after a brief examination, put his head through the bowstring and let it hang down his back. On the tablet at their feet, the carved diamonds began to glow. The air temperature quickly rose and the snow began to melt rapidly. The gray clouds evaporated, letting the sunshine through. Hieroglyphics appeared on the tablet. Jake read them aloud: "*Thou with the Lightning Arrow shall gain speed and agility. Be wise with this Weapon, for the Sage of Weather has created it for great Power. It shall show you the way to where you shall journey next.*" Jake looked up at the others who were staring awkwardly back at him.

The stone tablet dissolved in a swirl of brownish light and then vanished without a trace. The stone platform beneath the teens' feet began to glow, and then suddenly winked out of existence. They fell at least ten feet, giving them a slight jolt, but they were able to float back up in the air before they hit the curved roof of the building. They glowed briefly as they changed into their older form, costumes on.

"Well, let's get going to the Statue of Liberty," said Jake, leading the way. They approached the statue and began to ascend upwards. They gazed into the windows of the statue's head and were grateful to find no one there because of all the snow. The teens landed on Lady Liberty's crown.

"Let's go closer and check it out!" said Rachel, jumping from the crown to the statue's raised hand. "Yaaahoo!!!" she cried as she soared upwards into the white flames. She turned around. "It's okay!" she hollered. "It's more like a cool rush of air than a heat wave!" The others stared at her, unconvinced. Rachel laughed. "Come on guys—I mean, I know I can survive in flames, but I can still tell what's hot and what's not!" The others looked at each other—hesitated, then flew towards Rachel and hovered next to her. A blurred image appeared in the dancing white flame. It slowly became more visible—it was a very big ship. In fact, it looked like a cruise ship. It seemed to be floating in the New York Harbor near where all the transportation ships stayed. The image suddenly vanished, and the white flame grew smaller and smaller until it was finally out.

"A ship," said Mike. "Is that where we go next?"

"It sure is!" yelled Becca. "I'll meet you guys there. We obviously have a long journey ahead of us. I'm going to go back and get our stuff and explain everything to my parents—I think it's time."

"Are you sure?" asked Toni, incredulously.

"I agree," said Josh. "They have to know sooner or later—the longer we hide it, the harder it will be to explain. I'll go with you, Becca." Becca nodded as she dove off the statue. Josh jumped down and landed on a white Pegasus several feet below. They were quickly off.

Jake sighed. "With Becca gone, we'll have to use some normal human techniques to find the ship...like asking for directions—or just *looking* for it."

"Well," laughed Toni, "it can't be that hard to find—we can just search from above." They headed for the shoreline in search of the next part of their incredible adventure.

Chapter 13—When Darkness Comes

Becca and Josh landed in front of the hotel and walked through the doors nodding to the doorman. They took the elevator up and waited patiently. "So how are you going to tell them?" asked Josh, leaning up against the elevator wall.

Becca sighed. "I—I don't know yet—I'm sure it'll come to me." Suddenly the lights went out in the elevator and it came to a stop. They looked at the monitor, which was the only visible light, to see what floor they were on. They were only on the second floor! "But how could that be?" asked Becca. "I mean—we were in here for about fifteen seconds!"

Josh held up his hand and it began to glow. He moved his hand toward the elevator buttons, and gazed at the emergency phone. He picked it up just as it began to ring. A voice answered "*Hello?*" There was a click and the line went dead. "Hello? Can you hear me?" asked Josh. "HELLO!?" Josh hung the phone up and glared at Becca's glowing eyes. She raised her hands; the top of the elevator bent upwards, and peeled off, letting them see up into the elevator shaft. Becca soared out and entered the darkness of the shaft—the only light visible was through the cracks of the elevator doors on each floor. Josh flew quickly behind her.

They stopped at the fifteenth floor doors. Becca waved her hands again and the doors wrenched opened. They landed cautiously in the hall and looked around. It was dark everywhere and they could barely see. The walls looked like they had black paint all over them, but when Becca touched them she could feel the damp fog between her fingers. It was very cold, and Becca and Josh felt as though all life were being drained out of them. They shivered as they looked at each other. "Why is it like this?" asked Josh quietly.

Becca sighed, "It must be a power outage or something." She rubbed her hand against the darkened walls, and then removed it, studying it. Black fog was circling around her hand. She shook her hand and the fog floated away.

"How do you explain that?" asked Josh warily.

Becca shivered as a chill traveled down her spine. "Let's just go." The two began to walk down the hall very quickly. When they reached their room, Becca held out her arm in front of Josh to keep him from reaching for the doorknob.

"What is it?" asked Josh.

"Something isn't right—look!" She pointed down toward the crack at the bottom of the door. Shadows were crawling out all along the floor like thick smoke. She took a deep breath and threw the door open. Becca and Josh grew scared. The room was completely dark—and the same eerie black substance that had trapped Becca, Toni, and Jake in the park was floating around everywhere in strands and steamers like cobwebs. The window facing the park was thickly coated with frost, blocking out most of the light.

"Mom!? Dad!?" She began to search every room, but they were nowhere to be seen. Becca ran over to Josh, a look of panic upon her face. "They're not here! They wouldn't leave us without letting us know or leaving a note!"

Josh looked around the room. "Relax—they probably went looking for us because of the power out—" He paused to stare at the frozen window. His pupils dilated and he became motionless. Becca slowly turned her head toward the window. Dark shadows, like leeches, were visible on the other side of the iced window!

"*That's impossible,*" thought Becca, "*they would have to be on the outside of the glass!*" The shadow leeches began to travel all along the window, their writhing leaving black, bloody hieroglyphics carved in the ice.

Becca began to tremble in fear as she read aloud: "*Darkness has struck so that none shall remain. Your parents are gone, hearts broken in twain. Night, like a wraith, will come sooner than ever, and you will suffer a loss because you wouldn't surrender. Darkness will rule and Evil will reign—if you continue to meddle, you will never be sane!*"

Becca began to shake and she grabbed Josh's hand and held it tight. Her eyes started to water. The black, bloody hieroglyphics merged together, creating a single dark shadow whose surface rippled like oily pond water. Becca was shaking and breathing heavily. She gripped Josh's hand tighter. The screams of a man and woman echoed harshly through the room. She began to glow as she screamed, "GIVE ME BACK MY PARENTS!!! MOM!! DAD!!!" Josh held her back when she tried to beat on the glass with both fists. "NOOO!!!" she yelled, pushing him away. She began to cry and scream at the same time, the whole room shaking as she sobbed. Pictures tumbled from the walls, and flower-filled vases jigged along the tabletops before falling to the floor. The gilt mirror over the fireplace came loose and crashed to the marble hearth below, splintering into a thousand glittering shards. The whole building now began to shake, and Becca screamed even louder causing the immense window to shatter. The wall around the empty frame began to sag and fall away, chunks of concrete plummeting down to the sidewalk below. Clouds of dust came down from the ceiling like snow.

Josh gazed frantically all around him. "Becca, you must stop or you'll destroy the whole building!" he pleaded. Becca slid to her knees, crying even harder. A loud crack came from above as a wooden beam fell toward them. Josh quickly shouted, "*Levitarno!*" The beam froze in midair as though stopped by time. Josh picked her up and together they flew out through the shattered window. A sudden coldness gripped Josh as a dark form swept past. Becca fought to release herself from Josh's grip to chase after it. "No, Becca!" Josh cried, wrapping his arms more firmly around her.

A loud bang turned their attention back toward the hotel. It was still shaking badly and looked ready to collapse. Josh saw many panicking people down below running for their lives. Others, who were still trapped inside, were trying frantically to get the windows open and yell for help. Josh released Becca. "I have to go for a minute, but I'll be right back," he said giving her a gentle hug. He left her hovering limply above the neighboring apartment building, still sobbing quietly into her hands.

Josh looked back to where Becca was floating, and then back to the hotel. He shouted, "*GIANTS OF LORE!*" The sidewalk in front of the hotel began to glow as two huge brown figures emerged. The giants were muscular and had skin like brown polished granite. They walked clumsily toward the hotel and wrapped their arms around it to stop the shaking. The street was packed with cars honking and people yelling and screaming. At the sight of the giants, many people stopped in their tracks and gazed in amazement at the hotel. The flashing lights and the sound of wailing sirens filled the air. The giants gripped the hotel tighter, but it was no use! The building still kept on slowly shaking and breaking, and was about to collapse! Josh raised his hands as the giants disappeared in a blinding flash of green light with a popping sound like a very large light bulb breaking. He then shot his glowing hands out toward the hotel and shouted, "*Merendiet repero!*" A river of brilliant green light shot out of Josh's hands and traveled all around the hotel. Unbelievably, the cracks began to mend, and the beams began to repair itself. The building was fully restoring itself! He let down his arms and gave a faint laugh of satisfaction.

Josh returned to Becca and wrapped his arms around her. "I'm so sorry Becca—truly I am."

Becca began to cry on his shoulder. "*They're gone—she took them!*" She sobbed. "And now—I'm…*alone.*"

"You're not alone," said Josh, tears in his eyes. "As long as you have us—*you're never alone.*" Becca gazed up into his sparkling green eyes then hugged him even tighter. The warm wind blew around them as they floated motionless, arms around each other.

Chapter 14— The Arrival of the Ancient Protectors

Toni, Jake, Rachel, and Mike had finally found the ship in the harbor. It wasn't very hard to miss—it was massive! They landed on the dock next to the ship. As they got closer to the two lines of people waiting to get on the ship, they noticed something very strange. There were two ticket collectors, one at the head of each line. One was a human in a neat white uniform, but the other had a human torso on a horse's body! While the human took tickets from the line of humans, the centaur was collecting tickets from many hooded creatures.

He swished his tail to catch their attention then galloped over. "Greetings Sages—I have been informed of your arrival." His voice was very deep. The teens stared at him in fascination. Mike couldn't help stealing a peek at his hooves while he was speaking. "Welcome aboard the Meraintron Cruise Ship. Come right this way, and—"

He was cut off by two small, glowing objects that zoomed in front of him, handing him tickets twice their size.

"Thank you," said the centaur. "Welcome aboard the Meraintron Cruise Ship." The glowing objects flew up the gangway over the other passengers' heads and through the ship's entry doors.

"What was that?" asked Jake, stunned.

The centaur laughed. "Those are one of the thousands of species of Fairies."

"Mythical creatures can ride this ship?" asked Toni, highly amazed.

The centaur bent closer to Toni. "Mythical creatures use every human device that they deem useful. Humans can't see us—as you know—so *we* take *advantage*."

"That's smart thinking," said Mike.

The centaur scowled at Mike. "We are much more intelligent than any human, and are just doing what comes natural to a superior species."

Mike frowned. "Sorry."

"Your suite number is 5026, fifth floor, on the starboard side." He held his hand out, pointing up the gangway toward the wide open doors.

The teens walked up the ramp and they entered a large open room with three sets of stairs and two administration desks manned by uniformed crewmembers.

"Where exactly is our room?" asked Mike, gazing around the room, but not seeing any helpful sign whatsoever.

"It's called *asking*!" said Toni, walking up to one of the desks. A smiling blond-haired lady in a nicely pressed white shirt and black pants was flipping through a thick binder.

"Hello," said Toni kindly. "Could you please tell us where room 5026 is?"

The lady's smile widened. "Follow the staircase up to my left." She held her hand out to a wide staircase. "Go up two more floors and take another left. There will be numbers along the wall."

"Thank you!" said Toni, smirking at Mike as she walked up the staircase. Mike rolled his eyes and followed her and the others up the steps. They found their room easily enough, but realized they didn't have a key and the doorknob wouldn't budge. "It's locked!" said Toni.

"I'll take care of it!" said Rachel, holding up one flaming finger. There was the "*eh hem*" sound of someone clearing their throat behind them. Rachel hastily blew out her finger and put her hand in the pocket of her sweatshirt. They turned around and saw a tiny old man with long ears and a very wrinkly face like an old apple. He had long, gray, rather untidy hair, and small golden half-glasses perched on his long nose. His thin fingers had long, dirty fingernails. He was obviously a goblin, but was inexplicably dressed in a very nice black suit and vest. His long bare toes were visible, hanging out from beneath the cuffs of his neatly pressed trousers. The teens stepped back silently when the goblin gestured at the door. "Allow me," he said in a gravelly voice. He put one long index finger to the top of the door and slowly moved it down along the edge. As he did this, there were several clicking and clacking sounds. He nodded to the teens and walked off. Toni and Mike began laughing after he did the same thing to the door several rooms away, nodded at the teens, then stepped inside.

"That was the ugliest thing I have ever seen!" Toni laughed. Mike laughed even harder.

Jake turned the doorknob. "You guys need to get a life!" He opened the door and walked inside. It was the same room as the hotel suite they were previously in! The only difference was a line of dozens of small portholes instead of the huge window. "Unbelievable!" yelled Jake excitedly, slamming the door behind them. "It's the exact same suite as before!—How can that *be*?"

"Don't know!" said Toni, walking over to the couch and lying down. "I just want Josh and Becca to get back so I can go eat! I'm starving!" The others sat on the couch, turned on the television, and waited patiently.

About a half hour later, the door opened. Becca and Josh walked in followed by a porter pushing a cart full of their luggage. The porter unloaded the bags and left, closing the door behind him. Becca was pale and her eyes were red. Jake quickly got up and ran over to Becca. "What's *wrong*?"

Becca sat down on the floor with her back against the suitcases. "Well—I…I know what it feels like now to not have *parents…*"

Toni walked over, sat next to Becca, and took her hand. "Why—*what happened*?"

Tears rolled down Becca's face, but she managed to gain control of herself. "We went back to the hotel, but the room…there was nothing but darkness…we felt weak and cold, like we could never be strong or happy again. We went in our room…" Becca looked around her and was amazed that it looked just the same as the one in the hotel. She began to cry again, tears running unchecked down her face.

Jake knelt down. "We can ask for another room."

"No!" said Becca, wiping her face. "My parents were taken away by the Darkness! We saw it leave…the Darkness took them away…my parents were screaming." Her voice was a whisper. "I couldn't help myself hearing them in pain…I nearly destroyed the building…Josh was able to save it." She looked toward the wall of windows. "It left a riddle…some type of warning." Rachel gasped, and grabbed Becca's shoulder. They stared at each other. "It left you a message too?" Becca asked.

Tears formed in Rachel's eyes. "On the wall was black, bloody hieroglyphics. It was disgusting, like snail trails or something."

Jake squinted his eyes, and looked pensive. "What did it say?"

Josh spoke this time. "I can't believe I forgot—it was a warning: *We need your parents, they are a key—to unlock the Ancient Evil, that many soon shall see. As long as we have them, when no hope can abide-- the Darkness can take them, though they stand side by side.*" Josh paused. "It's weird how they said 'parents' when the Darkness only took our mom."

"It was probably referring to all of our parents," said Mike. Josh nodded but said nothing further.

Becca looked up at Josh. "*How could you forget that warning?*"

Josh looked intently back at her. "When I first saw it I didn't want to believe it. I tried to convince myself that it wasn't real. I guess it really got to me…"

Jake watched them both carefully. "The riddles…they're clues about what's happening. They need our parents for a specific purpose; to unlock some kind of an Ancient Evil. The riddle said that they were a key. That means that they weren't kidnapped just to harm us. But they left another clue—*when no hope can abide-- the Darkness can take them.* That has to mean that as long as they have hope, the Darkness can't hurt them."

Toni's eyebrows lowered in thought. "*Side by side*—that must mean—that our parents are there together! Maybe they can all help each other to keep their hopes alive…knowing that they are together."

"But why do they need them to unlock the Ancient Evil?" asked Josh.

"Because they need us," replied Becca, staring at the ground. "They're using them to lure us just where they want us."

"How do you know?" asked Rachel.

"I don't…" said Becca. She looked up at Rachel slowly. "But I just hope they don't get hurt." Rachel eyed her sympathetically. "It's all my fault that this happened," said Becca remorsefully.

Jake put his hand under Becca's chin and raised her head. "It's not your fault—it's not any of our faults. None of us were the cause of all this." Jake sighed. "We'll get our parents back—if we have to fight to the bitter end—we will finish this quest!"

Becca nodded. "Let's go eat—I'm hungry and we need to take our minds off all this, even if it's just for a little while."

"You do not know how glad I am you said that!" nodded Toni, letting go of Becca's hand and walking out of the room. The others quickly followed, Mike shutting the door behind him. He suddenly turned around and was about to lock the door but suddenly stopped, realizing he didn't know how to lock it. Noticing Mike, Josh walked back and raised his glowing green index finger. "*Warlock's Safe...*" He traced his finger down the crack of the door as the locks began to lock up again. He looked up at Mike grinning.

"Well," said Mike embarrassed, "you certainly have a very useful power." Josh laughed as he and Mike ran to catch up with the others. They all followed the flight of stairs at the end of the hall up one more floor and ended up in a bar. There were many groups of elves and humans talking and laughing. Glass doors at the other end of the room led out to a deck. Tables with big, green-striped umbrellas were arranged just outside the door and along both rails. There was a fairly large swimming pool and a hot tub with lounge chairs lined up around it. The teens gasped when they noticed that two sapphire dragons, about the size of large dogs, were also swimming in the pool, diving under and leaping over the other swimmers. The humans seemed completely unaware that they were sharing their pool with a pair of mythical creatures.

On the far side of the pool, under a white awning, were several heavily laden buffet tables. "There they are!" said Toni, dodging lounge chairs and little kids with pool toys to get in line. The others followed and packed their plates with everything they could fit. They found a table by the pool and began to eat hungrily. A noisy group of fairies took over the diving board for some kind of contest involving coins and an object that looked a lot like a radish. The humans were totally oblivious to the other creatures, even when a couple of the fairy game participants used one human's baldhead as a diving platform.

"You know," said Toni, through a stuffed mouth. "It seems like we only eat once a day and we're always starved because we're too preoccupied with all the other things going on."

"We'll get used to it," said Jake. "But yeah—it is weird." Toni was first to finish her plate, quickly followed by Becca.

Toni stood up. "Let's go swimming."

"We just got done eating, Toni!" said Mike. "Don't you know that you're not supposed to get in the pool for at least an hour or you'll get cramps!"

"You won't get *cramps!*" she said, annoyed. "That is a bunch of phooey stuff invented by lazy people."

"Okay," said Jake diplomatically, scooting back his chair. "We'll go once the ship starts moving."

The sound of an immense horn echoed all around, scaring some of the little kids and causing others to put their hands over their ears. The ship slowly started to move. Toni smirked at Jake. "Let's go, genius!"

Rachel got up and wiped her mouth with a napkin. "You guys go on ahead. I feel like exploring."

Becca frowned at Rachel, "Oh I'm so sorry Rachel—I completely forgot about that—I'll stay with you."

Rachel laughed and shook her head. "No, it's not that. I'm fine in the water—it's just I'm not in the best of mood to swim…"

Becca and the others stared at Rachel for several seconds. "Oh, okay…" said Becca, quietly feeling a bit embarrassed. Rachel smiled at them all and walked off.

Becca waved her hand as swimsuits appeared on all of them. "You guys ready?" They heard a crackling behind them and turned to find the little dragons blowing blasts of blue flames at each other. Every time they missed, a roil of steaming water showed on the surface. They were obviously having a ball. "Now I'm not so sure I want to get in there," laughed Toni. "I guess we have to be careful of being boiled like lobsters." Some of the other humans noticed the rising steam and quickly got out. One man walked cautiously around the edge of the pool trying to figure out where the hot water was coming from. The teens laughed, took a flying leap, and jumped in.

* * * * * * * *

Rachel made her way up to the tennis courts and then up to another smaller deck. She was at the bow of the ship with no one else in sight, so she could have her choice of the many white plastic lounge chairs. The ship was already far enough out that there was nothing to see but the bright sun sparkling on the deep blue water. It was a magnificent sight to see. There was a metal railing surrounding the deck, and Rachel imagined what it would be like to have a totally unobstructed view of the water. She looked around first to make sure no one was watching, then went to the very front of the deck and climbed up on the railing. She spread her arms out and let the wind take her away. Her eyes closed and sparks flew from her body. The sparks danced and spun around her in the wind as though moving to music. "*This is amazing*," she told herself.

A woman's soft voice came from behind her saying, "*Flare always loved the ocean.*"

Rachel opened her eyes as the sparks evaporated. She jumped down from the railing and looked around, but no one was there. "Hello?" she called out. She heard the voice behind her again.

"Hello, I am Flairen." Rachel whirled around again facing the ocean. In the air was a small, glowing red orb fighting the wind to stay hovered at eye level. Rachel thought it looked a lot like the fairies they saw down on the dock. The object was glowing so brightly that its true form couldn't be seen.

"Hello, Flare, I have come to join you," the voice said.

Rachel stared at the glowing orb. "*What*—how did you know I was Flare?"

Flairen laughed. "Because it is my duty to assist the Sage of Fire and Magma. The Ancient Sage told me, two thousand years ago, of your arrival. I have come to fight by your side. I am one of the Seven Royals of All Fairies. We Royals have always been the partners of the Ancient Sages." The red orb flew down and landed on the railing. "I came here to help—along with the other Royals who are on this ship seeking their Sages as well."

Rachel was silent for a few seconds. "How—how are you going to help us?"

Flairen laughed again. "We may be small, but we're a lot more powerful than we look. We also have a great deal of Knowledge that can lead you in the right direction. We accompanied the Ancient Sages when they were hiding their Power throughout the Earth."

"That's extraordinary!" replied Rachel. "If you *can* help us—it would make things a whole lot easier. Are you saying that you helped the Ancient Sages fight Darkness and spread the Knowledge of the Way of Life?"

"Yes," said Flairen. "And that is exactly what we will do again. The Ancients left us behind to guide you. We will be journeying with you forever. We will heed your every command." Flairen's ball of light suddenly stopped glowing and revealed her normal form. She had long, exquisite, curly red hair. On her back were two pairs of sparkling, red, flame-shaped wings. She wore an elaborate, long, red velvet gown that wrapped around her legs and draped to the floor. Her lips were as bright as red roses after a rain shower. She wore stunning jewelry of brilliant rubies.

"Oh, my God!" laughed Rachel in disbelief. "You're—you're *beautiful*!"

Flairen blushed. Her eyes were dark with a reddish tint as they glistened in the sunlight. "Thank you, Flare." Her eyebrows lowered, and she curtsied. "I almost forgot—I have a gift for you." She waved her hands and a large, glowing, red, circle of light appeared above Rachel's head. Once again, Flairen glowed brightly. Rachel looked around again to make sure no one was in proximity. As the light intensified, it exploded into flames.

"Now," said Flairen, "reach into the flames and remove your Weapon."

Rachel looked at Flairen in confusion, but did as she had been told. She put her hand into the flames and grasped the object tightly. The flames disappeared to reveal a long, magnificent spear. The spear had a silver blade at one end with a red plated grip in the middle. At the other end of the spear was a red orb with reddish fog whirling inside. The spear was made of strong, polished ironwood. Rachel swung the spear around her as the red orb began to glow. The spear burst into flames. Rachel spun it around her like a helicopter blade. It was as though she already knew how to wield it! The spear glowed briefly and disappeared in a puff of black smoke.

Flairen sighed. "It is almost as if I were looking at my old partner once again. I am the only one of the Royal Fairies who obtained a Weapon of the Sages. This Spear belonged to the Ancient Sage of Fire and Magma. It wields tremendous Power. Use it wisely, as I know you will."

Rachel nodded. "Should I show you where the others are?" she asked eagerly.

Flairen gazed past Rachel's left shoulder. "There is no need."

Rachel turned around and watched the approaching teens. Above them floated the colored orbed fairies, each glowing with their teens color.

"Hello, Thor," said Flairen, addressing one of the other fairies. "I see you have succeeded."

The white fairy next to Jake flew over to Flairen, his orb bobbing in the wind. "Hello, Flairen—I see that you also have succeeded."

"Yes, now we will be able to begin a new journey together," said Flairen.

"I wonder if Ororo was successful?" said the blue fairy, flying over from Toni.

"She'll have a hard quest, Misty," said the purple fairy, flying over from Becca. "Finding the apprentice of the Dark Pharaoh will not be easy."

"Wait a minute, Juhani!" said Becca, squinting her eyes. "Raven will be guided by a fairy, as well?"

The green fairy flew off Josh's shoulders and approached Becca. "Of course, Star. Ororo will help guide her to Serenity, but it will be difficult since she has the crystal of the Angel of Darkness. I doubt Ororo will succeed."

"Don't be so harsh, Merlin!" snapped the glowing yellow fairy, flying off Mike's shoulder. "Ororo will need our help. She has faith that Raven will turn towards the Light." He gazed over at Mike and then at all the teens. "She will succeed if you Sages are successful in completing your journey—your test."

"A test, Granite?" asked Mike.

"Yes," said Granite. "This is all a test—to see if you are ready to unlock your Destiny which lies in the Sages' Temple."

"So..." said Josh, "a test to see if we're to ready to accept our Destiny?"

"Precisely!" said Merlin.

"But we are ready!" said Toni, watching the waves.

"You may think you are," replied Misty, "but you have to know *who* you are, and that comes only from within. We are the only ones, besides yourselves, who will know if you are ready."

"What's in store for us?" questioned Josh. "I mean—at the Temple?"

Thor laughed. "Why Sages, don't you know what and who you are?" He flew higher in the sky, above all the others. The teens eyed him questioningly. "As the leader of the Royal Protectors of the Sages, I shall tell you. You are the chosen Protectors of the Earth and Galaxies, and also the Protectors of the Heavens. We shall prepare you for what is to come." He paused and gazed out to the sea. "Your next task approaches—in the morning we arrive." Thor and the other Fairies flew over to one of the plastic lounge chairs to get out of the wind. The Fairies stopped glowing and revealed their normal selves.

Merlin had long Elf ears and long blonde hair. He wore a long, green robe with linked golden plates around his wrists and neck. He had two pairs of green leaves on his back that acted as wings, and his eyes were the same bright green as Josh's.

Misty had short blue hair and wore a short, tight, blue silk skirt and shirt covered by a long blue cape with white fur along the edges. She had bracelets of silver plates around her wrists. She wore high-heeled blue boots that matched her pair of blue-feathered wings. Her blue angel-like wings were the longest pair of the fairies. When she flew, snowflakes fell from her glowing body. Her blue eyes were as bright as the open sea.

Juhani wore a long purple skirt and a short, tight purple top. Her blonde hair was worn tightly up in a bun, and her eyes were a dark violet. She glittered magnificently all over and had two small pairs of lavender wings. What was really interesting about her was the pair of small wings on the back of each wrist that flapped every time she moved her arms.

Granite had short black hair and tawny yellow eyes like a leopard's. His two pairs of yellow wings were as bright as the sun. He wore a sleeveless, black-armored shirt like Mike's, letting his muscular arms show. He had linked golden plates around his wrists and wore black leathery pants and boots.

Thor was the most unique fairy of all. He wore a silver-plated armored shirt and pants. He had long white hair and had three pairs of splendid opalescent wings. He held a silver staff in the shape of a lightning bolt, and wore silver wrist plates and lightning bolt-shaped silver earrings. His eyes were a bright pearly white, and he was quite muscular.

Even though they had lived for several millennia, they still looked as if they were in their early twenties. They were definitely very unusual creatures to the teens. By this time, the sun was going down, and it was painting everything with a rosy glow. It had been a long day for the teens, and Becca was still feeling depressed.

"Sleep here on the deck with us, Sages. Once the sun rises, we will begin our next journey," said Thor sleepily, lying down on the arm of the lounge chair.

"Where do we journey next?" asked Jake curiously.

"You will find out in the morning," said Granite, a bit annoyed. "Now we must sleep!"

"It's still a little early!" argued Toni.

"We'll need our sleep," said Becca. The teens looked at each other through tired eyes. Toni didn't argue with Becca, but merely nodded. Becca waved her hand and their sleeping bags appeared on the deck. They got in their sleeping bags and gazed up at the sky, watching the orange and pink clouds go by. None of them fell asleep yet—but they were silent. The sun sunk beneath the ocean as the sky grew dark and the stars revealed themselves as the day faded away. Slowly—their eyes began to tremble, and they were, at last, carried away by the sound of the waves into their dreams.

Chapter 15— Gateway To Atlantis

Morning approached, and the teens woke suddenly by the sound of Misty's voice. "In a moment Sages, we will come upon the City of Meraintron—an underwater city and home of the Merains. It is the gateway to Atlantis where Aquarius will acquire her Weapon."

The teens stood up and stretched with astonished looks on their faces.

"Atlantis?!" asked Mike, in disbelief and amazement. "You mean that the lost ancient city is real? It's still there surviving underwater all these years?"

Granite laughed. "Welcome to the Mythical world, young Quake." The others laughed as well.

"This is extraordinary!" yelled Becca. "Imagine all the great Knowledge we could gain today!"

"This is *sooo* exciting!" shouted Toni, running over to the railing and looking down into the ocean. That early in the morning it was smooth as glass. "I'm going to get my Weapon!"

"Yes." smiled Misty, proud to know that Toni was willing to work hard for what she needed.

Josh's eyebrows suddenly lowered in confusion. "How are we going to get there?" All of them looked at the Fairies with the same puzzled expression.

Misty flew from the deck of the ship out over the water. Her voice echoed across the waves. "*I am Misty—Queen of the Water and Ice*

Fairies. I am one of the Seven Royals, Protector of the Sage of Water and Ice. I wish to gain access to the City of Meraintron!"

Suddenly, two fish-like creatures came jetting up out of the water. They flipped high in the air and dove back down. The ripples they made glowed a greenish white.

"Come, Sages!" called Misty. The other Fairies flew to the teens' shoulders. The teens jumped into the air and flew toward Misty. They floated above and around the bright, glowing white circles of light on the mirrored surface of the water. The Fairies flew to the center of the group, and the teens watched them intently.

"Well, Aquarius," said Misty brightly, turning to face Toni. "Welcome to Meraintron—Gateway to Atlantis!"

The teens floated silently for several seconds, taking it all in.

"Alright!" said Juhani suddenly. "Here's how it works—we will land in the glowing rings of water. A force will take us down to the City. Do not move or else you will be sent right back up and not be able to use the portal again for another day. The Merains are very protective of their City—or I should say 'Kingdom'."

"Do not worry," said Granite intensely. "You *will* be able to breathe."

The Fairies landed on the teens' shoulders once again, and they all floated down into the water with a soft splash. They waited within the circles until they felt something slimy wrap around them, like snakes or vines. A transparent bubble, tinged faintly blue, formed around them. "Cool!" said Mike leaning against the curved surface to peer into the depths. With a jolt, they began moving smoothly downward. The water was quite warm and crystal clear. As the teens kept going deeper and deeper, they could see many different kinds and colors of fish swimming by. Surprisingly, they felt no pressure from the increased weight of the water as they went still deeper.

"We are almost there," said Thor. "It's just a *bit* deeper."

"Be prepared. There will be a brief period where we will move very swiftly. It is just a little further below us," said Merlin, searching the water beneath his feet.

"There is nothing to fear!" said Flairen, comfortingly. But by the look on the teens' faces, she could tell that they didn't exactly trust her opinion.

"We can talk!" said Mike excitedly. "And it feels as if I'm breathing real air—it's a bit *chunky* though."

"Yes," said Misty staring out further into the distance. "But no sudden movements—the guards are watching…"

The teens gazed around them through squinted eyes. Circling all around them in the distance were about fifty Merain guards. They were creatures with white skin and vivid blue tattoos all over their bodies. Their heads were human-shaped, but they had some fish-like features, such as gills and big, bulgy, greenish eyes. Running down their backs was a long eel-like fin, and connected to the back of each of their arms and legs was a thinner fin. They had human-looking feet, but with long webbed toes, almost like scuba flippers, that they used to propel themselves swiftly and strongly through the water. Some were dressed in shiny metal armor, but all of them held very lethal-looking spears with spiny collars around the shaft below the serrated blades.

"Why are they so overly defensive?" asked Josh, looking a bit worried.

"I do not know," said Merlin truthfully. "They were not this way two thousand years ago at our last visit."

"You guys are that *old*!?" asked Toni, astounded.

"We are far older than that!" said Misty, giggling. "We're the oldest creatures on Earth."

"You don't look that old!" said Jake.

"For us," explained Thor, "age doesn't change us on the outside. It changes on the inside."

"Because your Knowledge and Power increases," stated Rachel.

Becca laughed. "I was going to say that."

"You are both right," said Flairen.

"Get ready, Sages!" yelled Misty suddenly. "We are about to sink very quickly!" A different kind of force plunged them downwards as fast as a sinking boulder. The water around them grew dark as they moved further from the surface. The girls squealed in fear, but the guys raised their arms and whooped as if on an exciting roller coaster ride. They gained yet more speed until the only thing visible around them was the millions of tiny bubbles caused by their descent, twinkling like stars.

They reached the bottom with a soft thump, but before the silt disturbed by their landing cleared away, their bubble bounced back up several feet and stopped. Water sheeted off the sides of the bubble to reveal a spacious high-ceilinged chamber filled with light! The teens gazed around in wide-eyed amazement. They weren't under the water any more! The bubble around them quivered and rippled, then vanished.

The walls and ceiling of the enormous room were transparent and tinted slightly blue, like a larger version of the bubble elevator. Through its convex walls, they could see chains of hundreds of similar structures disappearing off into the gloom in every direction, like glowing strings of pearls. Outside some of the bubble chains were larger buildings that glistened in the light from some kind of torches. All of the bubbles and buildings looked clean and were highly polished.

The chamber had a floor of smooth, polished, white stone. There were small pools scattered about that seemed to lead to the ocean outside. Torches, hanging from carved strung brackets from the bubble wall, lit up the entire room. Merains, of all shapes and sizes, were moving in and out of the pools, unaware of the arrival of the teens.

"This is so amazing!" said Jake bewildered, studying every detail.

"I don't think *amazing* quite describes this, Jake," laughed Josh, hands splayed against the nearest wall. He pointed to what looked like a family of Merains approaching the bubble.

"It's absolutely dream-like!" said Rachel, leaning back to gaze up at the ceiling in wonder. Overhead, visible through the ceiling, were gently waving fronds of some deep red plant. Small fish dashed among the leaves.

There was a splash from the small pool beside the teens. A Merain flew out and landed beside them, drenching them all from the knees down. He wore a bright blue suit, and his smile revealed a menacing set of pointy white teeth.

"Welcome to Meraintron, home of the Merains. I am Cocon, one of many guides in this Kingdom. I am here to show you around and take you through the *bubbleways* to wherever you wish to go. The bubbleways will allow you to view the wonders of Meraintron in comfort. We haven't been getting many visitors lately, so it's an honor to be chosen to guide you." He bowed stiffly. "Are there any questions you wish to ask before we begin?" He spoke quickly and loudly, gurgling slightly between sentences.

"Umm..." said Jake. "Yes...we're looking for the way to Atlantis."

The grin was swept from Cocon's face. His bulging black eyes narrowed, and his gill flaps quivered. He looked rather offended. "I am sorry. That is *not* possible."

Jake glanced over at Mike and then back at Cocon. "Well, why not?"

"IT IS FORBIDDEN. THAT IS ALL I CAN SAY!" Cocon jumped five feet into the air and dove back into the pool, splashing them all again. "Hmm," said Jake, while a strong breeze dried him off. "That, was sooo *not cool!*"

"I wonder why we can't go to Atlantis," said Becca, arms crossed. "I thought you said everyone used to come to Atlantis?"

"I do not know," said Juhani. "Everybody used to be able to come to Meraintron to go to Atlantis, but security wasn't so tight then."

"Well, we are going anyway," stated Thor firmly. He didn't seem the slightest bit deterred by what Cocon had said. He seemed convinced that they were still going.

"He's right!" said Misty. "Aquarius needs that Trident—we will get it by *any* means necessary, if we have to."

"A TRIDENT!?" yelled Toni excitedly. "Oh, my God! I can't wait!" Toni's smile lowered into a frown. "What am I going to do with a—*Trident*?"

"The Trident holds tremendous Power and it will give you twice as much strength!"

"Won't the Merains get angry if we try to go to Atlantis?" questioned Rachel, concerned.

"Yeah!" Mike agreed. "And what if there's a good reason why we shouldn't go there?"

"You are supposed to be able to handle anything," said Granite, angrily. "Are you saying that you are not who you are meant to be?"

"Of course not," said Becca, forcefully. "So, how do we get there?" she asked turning to Juhani.

"We shall have to go speak to the King first," said Thor, flying off Jake's shoulder and over to the bubble wall. "We do not want those soldiers coming down upon us!"

"Ahhh," agreed Flairen. "Good thinking, Thor."

"So, where do we find the King?" Toni asked.

"The Palace is over there," whispered Thor, facing the wall. He was staring at the farthest bubble structure; one that was isolated from all the others. Piles of different sized bubbles rose like towers around an immense central bubble. There were no bubble chains leading up to it, so obviously, only Merains were able to get there. The bright, glistening flames from numerous torches inside lit up everything around it. It looked rather far away, and there seemed to be no way of getting to it—except by swimming.

The teens looked at each other, puzzled. "How were they going to get there?" asked Rachel.

"Let us go, then," said Merlin, flying past Granite and out through the wall. He now hovered outside surrounded by a greenish bubble. It seemed to be protecting him from the pressure of the water and allowing him to breathe. He gestured for them to join him. The teens hesitantly pushed through the wall, emerging on the other side in bubbles of their own. It was like walking through a sheet of cool water and coming out dry on the other side.

"Okay. Here we are," said Toni, her blue-tinted bubble bobbing gently. "So how do we get over there?" she said, pointing toward the palace.

"We walk," said Merlin, whose bubble began smoothly rolling through the water. They all gave it a tentative try, and soon were moving rapidly along.

"I feel like a hamster in one of those exercise balls," said Jake.

"I think this is what it would be like to walk on the moon!" exclaimed Becca.

After five exhaustingly long minutes of walking, which seemed like an hour to the teens, they reached the Palace. There were at least fifty Merain guards posted all around the towering stacks of bubbles, at the center of which, was one gigantic bubble.

Misty approached the gloomy looking guard nearest her. "We wish to see the King," she announced. Her voice was clear and strong, almost daring the guard to deny her request.

The Merain guard was silent for several seconds. "For what purpose?" he intoned, his dark eyes staying focused out into the ocean.

"We wish to gain access to the Ancient Kingdom of Atlantis."

"I am sorry—you cannot see the King." His voice showed no emotion.

"We must!" protested Misty. "It is most urgent!"

The Merain soldier's voice became louder. "You must leave right now. If not, you shall be taken away to jail. By force, if necessary!"

Misty flew back to the teens, her face pale.

"Well, what do we do now?" asked Toni, disappointed.

"My dear," said Misty, grinning. "We will see the King, even if *we* have to take *them* by force."

The teens approached a guard who stood closer to the entrance. This time Jake spoke, with Thor posing mightily upon his shoulder. "Let us pass if you do not want to get hurt!" he stated simply.

The guard looked menacingly at the teens, daring them to make a move. With a hand gesture to the others, the other guards stepped forward in a line with their spears pointed at Jake.

Jake's eyes began to glow fog white. He yelled to the other teens, "Protect yourselves!"

Thor laughed. "Yes, electricity does spread greatly in water!"

Jake looked back at the guards. "I'm giving you one last warning!"

The guard that Misty had spoken to ran forward and grabbed Jake's arm in a firm grip.

"*Fine!*" yelled Jake through clenched teeth. He stomped on the Merain guard's foot. The guard lit up like a Christmas wreath as bolts of electricity vibrated through his body. The bolts spread out, surging through the water, sending the other guards sailing backward. The wave of electricity collided with the bulging walls of the Palace, leaving a purplish iridescent mark, like a bruise, on the shiny surface. The pulse continued on until it faded out in the distance. The Merain guards were now lying on the ground, injured and unconscious, but not dead.

"Quickly now!" yelled Flairen, urgently gesturing toward the huge center bubble.

The teens stepped through the bubble wall and found themselves in a giant chamber that seemed to be lined with pure gold. There were twice as many guards inside, and they ran immediately to confront the teens. The teens' eyes began to glow as they got prepared to fight.

"Enough!" yelled a strong, deep voice.

The guards reluctantly lowered their spears and returned to their posts, where they came to attention, eyes staring straight ahead once again. Sitting on an ornate golden throne was a goliath Merain. He looked more like a fish than a human, and his skin had an unhealthy greenish tinge. He had a wide, toad-like face with bulging green eyes and rolls of fat down the sides of his baldhead, nearly obscuring his gill flaps. He was dressed in a flowing red robe of silk, trimmed in tiny golden tassels.

Lying on a cushioned platform to his right was a very pretty Merain girl in a pleated gown of purple silk. She was lying on her stomach among an assortment of elegantly trimmed blue pillows. She swung her greenish finned legs, seemingly more interested in her nails than the teens. Though still vaguely fishy, her head was more rounded, with delicate features. On her scaly wrists and ankles, she wore many thin, glittering bracelets of gold and silver. The rest of her abundant jewelry was gold inset with jewels of all colors.

To the King's left, on a smaller throne, sat an old balding man with a wispy white beard. He was obviously blind, since the pupils of his eyes were an opaque white. A round blue gemstone sparkled on his forehead. In his left hand, he held a thick wooden staff carved with swirling designs. Its one end curved like a shepherd's crook. His simple brown robes were long and cape-like.

"My hospital cannot support all my guards at one time," laughed the big Merain King. "I am King Midras, King of Meraintron. To my right is King Swenteon, King of Atlantis." Swenteon inclined his head and nodded. Midras' large, fleshy, purple lips kept moving up and down even when he wasn't speaking, as if chewing over his words or some invisible treat. The teens exchanged curious looks. "And to my left is my daughter, Princess Whisper." She looked up at them and smiled briefly before returning to her nails. "Once I saw the Ancient Fairies, I knew who you were and why you have come."

"Ahhh…can it *beee*?" said King Swenteon, leaning forward and smiling brightly, revealing squarish white teeth. He waved his palm in front of his face, revealing a twinkling pair of sapphire blue eyes. The teens gasped. "Yes it can! Welcome Thor, Juhani, Flairen, Merlin, Granite, ahhh…and Misty!"

"Hello, King Swenteon," smiled Misty, curtseying. "It is indeed good to see you again."

"And you," smiled King Swenteon. "But where is Ororo?" he asked, looking over the group carefully.

Misty sighed. "She's on a rather important quest like us—but a little more *complex*."

"I see," whispered King Swenteon. "So, you have come at last to retrieve the Trident and save Atlantis!"

"Save?" questioned Thor in disbelief. "Since when has Atlantis need saving? What is wrong?"

This time King Midras spoke. "A week ago, an evil presence—a Darkness—found its way into Atlantis, seeking the Trident. However, *it* could not get through the force field protecting the Trident. So *it* remains there, I can only assume, waiting for the Sage of Water and Ice to come for the Trident."

"I am afraid that is the truth," said King Swenteon sorrowfully. "The people cannot live where Evil lurks. It destroys their minds in the blink of an eye. They can no longer see their reflections in the Great Walls. So, my dear friend—King Midras—has been providing sanctuary for my people. He has been most gracious in allowing us to stay here."

"Does that mean we can go and get the Trident now—and rid you of the Evil also?" asked Toni strongly, prepared to do just about anything.

"Yes," replied King Midras. "But I am afraid three of you must remain behind to protect this Kingdom in case the Evil should enter here also. It is the only way to ensure the safety of the gateway while you retrieve the Trident."

The teens grouped closely together and looked to the Fairies for advice.

"You six must choose wisely," warned Merlin. "Each of you could affect the outcome, both positively and negatively."

"Well, obviously, Toni has to go," said Rachel. "I don't think I should, since my powers aren't too much of an advantage down here.

"Alright," said Mike, "then I'll stay too—it'll be easier for me to use my powers here for defense."

"Well," said Jake hesitantly, "maybe you should go too, Becca. It seems that Atlantis is a place for a powerful mind." Becca nodded.

"I should stay here too," said Josh. "This isn't really a situation where mythical stuff would be much help. You should go, Jake—water is defenseless against you!"

"Okay then!" said Jake. "That's that."

"It is decided!" yelled Thor loudly. "Cyclone and Star will be accompanying Aquarius to Atlantis. Quake, Myth, and Flare shall stay behind to defend the gateway."

"Very well," spoke King Midras. "My daughter will be accompanying you also. The entrance to Atlantis is sealed—she knows how to open it."

Whisper stood up at Midras' side, and then began spinning around, her bracelets jiggling madly. She vanished into a whirling cloud of miniature icicles, which blurred into a thick mist. She reappeared in front of the teens, startling them. Whisper laughed.

"Hello, Misty," smiled Whisper.

"Hello, Whisper. It is good to see you again," said Misty, circling her.

"As you can see," laughed King Midras, "my daughter has been granted special abilities. Only royal females obtain this sort of power."

Whisper snickered.

"The gateway shall now be opened!" howled King Swenteon. He passed his hand over his face once again and his sapphire eyes vanished, revealing only pure white orbs. He started chanting in a language unfamiliar to the teens: "*Brutah moniesta cosne wall ate, shall ton thy gatteaw!*"

The room began to violently shake—though the Merains and King Swenteon did not react. A glowing light appeared in the center of the room in the shape of a tall, wide archway. The area beyond the archway was in shadow.

"You may proceed," said King Swenteon.

Whisper smiled back at the teens as she walked through the light and disappeared into the shadows on the other side of the doorway. Toni, Jake, and Becca looked at each other in mild confusion. "Aren't we traveling in bubbles?" asked Toni.

"Those visiting Atlantis have no need for such creations. The water there is as easy to breathe as air," King Midras replied. The teens hesitantly walked through the doorway with Thor, Juhani, and Misty hanging tightly to their shoulders.

Rachel, Mike, Josh and the others stared at the lighted door through which they had entered. Mike broke the silence. "So…exactly what type of *Evil* are we preparing for, anyway?"

King Swenteon sighed. "Be prepared for any Darkness. This portal must remain open if your friends hope to get back. As long as it's open, anything can get in—and anything can get out. The other entrance shall stay sealed forever—unless you succeed."

Chapter 16—Where a Beast Master Lurks

Toni, Jake, Becca, and Whisper stood on a stone pathway on top of a ridge. Ahead of them, in the distance, was a colossal city made of ice. It spread out almost as far as the eye could see, and Becca guessed that it was five times bigger than New York City. It glimmered in the sunlight that filtered down from above. The water was so crystal clear that it was like looking through air. The teens looked up and could see the surface hundreds of feet above them. Clouds moved across the surface throwing shadows on the city below.

"We're not that far down," said Jake, gazing above him.

"Atlantis holds many secrets and mysteries," said Misty, looking out over the city. "The Kingdom—it has changed greatly from the last time I was here."

"Is the city *supposed* to be frozen?" asked Becca. "I mean—I've never pictured Atlantis this size, not to mention it being a city of *ice.*"

"This is the work of the Trident," said Whisper. "The Trident senses Darkness and fear among the People. It has unleashed some of its Power to protect the Kingdom. This Kingdom was so beautiful when I last visited here. We must be exceedingly careful—for the Ancient Trident to have unleashed this much power, there must be a formidable Evil present."

"We can handle whatever it throws at us," said Toni, forcefully.

Whisper smiled. "I'll take your word for it. Please—follow." She began to walk along the stone pathway. The pathway eventually left the ridge and crossed over a deep trench. The teens could see now that Atlantis was built on a series of flat-topped buttes that rose up out of the dark abyss below.

"It looks like the Grand Canyon, only underwater," exclaimed Jake in surprise.

"Actually," said Whisper, "this used to be the seabed, but a great cataclysm nearly a millennia ago split it apart. Much of the city had to be rebuilt."

The smallest towers of the city were taller than any skyscraper they had seen in New York! It was hard to believe that all the people from Atlantis were in Meraintron—a rather large Kingdom, but much smaller than Atlantis. All along the Kingdom's walls were many unusual trees, all very tall and very frozen.

After ten minutes of walking along the long, narrow pathway suspended over the trench, they finally arrived at a door in the Kingdom wall. The door was wide and tall with an ornate gold knocker and heavy hinges. There was a keyhole near one side, but no knob. In fact, the door looked like it hadn't been opened in a very long time, judging from its rough, barnacle-covered surface.

"This is not one of the main entrances," explained Whisper. "Not many people even know of its existence, since the outer wall of the City is very long and no windows open onto the courtyard inside."

"How are you supposed to open these doors, Whisper?" asked Toni, head and body leaning back, staring up to the top of the door. It was about fifty feet tall and just as wide.

Whisper and the Fairies laughed. "Yes," laughed Thor. "It is time."

Whisper waved her hand enchantingly and a blue light began to glow in front of her. She reached into the light and pulled out a cobalt blue ocarina. She placed it to her lips and softly played a lyrical, lilting song. Toni's eyes began to glow a very bright blue. Whisper stopped playing and handed the ocarina to Toni.

"This Song is called 'Shallow Waters'," said Misty, smiling brightly. Toni slowly played the piece—though this time it echoed all around, thrumming through the water. It was loud enough for anyone miles away, above or below water, to hear. Humming could be heard from inside the Kingdom. The door shook violently, knocking loose some barnacles, which spiraled down to the seafloor. Several large cracks zigzagged across the surface, first down the center and then over the whole door. Gigantic pieces of the door began to break loose and tumble down on top of them.

Whisper shouted quickly, "*VANISHING TUNDRA!*" The pieces disappeared before any could painfully hit the teens. "That's odd…it usually just fades away—I guess, now, there's no telling what's in store for us in the rest of the Kingdom." She turned to Toni, "By the way, the Sage of Water and Ice taught me that Song. We were good friends."

"How did you know her so well?" questioned Toni with interest.

"She would come along with Misty to learn more about the Kingdom and the Worlds Below. I was her guide and showed her many things. She taught me much in return. It was an experience that I'll never forget. We must go." She walked quickly through the doorway and into a huge snow-filled courtyard. Icicles hung from the eaves of the surrounding buildings and from the carved lintel of an arched doorway on the far side. Statues of angels lined the walls, each with a little plaque in gold on the pedestal. In the middle of the frozen courtyard floated the Trident.

The Trident stood up straight and was surrounded by a blue, rippling force field. The Trident's handle was made from a long, highly polished crystal of the deepest blue. The two outer prongs of the Trident were silver and the middle prong was gold with a blue gemstone at its base. Kneeling to the side of the Trident was a small figure in dark robes.

The teens heard a soft sob—she was crying. Her body shook with every breath. The teens approached cautiously and surrounded her. She raised her head slowly; pulling the hood from her face—Raven! Her face was paler than before, and her eyes were dark—blacker than ever. Her face was damp from crying, and she looked—afraid. Her hair was long and a deep unearthly purple. She began to speak calmly and quietly in a monotone voice. "Everybody fears me. When they look at me they scream and run—or, sometimes, curse." The teens were startled by the sadness in her voice.

Jake knelt down by her side and reached his hand out toward her. She moved her head back in fear, but then stilled, letting Jake wipe the tears from her face. "Maybe, it's because you have been working for Evil—it has corrupted part of you, but not all of you." Raven lowered her head as she cried even harder. "You can change, Raven. Didn't you have a life once where you were loved, and not feared?"

Raven frowned. "I—I can't remember—*Why*?"

"Look deep inside of you. Your Spirit is still within you, and it is fighting to be free," said Thor. "Find that which is hidden in your Soul."

Raven shut her eyes and a smile soon lit up her face. "I—I think I remember my mother. Her smile could light up the room, and was always joyful. She sang to me when I was sad or afraid. How—how could I forget something so beautiful?" she asked wistfully. She stared up at the ceiling for several moments. "And my brother—he was always there for me—*fighting for me.* Whenever I was afraid, he was always there to comfort me." Her eyes went wide. "What's happened to me?!" she asked fearfully. She suddenly began to glow an oily black as Shadows appeared beneath her feet. Her eyes began to glow and her voice grew deep with anguish. *"NO, PLEASE! DON'T PUNISH ME! I DIDN'T MEAN IT! NO!"* The Shadows surrounded her, climbing up her body, and covering her with a glowing black ooze. As they pulled her into the ground, she reached desperately out to Jake. *"HELP ME! PLEASE, HELP ME!"* she cried piteously. Jake tried to grab her hand, but she was pulled down into the puddle of Shadows, which winked out of existence, leaving a bare spot on the ground. She was gone. The Darkness had taken her.

Jake abruptly sat down and stared up at Becca and Toni. Becca knelt down and put the palm of her hand over the place Raven had been standing. "She wants to be helped. I was able to enter her mind for a short while, but I wasn't able to find the location of our parents." Becca stood up. "I still sense hope in her but Cleopatra has done terrible damage to her mind. We'll find our parents—and we'll save Raven!"

Toni stared at the Trident. "I wonder why she was taken away before she was able to get the Trident."

"It was because she had lost her focus," said Thor.

Jake walked over to the Trident and stuck his hand out to touch the force field. A white bolt of lightning shot from Thor, burning Jake's hand. Jake jumped back in shock and yelled angrily at Thor, "What was that for?! I mean, honestly!"

Thor flew from his shoulder without speaking. He landed on the ground long enough to make a snowball. He floated back up into the air and threw it at the force field surrounding the Trident. The force field caught and held the snowball for several seconds before hurling it across the courtyard where it smashed through the doors into the City.

Jake, Becca, and Toni stood there, stunned. Jake laughed. "Sorry!"

"I would never harm you unless it was absolutely necessary, young Cyclone!" sighed Thor, flying back to Jake's shoulder.

Toni stared at the Trident, dreamily. "If it's so dangerous and of such great value, why would they keep it in some courtyard?"

"Because, Aquarius," said Misty brightly, "Atlanteans have always thought of it as a symbol of Peace, not a weapon of destruction. Many visitors came to see the Kingdom Under the Sea and to experience its wonders. The people of Atlantis wanted them to see the Trident the way they did, so visitors would always feel welcome."

Toni stared at Misty for several seconds. "I can't help but noticing—you and the others have been calling the Ancients by our names—and the other mythical creatures knew our names—our second names—why?"

Juhani laughed hard. "I was wondering when you were going to wonder about that. I thought you would have asked sooner."

"Because," said Thor, "the Ancients who made you the Chosen gave you their own names."

The teens gasped. "But how can that be?" asked Becca. "We came up with the names ourselves!"

"You did," said Misty, "but with the help of the Ancients. The power that you have obtained contains part of the Ancients' spirits—and that spirit has become a part of you. Now, it is time to concentrate. Look closely at the center prong of the Trident."

They all stared at the blue crystal that was inset at the base of the middle prong. Whisper stepped forward for a closer look and pointed towards the crystal. "As you can see, this crystal of the Angel of Ice lies in the center prong."

Toni gasped. "So I've found all of my crystals?"

"Yes!" exclaimed Misty. "This means you only need to learn one more song for your ocarina."

"How do I get the Trident with the force field around it?" asked Toni.

Juhani laughed. "Concentrate on the stone and tell it to *open*."

"But that sounds too simple!" Toni said exasperated. "If it's that easy, how come no one else has done it?"

"It's simple for *you*," said Misty, "but not for anyone else. The spirit of the Ancient Aquarius is necessary to command the stone."

Toni laughed. "Okay then, OPEN!" The blue force field disappeared, leaving the Trident fully unprotected. "*Don't worry, Raven,*" she whispered. She held out her hand to retrieve it, but no sooner had she done this than a black whip wrapped around the handle of the Trident, lifting it high into the air. Toni gasped and jumped back in fright.

Floating in the air was a thin woman holding the Trident in her left hand. She wore tight, black leather clothing with gloves and high-heeled boots. She held a deadly looking bullwhip with silver spikes at the end of the lash. Her hair was long and white, and her face gave off a sickly glow, like phosphorescent mushrooms. Her eyes were glowing black. "Thank you, for the Trident. I am Espion, the Beast Tamer. I will be well rewarded for my work! It will help my Masters to defeat you once and for all!"

She cracked her whip into the air, creating a loud smack that echoed all around. The pair of doors at the far side of the courtyard opened silently inward, and two mighty, pure white saber-toothed tigers came lurking through. The teens began to walk slowly backwards toward the entrance behind them.

"Stay back, Whisper!" warned Jake. "I can tell these aren't ordinary beasts!"

"Of course they're not!" yelled Becca, frightened. "They've been extinct for a million years!"

Jake and Becca charged forward towards the saber-toothed tigers and Toni stood in front of Whisper to protect her.

A powerful gust of wind came soaring from Jake, sliding one of the tigers across the ground, plowing up little drifts of snow. It slashed its nails into the earth as it pulled itself through the blasting hurricane of wind. Its eyes began to glow as bright white beams shot from them towards Jake. A flash of white light blinded Jake as Thor used his magnificent staff as a bat, forcing the beams back at the tiger. The tiger flew back heavily through the air—smashing right through the ice of the City wall.

Jake stared at Thor, panting heavily. "Thanks!"

"It's my job to protect you!" yelled Thor, mightily.

Jake looked over at Becca who was raising her glowing hand. The other tiger was floating in the air—fighting furiously to get down. Becca shut her hand into a fist and the saber-toothed tiger's neck wrenched to the side with a horrible snap like a breaking branch. It fell heavily to the ground, unmoving. Becca gazed at Espion—hatred visible in her eyes. "Give back the Trident, you damned witch!"

"Foolish girl!" she screamed. "Look what you have done! You just created a Knight!"

Becca snapped her head around to where the two tigers lay. Suddenly, they transformed into a white light and merged together. In the light was a silver knight: half tiger, half man. He held a broad, silver-bladed sword in his clawed human hand.

Becca raised one eyebrow at him as though challenging him to make the first move. He smiled, showing terrible, pointed white teeth. She reached behind her and unsheathed her own sword. She swung it over her head as a purple glowing beam shot at the knight. The knight absorbed it with his own sword and shot it violently back at Becca. Juhani launched a cloud of misty purple fog in front of Becca that turned into a shower of purple flowers, absorbing the beam. Becca picked up one of the flowers, making it glow. She threw it at the knight, and it exploded in purple smoke, blinding him. Becca went soaring through the air, clashing her sword with the knight's own. Jake took his bow and reached for the silver arrow. He pulled back the wire and took careful aim at the knight's heart.

"Two against one!?" yelled Espion feverishly, still floating high in the air. "That isn't fair!" She pointed the Trident at Jake.

"WATCH OUT!!!" screamed Toni. She tried to run over to protect him, but she was too late. A blue electric beam shot out of the Trident and hit Jake and Thor straight on. He and Thor were frozen solid, covered with a thick layer of solid blue ice. The arrow, which had already left the bow, fell uselessly to the ground.

Becca lost concentration as she gazed at Thor and Jake. "NO!" she screamed. She waved her hand violently and the knight beast flew back and smashed into the wall. Becca stalked toward him, as he struggled to get to his feet. Her eyes glowed brighter than ever before and intense purple beams shot out, striking the knight in the chest. She swung her sword, cleaving through the side of his helmet. He fell to the ground, head twisted to one side and blood running down his face into the snow.

Becca looked over at Toni who was by Jake's side trying to use her Power to unfreeze them. "It's no use!" she sobbed in frustration.

Becca leered at Espion floating twenty feet above her. "*You!*" She raised her index finger and pointed it dangerously at Espion. "Release him!"

Espion laughed. "*Release* him? Now, why on Earth would I do that?" Espion floated down to hover five feet above the snow. "In fact—it's time I get rid of Atlantis, Meraintron, and you filthy, rotten, spoiled *brats!*"

She pointed the Trident at Becca and it began to glow. A purple force field appeared around Becca. The same icy beam struck through the field and hit Becca, freezing her solid like Jake and Thor. Juhani narrowly escaped.

"NOOO!!!!" screamed Juhani. She flew anxiously over to Toni. "You have to get the Trident! With that Weapon, she can penetrate any shield that you Sages, or any of us, use to protect ourselves!" She gazed at Becca and Jake. "You must hurry! It is only a matter of time before Star, Cyclone, and Thor become frozen for Eternity."

Espion pointed the Trident at Toni and a net of ice flew out over her, Juhani, Whisper and Misty. Toni grabbed Juhani around the waist and Whisper by the hand, pulling them in close. "Hold on to my cloak!" she instructed. The net fell over her and the others, but quickly melted away, not affecting them at all. Espion shrieked in disbelief and annoyance.

"The Trident won't hurt *me!*" threatened Toni. "Now, you're done for!"

Espion laughed. "Do you really think the Trident is my *only* source of Power? Well, if you think so—you are *wrong!*" Espion cracked her whip at Toni, but Toni grabbed it just before the silver lashes hit her in the face. The whip began to glow blue and turned into a thick, blue water serpent with crooked fangs. It leaped up and bit Espion on the neck. She grabbed the serpent and squeezed it tightly until it burst into black and gray flames. Espion threw the smoldering carcass aside as she said, "Fine, Aquarius! You wish to die playing games—then so be it! I don't have time to watch you suffer—but it would be *quite* enjoyable!" She raised the hand with the Trident in it, and spoke loudly. "*Serpents of Darkness, hear my call—Come forth at once to perish all!*"

Two thick, black, red-eyed serpents burst through snow-covered ground. Their bodies continued pouring out of the hole until they stood nearly fifteen feet high. Their long, oily black tails lashed feverishly as they screeched and snapped at Misty, Juhani, Toni, and Whisper with jagged silver fangs.

"*Kill them!*" whispered Espion. She walked away through the open doors leading to the pathway to Meraintron.

"Juhani!" yelled Whisper, "you must warn the others. Don't let Espion escape with that Trident! If she does, the Sages won't survive! You know the way to the Portal better than she does! Hurry!" Whisper sent a powerful surge of white light at the serpents, hoping to distract them so that Juhani could get away unnoticed. Juhani quickly disappeared in a flash of purple light.

"Let's go!" yelled Toni to Whisper. A churning vortex of water appeared beneath Toni's feet pushing her up above the serpent's heads. Surprisingly, Whisper did the same. As she traveled upward, Toni opened her palms wide, creating thousands of small icicles that shot out toward the serpents, piercing their skin. Pinpoints of silvery blood oozed out, but the serpents' flexible black scales surrounded and overlapped the wounds, healing them instantly.

The serpents, not capable of reaching Toni and Whisper physically, raised their heads and shot purple-black poisonous needles at them from their mouths. Whisper ran straight up the wall, dodging the needles. She flipped off the wall and landed on another jet of water, which put her down gently next to the doorway into Atlantis.

Toni quickly made a long dagger of ice and twirled it like a propeller, hitting every single needle coming at her. They ricocheted back at the serpents who manage to loop their bodies out of the way. Toni then blew a cloud of silver mist from her mouth at the serpents, who were unable to avoid it. They froze completely, sparkling in the dappled light from above. Toni smiled and landed next to them.

"Excellent, Toni!" yelled Misty. "Let's get out of here in case they get free."

With a loud crack, the tail of one of the serpent's whipped through the ice and sent Toni flying. Before she could hit the wall, Misty waved her hands and a soft bubble appeared as a cushion. Toni bounced off it, nimbly landing on her feet, chuckling in relief.

Whisper and Toni grew frustrated. How were they supposed to defeat the serpents if they kept healing themselves? "Toni!" cried Whisper. "Look up!"

Toni looked up over her head at the glittering icicles hanging from the eaves of the buildings surrounding the courtyard. Some were several feet long and as thick as Toni's wrist. "Misty!" she yelled, "get Whisper through the doorway and protect her. I have an idea!" She gestured quickly toward the way into Atlantis. Misty leaped off Toni's shoulder without question and flew over to hover in front of Whisper who had already gone inside. They turned to look out into the courtyard, a blue force field glowing around them. The serpents, who seemed to be attracted by the glow of the force field, slithered toward them. Their crooked silver fangs dripped black poison as their long, red forked tongues whipped in and out between them.

Toni's eyes flashed brilliant blue, and the courtyard began to shake as if there was an earthquake. "Hurry!" screamed Whisper when the serpents reached the entryway. The icicles hanging from the archway jiggled and chimed before cracking off at their bases and slashing down like a hundred spears. The icicles plunged into the backs of the serpents nearly cutting one of them in half. They screeched, shrieked, and writhed several times before finally lying still.

"You did it!" cheered Whisper. The force field disappeared as she rushed forward among the broken bodies of the serpents to meet Toni. One of the serpents began to glow black, and the icicles melted away. Its wounds quivered and rippled, healing yet again as the black scales smoothed over them like oil. Its eyes opened wide revealing a reddish glow. "Toni!" screamed Whisper, fear echoing through her. The serpent opened its mouth and snatched at Whisper. She hugged herself and screamed.

A huge rock crashed through the serpent's jagged teeth, wedging its mouth open. It thrashed wildly trying to free the rock. It crashed to the ground at Whisper's feet, driving her back with its whipping tail. Whisper gasped and pointed toward the door.

There at the entrance stood Josh and Mike with Granite and Merlin! Josh was holding the Trident! "Toni!" he yelled. The Trident flashed green as it soared through the air. Toni snatched it and held it tightly. The crystal on the Trident, along with the one on her head, began to glow and pulse. Toni twirled the Trident around and raised it high overhead as she floated up toward the ceiling. Glimmering blue light surrounded the Trident as though it were absorbing energy. Toni yelled as she threw the Trident with all her might down at the serpent. It pierced through just behind the serpents head, severing it from its body. Both serpents glowed then exploded into silver ash.

Toni flew down through the doorway to where Jake and Becca stood frozen in the courtyard, the others following.

"What happened to them?" asked Mike.

"Espion used the Trident against them!" yelled Granite. "Otherwise, Toni could have already unfrozen them."

Toni raised her head. "I just hope it's not too late!" She waved the Trident and an azure light began to surround them all. The ice glimmered and rivulets of melting water cascaded down its surface. With a final flash, Becca, Jake, and Thor collapsed to the ground. Toni and Mike knelt down next to them. "Are you alright?" Toni asked, tears in her eyes.

Mike helped Jake to rise shakily to his feet, while Josh and Toni helped Becca. Misty flew down and hugged Thor. "We're fine," said Jake, shaking his head and shrugging his shoulders. "What happened? Where's Espion!? Is everything okay?" he asked hurriedly, looking around.

"It is now," smiled Toni. "But now I must complete my final task!" Toni shut her eyes as she slowly floated high above the others holding the Trident out in front of her.

"What is she doing?" asked Josh, gazing up at Toni.

"She's going to free Atlantis from the Darkness," whispered Thor. Toni let go of the Trident, but it still floated in front of her as though it were held up by some invisible force. Toni raised her hands as her cloak covered her completely and her hood slid up over her head. Her eyes glowed brilliant blue from within the shadow of her hood. She lifted her hands upwards and spoke with another's voice, but this time it was a different voice than before. "*ATLANTIS—CITY OF THE SEAS, YOUR CURSE SHALL BE BROKEN*!"

The Trident raced down and stabbed its prongs into the seafloor. A sapphire light spread out from the Trident. As it traveled outward, everything it touched lit up brightly. The ice was melting and revealing many things in the light. Flowers, trees, statues and fountains were everywhere, shining brightly. The sun beamed throughout Atlantis, showing its true inner beauty as if for the first time. Everything shimmered and glistened. Peace and serenity traveled with the light, carried like a gust of fresh air. Atlantis was free.

Everything about Atlantis made the teens feel welcome and at home. Toni floated down and pulled the Trident out of the ground. The teens were awed. Whisper giggled. "It is truly a most remarkable place. And with the Song I have passed down to Aquarius, you will be able to gain access to Atlantis on your own."

When they had all gathered at the pathway to Meraintron, Whisper said, "you do not realize how grateful I am for all that you have done. And King Swenteon probably has a thousand more thanks to give!"

"We're glad to have met you, too, Whisper," said Toni, hugging her.

"Yes," said Josh. "It has been a wonderful experience for all of us. But we can't forget about Espion. Rachel is guarding her back at the Gateway."

"Oh, yeah!" yelled Mike. "Juhani appeared and warned us right before Espion came through the portal."

Whisper laughed. "I knew she would be successful."

"Whisper?" asked Mike suddenly, something on his mind.

Whisper turned her head to look at Mike. "Yes?"

Mike grinned. "How old are you?"

Misty laughed very hard as she eyed Whisper. "Well," said Whisper. "I'm not *that* old—I mean..." She smirked at Misty. "I am only four thousand, one hundred and sixteen years old," she said defensively. The teens' eyes widened in surprise. "Well if you think that's old, my father will be fourteen thousand, three hundred and sixty-two next month. Only the people of Atlantis live longer," she said proudly.

"For goodness sake, Mike!" laughed Granite. "What is it with you and age?"

Mike said nothing, but simply folded his arms and walked out of Atlantis with Granite perched on his shoulder. The others followed along the pathway, but couldn't believe what they were seeing. Instead of a dark abyss on either side of the path, there were fields of colored sea lilies and blue and green algae, like grass, through which schools of tiny fish darted.

Becca gasped, "This is the most incredible thing that has ever happened to me. I want to come back here someday—and learn more about the Kingdom."

"Oh, you'll come back," said Thor. "It is your Destiny."

A current wafted along, like a breeze, riffling the grass. Singing, humming, and whistling could be heard from all around. Flying fish, like bluebirds, zipped over their heads. Neighing echoed across the meadow, and the teens turned to see a herd of white horses with silver horns on their heads. The largest one looked in their direction and snorted. The teens gasped. Never before had they seen a unicorn in real life, only in books, and certainly never imagined they would find some under the sea! But now they knew that fairytales and mythology were real.

Josh stepped off the pathway into the field. He put his hands to his mouth and blew out a cloud of green mist. White doves flew from the mist and circled around the unicorns. The biggest unicorn shut its eyes and nodded, its thick white mane floating around its head like a cloud. It turned and galloped gracefully along with the doves, the rest of the herd following with flowing tails. "I have never seen a creature more beautiful than that," said Josh, eyeing the unicorns." He returned to the pathway and they all climbed silently to the top of the ridge for one last look at Atlantis before stepping through the portal.

Chapter 17—Painful Knowledge

The teens were once again in the throne room of King Midras. In the center of the room stood Rachel and Juhani, with Flairen resting on Rachel's shoulder. Rachel was floating in the air and her hands were glowing red. She was controlling a dome of fire over Espion, who was tightly bound with green vines. Amongst the fire were unique black symbols.

"What are those?" asked Jake, pointing.

"Well," said Josh, "much of my power is Elfin. Those are ancient symbols that are used to block Evil. Espion wouldn't be able to get through the fire without serious burns, but the symbols are an extra precaution."

"That was good thinking," laughed Becca, amazed. "You never know what trick this chick has up her sleeve." Becca jumped back suddenly when Espion broke loose from the vines. Espion ran at the wall of fire, but green lightning from the symbols pushed her back. She screamed in pain and fury.

"Idiots!" yelled Espion. "I am the most powerful Beast Master in this world!"

"Actually," said Toni, "I disagree with you there. The most Powerful of all Beast Masters would have to be Myth." She looked over at Josh. "I mean—he managed to capture *you*."

Espion screamed in rage again. "This dome will not hold me forever!"

"She's right," said Becca. "Are we going to keep her like that?"

"Are you kidding!?" yelled Rachel annoyed. "I can't stay up here for eternity!"

The others looked up at Rachel and laughed. Juhani flew from Rachel's shoulder and landed on Becca's. Becca smiled. "Good job, Juhani."

"As to you, Star," acknowledged Juhani. "We could not have done this if we were not a team."

Josh walked over to Mike. "Hey, I need a *mosaint* leaf."

"That's the spiny kind, right?" asked Mike, looking at Josh inquisitively. Josh nodded. Mike raised his hand and a thick, spiky green leaf with a smooth underside appeared and floated over to Josh.

A black liquid streamed from Josh's finger as he began to paint another symbol on the leaf. Josh smiled as he held up the leaf. "The Ancient Chinese Scholars were brilliant!" He looked up at Rachel, sweat now beading on her forehead—she was straining herself to keep the flames going. "Yo, sis! That's enough—subdue the fire!"

"I hope you know what you're doing!" she yelled, aggravated.

"Oh, he does," laughed Merlin.

Rachel lowered her arms and the fire collapsed instantly into smoke. Espion grinned and began to chant in an unknown language. The *mosaint* leaf began to glow green as it soared through the air without any resistance. It hit Espion in the forehead, and she stopped talking and became still.

Josh slowly walked over to Espion. He pulled the leaf carefully off her forehead, revealing the black symbol. "As long as she has that tattoo upon her, she will never be able to speak or move again," Espion moaned softly.

King Midras and King Swenteon got up from their thrones and approached the teens. King Midras appeared even bigger up close. He was at least three times the size of Jake. "Sages!" said King Swenteon, with a wide grin on his face and shining in his sapphire blue eyes. "You have saved my People and my Kingdom. The Ancient Sages told me you would arrive to rescue us from Darkness. You must be very special for the Ancients to have chosen you. I bless you with a thousand, thousand thanks! Because of you, my People can live in Peace once again! We would be most honored to have you visit At~~lantis in~~ the future," he said, bowing deeply.

"And you are welcome to visit my Kingdom also, anytime you please," said King Midras, inclining his head because his enormous girth wouldn't allow him to bow. Whisper ran over and hugged her father. "I am proud of you also, my princess. You too, have done very well." He sneered at Espion. "Guards! Take her to the prison and make sure she is well guarded!"

The guards that stood inside the door to the throne room carried Espion away.

"How can we ever thank you? What could we possibly give you to repay you for what you have done?" asked King Swenteon.

"What we really want from you," said Jake, looking at the others, "is for you to continue believing in us."

"Yes," said Toni, "everyone who is counting on us gives us the strength to continue fighting against evil. We may not know where our final destination lies—but we have enough faith in the Good of people to get us through the difficult path that lies ahead."

"We have our own cause to fight for," said Josh, tears in his eyes, "making sure that our parents are returned unharmed. Do you know where Cleopatra is—do you know where our parents are?" The room fell silent as everyone stared at the floor.

The bright smile faded from King Swenteon's face. "No—I'm afraid I do not."

Whisper's eyebrows lowered. "Actually, I might," she said quietly.

"You do?" asked Josh, with hope in his voice.

"Well, I remember something I heard, something from my mother—where Darkness lies. My mother was a traveler. She told me many stories of her adventures before she died. She was the oldest living Merain—she died of old age."

"I'm sorry," said Mike. "You must have been very close to her."

"Very," said Whisper sadly, "but I feel her watching over me. I remember her saying that there was a temple with a source of Power large enough for all living beings. It is the temple that many fear—including some Darkness. All I know is that it's in the shape of a triangle. She drew one with the index finger of both hands—located high up in the sky."

"You must mean a pyramid! The only pyramids I know of are in Egypt," said Rachel, taken aback.

"No, I don't think so," said Whisper, looking up at the ceiling, thinking. "I am sure it is not there, or Mother would have said so, since she traveled often to Egypt. All I can tell you is that the pyramid is somewhere many would not think of looking: somewhere in the eastern hemisphere of this Earth.

"We must go look then!" yelled Becca.

"No!" snapped Juhani. Everyone turned toward her, stunned at the outburst.

"What?" asked Becca, bewildered.

"You have much to learn!" shouted Juhani. "You have to gain more Experience, you must learn how to stand up to a powerful Evil such as the one that lurks there!"

"We're ready!" yelled Becca angrily.

"No!" Thor interrupted. "Juhani is correct. If you went there now without the benefit of more Experience and Power, Cleopatra will surely destroy you all, including your loved ones."

"So you're saying that we must obtain the Final Power from the Temple of Destiny?" asked Mike.

"No," said Granite. "Before you earn the Final Power you have to save your parents."

"The Final Power," said Misty, "is something much more difficult and… 'unique' than what you have now. If you attempt to use it without the required Experience, you will only become weaker."

"Then why do we even need to bother with the Final Power?" asked Becca, sounding even more confused and angry.

"You do not understand!" said Flairen. "The Final Power is linked to who you really are. It's different, like Misty said. It is something that will be of use to everyone, including yourselves."

"Star," said Juhani calmly, "do you remember in Atlantis when Raven was confused and feeling pain?"

Becca sighed. "Yes."

"That was because Cleopatra had taken over her mind. If you go now, without proper training—she will be able to brainwash you *all* in order to get the Final Keys for herself! If you go with the Keys AND the proper training, you will have a much better chance of success! Just remember: Raven still has hope—you Sages are her hope…"

"You're right," said Becca, tears flowing from her eyes. "Sometimes I guess the truth has to be painful."

"Which is why," said Granite, "you must overcome the pain and look for the advantages and positives in life."

"Then we must continue on our quest!" agreed Toni, tears in her eyes.

"But… how do we know for certain if we'll succeed?" asked Rachel, unsure of herself.

"We don't!" said Mike, grinning. "But they're right. We have to follow the path to our Destiny that gives us a better chance to succeed."

"And we will succeed," said Jake strongly.

"And all of us will fight together to the end," said Becca.

"And we Royals will be by your side in any situation!" said Thor, powerfully, in his booming voice.

"We know you will," said Toni. "We have faith in you. I can speak for everyone when I say that you're the ones, besides ourselves, that we count on and trust most," she said fondly. "Okay then, where do we go next, if we can't go look for the pyramid?"

"To the Kingdoms in the Sky, where Jake will receive the Crystal of Wind, and Rachel will receive the Crystal of Magma located in the volcano," said Thor, now looking above him. "It's a long way from here."

"Kingdoms in the sky?" asked Jake with curiosity in his voice.

"Wait a minute," laughed Rachel incredulously. "A volcano in the sky?"

"The Kingdom is hidden from people who live on the land," said Granite. "The Bird Riders are well prepared to guard and protect the Crystals that the Sages left in their care."

"But what are these 'Bird Riders'?" asked Becca.

"Ahhh…" sighed King Swenteon. He began to pace back and forth, trying to think. "I have heard of them in rumors and tales told around the court of Atlantis."

"Do not tell the young ones," Flairen beamed. She looked at Rachel. "We want it to be a surprise."

"Yes," smiled Juhani. "It will be a wonderful surprise!" The teens began to cheer up, knowing that they had another incredible journey ahead of them. They could only imagine what incredible things await them.

"You must get some rest now," King Midras bellowed, clapping his hands loudly before sitting back down on his golden throne. "Take them to the special Sleep Chambers," he said to two Merains ladies with sashes of seashells who suddenly appeared from behind the throne. "After all you have done for us, you should get some rest before continuing on your journey."

It was true. The teens had had a rather busy day and they didn't realize, until now, how tired they were. They waved good-bye to the Kings as they followed Whisper and the ladies with the sashes to the sleeping chambers. She led them through many hallways and through several bubbleways until they finally reached a large room with white carpet.

There were six water mattresses built into the floor and at the far end of the room was a large table laid with silverware and glasses. A long table along the back wall was filled with pitchers of water, bowls of fresh fruits and vegetables, and platters of cooked meat. The ladies immediately began piling the beds with pillows and blankets and adjusting some dials on the wall next to the door. They then laid out pajamas on each bed, bowed to Whisper, and quietly left the room.

"Welcome to the Sleep Chamber. How many days would you like to rest here?" asked Whisper.

The teens looked at Whisper in confusion. "Well," said Jake, "we're only staying here for the night."

"Program it for a week," said Thor. "I will explain it to them later. They are going to need rest." Whisper nodded, adjusted some more dials, then bid the others farewell.

Without thinking, the teens ran to the food table and began to pile warm white plates with the delicious-looking food. They sat down at the table and began to stuff their mouths with food. The Fairies sat down in the middle of the table and shared an apple since it was the only food exactly their size.

"Okay," said Mike, shoving a large portion of steak into his mouth. "What do you mean a week?"

"Mike!" yelled Becca annoyed. "Could you stop shoving food in your mouth if your going to talk?!"

Mike swallowed with difficulty. "Fine, you crazy woman!" The others laughed. Becca scowled at him. Mike looked at the Fairies. "So, do you really mean we're going to spend a week in here?"

"This is a special chamber which allows you to sleep for a given amount of time. We programmed it for a week because you need *LOTS* of rest!"

"But what about the ship?" asked Josh. "And all our stuff? If we're not there, what will happen to our stuff? How will we know where the ship will be?"

"The ship only has one route—it goes back and forth to Africa from New York City," said Merlin. "We will inform the cruise line, and they will keep your belongings for you."

"Then I guess it's alright," said Rachel. "I mean I usually sleep in late—but a week—gosh—that's a long time!"

"I feel so tired right now that I might be able to actually sleep for a week," laughed Jake. "I'm going to bed—I always get tired after I eat a lot." He ran over to the mattress and jumped on it as though it were a trampoline.

"Good night, young Cyclone," bellowed Thor. "Sleep well! And to the rest of you also." The others bid each other goodnight as they followed Jake to bed, one by one. The teens fell asleep almost instantly. The lights in the room dimmed until it was totally dark except for the bright glow of the Fairies.

Merlin sighed. "Do you think Ororo has reached Raven yet?" he asked, flitting over to examine the bowls on the side table.

"I do not know," whispered Thor.

"She *has* to reach Raven," murmured Granite. "We all know that Cleopatra cannot be defeated without Raven."

The Fairies fell silent. Misty looked out towards the ocean, "She's confused. Maybe she will realize who she really is once the Chosen have come to her. Maybe when she sees them—all of them together and working as a team, maybe then she will realize that she's not so different after all." Merlin returned to the table with a carrot in each hand.

Thor looked over at the teens and sighed. "I know Jasmine is watching over them this very moment."

"When Jasmine told us of their arrival," said Juhani dreamily, "a smile as bright as the sun appeared upon her face. She acted as though they were her own—*children*." The teens were tossing and turning in their sleep. The Fairies hovered above them.

"Let's give them good dreams these few nights," smiled Misty, gently placing her hand on Toni's forehead. The others floated down to the teens and curled up among the cushions. "We will be with you always, young ones," said Misty. "For that is *our* Destiny."

Chapter 18—An Unforgettable Ceremony

Becca pushed her covers off and sat up. She heard a soft thud behind her. Juhani rubbed her hand over the back of her head. "*Sorry*," Becca whispered, "*I didn't realize you were sleeping on me.*" Juhani smiled brightly at her. Becca rubbed her eyes and looked around at her fellow sleeping companions. "Wow!" Becca closed her fists and flexed her muscles. "I feel so alive with energy, and I feel *stronger*."

Juhani glowed bright purple as she stood up, looking straight into Becca's eyes. "Sleep helps restore both your mental and physical strength—now you know why it was wise to make that decision, yes?" she said, sounding very motherly.

"I guess so," laughed Becca. "I just can't believe we actually slept a week—and not to mention hundreds of feet below the sea." Becca felt the blankets move next to her as Mike rolled over then sat up, an irritated look on his face.

"Could you be any louder?" Mike asked angrily, his hair messed up.

"SORRY!" bellowed Becca loudly. "YOU ONLY SLEPT FOR A WEEK! WHAT WAS I THINKING BEING LOUD AND WAKING YOU FROM YOUR ENDLESS SLUMBER?!"

Mike scowled at her and reached for the pillow next to him. He threw it at Becca, pelting her in the face. Granite, who had been sleeping inside the pillowcase, tumbled out in midair and flopped down face first among the blankets. Grumpily, he flew into the air, head still hanging down tiredly, and went over to check if any fresh food had been laid out yet on the buffet table. He grabbed an apple and returned to Mike's shoulder.

Jake took the pillow off his head that he used to keep the sound out. "Are you guys arguing already? Come on!"

Mike said nothing, got up, walked past Becca to the buffet table, and grabbed an orange. "*She* started it," he said testily.

Thor laughed mightily, his voice echoing in the nearly empty room. "Come, young Cyclone—and the rest of you also. You must eat now—we have a long day ahead of us and you'll need all the strength you can get!" No one answered—they just simply pulled their blankets over their heads. Thor chuckled. "You know, it surprises me that the lot of you are still tired after a week of sleep. If you don't get up, I'll make you get up!" He heard a soft mumble from Jake. "*Just try it.*"

Granite snickered. "I hope I didn't hear what I *think* I just heard."

Thor flew into the air and raised his glowing, silver lightning bolt staff. His white hair blew around frantically in the sudden wind. A small gray thundercloud appeared in the room, and lightning struck with a loud crash. A gray cyclone appeared from beneath the cloud, lifting Josh, Rachel, and Jake out of bed, blankets and pillows swirling around overhead. They screamed at the sudden commotion that tore them from a sound sleep. Jake's white hair stood on end and shone brightly with each blaze of lightning. His eyes flashed white and the gray storm cloud disappeared along with the cyclone that was lifting him and the others. A last tricky bolt snaked down and cracked Jake on the butt, before disappearing. They all fell to the ground heavily. "Ow!" Jake looked over at Thor, impressed. "I didn't know you had those kinds of tricks up your sleeve."

Becca bent down next to Mike, grinning. "Is it just me, or is Jake starting to look exactly like Thor?"

The doors to the sleeping chamber crashed opened, smashing into the walls. Whisper came running into the room out of breath. "Sages! You must hurry! The Beast Master, Espion, is escaping!"

Jake stood up suddenly and glared at Whisper, worried. "What are you talking about?"

"Everybody! Follow me! Quickly!" she yelled, bounding out of the room, but this time through the wall of the bubble. The teens glowed briefly as they took on their older Power forms, costumes and weapons appearing from thin air. The Fairies flew over to the teens as they ran after Whisper into the deep blue, fear spreading amongst them. How could Espion have escaped? They had just battled her and won—how were they supposed to do that again?

Instead of Whisper making her way to another bubble on the ground, she began to ascend almost immediately toward a very fascinating tower at the back of the Palace that they hadn't noticed before. A solid tower of coral held up a spectacular luminescent bubble—far larger than any of the other tower bubbles. Whisper swam quickly using her webbed feet and toes, nearly as fast as a dolphin. The teens began to swim upwards, but the weight of their costumes and weapons made it extremely difficult to ascend. Jets of water suddenly lifted them through the water to catch them up to Whisper. The teens looked over at Toni who was glowing a bright blue and obviously concentrating hard on controlling the jets. They soon reached the top of the tower and entered through the wall of the bubble just as Whisper had done moments before.

They stood in a broad hallway only several yards behind her. She suddenly stopped in her tracks and stepped aside, revealing a wide aisle that stretched between hundreds of rows of chairs. A red carpet was unrolled down the aisle and all the way up to the foot of a short marble staircase at the end leading up to a platform. On the platform were the thrones of King Midras and King Swenteon. King Midras was standing up, and King Swenteon was sitting down—but they were both gazing proudly at the teens. Along the aisle, thousands of Merains and Atlanteans stood watching the teens expectantly. The teens' jaws dropped, and the Fairies chuckled. They all turned to look at Whisper—the room was completely silent.

"*Whisper*?" asked Jake, nervously. Whisper smiled back at him as she began to clap. The Fairies flew off the teens shoulders, hovered above Whisper's head, and also began to applaud. The room suddenly filled with applause. Cheers and whistles erupted from the crowd, causing chills to creep down their spines. They felt noble and wonderful. It was a great feeling to see and be seen by these beings who were of such great importance—those who looked up to them for their safety. It felt like being accepted and loved by their own families.

The teens stared around at the crowd and then up at the two great Kings of the Sea. King Midras' voice could be heard over the crowds, "Come forth young Sages—come and accept our gratitude—you are *heroes*!" The cheers roared louder than ever. The teens hesitated, but then walked forward, embarrassed—but grateful. They walked slowly down the aisle, shaking hands and accepting flowers from small children. They made their way up the stairs, approaching the Kings, who looked nobler than ever. They wore long, bright silver robes that made them look majestic and regal. Their eyes shone as brightly as the silver crowns upon their heads. When they reached the top step, the cheers and applauding slowly came to a stop as the crowd moved in, completely blocking the aisle.

King Midras stood up straighter and looked out over the crowd. "People of Atlantis and Meraintron," bellowed King Midras. "These are the future Saviors of Earth. Whatever Fear and Evil comes our way—the Sages will be here to send it away!" The cheers began to roar again so that they echoed throughout the room, but then it fell silent once again when King Swenteon left his throne.

He approached the teens with his hands outstretched in greeting. "I have a small token for you Sages," he said, eyebrows raised. "It is a small reminder of how much our People appreciate all that you have done for them." He raised his glowing silver hands and a silver mist appeared in the air between them. The mist died away, revealing six sets of wrist plates made of linked rectangles of purest sapphire. "These wrist plates were made by an Ancient magic of our kind. They are thought to be indestructible." He looked down at the teens' wrists and realized that all the teens, except Rachel, already had wrist plates on. He grinned. "I hope you don't mind trading with me." Becca, Jake, Mike, Toni, and Josh all smiled as they snapped off the plates on their right wrists and let them fall to the ground.

As the first sapphire plate floated down onto his palm, King Swenteon took hold of Mike's wrist with his other hand. "The Guardian of Earth!" he declared, snapping the sapphire plate firmly onto Mike's wrist. As he did this—a black symbol began to engrave into the plate. One by one, he put the plates on the teens' right wrists until he finally got to Toni. "Guardian of Water and Ice, the true Savior of Atlantis!" The roar of the crowd was so tremendous, that Toni's cheeks went red and her eyes filled with tears when King Swenteon snapped on her sapphire wrist plate. When the teens bowed politely to the kings, the cheering echoed so loudly through the room, that it made the room shake.

King Midras gasped. "Sages, do not bow to us! We are the ones who should be bowing to you—for you have saved our Kingdoms." He looked at King Swenteon and they both bowed to the teens.

Whisper appeared from between the thrones and walked with great dignity over to the teens—mature enough to know her position among royalty. The Fairies accompanied her and landed on the teens' shoulders. Whisper waved her hand wide over the teens, sending out a blue sparkling mist from her fingers that settled on them like glitter then vanished. It felt cool and made the teens shiver. "When this Magic is sprinkled over you, it will give you Luck and let Peace surround you. I wish for you to find both on your noble quest and as you make your journey toward—as the Ancient Aquarius once told me—your Destiny."

Whisper closed her eyes and cupped her palms together in front of her. As she raised her glowing hands up toward the ceiling, a pulsing, glittering ball of light rose up out of her palms and floated up through the bubble overhead. It ascended up through the water—higher and higher above the ocean until it whirled apart to spread all across the brilliant blue sky. Whisper lowered her hands, breathing deeply, but smiling. "That one takes a lot of strength out of me," she said softly so only the teens could hear.

The audience was silent then rose to their feet applauding wildly. King Midras raised one hand in dismissal to the crowd then turned to take Whisper by the hand. They lead King Swenteon and the others back between the thrones, the crowd chanting and singing behind them.

They passed into a small room, but well-appointed room and a guard closed the door behind them. Whisper turned to face the teens, extending an open hand to Misty, who flew off Toni's shoulder. She raised Misty to her cheek and kissed her. "It was good seeing you again Misty. When you get the chance—when the world isn't in peril…"

Misty smiled brightly, a tear rolling down her face. "Of course, my dear friend. I will always visit." She flew off Misty's palm and landed back on Toni's shoulder.

"Thank you," said Toni, "for showing us a world far beyond our wildest imaginations—and thank you, most of all, for being our friend."

Whisper's eyes became damp, and she began to tremble. "Of course. It was my pleasure to meet you all." She wiped her eyes with one scaly hand, bracelets jingling merrily. Another loud cheer was heard from the throne room. "The celebration will go on for days. It is a shame you are not staying to enjoy it." Turning toward an archway at the other side of the room, she said, "the light will take you back to where you need to be." She stepped back and bowed.

The teens stood there in silence for several moments, and then they all hugged Whisper, shook hands with the Kings, and went out through the archway. At the bottom of a short flight of stairs were four brilliant circles of light. Before the light took them back up, they bid another farewell to the creatures they had never dreamed of meeting. They skyrocketed upwards, zooming through the water. They shot up through the waves and landed on the empty forward deck of the cruise ship, exactly where they had departed from!

"Wow! Talk about timing!" exclaimed Mike.

Rachel suddenly ran as fast as she could to the railing and vomited out in the ocean. Josh ran over to her as the others cringed in disgust. Flairen rubbed the back of her head and Josh put his arm around and her. "Are you alright?" he asked.

Rachel nodded quickly. "That last skyrocketing really got to me."

Toni walked over to Rachel and took her by the hand, leading her away from the others. "I'm going to go clean her up a bit." Several minutes later Rachel and Toni came back, Rachel looking more refreshed than ever. She smiled at the others as they all looked out to the sea.

A warm, humid breeze whipped by. They all agreed that no matter how amazing the Kingdoms Under the Sea were, and how welcome they felt, it was still good to be back on the surface breathing fresh air again. The waves were calm tonight, and the sunset made the sky a bright red.

A small kitten of fire leapt along the railing. Rachel laughed as it chased after a fireball she had created. The kitten batted the ball over the edge, where it puffed into smoke before hitting the cool liquid far below. Sleek, blue creatures began to emerge from the waves, jumping in and out of the wake created by the ship's bow cutting through the water. Becca, Jake, Toni, and Mike had admired the dolphins ever since their encounter with their mutant friend, Crystal. Seeing the dolphins again reminded them of her.

"I hope she's doing okay." Becca's eyes were only half-open as she gazed at the dolphins, mesmerized.

"Crystal?" asked Jake, although he knew the answer to his question already. Becca nodded. "I wouldn't worry about her. She has a good heart—and strong hope. She's made it far in her life without much support—so why wouldn't that still be true?"

Josh's eyes began to glow a bright green. The dolphins whined and happily hummed a high-pitched tune back at him.

Toni looked at Josh and smiled. "What did you tell them?"

Josh sighed as his eyes went back to normal. "I simply let Peace enter their minds, letting them know that we think they are such beautiful creatures."

"So you gave them a gift of Peaceful Knowledge," sighed Rachel, putting her arm around her twin brother.

"Precisely," he replied. The glow of the setting sun tinged everything around them pink as the sun sunk beyond the horizon. Darkness settled in, and the stars were eventually revealed. Mike yawned deeply.

"Young Quake, you are getting tired already? You just slept for a week!" muttered Granite. "But, it *has* been an exhausting few hours."

"Are we sleeping out here again?" asked Jake, turning his head toward Thor.

Thor grunted. "Well, I have to admit—it is nice out." He raised his head and gazed up at the stars. "The stars are all different from each other. Did you know that the stars are in a different position every second of every day? So, whenever someone is born, the stars are different each time around, giving everyone their own individual Destiny. You may see them as being still—but the Great Ones look beyond that. The stars are all powerful and full of life. They represent the great gods and warriors that have fought battles to spread Knowledge. Whenever you are lost—the stars will always show you the way. In time, you will learn to read them. It will be one of the most important things you will ever learn."

They were all silent, thinking about what Thor had said. "When I see stars, I picture what's beyond them—what new adventures and new things are waiting to be discovered just beyond them," whispered Jake.

"Someday," said Thor, now staring at Jake from the foot of his lounge chair, "I promise you, I will take you beyond the stars."

Becca made their sleeping bags appear and the teens laid in them, still looking pensively up at the stars. They were picturing what mysteries could lie beyond them, but also about Thor's beliefs about Destiny. They knew that part of his religion was believing, without question, everything the stars told him. The teens had their own kind of religion, but spiritual ways could always be added to it, making it a more wonderful and adventurous sort of belief.

The sound of the waves echoed all around. The breeze grew stronger, and the waves sent mist in the air, making the teens feel relaxed and comfortable. Their eyelids began to twitter as their Spirits carried them away into fascinating dreams.

Chapter 19—Unique and Powerful Birds

Immensely loud screeching rudely awoke the teens. They got up, looking frantically around, trying to find out where the sound came from. The Fairies were huddled together on the railing, searching the sky.

"What was that?" Josh asked, still shaken.

Merlin laughed. "That, my boy, is the ticket to your next destination." The teens looked above them and their jaws dropped. Soaring gracefully above the ship, was a gigantic bird the size of a city bus. Its rainbow-colored tail feathers fluttered behind it in the wind like a tail of a kite, at least twenty feet in length. It had a blue-feathered body the color of the sky and its yellow eyes were as bright and shiny as the sun. Its lethal talons bobbed and swayed with every majestic flap of the forty-foot wingspan. The teens gasped. What more amazing creatures were in store for them? They had never seen a bird more beautiful!

"What is it, Josh?" asked Becca, eyes wider than ever.

Josh was silent for several seconds. "It's a very rare mythical bird known as a 'Rainbonian', for its rainbow ribbon tail feathers. They're known as the 'Bird of Wind'."

"Awww...very good Myth!" laughed Merlin proudly.

"Why—why is it here?" Rachel took a few steps back—she looked afraid.

"Well, it's waiting for us!" said Flairen, brightly. "Don't be afraid—it's a bird of Peace."

"Waiting for us to do what?" Toni asked, now focused on Flairen, confused.

"That bird came from the Kingdom in the Sky where we are heading," said Granite. "The Kingdom is known as 'Skytania'. The Skytanians worship this bird—it's part of their religion. The Rainbonian was probably journeying back to its home and sensed that we were heading to the Kingdom. It's offering us a ride."

"And how, exactly, is it supposed to give us a ride?" Mike asked nervously.

"Well," said Granite, "not only do the Skytanians worship the Rainbonians, but also the Seven Sages, since the Rainbonian's tail feathers match the color of each Sage. So, as for you, young Quake, grab the yellow ribbon tail feather."

The Rainbonian seemed to understand Granite because it lowered itself closer to the deck where the teens were standing. The tail feathers now touched the deck, whipping wildly all around in the wind. Granite flew over to Mike and grabbed tightly to his shoulder. Mike made a snatching grab for the yellow tail feather—it was pure luck that he caught it on the first try. He looked over at the others, waiting patiently for them. He clutched the feather tightly, not letting the wind take it from his grip.

"What about all our stuff?" asked Becca concerned. "Are we going to be coming back like last time?"

"Yes," said Juhani, getting a tight grip on Becca's shoulder. "We'll come back to this ship."

Becca waved her hand and the purple tail feather soared right to her. She grasped it tightly and watched as the others ran around the deck trying to grab theirs. Jake and Rachel were also able to snatch their ribbon tail feathers without any misfortunes, while Josh and Toni had a little more difficulty. Unfortunately, the green feather whipped Josh in the face—but he managed to seize it quickly. Toni also had a bit of a misfortune: as she took a running leap at the blue feather lashing overhead, she tripped and fell flat on her stomach, but miraculously managed to land on the feather and hold it tightly in both hands.

The Rainbonian called out to the sky with another loud screech, looking down to make sure that they were all in place. The teens glanced around and realized that an extra tail feather was still flapping in the wind: a black one.

Jake thought about it for several seconds and then shook his head, hearing another loud screech from the Rainbonian. "Hold on guys!" warned Jake. "I have a strong feeling that this is going to be another wild ride!" The teens closed their eyes, waiting for the take off. With a sudden gust of cool wind from the enormous blue wings, the teens were swept off their feet. They were being pulled quickly, and yet, gracefully, through the air. It was difficult holding on, but it was an experience like no other. They were pulled through the clouds into the wind. The ship was falling quickly out of sight as they began to gain more and more speed and altitude.

Mike and Rachel were having a blast. They were laughing hard and swinging back and forth on the feathers, ramming into each other like kids on playground swings. Granite and Flairen, however, were screaming in fright, trying desperately to hold on.

"Come on you guys, cut it out!" yelled Becca. "You're giving Granite and Flairen heart attacks!" Mike and Rachel continued laughing but stopped swinging. Suddenly, the Rainbonian made an angle upwards. The teens snapped at the ends of their feathers like bungee jumpers as a huge whiff of heat rammed past their feet. They looked down and realized that it was a giant ball of fire! The teens heard an ear-blasting shriek echoing in the distance. They gazed ahead of them and saw, to their horror, a giant Phoenix. It had blood-red feathers and dark yellow eyes, and its wings and tail were trailing a blaze of fire.

"Oh no!" yelled Merlin, frightened. "It can't be!"

"Why are you so scared of it?" asked Rachel, now concerned. "It's only a Phoenix."

"That's the Birandian Phoenix..." Merlin paused, listening to the birds exchanging shrieks, hisses, and assorted screeches.

"What is it?" asked Toni impatiently.

Merlin looked at the others. "The Kingdoms in the Sky—there are three—but two of them are at war...the Skytanian Kingdom and the Birandian Kingdom—the precise ones that we have to travel to!"

"That's just great!" yelled Mike. "Perfect time to visit...WHEN THEY'RE AT WAR!"

"Should we abandon the Rainbonian then?" asked Josh, looking below him. "I do prefer flying on my own."

"No!" snapped Merlin. "We have a better chance of not getting hurt if we stay on the Rainbonian!" The teens exchanged worried looks.

The Rainbonian stopped suddenly in midair and gazed at the Birandian Phoenix. It was about one hundred meters away, also hovering in place.

"What's going to happen, Merlin?" Josh asked, looking worriedly at Merlin.

"Never does the Rainbonian attack when innocents can be hurt." Merlin was speaking very calmly as though he was also curious about what was going to happen next. "It will only attack to defend itself and get us to safety. These are very intelligent and caring birds."

The Phoenix shot another fireball from its wide-opened beak. However, the Rainbonian didn't move.

"Move, you damn bird!" yelled Mike, nervously. But the Rainbonian didn't budge. The fireball was fast approaching until the Rainbonian opened its mouth and shot a ball of wind right back at the Phoenix. It hit the fireball causing a loud, cracking explosion. The force blew the teens back, but they managed to hold on tightly. The air got cooler, and the sky, darker. It began to thunder, and then rain. The wind picked up, and the Rainbonian flapped its wings harder.

"What are you doing, Jake?" yelled Toni, through the powerful wind.

"It isn't me!" Jake yelled, looking at the Rainbonian. "I think it's the bird—look at its eyes!"

The teens gazed up at the Rainbonian's eyes. Its eyes were no longer yellow, but a glowing, ghostly gray. It screeched louder than ever, forcing the teens to squint their eyes, since they had no way to cover their ears. The winds grew even stronger until a mass began to emerge from beneath the gray thunderclouds above. A tornado was forming! The tail feathers of the Rainbonian were blowing violently, sending the teens flying in every direction. They held on with all of their might. The tornado made its way toward the Phoenix.

The Phoenix's whole body was engulfed in flames as it vanished with a wisp of smoke. The tornado died away, and the wind returned to normal. The sun appeared, and the gray clouds evaporated. The

Rainbonian screeched loudly again as it continued its ascent into the sky. The teens were still in shock at what had just happened. They couldn't believe it! How could a mere bird, though a giant one, have so much Power—almost as much as Jake?

They glanced up ahead of them in the distance at three dark objects, floating far apart from each other. The Rainbonian made another loud screech as it sped up toward the first of the black objects. As they got closer, the teens could easily see that it was one of three very large Kingdoms floating in the sky! The middle Kingdom floated much higher than the other two, apparently held up by the thick layer of clouds below it. As the Rainbonian carried the teens yet closer, they could see that the other two Kingdoms were supported by thousands of slowly spinning propellers underneath their rocky, domed bottoms.

Each of the Kingdoms seemed to have a different sort of environment. The teens could see that the closest one had many open fields of grasses and flowers, as well as numerous gardens and fountains. There were many buildings of gold, white and red surrounding a palace of red and white. A fantastically tall tower stood in the very center of the Kingdom. It stretched so far up into the clouds that the top was not visible.

Forests of pine trees, similar to the ones on Earth, covered the snow-peaked mountains of the middle Kingdom. A castle of dark green and white was visible surrounded by many outbuildings and gardens.

The last Kingdom was still a long distance away. It seemed to have a rocky surface and a large volcano rising from the center. It was still extremely beautiful, as the buildings were made from pure white stone, and the magnificent castle was by far the largest of all the other Kingdoms.

The teens were amazed to see that a wide stone bridge led from the Kingdom with the tower to the mountainous green Kingdom. There was also a stone bridge arching upward from the Kingdom with the volcano to the green Kingdom. Strangely—there was no connection between the volcano Kingdom to the Kingdom with the tall tower.

Thor broke the silence to explain. "The Kingdom with the large tower is Skytania—home of the Skytanians."

"And the Kingdom with the volcano," said Flairen, "is the Birandian Kingdom—home of the Birandians."

"And the Kingdom above the other two," smiled Merlin, "is the Emerald Kingdom—home of the Moniques."

"This is the surprise!" yelled Juhani excitedly. "Many Mythical beings come to the Emerald Kingdom to either watch or enter the Race of Flying Creatures."

"A race?" asked Josh, highly interested.

"Oh, yes," Merlin beamed. "It is highly dangerous and many Beings compete—using any means necessary to win."

"Wow," laughed Becca. "They must be really *obsessed* with winning."

"Except no one has," Thor sighed.

"What do you mean no one has won?" asked Toni confused. "I thought that it was a popular race?"

"Oh, it is a popular race," said Misty, "but no one has ever finished it. The race is only held every decade, and because the course is so complex and difficult, no one has ever completed it."

"Will we get to see it?" asked Josh. "I mean every ten years—this is the first one in our lifetime."

"We'll see," smiled Merlin, indulgently. "If we have time." Josh nodded and began daydreaming about what kinds of objectives could be thrown at the contestants to make the race so impossibly tough? It was something he had to find out.

Chapter 20—The Skytanian Kingdom

The Rainbonian circled once above the Kingdom of Skytania before descending toward a field full of many different kinds of wildflowers. The Rainbonian landed gracefully while the teens crashed and tumbled, the scents and colors of the flowers blurring.

A girl with long red hair was watering some flowering hedges along the edge of the meadow with a large silver watering can. The girl eyed the teens warily with her large blue eyes, and then watched the Rainbonian take off and soar up into the sky and vanish. She wore a knee-length purple dress with many layers of ruffles under it. She looked as if she were someone rather important. She walked over to the teens and smiled brightly. The teens untangled themselves and stood up, brushing dirt off their clothes. "Hello, and welcome to Skytania. I am surprised the leader of the Rainbonians picked you up. There must have been a very important reason."

Jake stepped forward and smiled at the beautiful young girl. She looked no older than any of the teens. "We're here to—"

"Explore, and see the race!" Josh cut in, making sure he didn't reveal anything.

"Ahhh…" she sighed. "I should have known. It is still curious that the Rainbonian chose to bring you here—but still, I am honored that it chose you. I will happily give you a tour of my Kingdom, if you are interested."

"Your Kingdom?" asked Becca. "But how old are you?"

The girl smiled. "I am sixteen years of age—my name is Simone, Queen of Skytania."

"It's an *honor* to meet *you,*" smiled Mike.

"Thank you. Please follow me. I have just finished my watering and hope you will join me for tea." She began to lead them across the field of flowers toward a city in the distance. It was a beautiful day. A breeze was gently blowing, carrying leaves and flower petals along with it. Some kind of colorful birds, like swallows or doves chattered around them. The sun was shining a brilliant gold and there wasn't a single cloud in the sky to mar the fabulous expanse of blue.

Becca caught up with Simone and walked beside her. She took in the calm and beauty of the scenery. "I understand that you are at war?" asked Becca, curiously.

"Yes, sadly, that is true," replied the Queen. " I am not one for war, but I *will* defend my Kingdom when necessary."

"Do you mind telling us the cause?"

Simone sighed. "The Birandian Kingdom has been sending fire attacks at us. We do not know why. We cannot talk to them because they have destroyed the bridge between our Kingdoms. They are the ones who started the war without provocation."

"Why would they just attack you?" asked Josh, confused. "It doesn't make any sense. They have to have had a reason for doing so." They were now walking along on a yellow dirt road that meandered its way through several more meadows and over a wooden bridge. The brook sparkled and foamed as it tumbled over the rocky stream, and dragonflies lazily buzzed and dipped among the cattails on the bank.

"We do not know why they would just attack us," said Simone. "Our two Kingdoms have always gotten along until just recently. The Phoenixes and Rainbonians have also been acting strange and are even attacking each other. It is not their normal behavior, and my people think it is an omen that something bad is going to happen. Many are scared—I fear for the worst."

"Will the Emerald Kingdom help you?" asked Jake, gesturing toward the green Kingdom. They were now all walking along a white gravel pathway that led through what looked like a park, as there were now some small trees nestled among the carefully tended flowerbeds.

"In the written Legend, it says the Chosen Ones will aid our Kingdom and bring Peace to the Sky."

"Legend says that?" asked Jake.

Simone stopped in her tracks. "It is true! The Ancients of Skytania read the future and they are always right. Just because it hasn't happened yet..."

"Well, we believe you. And it does look like your Ancients were right, too." Jake smiled at Simone.

"What are you talking about?" she asked with sudden curiosity.

"We are the Chosens." Becca smiled.

Simone laughed. "You are much too young to be the Chosens." Her eyebrows slowly lowered and her blue eyes flashing in the sunlight. "How *dare* you try to impersonate someone you are not—how *dare* you try to manipulate me!" The teens were taken aback. Jake looked at the others as he began to glow. The others did the same, and the Fairies, who up until now had stayed invisible, lit up like mini suns before showing themselves.

Simone stepped back. "How did you...no it can't be!...the Fairies—is it really?" She looked more closely at the Fairies. "You *are* the Royals... The Ancient Protectors."

"We'll do our best to stop the war and solve the mystery behind it," said Toni, smiling confidently.

Simone smiled even brighter. "I am sorry about the way I acted. I had no—"

"It is alright!" said Thor, cheerfully. "No harm is done."

"Very well, then!" Her body was still tense and anxious, and her voice was a little shaky. "Please, come to my Palace immediately."

The path now passed by many normal-looking, Earth-like, homes along the shores of a large lake. They soon arrived at a long stone bridge that crossed over a series of ponds leading to the entrance to a palace of the same simple white blocks of stone. The ponds were home to at least fifty spectacular black and white swans that cruised gracefully along on the crystal clear water.

For being so simply constructed, the Palace of Skytania was astoundingly beautiful. The pathway changed to cobbles of white stone as it ran between rows of white columns intricately carved with flowers, vines, and birds. The cobbles gave way to a wide staircase of polished white marble with a silver railing running up either side. The posts that supported the railings were carved into Rainbonians with jeweled eyes. The second level of the Palace was ringed with more columns with white fabric stretching between them overhead. These covered terraces looked out over the ponds and fields of flowers. Many people were seated at small tables under the awnings enjoying the breathtaking view. After passing under three colonnades, also of white stone, the group arrived at a set of narrow silver doors.

The doors opened for Simone from the inside, and she lead the teens through a courtyard containing beds of stunning wildflowers and white marble statues laid out in precise geometric patterns. A muffled screech from above drew their attention upward where they saw many Rainbonians resting on clouds that hovered in thick staggered layers over the palace. The silver-white tower rose up from somewhere ahead to soar up above the Rainbonians.

The teens quietly followed Simone through another set of doors, and finally ended up in a red-carpeted room with red velvet wallpaper. Several overstuffed sofas covered in white linen were arranged around a low polished wood coffee table in front of a fireplace. Tasseled cushions in different patterns of plum and white were arranged along the backs of each sofa. The walls were hung with numerous paintings of all different sizes and styles, each in an ornate gilt frame. A little plaque under each one listed the title and gave a brief description. Most of the paintings seemed to contain either Mythical creatures, some old-fashioned looking people in funny hats, or groups of exquisite angels.

"Wait here," said Simone. "I will get us some tea." She left the room through yet another set of doors. While she was gone, the teens walked around the room looking at the artworks.

"This one says that it's of the Ancient Sages!" exclaimed Rachel, looking up at the artwork hanging over the white marble mantel. They others gathered excitedly around to examine the painting. It showed seven rather ordinary-looking people being given something by a group of glowing Fairies.

Simone entered the room again holding a round silver tray with porcelain cups on saucers. The teens sat down on the couches in front of the fireplace, while the Fairies flew down to stand on the wooden table in front of them. A butler with long black hair wearing a black suit held the silver tray while Simone filled the cups then passed them to the teens. There were even small porcelain cups of tea for the Fairies. They were a bit surprised, and thankfully accepted the tea. After placing the silver tray on the table, the butler then grabbed a very large cushioned chair that looked impossible to carry from the other side of the room. He brought it over to Simone and after brushing it off and fluffing the pillows, gestured for her to take a seat. He bowed to her when she sat down, and she thanked him quietly. She looked at the expressions on the teens' faces.

"Oh!" she laughed. "This is Raymond and he's an Earth Elf. Earth Elves have enormous strength," she paused in thought. "Then again I think all Elves have enormous strength," she sighed as Raymond nodded wordlessly and went to stand beside the door. The teens smiled as they carefully sipped steaming tea. "My Kingdom would be most thankful for your help. It would be a miracle if you could figure out what has been happening here and help us find a Peaceful solution."

"We'll do all that we can," said Jake. "But you mentioned that strange things were happening. Could you be more specific?"

Simone put her cup of tea down on the table where the Fairies were resting. "Yes, of course. The King of the Emerald Kingdom has been going off by himself for the past few weeks. I do not know if it's because he is planning for the race tomorrow...or if it is something else. As I said before, the Birds are acting strangely also—something is definitely wrong."

"What do you want us to do?" asked Toni.

"I would like you to secretly investigate the Birandian Kingdom, the Emerald Kingdom, and my kingdom. Find out as much information as you can about anything mysterious. You will have to split up if you wish to cover all the Kingdoms. You must try to find out what is wrong with the Emerald King and discover why he is not acting—*himself.* Unfortunately, the only way you can get close to him is if you are a contestant in the race."

Josh's face suddenly lit up with excitement. "I'll enter! I have just the kind of skills necessary. Who better than someone who understands the ins and outs of Mythical creatures?"

"Very well," said Simone. "It is a good way to get close to the King. Very quickly, I want you to know that I know the true reason why you are here: You want the Crystals."

"How did you know?" asked Becca, although she wasn't surprised.

"The written Legend," Simone beamed. "It states that your reward shall be the Crystals. But the thing is, the Crystals are our only source of Power and Protection. Once removed, only the Sages can replace them with a Power great enough to protect us once again." Simone closed her eyes and sighed. "We are at war—we need the Power or we will surely be defeated."

"But the Birandian Kingdom also has a Crystal. That's its only source of Power as well!" said Rachel. "I need to retrieve that Crystal, but maybe if…"

"Yes," said Simone, her eyes widening. "Perhaps you could take both Crystals and have both Kingdoms powerless—so we are both equally weak. Perhaps that would slow the war down!"

"And in the mean time," said Josh, "Toni and I will go to the Emerald Kingdom, and I'll enter the race. Something tells me the King must have some idea what is going on."

"Becca has agreed to go with me to retrieve my Crystal," said Jake. "So, that leaves Mike and Rachel to go to the Birandian Kingdom. They can retrieve the Crystal and investigate at the same time."

"I must warn you," Simone stood up, eyeing Becca and Jake. "The Crystal is located at the top of the Tower of the Ancients, and there is a great Guardian protecting it. The Ancient Sage created the Guardian so that no Being could take our Power—it is unstoppable. However, it is written that only true Sages will be able to defeat it and retrieve the Crystal."

"Don't worry. We'll retrieve it and protect the Kingdoms," said Jake stoutly.

Flairen flew into the air, her body glowing brightly. "I am sure there is also a Guardian in the volcano," she said worriedly.

"We'll be fine," said Rachel, smiling at Mike. "We'll come back here as soon as we can to let you know what we've found out. We'll discover the reason for this war."

"Very well," said Simone. "But I must also warn *you*. The Birandian Kingdom is lead by a General rather than a king or queen. The General's name is Bulkest. Be careful around him—he has a wrath stronger than a bull and a temper to match."

The teens stood up and put down their teacups. The Fairies floated to their shoulders. "Rest here for the night—in the palace. The race doesn't start until tomorrow afternoon. You can leave in the morning. I have to leave now and meet with my council. The guest rooms are just along the hall." She pushed aside a white lace curtain and looked out one of the windows. "It is still early. You are free to explore the Palace and my Kingdom—but if you leave the Palace, please be sure to return before dark. The guards know who you are, so there shouldn't be any problems. My butler, Raymond, will show you to your rooms now and will assist you in any way he can."

"Thank you," said Toni gratefully.

Simone smiled and walked out.

Raymond approached the teens. "Your rooms are through those doors," he said pointing to the other end of the room. Shall I lead the way?"

"No, thank you," said Mike. "I think we want to explore the Kingdom for awhile."

The butler nodded again and said, "the marketplace is very interesting and is quite near. Let me know if you need anything." He turned and left the room.

"It doesn't make any sense that Simone doesn't know why her Kingdom is at war. And it doesn't make sense that the Emerald Kingdom isn't a part of it, since they are still communicating with both the Skytanians and the Birandians." Josh shook his head.

"I want to find out more about this Kingdom in the Sky," said Becca, a smile lighting up her face. "Let's go!"

The teens left the Palace and went to visit the central marketplace of the city as Raymond suggested. It was a tad crowded, but that was probably because of the upcoming race. It was clean—no pollution—no litter—and the people were very friendly. The teens saw some odd-looking creatures that they didn't recognize, but Josh was happy to tell them what kind of Mythical Beings they were. They stopped at a food market and tried some of the local specialties, though only the Fairies thought it was delicious.

They explored many shops selling armor and very unusual home utensils. In the center of the marketplace was a large memorial fountain. It was carved all of white stone with flecks of silver and was uncommonly beautiful. There were seven large statues of Angels—they were probably the Ancients. Water floated in the air above them, rather than at a pool at their feet, though some of it fell back to earth and ran down into a drain in the pavement. It was very magical, indeed. The teens continued walking through the city until they passed through to the other side and ended up in a flat, empty, field of magnificently lush green grass. The teens laid down on its cushy surface and gazed up into the clouds, where the Rainbonians hopped and played.

They made sure they were back to the Palace before dark, and the guards let them pass without difficulty. Raymond, surprisingly, met them just inside the door and happily showed them to their rooms. The guys slept in one room and the ladies another—their Fairies with them. The room fell dark quickly—and the wind began to whisper and howl outside, carrying the scent of grass and flowers in through the open windows. They were all quite comfortable, but their minds were filled with what was going to happen the next day.

Chapter 21— Split and Investigate

The teens awoke to bright sunshine and bird song. They got up instantly and met in the room with the paintings where breakfast was laid out on the coffee table. After a quick bite, Becca suggested, "Let's get going. We've got a lot to do today." They made their way down to the courtyard doors without any difficulty. "If any of you need to contact me for something important, call my name in your mind. I'll be able to sense it. But only contact me if you absolutely need to. It takes strength from me when we're far away from each other." The others nodded and they exited the palace into the statue garden. They all breathed in the sweet scent of flowers and fresh air that were still damp and cool from the night. Gardeners moved about busily pulling weeds, watering, and cutting bouquets.

"We will meet here when we are done," said Thor. "Don't forget to check thoroughly around the Kingdoms and make sure you question as many people as you can without drawing too much attention to yourselves. We need any information that can help solve the puzzle of this *weird* war."

Becca and Jake watched as the rest of the group crossed the stone bridge over the many ponds where workers were sweeping the paths and feeding the swans. When they had left the Palace grounds and reached the open fields, Mike and Rachel were off in the air to the Birandian Kingdom—Josh and Toni to the Emerald Kingdom. Jake gazed at

Becca as she began walking along the path to the tower, glistening signs pointing the way.

"I guess we're not going to go ask questions first?" asked Jake, staring at Becca, wondering why she wasn't heading back to the main part of town surrounding the marketplace.

Juhani chuckled. "Star has her ways."

Becca shook her head. "I am almost positive that we'll gain no information there. Queen Simone is telling the truth. I entered her mind. I know I shouldn't have without asking permission, but I had to. It's up to the others to solve the case. All we can do is successfully retrieve the Crystal from the top of the tower."

"You did what you needed to," Juhani smiled. "When you enter one's mind only for the purpose of gaining Knowledge that will help you and hurt no one else, then it is okay. Do not pressure yourself, Star." Becca nodded as she continued along the path that began to incline up a steep hill covered with an immaculate green lawn whose surface was studded with white star-shaped flowers.

Jake's eyes dashed along the tower and followed it as high as he could. Looking at it made him feel as though he were about to fall over backwards. "We have to go to the top of that?" he looked at Becca with concern.

Thor laughed. "It will be good exercise for you, Cyclone. It is good training for your skills."

Jake turned his head and leered at Thor. "Good *training*?"

Thor smiled. "You still have much to learn, young one."

Jake's eyes widened. "Can't we just fly up?"

"We can, but I would feel more comfortable climbing it. Remember what Simone said about the Guardian," Becca assured. "This way we look like any other tourist visiting the sights of Skytania."

"Let's just fly!" Jake flew swiftly, making his way to the base of the tower. Becca was on his tail as they ascended straight up, perfectly parallel to the tower. Several minutes later, clouds began to whip past them, yet the top of the tower was still nowhere in sight. They sped up and continued flying for several more minutes until they saw a wall of gray storm clouds and flashing bolts of lightning gathered around what seemed, at last, to be the very tip of the tower. The wind had gotten harsher and the cold pierced their skin. The Fairies had to grip even tighter to the teens' shoulders to keep from being blown away.

"It's horrible up here!" Becca shouted. "You know, I believe the inside of the tower would have been safer!"

"Well let's see how far we can get. If it doesn't work out, we'll head back down!" yelled Juhani.

The wind grew stronger and the teens fought harder to move through the frigid air. They carefully approached the massive storm. They got ready to enter it, but suddenly hit a white barrier, and they ricocheted off about ten feet. A purple lightning bolt struck at them, but Juhani saw it coming. She quickly threw her arms up, creating a purple force-field barrier to protect herself and the others.

"Thanks!" Jake yelled, relieved. "I think maybe we should have taken the stairs!"

Becca began to yell in annoyance. "That's what I said in the first place!" She dove down quickly, Jake on her tail, laughing, narrowly missed by another bolt of lightning.

* * * * * * * *

Rachel and Mike were in the air, making their way to the Birandian Kingdom. "Why is it taking so long to get there?" Rachel glanced ahead of her at the Kingdom. "I mean, I can see it perfectly."

"Relax!" Mike laughed, hovering on his giant green leaf right beside her. His hair was blowing madly behind him.

Flairen chuckled. "He is right. We haven't been flying that long, and the Kingdoms are a great distance from each other."

Rachel raised her eyebrows and rolled her eyes. "Why should we even interfere in this whole war thing?"

"Because it is the right thing to do, and it is part of your Purpose for being." Flairen beamed at Rachel.

"Well, once I get this Crystal—" A red glow appeared on Rachel's back as she unsheathed her spear and swung it violently around behind her. It made a loud clash as it met the sword of one of the many bird-like humans that were suddenly flying behind them. There were about twenty of them, and they had feathered wings extending from their backs that ended in normal human hands. Their arms and legs were bare and muscular, but they had feathers for hair and beaks for mouths, and some even had facial hair. Their fingers and toes had large talons, and long tail feathers were sticking out from beneath their heavy armor.

"Those are obviously the Birandian Kingdom's soldiers," yelled Mike. The weird bird creatures looked angry. Their eyes were squinted and their feathery eyebrows lowered.

"What do you think you're doing?" yelled Rachel angrily at the bird who had swung a sword at her. He was bulky, but more fit than the others. His face looked stronger and healthier than the rest—he was obviously the leader of the group.

"You are not welcome in our Kingdom!" the Birandian yelled. His voice was deep and raging.

Granite flew off Mike's shoulder and hovered in front of the Birandian. "We have just come to seek information—"

"So, you admit you are spies for the Skytanian Kingdom!" he yelled, fuming.

"No!" protested Mike. "We are just—"

"Attack! Death to the spies!" yelled the Birandian leader. The rest of the soldiers hurled themselves forward at Mike and Rachel, swords striking at their hearts. Rachel's eyes glowed with fire. With one strong wave of her arm, a burst of burning red-hot liquid flame shot out, causing an explosion that hit the Birandians. The leader and the rest of the soldiers were pushed back by the force, screaming in pain and terror.

"We don't wish to fight you!" warned Rachel. "But we will defend ourselves by any means necessary."

The Birandian bird leader glared at them. "You are one with strong Power. Your Power is great—but Evil! We are vowed to protect our Kingdom from intruders like you!" The Birandian birds raised their swords and red beams of light shot from them.

"You don't understand!" yelled Flairen, with annoyance in her voice. "We are here to find information about how this war started. We mean you no harm!"

The Birandians simply ignored her. Loud screeching echoed through the air from below, as a burst of fire erupted from the volcano. Five large black shadows flew out from inside of it, rapidly gaining altitude. Everyone paused to watch for several moments. The Birandians backed off some, but still didn't seem like they were going to allow Mike and Rachel to enter the Kingdom.

The two teens looked warily at the volcano, eyebrows raised—curious, yet still thinking how to get through to the Birandians.

"They don't get it!" said Rachel, through gritted teeth.

"We'll make them get it!" Granite replied.

"How?" Mike was staring at the dark objects through squinted eyes, trying to figure what they were.

"First, fight them off, and then enter the Kingdom. They will see that we mean them no harm." Granite flew to Mike's shoulder.

Mike looked over at his shoulder where the Fairy stood with crossed arms. "Whatever you say, Granite."

* * * * * * * *

"The Kingdom is fantastic!" yelled Toni, excitedly staring at the magnificent towering buildings of the Emerald Kingdom. They had easily entered the Kingdom and had been warmly welcomed by many Beings of all kinds.

"It is certainly as magnificent as it was many years ago when I last visited," said Misty brightly. She turned her head toward Merlin who was resting on Josh's shoulder. "Wouldn't you agree, Merlin?"

"Actually..." replied Merlin. "I have to disagree with you—it is far more amazing than before."

The Emerald Kingdom glimmered in the sunlight, sending rays and sparkles of green everywhere. The streets were crowded with many Beings who were talking excitedly about the upcoming race. It was obviously the topic on everyone's minds.

"It's going to be amazing!" said one creature with a leopard's lithe spotted body. "I've come to every one for the past one hundred and twenty years! I bought my ticket over a year ago. I can't wait to watch it!" The teens smiled at his enthusiasm.

"There's the palace!" Josh exclaimed, pointing ahead of him at a large building built of slabs of dark jade green polished stone. Clouds of white doves circled the many towers of different heights along its outer wall. Fountains of white marble reflected the green light in their splashing waters. Just to the right of the palace gates was a small wooden booth where many Beings were standing in several long lines. "Is that where we sign up?"

"I believe so," said Merlin. "It never hurts to look." They walked on the wide gray stone pathway, glancing in shop windows along the way. Most of the people in the streets appeared to be happy and there was no talk of war. Shopkeepers often came out and greeted the teens as if they were long lost family, trying to guide them into their stores. It was hard to believe there even *was* a war going on.

"You know," said Josh, glancing at the different kinds of Beings walking by him and at all the stunning buildings. "This Kingdom is truly amazing, so why would they stand by while their two glorious neighboring Kingdoms create a war with them in the middle? I have a strange feeling it might have something to do with the race. It makes sense why they wouldn't help out in the war if it would disturb such a moneymaking tradition. A big part of the economy probably depends on it. After all, it's the biggest event of the decade."

Misty hummed in agreement. "First thing, Myth, is that we have to enter you into the race. It's the only way you'll be able to get near the King, since he takes a personal interest in all the contestants." Misty looked over at Merlin who only grunted, deep in thought. "The King should have a pretty good idea of what's going on. You have to question him carefully. From there, Aquarius and I shall have a look around to find information or anything—*suspicious*."

"Sound's like a plan," said Toni. They reached the palace. It was heavily guarded by human-like people. Josh and Toni got on the end of the left-hand line and stood patiently waiting, eavesdropping on the conversations of the other contestants and watching the crowds. After about an hour of waiting, it was finally Josh's turn. There was a human man in the booth who looked like he was enjoying himself, laughing and joking with the Beings at his window. Josh walked forward. "I would like to sign up for the race."

"Of course you do," said the man behind the counter in a low-pitched voice. "Otherwise you wouldn't be here! Very well, here are the rules." He pushed a piece of paper toward Josh as he recited them. "You must use a flying creature if you are not capable of flying yourself. You must try to complete the course without harming any of your opponents. We are not responsible for any injuries that will occur—I mean…*might,* occur." Josh's eyebrows rose. "If you do not have a flying creature of your own, speak to the Warlock in the hut bordering the Emerald Woods. He will provide you with a creature for a fee. Here is a map of the course. Follow the course as fast as you can, avoiding any injuries. There will also be challenging puzzles and objectives along the way—but the reward will be great. The King has high hopes that this will be the year that someone will finally complete the course." He put a long sheet of paper on top of the sheet of rules and held out a green pen to Josh. "Sign this contract acknowledging that you understand the rules." Without hesitating, Josh took the pen and signed his name. The man quickly took the contract and added it to an enormous pile in a box on the floor behind him. He then pulled a silver bracelet with an engraved wrist plate out from under the counter. "You need to wear this wrist plate to let the King know you are an official contestant."

The man glanced at Josh's right wrist, which already had the sapphire plate that King Swenteon had given him as a gift for saving Atlantis. "I see you already have a plate on your right wrist. Very well, put it on your left." Luckily, Josh wasn't in his costume because his left wrist would have had a gold plate on it. Josh took the gleaming silver plate and snapped it on his left wrist.

"What are the prizes?" asked Merlin in interest. Josh scowled at him. "Well, I was just curious."

The man laughed. "I'm surprised you don't know by now, since it's the biggest prize we've ever offered: one thousand gold pieces, useable in any Mythical kingdom. Plus a rare and powerful item."

"Yes?" asked Merlin curiously.

"A magical Boomerang. The King's warriors conquered the Wood Elf King and stole the Boomerang from amongst his treasures. It possesses great Power and is worth a fortune! It would make a man richer than the King!"

"Gods and Goddesses!" yelped Merlin. He quickly grabbed Josh's ear and pulled him back, forcing Josh to nearly tumble over backwards.

* * * * * * * *

"How much longer!?" yelled Jake, breathing heavily. The inside of the tower was lit with torches, and the stairway was narrow. It kept going in a circle, making the teens dizzier by the second.

Becca moaned. "I think I'm going to barf!"

Jake laughed. "Well, do it in the opposite direction of where I'm walking!"

Becca's face lit up with an idea. "Why don't we just fly up?"

Jake stared at her for several seconds as though she were crazy. "I think flying in a spiral at high speed is a very bad idea." Jake sat down a few steps above her. "Well, isn't there anything *you* can do?"

Becca rested her head on the wall, thinking. "Well, there is one thing, but I'm not sure it will work."

Jake stood up suddenly. "Try it—anything that can help us."

"Make sure you know what you are doing," Juhani warned.

"Yes," said Thor. "You don't know what ancient magic this tower possesses."

"Okay," Becca stood up and shut her eyes. Her body began to glow as she raised her hands. Suddenly, the stairs folded together, making a slick, sleek slide. Becca and Jake, along with their Fairies, fell to the ground and began sliding down, rapidly gaining speed by the second.

"WHAT DID YOU DO, BECCA!!!?" yelled Jake angrily.

Becca shook her head as she tried to slow herself by trying to grip the wall, but it was no use. They were going too fast. "I tried to make the stairs into an escalator—it obviously didn't work!"

"Obviously!" yelled Jake. They slid faster and faster. Soon, they were too dizzy to try and stop themselves or get into the air.

Becca suddenly became angry also. "You said to try something that could help us!"

Jake yelled, frustrated. "I said *if* it would *help* us!"

"Calm down," said Thor patiently.

"Yes," said Juhani. "We're never going to solve anything with you guys screaming at the top of your lungs at each other."

"Well, we're never going to solve anything like this either!" yelled Jake.

Becca and Jake continued yelling at each other all the way down. Thor and Juhani, wisely, didn't get in their way. After five minutes of sliding, the teens landed roughly on the hard stone floor at the bottom. They stood up and continued yelling.

Thor and Juhani immediately leaped off their shoulders and flew high up in the center of the room. Jake and Becca stopped yelling long enough to glance around to see where they had gone. The teens were abruptly silent. Their mouths gaped and chills ran up their spines. They couldn't believe where they had ended up. A place very similar to somewhere they had been before.

* * * * * * * *

The dark figures came closer, and Mike, Rachel, Granite, and Flairen could now tell that they were Phoenixes.

"Come!" beckoned Flairen urgently. "We must hurry and make our way to the Kingdom."

Rachel and Mike looked at each other intently before dodging around the Birandian soldiers and diving steeply down toward the Kingdom. Surprisingly, the soldiers didn't chase them. Glancing behind them, the teens saw the Birandians hop on the Phoenixes and ride them as though they were domesticated. They flew as fast as they could with screeches echoing behind them. Rachel and Mike could feel the heat of the Phoenixes approaching quickly and hear the angry shouts of the Birandian soldiers.

Mike could also feel Granite's tension. He was holding on to his shoulder tighter than ever. "We are almost there!" yelled Granite. "Just a little farther!"

A loud blast, like the sound of a blowtorch, filled the air. Mike glanced over at Rachel. "LOOK OUT!!!" He threw his arms out and vines sprouted from his hands, snatching Rachel like a snake and quickly pulled her towards him. He caught Rachel in his arms as she narrowly missed being scorched by a fiery flare from one of the Phoenixes.

Rachel smiled as she looked up into Mike's blue eyes. Suddenly, a mass of Birandian soldiers came soaring up towards them from the Kingdom. The teens found themselves confronted by a wave of what seemed like at least a hundred flashing, glittering swords that were raised and pointed lethally at the teens.

"Careful you two!" Flairen warned. A fiery wind shot above them as the soldiers riding the Phoenixes soared over the teens and down into the city of Birandia. The mighty, glowing red Phoenixes turned around, prepared for anything coming at them.

"Give them a warning before you attack!" yelled Granite, the rising wind drowning his voice.

Mike stared at him shocked. "You want *us* to attack *them*?"

"You can knock them out with one strong blow if you combine forces."

Mike stopped in midair and Rachel flew up next to him. "What are we going to do?" she asked, staring ahead.

"We're going to attack them." Mike's eyes began to glow a bright yellow as his voice echoed all around. "This is your last chance! We do not wish to fight. We are the Sages of the Heavens, and we will do what we must!"

The Birandians' swords began to shine a ferocious red. Mike looked over at Rachel, whose eyes were glowing with dancing flames. "*Fine*!" he whispered in rage.

Rachel suddenly burst into flames and screamed with all her might, "*RAGE OF THE PHOENIX*!" A red fireball glowing with magma shot out of her hands. Extraordinarily, Mike burst into yellow flames himself as he unleashed a burst of Power mightier that he had ever used before. "*NATURE'S WRATH*!" A gigantic ball of yellow flame shot out from his hands, and combined with Rachel's flaming ball of magma. The massive flaming ball was about one-eighth the size of the entire city and glowed as brightly as a second sun. The Birandians sword beams merged together to form an equally large ball of energy.

"OH NO!!!" yelled Flairen, terrified. "We didn't realize the two of you could unleash that type of Power yet!"

Granite howled, "The force will certainly tear the Kingdom to shreds!"

*   *   *   *   *   *   *   *

"What is it?" asked Josh, embarrassed at what Merlin had just done. He stood up from the ground and scowled at Merlin, who was floating in front of him. Toni and Misty were next to him also eyeing Merlin warily.

"The Boomerang!" whispered Merlin harshly, while pulling Josh away from the others in line. "It's the Weapon of the Sages—the one you *need*! The Boomerang was given to the King of the Wood Elves by the Sage of Mythical Creatures to protect and guard from those who would use it for Evil!"

Misty sighed as if she knew what work was ahead of them. "If anyone gets their hands on that Boomerang and uses it..." She paused. "Who knows what could happen," she said in desperation.

Josh glared at Misty. "So, now you're saying that I *have* to win the race?"

"Yes," replied Merlin. "Or the Boomerang could fall into the hands of Evil. I am surprised that the Elf King has been destroyed. He was extremely powerful. We must consult the Warlock to find you a strong and agile beast to fly," he said thoughtfully.

Josh grinned. "Well, I can manage that!"

"*No!*" said Misty abruptly. "If you create a beast, you would have to use additional Power to think for it. In this race, you will need more than one mind, and it is too risky if someone finds out. We need to ask the Warlock." Josh nodded.

Toni beamed suddenly. "I've never met a *warlock*...for all I know anyway."

After asking directions, Toni and Josh walked the short distance to the Emerald Woods. It reminded them of back home in Flagstaff with its fragrant pine smell. They rang the bell on the plastered wall next to the door of the small thatch-roofed hut and went in when they heard a gruff "Enter!" from within.

The hut was very warm inside and filled with a pungent smell that made Josh, Toni, and the Fairies choke. A fire was burning in a wide fireplace big enough to stand up in. Kettles and cauldrons of different sizes and colors hung from hooks over the flames. Pots and pans simmered over a collection of small burners on a cluttered granite-topped workbench along the back wall. Much of the remaining wall space was taken up by shelf upon shelf of bottles of potions. Bunches of dried plants, flowers, and unidentifiable bits of who-know-what hung from the beamed ceiling. It reminded Toni of what she imagined the inside of a witch's house would look like. There were also tall stacks of books everywhere, piled in chairs and jumbled in boxes under the table.

Behind a long wooden counter was a man sitting on a high stool with long gray hair growing from the sides of his head. He was writing on a piece of parchment with a large quill pen and grunting as he wrote. He was bald on top, and had a long, pimply, sweaty nose. He was about Toni's height and wore an ink-stained rough woven shirt of some grayish material that might have once been white. He stopped briefly and tapped the end of the quill thoughtfully on the shoulder of his brown leather vest.

"Hello?" Misty called out.

The Warlock fell backwards off his stool and landed quite hard, his booted feet pedaling in the air as he tried to get up. Josh and Toni clenched their teeth as though feeling the pain. He finally got to his feet and brushed off his brown plaid trousers. He chuckled happily and quickly trotting over to the two, gleefully rubbing his hands together. He greeted them warmly, and shook their hands tightly, enfolding them in both of his big hairy-knuckled hands.

"Welcome, welcome! I am Jeeves, Warlock of the Emerald Kingdom. I can create almost anything!" Toni and Josh tried not to gag. His breath smelled as bad as the inside of the hut, and he unfortunately breathed toward Josh and Toni rather heavily in his enthusiasm. "I am assuming you need a beast to fly. If so, count yourself lucky. You are the first to come today."

"Well," said Josh, "I can actually create my—"

"Yes, we do need a beast!" said Merlin grinning, cutting off Josh and pushing him aside.

"Awww...good, good—usually contestants have their own beasts, but I can give birth to any kind and make them real, if you know what I mean." Jeeves winked at Josh.

"I have to win this race!" said Josh sternly.

Jeeves eyed him. "Everybody does, but something tells me that this will certainly be the best race in a long time. I sense your will is great. I have high hopes for you!"

"Well, thank you," said Josh gratefully, "I appreciate your kindness."

Toni walked over to the counter and pulled a stool out from under it. She sat down and said, "we need a beast that is fast moving and fast thinking. AND we need it to be something magical that can help protect him."

Jeeves stared at Toni and held up his index finger, pointing it at Toni. "You are a strong-willed young lady. I think I have a beast that meets all of your requirements—a beast that almost finished the race all on her own several races ago!" He bustled around behind the counter and started to dig through one of the boxes of books. "However, Evil destroyed it!" He slamming down a big leather-bound book on the counter. "Darkness despises that which is rare and valuable or beautiful." He started paging frantically through the book as if searching for a particular page. "Ah-ha! It will cost you a great fortune if you wish to use *this* beast."

Misty coughed. "Well, the truth is—we don't have any money."

"WHAT!?" Jeeves fell backwards off the stool again, laughing rather hard. He got up, brushing dust and several very long-dead spiders off his stained shirt. "No money?" he chuckled.

"Hang on a second!" said Toni, quickly putting her hand in her pocket. She had pulled out the fifty-dollar bill that she had received from Becca's parents at Islands of Adventure for souvenirs and food. She didn't have time to spend it because of what happened with the Goths. Josh's face lit up once he saw the bill. "Will this be okay?" asked Toni, holding out the bill toward Jeeves.

Jeeves stared at the bill, a look of disgust on his face. "I cannot spend Human money in Mythical lands!" Toni slowly let her arm down as she put the money back in her pocket. Jeeves squinted his eyes in thought, "I'll tell you what." His voice was calm. "Which do you *really* want of the prizes?"

Josh and Toni stared at their Fairies. "The—*Boomerang*," said Merlin clearly.

"Well," said Jeeves, "the other prize is one thousand gold pieces. It would make a man rich!"

"You want the gold pieces, don't you?" asked Toni smiling.

"I will give you the beast, if you give me the prize money. I am a poor man with no family or friends—a bit of money would help." Jeeves stared at Josh as though he would never accept the bargain.

"Deal," said Josh, holding out his hand. "The gold is worthless to us." Jeeves's face lit up with excitement as he shook Josh's hand. "But if we don't win?"

Jeeves let go of Josh's hand and leered at him, eye to eye. "You will, and it is a chance I'm willing to take. So, I have your word?"

"Yes," said Josh, "I promise!"

"Good!" yelled Jeeves ecstatically, clapping his hands together once. He held out his hand toward the middle of the room and a giant black cauldron appeared. He walked over to the fire and hunted among the pots until he found one of boiling water. He grabbed the pot in his bare hand and swore loudly as he ran and poured it into the cauldron in the center of the room. He quickly dropped the now empty pot.

"*It was hot,*" he whispered. "Okay, now if I remember the main ingredients—oh yes!" He held his hand up, and a bottle of silver liquid came soaring from the shelf into it. "First, a pinch of Sphinx's saliva!" He poured half of the liquid into the cauldron, making it hiss and smoke madly. Jeeves snapped his fingers and a green flame started licking out from under the pot. More potions came zooming over to him and he poured what seemed to be random amounts from each into the smoking kettle. "Serenities' Dream, a pinch of Goods, liquid salt, and a single Moon's Tear," he intoned, as a puff of pink mist rose above them in the shape of a pink rabbit with floppy ears. Jeeves looked over at the four and smiled. "You said you wanted it to hold magic. Is there a personal belonging or substance you wish to put in the cauldron?"

Josh stepped up to look in the cauldron. A cloud of misty green shamrocks formed overhead as the contents bubbled and steamed gently. Josh rubbed his palms together over the cauldron, and small green stars landed in it. Josh looked over at Toni. She walked over to him and touched his hand. A snowflake formed the size of Josh's palm and he walked over and put it into the cauldron. The liquid inside the cauldron began to swirl as it turned a greenish blue. Glittery streams of green and blue steamed out of it.

"Now," said Jeeves. "For the final two ingredients." He slowly walked over to his desk and pulled out a small, wooden polished box from a drawer. He opened it and picked up a white feather and a small silvery-white triangular cylinder made of some kind of horn or bone. He walked over to the cauldron and put in the items. He then held his hands up over the cauldron and shut his eyes. "*Mungia patronea mun sientence!*"

The cauldron began to shake and it broke in many pieces. Standing in the middle of the room among the shards was a creature far more lovely than any they had ever seen before. Its beauty lit up the room, and its breathing filled them with Peace and Serenity. It was unbelievable, and yet no one could utter a sound.

Jeeves smiled brightly, knowing he'd done an outstanding job. "I shall call him *Gladius—Unisus of Light!*"

* * * * * * * *

"It can't be!" yelled Becca, shocked.

"Oh, but it is!" said Juhani. "It's an exact replica of the inside the Temple of Destiny!"

The teens walked across the room until they reached the platform, their footsteps and voices echoing. This time, the marble tablet was inset in the floor on top of the platform instead of resting on a golden pedestal. Jake looked up and out through the stained glass windows overhead and saw huge gray storm clouds with bolts of purple lightning zigzagging from them. "We're at the top of the tower!" he exclaimed. "How can that be? How could we possibly have gone down to go up? It doesn't make any sense!"

"The tower," said Thor, "knew that Star was here because of the magic she used. It allows any of the Sages to progress to the top. Like I said—this tower is full of ancient and unusual magic!"

Jake turned and faced Becca. "Looks like I owe you an apology."

Becca laughed. "It's alright—I was just as angry at myself as you were at me!"

Thor and Juhani flew to the far end of the room toward the large silver door. It looked as though it had never been opened. Many hieroglyphics were engraved on it, and a large hole was in the middle, approximately a foot across.

"Is that the one we have to go through?" asked Jake, staring at the door.

"Yes," said Thor.

"How do we *get* through?" asked Becca, now staring at Juhani and Thor.

Juhani sighed. "We cannot tell either of you."

"And why is that?" asked Jake, not believing what he was hearing.

"You have to use your inner Knowledge," said Thor. "There will be times when you have to solve things for yourself."

Becca and Jake walked over to the doorway and traced their hands over the hieroglyphics. They examined every detail closely.

"I sense great power beyond this door..." said Becca. Her eyebrows suddenly lowered. "It's almost the same feeling I had when we were in the temple."

Jake shut his eyes. "It's as though...I feel something alive back there. Okay—I'm going to try to open it." He shot his white lightning from his hands toward the door, but it bounced off and scattered across the room. He looked at Becca, who had a glowing purple force field around her. Jake laughed. "Okay, so that didn't work. How about—*Open!*" Still nothing happened. Jake took a deep breath and blew hard on the door. The force of a tornado came out of his mouth. Becca and the Fairies went flying, but besides that, nothing happened. "*Sorry*!" he said, picking up Thor and dusting him off.

Becca rolled her eyes as she pushed herself up. She examined the door closely. "Why don't we read what it says?"

Jake went red. "That would make sense." He squinted his eyes and examined the door once more. "*In order to open the door leading to the Crystal of Wind, play the Song of Force.* I know one Song, but it's 'Fantasia on the Dargason', and that's the Song of Lightning. I don't know the Song of Wind."

"Very good," said Thor. "You are getting warmer."

Becca walked to the center of the door and put her arm through the hole. "What is this?"

Jake walked over to her and looked through the hole. "It looks as if something goes through there—that's it!—our journey went through a sequence of order. Before I came here, I obtained my Weapon—my Weapon is the key!" Jake ran over to the platform in the center of the room and stood in the middle of the fourteen carved diamonds.

"What are you doing?" asked Becca, walking over to him.

"You'll see." Jake took out his ivory bow and reached for a silver arrow. He notched it onto the string, and pulled it back. The arrow began to glow white as it grew with the static of silver lightning. The glowing silver arrow left the bow and whispered across the room through the hole.

Music poured suddenly from the glowing white hole, filling the tower with sound. It rang in Jake's ears and echoed through his head as he memorized the tune for his ocarina instantly. The tune stopped as soon as Jake moved the pearly white ocarina to his lips. They could hear the wind and thunder from outside once again. He began to play the tune, his eyes glowing brighter white by the second. The door shook as it moved upwards into the ceiling, revealing a large stone deck in the center of the storm. Purple lightning danced and flickered across the gray sky, and thunder shook the stone beneath their feet. High above the middle of the deck floated a small platform.

* * * * * * * *

"PROTECT YOURSELVES, YOUNG ONES!" yelled Granite. But suddenly, two giant birds appeared between the forces, swallowing the blasts whole. It was the leader of the Phoenixes, and the leader of the Rainbonians. Their mere presence lit the skies, giving off a feeling of peace. Both birds exploded into flames.

The Birandians stood still in shock. Rachel and Mike were in disbelief. A bright blue and red light formed where the birds had been. They swirled around each other once, becoming mistier, and then set off in opposite directions. The blue vapor set off toward the Skytanian Kingdom and the red vapor traveled down to return to the Birandian Kingdom.

"What is it?" whispered Rachel to Flairen, who was resting on her shoulder.

"Their Spirits," said Flairen calmly.

One of the Birandians moved toward Becca and Rachel. He was much bigger and more muscular than the one they had seen before, nearly seven feet tall. He came close enough to the two that they could almost touch him before Rachel pulled out her spear and pointed it at him. He flew back a couple of feet, in caution. "I am Bulkest, the commanding General of this squadron. What is it that you want?"

Rachel lowered her spear. "Answers. Why are you at war?"

Bulkest stared at Rachel for several seconds, not expecting to hear the words he had just heard. "The Skytanian Kingdom has been sending terrible tornadoes upon our land, destroying homes and lives!"

The teens paused. "But how do you know it wasn't naturally caused?" asked Mike.

"Because!" he yelled angrily. "Never have tornadoes even approached our lands in hundreds of years. The cyclones come and go, in all shapes and sizes. The Phoenixes—they have been acting strange."

"But Skytania doesn't know why they are at war!" yelled Mike. "They said they've never attacked you, and that you attacked them!"

"That's impossible!" yelled Bulkest, not believing Mike's words. "We wouldn't have attacked them if they didn't attack us first! They were the ones who broke the peace."

Rachel leered at him angrily. "Have you ever tried communicating with them to see what's going on!?"

"They destroyed the bridge!" bellowed Bulkest in reply.

"They said you destroyed it!" protested Mike.

Bulkest's eyes squinted at the two. "If neither of us destroyed the bridge—then *who did*?" There was a very long pause.

Rachel sighed. "You have to stop fighting," she said calmly.

"We can't! Our Kingdom does not trust them anymore."

Mike eyed Bulkest. "Then we are on our way to obtain the Crystal."

"What!?" yelled Bulkest, a petrified look on his face. "That Crystal is the source of all our power! Without it, Skytania will destroy our Kingdom!

"It will not," said Rachel. "Our friends are obtaining the Crystal from the tower in Skytania."

"They'll never destroy the Beast—nor will *you*!" Bulkest grinned.

Mike smirked. "They will, and so will we!"

"You must not take the Crystal!" begged Bulkest.

"Are you going to try to stop us?" Mike yelled. "And risk destroying the Kingdoms!"

Rachel looked at Bulkest in disgust. "Think about others more than yourself, for a change. Look around! No one wants to fight!"

"We're getting the Crystal!" said Mike firmly.

Bulkest sighed. He knew the teens were not going to leave without a fight. "Then I have no choice but to let you go. I cannot risk having my Kingdom destroyed by you." He pointed down towards the volcano, pointing out where a nearly invisible stone staircase was carved into the side.

Rachel and Mike turned toward the Kingdom and began to soar off. The other soldiers moved out of the way, letting Mike and Rachel pass. They soared through the Kingdom, seeing many Birandians run into their homes out of fear. The teens came to the base of the volcano where they found the beginning of the long stone stairway going up the side of the cone. They flew above the stairs, following it up to the top, where they found a large black stone door hidden among the rocks. In the center of the door was a large hole, about a foot across. They landed and stared at the hieroglyphics carved on the massive stone door.

Rachel began to read aloud. "*Thy Sages only may pass through; by your worth you must prove that this is thee. The Ancient Spear is the key to penetrate the door.*" Rachel looked over at Mike as she reached back and grabbed her Spear from her back, aiming it at the hole. The Spear burst into glowing red flames, and Rachel stepped back then threw it with all her might. The Spear went arcing through the hole. The hieroglyphics upon the door began to glow red, symbol by symbol, and the door shook as it made its way upwards into the earth of the mountain.

Mike and Rachel walked bravely through the door with their Fairies, and the door slid closed behind them with a bang. It was burning hot inside the cave, even though high up the sloped ceiling opened onto blue sky. It was so hot that Granite had to put a special barrier around Mike, making him resistant to the heat. Rachel however, did not need any such protection. They stood on a stone pathway that led to a wide circular stone island in the middle of a pool of bubbling, sizzling lava. In the center of the island was a glowing red crystal that rested on a stone column. Around the column, lay curled a large sleeping red dragon, smoke puffing gently from its nostrils and mouth.

Chapter 22— Beasts

"It's magnificent!" Josh exclaimed, gazing at the beautiful beast as if it were the most splendid thing he had ever seen. The beauty of the Unisus was simply extraordinary. Its silver-feathered wings stretched across the room, fifteen feet in length. Its glorious, glowing white fur was so pure that it would be invisible in the snow. The two-foot long silver horn extending from its forehead, gave it a look of fearlessness and undeniable strength, yet its large, turquoise eyes were filled with passion. Its neck was sleek and well-muscled, leading down to a broad chest mightier than any great shield. Its well-proportioned legs ended in silver hooves that were strong and well built. Its flowing white mane and tail seemed to show its true inner beauty in the glistening pearly highlights. The Unisus began to paw the ground and toss its head. Its horn nearly touched the beamed ceiling, knocking several dried bundles to the floor.

"This is a rare beast," said Jeeves. "A rare breed indeed—half Pegasus and half Unicorn.

Toni stared into the Unisus' eyes. "I've never seen anything like it, nor ever will." She walked carefully over to the Unisus and began to pet its neck. "It's so incredibly beautiful."

"So, you're going to call it Gladius?" asked Josh.

Jeeves eyed Josh warily. "I liked the name—is it alright with you?"

Josh laughed. "It most certainly is." Gladius walked over to Josh and nudged him with its velvety soft nose to show that it wanted to be petted. Josh rubbed his hand over the warm, white nose and gazed into the ocean blue eyes—their souls were being connected—they were merging into one.

Jeeves suddenly held up his wrist and glanced at his watch. He let out a howl. "You're going to be late!"

"Where do I go now? Is the race starting already?" asked Josh. He paused to stare at Gladius, and then looked around the hut. "More importantly, how are we supposed to get Gladius out?"

"You meet the King in the courtyard along with the other riders. Gladius will be able to get out fine." He winked at Josh. "Just leave it to me." He quickly waved his hand at the ceiling and whispered, "*Montechision*." The ceiling to the hut suddenly disappeared, revealing the bright blue sky with many puffy white clouds.

Gladius stretched her long wings and they shimmered in the sunlight. Josh ran over to Gladius and hopped on her back. He looked over at Toni and held out his arm, grabbing her just above the elbow to help her up.

"Thank you," Misty hollered to Jeeves.

Josh looked down at Jeeves. "I will be back with your one thousand gold pieces—I promise!"

"Before you go!" yelled Jeeves. "No one is to know where you got this Unisus."

"Got it!" yelled Josh.

Gladius leaped off the ground and took flight into the bright outside. It felt smooth riding her, as if the two were dancing in the air. Josh held on to her neck while Toni held on to Josh.

"Hey?" asked Toni suddenly, having a tight grip around Josh's waist. "Is Gladius a boy or girl?"

"A girl."

Toni looked over at Misty, questioningly. Misty shrugged. "How do you know?" asked Toni.

Josh turned around and stared at Toni. "After all, I am only the Sage of Mythical Creatures."

Toni said nothing, just kept looking at the gorgeous scenery slowly passing below them.

Josh held his arms out to either side and closed his eyes, letting the wind blow past him. "This is such an awesomely comfortable ride!"

Gladius made her way to the Emerald castle, flying high and gracefully before descending to the courtyard.

"Well, it's easy for you to say," Toni sneered. "I get the *rear*."

Gladius landed elegantly in the courtyard beside a stone statue of a man wearing a crown and petting a very small dragon. Many of the other race competitors stood with their flying creatures and watched in awe as Toni and Josh slid off with their Fairies. Most of the competitors looked human-like, including a man riding a Rainbonian. The only exceptions were a Birandian with a Phoenix and a tall Elf with a lovely opalescent white dragon the size of a large horse. There were an amazing range of flying creatures from a pair of regal-looking griffins and other odd bird creatures to a few gruesome bug creatures. There was even a seven-foot tall Fairy who seemed to be able to fly by himself!

Doors opened at the far end of the courtyard nearest the castle. A tall, muscular young man with short black hair appeared at the doorway. He looked to be about the teens' age. Behind him was something that Josh had never seen before, but because of his Power, knew to be a Nightmare. The Nightmare was a pitch-black horse with flames for its mane and tail. Flames also wreathed its steely hooves, which trailed from its flared nostrils, and smoldered in the depths of its gleaming dark eyes. It gave off the presence of Darkness and Hate. It followed behind the boy as he quickly walked over to join the rest of the group.

"Josh, be careful of the Nightmare," warned Merlin. "I know a lot about these creatures." Josh and Toni stared at Merlin, confused and cautious. "They are wild and restless creatures. They roam the world doing Evil and haunt all those who dare to look it in the eyes."

Josh and Toni looked over at the approaching Nightmare. "How does it fly?" whispered Josh.

Merlin grunted. "Although they have no wings, they can fly with great speed using magical abilities. They seldom allow others to ride them." Merlin stared at the boy with the jet-black hair walking next to the Nightmare. "It is known that only powerful Evil creatures can tame them." The boy and the Nightmare stopped next to Toni and Josh. They could feel the heat from the smoldering flames.

The boy looked at Toni and Josh and then at Gladius, most disdainfully. "Where did you get a creature like *that*?" his voice was dark and deep. Merlin did a fake cough, as if to remind Josh of his promise.

"Umm..." mumbled Josh. "Where I come from, we breed creatures such as this."

The boy looked at Josh questioningly. "Are you sure?"

Josh smirked. "Do you think I'm lying?"

The boy squinted his eyes and shrugged in displeasure. He turned around and began to pet the Nightmare—the flames lowered as he did so. "The name is Drake. Get in my way and—I swear it—you will *pay!*"

Toni laughed, taken aback by what she had heard. Drake turned around and sneered at Toni.

"Stay out of his way," whispered Misty to Toni. Then louder, "Well, Josh, you'll just have to show him what you are made of on the—"

The far doors opened once more, but this time walking out was a tall man wearing a glorious golden crown and exquisite emerald robes. He wore a lot of jewelry, all of it with dark green stones. A heavily encrusted jeweled crown contrasted with his white beard and hair, matching almost exactly his brilliant green eyes. He looked as though he were in his early sixties.

Beside him was a very tall, bulky man. He had long, black, raven-like wings growing from his back, and his eyes were so dark they seemed to be full of shadows. A mighty sword hung from a wide black belt around his waist. Five guards walked in step behind the two. The pair made their way to the contestants and stopped several feet in front of them.

"Welcome!" yelled the King joyfully. "I am King Absoulah, King of the Emerald Kingdom, for those of you who don't know. This is the one hundredth Race in the Sky!" The challengers roared, cheered, clapped, and whistled loudly. "I shall explain the rules to you quickly." He looked around, eyed each of the contestants, and stopped abruptly, his eyes on Josh. "If you are caught not following the rules, you will be disqualified and charges will be brought against you." He paused and stood up straight, checking his watch. "Thousands of Beings have come to the Emerald Kingdom to watch the race that will begin in fifteen minutes. They deserve to watch a fair and enjoyable race." He walked closer to the contestants so they could hear him more clearly. "You have to follow the given track in the sky all the way to the finish line. Shortcuts are *not* allowed. There will be difficult objectives in your path that you *must* get through. If you fail to complete an objective, you will be eliminated. You may use any power to help you get through the path, but you may *not* use it against other competitors. Bulkum and I shall be watching each of you closely. Protect yourselves from harm—and do not *die*. Whoever reaches the finish line first, wins." He paused for a moment and looked up to the clouds. "That is, if you *do* finish. But I have high hopes…" He eyed the contestants again. "Are there any questions?"

Toni raised her hand, but Josh nudged her with his elbow. "This isn't school!" he whispered.

"Yes," said the King pointing at Toni. "The young miss with the black hair."

"Umm…" said Toni, "I am one of the—*observers* from another Kingdom…" She looked to the sky, trying to think. "You sent for me from my home Kingdom in—*Twileken,* to *observe.* Would you be so kind as to let me accompany you to the viewing area?"

The King didn't say anything for a moment, but stared at Toni through squinted eyes as if trying to remember. Toni grew hot, hoping that her plan would work. The King's face suddenly lit up, and he broke the silence. "I don't remember sending for you, but my mind has been forgetful lately, so—absolutely! In fact, you can be my guest in the stands. You can come with me where you can see the entire race! It is an offer that is too good to not accept!"

Toni smiled as she winked at Josh. "Thank you."

Misty nudged on Toni's neck. "Good thinking!"

King Absoulah looked around again to each of the contestants. "Are there any more questions?"

"Yes," said Josh. "I have a question. Where is the finish line to the race?"

The King smiled as he put his hands behind his back and looked to the sky. "In between the Skytanian and Birandian Kingdoms."

Both Misty and Merlin quietly gasped. "*Where the bridge was!*"

* * * * * * * *

Jake and Becca made their way outside and walked into the storm. The winds whistled and screamed past them, and Becca could barely keep her footing—but Jake, on the other hand, walked right along with the wind as if defying it to knock him down. The two stared at the floating stone platform above them, which was glowing a brilliant white. Then, from the shadows under the floating deck came a resonant female voice, as if three people were speaking at the same time.

"*Who dares come here and disturb the sleeping Crystal?*"

Jake stepped forward without hesitation. "It is I—the Sage of Weather. I have come to obtain my Crystal."

The voice spoke again, but it was deeper and louder—Becca shivered as the voice traveled up her spine. "*The last being who came here said he also was the Sage of Weather. He lied so I killed him. Only the Sage of Weather can defeat me, for I was created by the Ancient One.*"

Jake stared deeper into the shadows, trying to locate the source of the voice. "So how do I prove myself?"

The voice laughed. "*Destroy me—if you can, then I will know who you truly are. For I am the Mistress Guardian of this tower, known as the Legendary—*"

But this time, Thor finished her sentence. "Three-Headed Sphinx."

The lightning struck, illuminating the shadows under the floating platform. In the gloom stood a sphinx with three human female faces and a monstrous lion's body three times bigger than normal. Its body and mane were bright white. The lips were golden, and the eyes were a piercing blue, and upon each forehead was a diamond.

The three faces smiled. "I see that I have four beings to defeat—very well, I enjoy a challenging fight!" The Three-Headed Sphinx stepped forward as Jake and Becca cautiously stepped back. The Sphinx opened its mouths to reveal white glows within. Three beams of energy hit Jake and Becca without warning. They were hurled through the air and smashed into the wall next to the doorway. The Sphinx charged, and then leaped into the air, getting ready to pounce. Becca got up quickly and shot her own purple beams from her eyes. The Sphinx was hurled back and landed painfully on the stone floor.

Jake got quickly to his feet. Thor and Juhani were clasping tightly to the teens' shoulders, paying close attention to everything going on.

Jake and Becca charged the Sphinx, but it went into a spin, creating a powerful gust of wind that sent them both hurling back against the wall again.

Jake's hands began to glow and white bolts of lightning streamed from his fingers to hit the Sphinx. It didn't do any damage whatsoever! The Sphinx's open mouths began to glow again, but this time Jake and Becca knew what attack was coming. They raised their hands, the powerful blows bouncing off their wrist plates, sending them violently back at the Sphinx. The Sphinx dodged agilely and remained unhurt.

Becca reached behind her, unsheathed her sword, and ran at the Sphinx. She swung her blade hard and with fury. The Sphinx stuck its paw out, catching the silver blade. It then clawed at Becca's chest with its other taloned paw, blood going everywhere. She screamed in pain and horror. Juhani sent beams of lights at the paws, but it had no effect.

A whistling, glowing arrow took to the air, striking the Sphinx in the shoulder and piercing straight through. Golden blood began to drip, and it lost its grip on Becca's sword. Becca yanked the sword back and returned to Jake cradling her bloody chest.

"Are you alright, young Star?" asked Thor, concerned.

"I'm fine," said Becca quickly. "The beast is very powerful and smart, but thanks to the quick thinking of Jake…"

Jake nodded. "No problem—but it seems it has an advantage on the ground… but what about in the sky?"

"Good thinking, Cyclone," Juhani agreed.

"Very well," said Thor. "I have a plan…"

* * * * * * * *

"How are we supposed to get past that thing?" asked Rachel. The red dragon was fascinating, but it looked very lethal to the two teens and also to the Fairies. It was as large as the dragon they had battled at Islands of Adventure, but this dragon had four legs and looked fiercer. It was also real. Its long, sharp, golden teeth were visible around the edges of its closed mouth. Its scales glistened in the orange light from the magma. Its black iron claws and the horns on its head were as dark as smoke. Its head was the shape of an arrowhead and it had rows of spikes running along the jaw ridges and continuing down its spine. Its wings were red, long and leathery-looking. Fire was spouting in delicate wisps from its nose with every exhale.

"Why did the Ancient Sage put a dragon here?" asked Mike.

"Actually," said Granite grinning, "they didn't. The Birandians probably put it here for extra security."

"They are pretty smart," said Rachel, eyebrows raised.

"Indeed they are," said Flairen beaming. "The only Being created by an Ancient Sage to protect the Crystals in these Kingdoms is the Being atop Skytania Tower."

"But that's where Jake and Becca are!" exclaimed Mike. "So that means they have to defeat their own Beast?"

"Well," said Granite, "not necessarily…"

"Umm….guys?" asked Rachel, voice shaky. She could hear Flairen gasp in her ear.

"Hold on," said Mike, eyebrows lowered. "What do you mean not *necessarily*?"

Granite laughed. "As in—"

"GUYS!?'" yelled Rachel.

Mike turned toward her, annoyed. "What?"

"Well," said Rachel, eyes fixed ahead of her on the dragon, "feel free to talk as *loudly* as you want now. The dragon just woke from its slumber."

The dragon uncoiled and stood up, stretching and yawning like some kind of demented cat. It was enormous standing up, and its eyes were a deeply burnished ruby red.

"So much for a sneak attack!" said Mike irritably.

The dragon charged at them, lightly leaping over the moat of molten lava. Mike and Rachel flew up into the air, hoping to get out of reach. The dragon spread its enormous wings and took flight after them. Rachel paused to unsheathe her Spear and pointed it at the dragon. The glass ball glowed and a beam of fire shot out of the blade of the Spear.

The dragon opened its mouth and sucked in Rachel's flaming attack. A puff of smoke came out of its ears. It howled loudly, shooting fire from its mouth. Boulders appeared around Mike and Rachel, creating a barrier. The blast hit the boulders with great force, turning them to pebbles and pelting Mike and Rachel head on. They were slammed into the cave wall, dust filtering down over them. Rachel raised her glowing hands and a large mass of magma from the moat flew into the air, hitting the now circling dragon.

"Good one, Rachel!" yelled Mike.

She lowered her glowing hands and the lava fell back into the moat. The dragon still floated in the air. Mike, Rachel, Flairen, and Granite stared at it, not sure what had just happened.

"Well," said Flairen, "I don't think that did it."

The dragon roared again, shaking boulders down from the ceiling high overhead. Mike's eyes flashed yellow as the boulders stopped in midair and hurled themselves at the dragon. The dragon shielded itself with its wings, but slammed into the sloped wall on its back. Mike's hands glowed yellow as he threw orange exploding roses at the dragon. The dragon dodged the roses, hurling itself into the pool of magma. A large explosion echoed all around as a giant hole appeared in the cave wall. Mike and Rachel looked around for the dragon to emerge from the magma, but it didn't. They floated nervously down to land on the island, watching closely for the dragon to emerge.

The Crystal suddenly glowed brightly, as if feeling the intensity of the moment. It seemed to sense Rachel's presence because every time she took a step, it flared even brighter. "Get the Crystal! Now!" yelled Flairen suddenly.

Mike ran toward the Crystal, but suddenly the stone cracked violently beneath him as the dragon emerged. It struck brutally at his chest with its teeth and claws, sending him hurling yet again through the air. A powerful blast of fire echoed from Rachel's hands, striking the dragon viciously and pushing it back from Mike. The dragon began to walk against the powerful force of the flames!

"It's invulnerable to flames and magma!" yelled Flairen. "The only way we can destroy it is if we get under the scales!"

Rachel's muscles clenched as her voice echoed around the cavern, "very well!"

* * * * * * * *

"Let's be on our way to the track!" yelled the King, thrusting his hand up in the air. "Let the race begin!" The riders quickly mounted their flying creatures, anticipation and excitement echoing through every nerve of their bodies. Josh didn't know where to go, so he hopped on Gladius and followed the other contestants. He waved goodbye to Misty and Toni as he glanced ahead of him at the white dragon with the Elf rider. He had never seen a Being ride a domesticated dragon. He was quite fascinated.

Toni stayed behind, but surprisingly, so did Drake. Drake walked over to the man with black wings and whispered something in his ear. The man squinted his eyes shut in disapproval and then nodded his head sharply. Drake grinned and hopped onto his Nightmare. They took flight, and followed after the rest of the contestants. What was interesting about the Nightmare was that it galloped through the air as though moving on a solid surface.

Toni and Misty focused once more on the man with black wings. "Your Majesty?" asked the man.

"Yes Bulkum?" replied the King, walking closer to him.

"I have to run a quick—errand." Bulkum stared off into the sky. "I will return shortly."

King Absoulah nodded. "Very well—you'll know where to find us."

Bulkum spread his black wings—they looked larger than before—and took off into the sky. He was heading in the same direction that Josh and Toni had come from. King Absoulah looked over at Toni and Misty—they were the only ones left in the courtyard.

"What are your names?" asked the King, with a bright smile.

Misty nudged Toni's neck. "Oh…" said Toni. "I'm—*Aqua* and this is my partner *Mist.*

King Absoulah nodded. "It is nice to meet both of you—Mist and Aqua. I am thrilled to have a royal observer inspect my Kingdom and watch the race. It is an honor." The King bowed.

"Oh…" said Toni, blushing. "I'm no *princ—*" Misty nudged her again. Toni's eyebrows lowered. "Well apparently I am—well, it is an honor to meet you, your Majesty." Toni curtsied awkwardly. She could not believe that the King actually thought an *observer* was someone of royalty. She didn't even look like someone royal. She was only dressed in pants and a shirt.

"Well, come with me," said King Absoulah. "I know a *quicker* way to the stands."

Josh had found a place in mid-air at the starting point of the race in between a man riding a Hippogriff and the Elf riding the white dragon. Josh looked around, confused, because he knew nothing about the kind of obstacles he might encounter. He hadn't even had time to look at the map of the course!

"When do we find out what to do next?" whispered Josh to Merlin.

Merlin laughed. He sounded excited and happy. "The King will let us know, and hopefully Aquarius will get some information from him." Beings were sitting in the stands hovering on either side of the starting point, and crowds of people lined the streets of the city. There were small, glowing black balls showing the boundaries of the track. From Josh's point of view, there didn't seem to be any obstacles. He could easily see small shadows of the two Kingdoms in the distance. He began to wonder how the crowd got to the stands—there were no stairs leading up to them, not even a simple ladder.

Toni and the King ended up in another courtyard. High above them were the roaring crowds in the stands. Ahead of them was a platform with three ornate cushioned chairs with high backs. In front of the chairs was a table with bowls of fruit. The King stepped up on the platform and sat down in the center chair. Toni sat in the chair to his right, while Misty perched on the high back. Toni looked around, confused. Why were they sitting—she thought they were going to take a shortcut to the stands. She turned to the King. "How are we going to see the race from here?"

The King laughed. "*Watch...*" He pushed a button on his throne. Suddenly, the platform jerked upwards into the air. It soared high behind and above the stands. It stopped where they could see everything. The crowd, seeing the King, stood up, cheering.

"Did you see the entrance?" asked Merlin excitedly.

"I did!" yelled Josh. "That sure answers my question!" Merlin laughed.

As the King stood up, the crowd fell silent. His voice echoed loudly as if he were using a megaphone. "*This course is the most difficult one yet. It was made by the best designers from all around our world.*" The crowd roared in approval. "*I expect a fair and enjoyable race.*" King Absoulah raised his hands. "*On the count of three, you will race to the finish.*" The

King sat down, and the crowd roared again. The King leaned over to Toni. "Our platform will move with the contestant in the lead. The stands will not, but they can see it on a special monitor. I am the judge of the race. We get to see everything. You and your friend, Mist, are lucky, Princess."

"Well, thank you," said Misty gratefully. She nudged Toni's neck.

"Yes," said Toni, "I'm very grateful." She rolled her eyes when the King turned his head to watch a black object soar up behind the platform. Bulkum landed on the platform with a thud that made Toni and Misty jump. He sat down on the chair to the left of the King.

"Sorry, I'm late," he apologized.

"That's alright," said the King. "You haven't missed anything. The race is just about to begin." The King stood up again.

Josh tightened his grip on Gladius' mane, watching and listening to the King carefully. He heard the King speak loudly.

"*The count off shall commence—one—two—THREE!*"

Josh took off. He was in the lead by a hair. There was plenty of room to fly, but he was still careful. Suddenly, out of thin air, trees began to appear. One appeared in front of Gladius making her lunge frantically to the side. She narrowly missed it. Josh was in about eighth place now and Merlin was griping his shoulder tightly.

"I have a question…" said Toni, as the platform quickly moved with the leader. The leader was beside Josh riding the Hippogriff.

"Yes?" asked the King, fixing his eyes on Toni.

"You mentioned that the competitors could use powers to get them through the race. Does that mean they can use *any* power?"

"Absolutely!" said King Absoulah. "That is the fun of the race. You must get use to your inner Knowledge as well as your skill!"

Josh raised his glowing hands and shouted, "*THE EYE OF TRUTH!*" He was now able to see the trees, and direct Gladius with his mind when and where to turn. He was steadily catching up to the leader, because he seemed to be the only one that could see the trees. Many of the contestants who were riding insect-looking creatures kept hitting trees and falling.

Toni screamed as she saw the riders of a huge green june bug and what looked like a giant horned beetle go tumbling down after striking a tree.

"Don't worry, Princess," whispered King Absoulah to Toni. "This is the fun of watching the race!" Toni's eyebrows lowered. Watching people fall to their deaths wasn't entertaining for her or Misty.

* * * * * * * *

The Fairies flew off Jake and Becca's shoulders. "Juhani and I will distract the beast while you throw fire from above!" yelled Thor quickly. They flew off toward the Sphinx and begun throwing flashing lights in the three faces. The Sphinx howled in annoyance and began swiping the air with its paws, trying to rub away the lights.

"Let's go!" yelled Becca, flying up into the stormy sky.

Jake shut his hands and the black clouds above him began to rotate. The clouds bulged and churned, making their way down to the deck where the flashing lights kept flashing around the Sphinx.

"Get out of the way!" yelled Becca.

Thor and Juhani quickly flew away from the Sphinx. That instant, a deadly black tornado dropped down out of the sky and struck the Sphinx. A glowing, white light appeared at the base of the tornado. It began to fold inwards as though turning inside out, traveling upwards at a slow speed. Three, white glowing diamonds appeared. Thunder echoed more loudly, and the tornado began to spin faster, gaining strength. Black lightning struck out from the tornado, striking Jake violently in the chest. It streamed through his body. He screamed loudly in pain, but the wind blocked out the sound. Becca screamed in horror. She swung her sword madly back and forth, as purple kinetic energy beams flew at the glowing Sphinx, hitting it and pushing it out of the tornado. It crashed to the ground near the edge of the deck.

Meanwhile, Thor and Juhani quickly flew over to Jake and each held one of his hands to keep him afloat. Becca landed on the deck near the crouching Sphinx. Becca raised her glowing hand up off the ground with an invisible force. "You will be defeated now. When I close my palm, your neck will snap as easily as a twig."

The Three-Headed Sphinx laughed. "You don't understand, little girl. Only the Sage of Weather can destroy me!" Its mouths began to glow a bright white as yet again, lightning shot out from the heads, striking Becca in the face. She flew back, hitting the wall to the tower. She was unconscious.

Jake slowly opened his eyes. In the distance, through the clouds, he saw a blue glowing light traveling toward him. It swam through the clouds headed right for him. Jake's eyes lit up as he gazed into the light. His body felt a soothing Serenity enter it. His mind had become part of another's and he heard the Song of the Rainbonian swim through his soul. Thor and Juhani flew back away from him slowly.

Jake was no longer glowing white, but a magnificent royal blue. An outline of a large bird in glowing light surrounded him. The Spirit of the Rainbonian spoke through his mouth. "*You are a true Hero. I have gazed into the Heavens, and your Destiny is strong. You must fulfill it, for you are the Ancient Sage of Weather.*"

Jake raised his glowing blue hand. The light surrounding his arm made it look like a wing. The entire storm began to change into fluffy white clouds, giving Light instead of Darkness. The clouds circled around Jake's glowing hand. A wide, electrifying beam shot down, striking the Legendary Three-Headed Sphinx. It collapsed and lay still. The storm slowly evaporated, revealing the bright afternoon sky. The Rainbonian Spirit left Jake and traveled up to the floating deck where the Crystal rested on a white velvet cushion. The Crystal grew brighter as the Spirit sunk down into it and they merged. The Crystal shone strongly, lighting up the sky like a beacon.

Jake soared down to Becca, followed by Thor and Juhani. He knelt down and touched her face. Becca slowly opened her eyes and gazed into Jake's. A tear rolled down her face as she hugged him tightly in relief.

"Are you alright, Becca?" asked Jake, still hugging her.

"Yes," said Becca slowly. "I'm glad you're okay."

They let go of each other and looked over to where the Sphinx lay. They walked over to it and looked down at it. The three heads turned toward Jake slowly. "*Destroy me now. Take your final blow, for you have truly defeated me.*"

Jake stood there for several seconds in silence, but then he said sternly, "NO."

The Sphinx gazed at him in shock, unable to believe its ears. "*But why? You are clearly more Powerful.*"

Jake smiled. "My Destiny is not to kill the innocent. You were created by the Light to protect Good. Now I want you to protect Skytania."

The Sphinx glowed a bright white as it slowly stood up. It towered over Jake and Becca. It looked down at them, smiling.

"*You are truly one of the Chosen. For you have not killed me, but spared my life when you could have easily destroyed me. The true Sage of Weather would have also spared me. Because of your decision you shall gain Knowledge, for I know the Truth of the situation.*"

Jake and Becca stared at the Sphinx, confused, but yet eager to hear more. "*There is a spy in our Kingdoms who has Power of great Evil about him. He has been attacking Skytania and Birandia to confuse the two Kingdoms and make it seem as though they hate each other. He plans to reveal what he really did, but blame it on the Innocent One. This spy has taken control to do Evil things. If the Beings of both Kingdoms don't learn the Truth, the Innocent One will be banished, and the rest will be led down the Path of Darkness. The spy will obtain the Ancient Power unless you stop him. You must reveal the Truth and stop the war.*"

"How?" asked Thor. "What direction must we go?"

"*Go to where the bridge once connected the two Kingdoms. That is where the fighting will begin. Bring the Crystals of Wind and Magma to the bridge. That will stop the fighting. It is also where the winner of the Ancient Race will gain the Ancient Power as a prize. Now go, obtain the Crystal. For you are truly the Sage of Weather. Farewell...*"

"Before you go," said Jake, "could you release the Power needed to protect Skytania when the time comes?"

The Three-Headed Sphinx smiled. "I shall, if that is what you wish." The Sphinx bent its knee and bowed.

Jake nodded. "Thank you."

The Sphinx became a bright light and took off into the sky. "*Good luck, young Chosen...*"

Jake's eyes followed after the light from the Sphinx. "Let's hope Josh wins."

Becca put her arm around Jake. "He will..." she whispered. "Now let's go get that Crystal!"

Chapter 23— Eruptions

Mike got up from the ground and flew over to Rachel. Tied tightly around his chest was a giant green leaf bound with vines. Blood was seeping through it, but it was slowing the bleeding.

"Are you alright?" asked Flairen.

"I'm fine," said Mike sternly. "But I'm beginning to get annoyed."

"Flairen is right! We have to get under the scales!" yelled Granite. He looked at Rachel. "You and Flairen have already figured out that the dragon is impervious to flame and magma. I should have remembered this from the beginning. It is a red dragon—it can withstand any heat, including the temperatures of the hottest magma. Dragons love jewels and precious gems, and they will not let anything get in between them and their treasure. I am sorry I didn't warn you."

The dragon wrapped itself around the glowing Crystal and laid down once again. It watched Mike and Rachel closely and cautiously. The two were a bit surprised that it didn't keep attacking them. It was more obsessed with guarding the Crystal than fighting.

Mike suddenly broke the silence. "I know what to do," said Mike. "Rachel, get ready to use the Spear!" Mike quickly flew over to the dragon's island and landed. The dragon got up and opened its mouth wide, getting ready to crunch Mike. Mike suddenly shot a vine from his hand and wrapped it around the dragon's mouth, snapping it shut and tying it closed. The dragon pawed frantically at its face, moving its head so violently that it tripped and fell to the ground, still trying to open its mouth. Mike waved his hands up and down and back and forth wildly. Thick vines sprouted from the ground, wrapping tightly around the dragon, forcing its wings down across its back. The dragon was now pinned to the ground.

Rachel quickly flew over and unsheathed her Spear. She spun it in circles in her right hand as she landed on the dragon's back. She raised the spear up, the steel blade shimmering with orange light reflected from the magma. Suddenly, the spikes on the dragon's back snapped straight up, revealing sharp edges. As the spikes shot up, Flairen tried to get in front of Rachel to take the blow—but she was too late. The spikes stabbed Rachel in the stomach and out through her back. Blood began to pour out in torrents. The dragon broke itself from the vines and raised its wings, knocking Rachel and the Crystal into the lava.

Mike, Granite, and Flairen screamed in horror. Flairen dove into the magma after Rachel, who was sinking quickly with the Crystal wrapped in her arms. "NOOO!!!" screamed Mike. Tears rolled down his face and he clasped his arms around his head and began to wail. The ground began to shake violently. The sloping walls were cracking, along with the ground where Mike was standing. Boulders fell from above onto the dragon, and it roared in displeasure. The lava began to rise very quickly in the moat.

"Your Power has triggered an eruption!" yelled Granite, glancing around him in every direction. "We have to get out of here!"

"NOT WITHOUT THEM!" Mike bellowed, pointing to the lava.

"Their gone!" yelled Granite. "And I'm not going to lose you, too!" Granite shot a beam of yellow light at Mike and raised him into the air. Mike struggled to get back down, but it was no use. Granite carried him with the light up and out of the cone of the volcano toward Birandia. Loud bangs echoed everywhere, and fiery boulders began to fall from the sky. Above the Birandian Kingdom hung a veil of smoke and falling ash. But surprisingly, the smoke and ash stayed only above the Birandian Kingdom, not drifting elsewhere. The volcano was erupting and the Kingdom was in danger.

* * * * * * * *

Josh had successfully passed the tree course. Loud bangs filled the air. He glanced around him, frantically, thinking that it was another part of the course, but then he looked ahead of him and realized the volcano in the Birandian Kingdom must be erupting!

He knew Toni realized it too, because he could pick out her scream anywhere. He hoped Mike and Rachel were alright, and knowing them, he was sure of it. But for now, he had to focus on the race. He looked ahead and behind him. Only six others remained on the course: the Elf with the white dragon, the tall fairy, the Birandian with the Phoenix, the Skytanian with the Rainbonian, the man riding the Hippogriff, and Drake.

Toni looked at Misty and whispered in her ear. "Those explosions.... I think they're from the volcano!"

Misty sighed. "Do not worry. Mike and Rachel are probably dueling with the Beast. They know how to take care of themselves."

"Beast?" A loud cracking sound filled the air. Toni gazed back at the track and realized that Josh and the other competitors, except Drake, had crashed into a black force field. Drake was glowing black and laughing. Toni yelled in protest. "Your Majesty—he cheated!" King Absoulah didn't say anything. Toni stared hard at him. His face was pale and his eyes were white. "*Your Majesty?*"

The King spoke, but his voice sounded cold and dark. "It could not have been him." Toni and Misty could have sworn that they heard a second voice mixed in with the King's own.

Toni stared at the King. "Your Majesty, I have been meaning to ask you—what started the war between the Birandian and Skytanian Kingdoms?"

The King spoke in the same unusual voice, still looking straight ahead. "Skytania has been jealous of the Birandian Kingdom's Power and their relationship with my Kingdom. Skytania attacked and the war began..."

Toni said nothing, but continued watching the King. Misty bent down to Toni's ear. "*Something isn't right...*"

Josh got back in the race and managed to keep his place in third. He whispered an Ancient saying, "*DRAGON'S GIFT*!" Gladius began to glow. She picked up speed, flying faster through the air; faster than ever. He passed both the Elf and Drake, whose face grew red with anger. Drake began to kick his Nightmare harder in the sides, telling it to speed up. Suddenly, dark shadows appeared right above the riders.

"What are they?" asked Josh, glancing worriedly at the Shadows.

Merlin began to glow. "I sense horrible beasts. Defend yourself—they are... *Vampires*!"

The Shadows came closer and the Vampires were now clearly visible. There were at least twenty of them. Fire and wind attacks began to shoot up into the air, but the Vampires simply disappeared and reappeared closer. Suddenly, one appeared right in front of Josh. Josh opened his mind to the Vampire and took control of it. The Vampire flew off, attacking the others of its kind.

"A useful technique," Merlin laughed.

Josh looked behind him and saw two riders and their birds fall through the sky. It was the Hippogriff and its rider, and the Phoenix and its rider. The Birandian took flight, following his Phoenix downward. All the creatures were bleeding at the neck, except for the Birandian who abandoned his Phoenix. The Phoenix shrieked pitifully one last time, and died. The Vampires noticed the Birandian, and four of them surrounded him. The Birandian screamed in horror, but Josh raised his glowing hand, and the Vampires turned into bats and flew away.

For some reason, no Vampires were going after Drake. He didn't even bother to look around him to make sure the Vampires were not near him. He was far in the lead. The Fairy contestant had a protective force around him, preventing the Vampires from harming him. The Skytanian rider waved his hands, blowing seven Vampires twenty feet away from him with a powerful burst of wind. The Elf's white dragon was tearing apart any Vampire that got near it with its claws and teeth. There were seven Vampires left and they were speeding up after Josh.

"Watch your back!" warned Merlin. Josh's eyes began to glow. Suddenly, sparkling light shimmered around him. Blue Pixies appeared with silver arrows strung to their bows. They were easily twice the size of Merlin, and had completely furless flesh. The Pixies swarmed around the Vampires and fired their silver arrows, piercing the Vampires' hearts. Those struck by the arrows burst into flame, shriveled up into ash, and blew away. They were racing in a clear path once again. The rest of the contestants including Josh caught up to Drake, a hair behind him.

"But why would they do that?" asked Toni, with disbelief in her voice. "How could Kingdoms attack each other only out of jealousy? These Kingdoms are supposed to be close. The Queen of Skytania has said that she doesn't know why there is a war. She has protested that she has not attacked the Birandians!"

"The Queen," said the King coldly, "is a liar and too young to rule! She is not equipped with the proper Knowledge to advance her Kingdom toward success. She will do anything to get others to pity her."

Gray storm clouds approached. A violent wind struck, throwing the riders off guard. Thunder boomed and rolled, and lightning blazed. Suddenly, the Skytanian flew past Drake and Josh, barreling along with the wind on his Rainbonian as if they were a part of it.

Josh glanced at the tall Fairy who was struggling to fly beside him. He was barely moving through the wind. Suddenly, he lost control and flew back violently, flipping and turning. Josh turned back around and held tightly onto Gladius's mane. Lightning was striking everywhere without pause. Josh waved his hand and a transparent protective shield appeared around them, enabling Gladius to fly more easily against the wind.

Drake raised his glowing hand and lightning began to strike at Josh's shield. It ricocheted off, hitting the Rainbonian. The Rainbonian screeched in pain and slowly fell, along with the screaming Skytanian. Red shimmering wings sprouted from the Skytanian and flew quickly back toward his own Kingdom.

Josh was flabbergasted. "How did it do that?"

Merlin laughed. "Many species have different capabilities as you will soon learn. And some are only accessible under pressure."

Josh glanced over at Drake who was laughing hard. Josh clenched his teeth. He wanted to cause Drake unbearable pain. He wanted Drake to feel the pain he had caused others.

"Your Majesty!" protested Toni, now on her feet. "That boy cheated again!"

King Absoulah sighed. "I did not see anything..." Toni looked at the King coldly. She said nothing and sat down slowly, eyebrows lowered.

"*Control yourself!*" whispered Misty.

Toni sighed. *"I can't stand seeing someone cheat—especially when he's trying to kill the others!"*

Misty sighed. "*I agree with you, young one, but we both know something isn't right—let's keep our cool...*" Toni nodded as she looked back out to the race.

There was only Josh, Drake, and the Elf left now. A shimmering white glow appeared behind Josh. He turned around and found that the dragon was glowing along with the hand of the Elf. The Elf suddenly bellowed into the darkened sky. "*THE ELVES' RITUAL!*" The storm began to swirl and circle, forming into a hurricane. But instead of the winds getting stronger, they subsided. The thunder and lightning subsided as the clouds began to break apart.

The contestants were in a clearing once again. Drake placed his hand above his Nightmare's fiery tail. Black lightning streamed out of his fingers, striking the Nightmare in the behind. She neighed in pain and started to gallop mightier and faster, moving quickly ahead of Josh. The Skytanian and Birandian Kingdoms came closer into view—they were almost there!

But suddenly, Gladius froze in midair, not moving a single muscle. Josh looked around and saw that the same effect was upon the other riders. They all started to spin like tops, gaining speed by the second. A black vapor appeared and enveloped them. Josh saw nothing but darkness.

"Where do I go now?" he asked Merlin. He could only see a faint glow coming from Merlin and Gladius.

"Well," said Merlin, "you can't go straight, because the spinning put you off guard. I suggest you pick a direction and fly..."

Josh shut his eyes, trying to find some Power within himself that could lead him. Suddenly, he could see a white light floating towards him in his mind. He opened his eyes—the Legendary Three-Headed Sphinx was looking directly at him.

"Are you here to show me the way?" Josh asked it.

"*Yes*," she said. "*You are a god of our kind, the Mythical Father of Beasts. I shall show you the way if you answer my riddle...*"

* * * * * * * *

Jake grasped the Crystal in his hand. It shimmered into many stars and appeared on his forehead. He felt his Strength and Wisdom increase, for the Ancient Rainbonian was another Spirit that was now part of him.

"Now, let's go!" yelled Thor. Becca and Jake took flight and flew over the edge of the stone deck. They felt no force field holding them back, so they floated quickly downward. After several seconds of a fast descent, they landed on the grassy field surrounding the tower. They gasped. Thousands of Skytanian soldiers were walking toward the edge of their Kingdom, and hundreds of Rainbonians flew in the air above them, flying steadily to their pace.

Suddenly, loud explosions filled the air from the Birandian Kingdom. Boulders of fire were erupting from the volcano! The boulders soared through the air like a meteor shower, heading right for the Skytanian soldiers!

Becca gasped. "We have to do something!"

A bright, white light flashed. The Crystal on Jake's forehead was glowing and pulsing with light. He raised his arms and spoke from his soul. "*GRAVITY WIND AURORA!*" A white force field of wind appeared around the Rainbonians. The soldiers stopped marching and looked over at Jake in surprise. They were truly amazed at the Power he had just unleashed. The boulders crashed into the force field—it was working—the force field was holding strong. Jake continued holding his arms up, keeping the force field intact. The soldiers looked up and then straight ahead. They began marching quickly once more. "You must not fight!" yelled Jake, the Crystal on his forehead still glowing as brightly as before. The soldiers were not listening, or if they heard him, they were ignoring him—they simply kept marching. Suddenly, loud cracking noises filled the air. Becca and Jake looked up at the force field, and realized that it was cracking! Twice as many flaming rocks were striking it now.

"You must do something!" warned Juhani to Becca.

Becca soared into the air. "I'm already on it!" Becca flew right below the force field, observing it closely. The force field was about to give way any second. The soldiers would be in danger if the force field broke. The Rainbonians were fine because they had already reached the end of the Kingdom. Becca soared down to the ground toward the marching soldiers. "You must run!" she yelled. "The barrier is about to collapse!" The soldiers stopped and gazed up at the cracking force field. "*RUN, YOU IDIOTS!*" she screamed. The soldiers began to run, but it was too late. The barrier vanished and the boulders began to fall. Becca shot her glowing hands upwards, stopping all the boulders in midair. She was shaking and her eyes were squeezed shut. It was a lot for her to be carrying. The soldiers had stopped again and looked at Becca, stunned.

Jake ran over to Becca as a flare of blinding white flashed from his eyes. A powerful wind hit the soldiers that were under the boulders, pushing them through the air and out of the way of danger. Becca lowered her hands, letting the boulders fall heavily to the earth.

Juhani and Thor glanced over at the soldiers and came to a stop at the edge of the Kingdom. Juhani began to glow very brightly as she shut her eyes. "*The volcano is erupting—the Birandians are half way to Skytania—they are getting ready for a battle!*"

"But how are they going to get out there?" asked Becca, looking at the soldiers curiously.

Jake looked to the sky and stared at the Rainbonians. He pointed to them. "Maybe they'll take the Rainbonians."

But he was wrong. What happened next was unexpected. Bright spots of light appeared on their backs turning into fairy wings. The soldiers jumped off the edge of their Kingdom, and glided to the Birandian Kingdom. The Rainbonians landed on the ground near the edge of the Skytanian Kingdom. They then closed their eyes as though sound asleep.

"Why are they just sitting there?" asked Jake, curiously watching the resting Rainbonians.

"I don't know," said Becca. "But I know we don't have time to stand around to find out. We have to get to Rachel and Mike before the two Kingdoms attack each other! We have to stop them—we need the Crystal of Magma!"

"Well, are we just going to out-fly them?" asked Jake, knowing that would be impossible.

"No!" said Becca sternly. "I can see the edge of the Birandian Kingdom." Her eyes were squinted shut. "I can teleport there, right Juhani?" Juhani said nothing, but merely nodded. "Very well…." said Becca grinning. "Grab hold of me guys!" Thor flew over and landed on the shoulder opposite Juhani. Jake walked over and grabbed Becca's hand as a bright purple light illuminated them—they were gone in a flash.

* * * * * * * *

Mike and Granite were running away from the volcano as fast as they could. "You don't understand Granite!" yelled Mike, tears in his eyes. "We have to go back for them!"

"It's too—*too late*!" said Granite. A sudden flash of purple caught Mike's eyes at the edge of the Kingdom. Jake and Becca came soaring through the air toward them. They landed right in front of him and stared at him.

"Well, did Rachel get the Crystal?" asked Jake anxiously. He looked around, but there was no sign of Rachel or Flairen. "Where is she?"

Mike lowered his head. "She was knocked into the magma by a red dragon. Flairen and the Crystal went with her." Becca screamed, and Jake gasped.

Tears filled Becca's eyes. "So she's—*gone*?" Mike said nothing. "But what about Josh—and the war—good heavens...she *can't* be *dead*..." Tears rolled down her face.

The Birandian Kingdom suddenly shook violently. Birandians ran out of their homes and flew into the skies, carrying bags of food and personal belongings. An ear-splitting roar filled the air. The volcano had exploded its top off! The enormous piece flew high into the air! The teens followed it with their eyes, gasping in horror.

"It's going to land!" warned Thor.

"We do not want this Kingdom to be destroyed!" yelled Juhani.

"But how can we stop that!" said Mike, totally shocked. "Look how colossal it is!"

"Young Quake!" bellowed Granite. "Are you forgetting who you are? You are the Sage of Earth. This is your Power. You can save this Kingdom!"

The ground shook under Mike as a large piece of earth lifted him off the ground. He soared like a rocket with his fists in front of him. Granite was clenching fiercely to his shoulder. Mike looked ahead of him at the blown volcano top and realized that it was decelerating quickly. A yellow mist circled Mike's arms then shot like a beam toward the top. The beam quickly circled around it, and the volcano piece began to glow brightly. Mike stopped it in midair. He flexed his arm muscles as though getting ready to lift something heavy, and raised them slowly with much force. His muscles were flexing so much that his arms began to sweat and grow twice the size of what they normally were. Mike's arms began to slowly bend—it was as if he was really holding the boulder. The volcano piece slowed, but it was still falling.

Mike's teeth clenched and the earth he was standing on rose. Granite's body flashed four times as though signaling. Becca shrieked as four walls of earth shot upwards from around her and Jake, soaring to where Mike and Granite were. The walls flew past Mike about twenty feet and then stopped, creating four giant pillars.

Mike shot yellow beams from his eyes at the volcano piece. He screamed loudly as yellow beams shot from his arms, hitting the falling chunk of rock. The piece braked to a halt, floating in the air ten feet above the pillars. Mike shut his eyes and the beams died away, letting the huge piece of rock slowly float down to rest on the pillars. Mike collapsed on his earth mound as it began to fall. Granite lay on his chest, exhausted. Mike was falling rapidly now through the opening between the four pillars. Just before he hit, the earth mound he was lying on stopped, and then softly collapsed into a pile of dust.

Jake and Becca ran quickly over to him. Mike slowly opened his eyes and gazed up at the large volcano chunk resting on the four pillars. He gasped along with the others. He couldn't believe that he actually did it, nor could he believe what was happening now!

* * * * * * * *

"What happens if I don't answer the question correctly?" asked Josh.

"*Then,*" said the Sphinx, "*you will be lost in the Darkness forever.*" Josh paused for a moment as he let the fear swim through his insides like spiny fish.

Josh hesitated but then spoke. "If I answer the riddle correctly, will you free those from the Darkness who cannot find the Way?"

The Sphinx smiled. "*I shall, but only when you pass the finish line*—if *you do.*"

Merlin grunted. "Will I be able to help the young one with the riddle?"

The Sphinx sighed. "*I am afraid not.*"

"Then, so be it," said Josh sternly. "Tell it to me…"

The Three-Headed Sphinx shut its eyes, but through its eyelids came a bright white glow. "*A Legend begins yet again. A legend of Truth and Destiny. It was a past of Skill, a future of Hope, but a gift of Love. The Strength of an ox, the Courage of a lion, and the Wisdom of a scholar. But this time, what is born?*"

"How are they supposed to get out?" asked Toni, fear spreading through her. She began to think of all the horrible things that could happen to Josh if he was stuck in the Darkness. She didn't want to speak of the worst—but she *feared* it.

"They can't get out!" said King Absoulah coldly. "Only the one with the Power of Darkness can get through the *Dark*."

"That's unfair!" Misty bellowed. "We must help him, Aquarius!" At these words, both Bulkum's and the King's eyes widened. Toni stood up sharply from her chair and glided on an ice pathway, leading them into the Darkness.

* * * * * * * *

The boulder on the pillars was glowing a bright red. Lines of magma began to carve out symbols in hieroglyphics.

"I can't read what it says from here," said Becca. But then suddenly, the boulder began to shake, and a loud female voice filled the air.

"*A PHOENIX IS ALWAYS REBORN!*" The boulder burst open like a flaming egg as Rachel flew out, glowing brightly with the Spirit of the Phoenix surrounding her. The red Crystal was on her forehead, and Flairen rested on her shoulder. She was wearing her warrior's costume and in her older form. Her wounds were gone, and not a single trace of a scar was in sight. Her hair was fire, and her eyes glowed red. A faint smile graced her glowing features. The pieces of the boulder knit themselves back together where Rachel had broken free.

The teens were flabbergasted. Rachel gazed over toward where the Skytanians and Birandians were getting ready to meet in battle. The Kingdom shook again as lava burst out from the volcano like a fountain.

It was no ordinary eruption. Rachel's hands were glowing—she was *controlling* it.

The others were unsure what was happening. They thought another eruption was occurring, but the lava began to travel through the air like a snake. Rachel pointed her hand in between the Skytanians and Birandians. The lava formed into a thick wall as it traveled between the two forces, separating them. Rachel turned her head so she was looking down at Jake. "It is time we show them the way!"

Jake glowed strongly, still in his costumed older form. The Crystal on his forehead began to glow again as a bright blue light formed around him in the shape of a giant bird. The Spirit of the Rainbonian was glowing around him—guiding him.

* * * * * * * *

"I can't see anything!" said Toni. She held out her glowing hand like a lantern trying to light the way, but it was no use.

"Use the Trident," Misty said simply.

Toni began to glow even brighter as she unsheathed the Trident. She held it in the air and chanted, "*Show me the way to the Mythical One.*" The Trident soared from her hand and the crystal on the middle prong began to glow. It spun around quickly and pointed to the left. Toni grabbed the Trident and began to fly in that direction.

Josh fell silent in thought. "Can you repeat the third line?"

"*It was a past of Skill, a future of Hope, but a present of Love.*"

Josh's eyes narrowed in thought as he sighed. "So it has to be something with all those descriptive deeds. *Strength, Courage, Wisdom, Truth and Destiny.* If it begins yet again, that means the power has been passed down." Josh fell silent again. "THAT'S IT!" he yelled excitedly. "It's describing us, the New Sages. But what we really are deep inside—heroes."

The Three-Headed Sphinx smiled brightly with her three faces, revealing three mouths full of sharp white teeth.

Toni collided with Josh, nearly knocking him off Gladius. He regained his balance and stared at Toni in confusion. "What are you doing here!?"

Toni said nothing. Instead, her eyes were fixed upon the Three-Headed Sphinx. Toni's hand was glowing blue, as if getting ready to attack.

"No!" said Josh suddenly. "She's showing us the way out..."

Toni's hands stopped glowing. "The way out—but King Absoulah said it was impossible!"

The Sphinx spoke this time. "*You can only get out of the Darkness if you head in the right direction the first time. But now, they shall show you the way.*" The Sphinx disappeared. A white and a red light now glowed brightly in the distance.

"That's it!" yelled Josh, pointing to the left. "The red beam is the Birandian Kingdom and the white is the Skytanian Kingdom. We have to go in between the lights—that's where the finish line is located. Get on, Toni!"

Toni hopped on Gladius behind Josh and they flew off toward the glowing lights. Toni grabbed her Trident at the last second and sheathed it behind her. The Darkness around them began to disappear. They were flying in a clear sky once again. The sun was setting—dusk had come. They could see Jake and Rachel floating in the air with their Crystals glowing bright. The soldiers from both Kingdoms stared up at them. A purple and yellow light traveled up to Jake and Rachel—it was Mike and Becca.

Suddenly, a sharp pain went through Josh and Toni. Black lightning was powerfully and painfully striking them. Gladius stopped in midair, neighing in pain and distress. Josh and Toni looked at Drake who was now flying ahead of them. "We're never going to catch up!" said Toni, clenching and unclenching her body trying to ease the pain.

"Remember when we made Gladius?" asked Misty quickly. "You both added your own special Power from inside to make Gladius unique. Unlock the Power within Gladius and it might unlock something entirely new."

Josh turned around and stared into Toni's eyes. He grabbed her hands as they both began to glow. Their blue and green merged together creating a yellow light. They touched the head of Gladius and she began to glow yellow also. Her horn and wings grew twice as long and a golden halo appeared above her head. Gladius flew rapidly toward the finish line at an incredible speed. They were now right on Drake's tail. Toni and Josh had almost reached the finish line, when Gladius began to gallop. Josh looked below and realized she was galloping on ice. Josh looked behind him and saw Toni grinning as her eyes glowed brightly. The ice formed into a ramp and Gladius jumped magnificently off it, landing in the air in front of Drake. They passed the glowing golden line in between the two Kingdoms…Josh had won!

Chapter 24— The Zarroken Gem

The soldiers' eyes, from both Kingdoms, were now fixed upon Josh and Toni. Bulkest flew over to King Absoulah. "This is your *finish line*?"

King Absoulah grinned. "Why—*yes...*"

Bulkest looked at the evaporating golden line. "This is where our bridge once stood..."

"Well, I had to remove it," said the King, smirking with pleasure.

"It was *you?*" asked Bulkest, eyes narrowed in rage. "Well, that means Queen Simone wasn't lying!" He turned his head to Simone who was approaching. Her hair was now curly, her wings longer than the rest, and she wore a golden crown and golden armor.

Simone faced Bulkest. "I have been trying to tell you that we haven't been attacking you—but *YOU WOULD NOT LISTEN*!" She opened her eyes, which were red with anger. "Don't you see what fighting leads to if you do not talk matters through?"

Bulkest's eyes grew wide. "But if you haven't been attacking us—than who has, and why?"

King Absoulah laughed darkly. "Now your Kingdoms are *worthless*. The Emerald Kingdom is far wealthier and our economy is growing. So...I removed the bridge for a finish line—and a place to *expand* my Kingdom."

Bulkum stepped up on the platform and walked over to the King. He spoke loudly to Queen Simone and Bulkest. "Our King has betrayed us! Never have our People wanted this. We must get rid of him, and I will be the new King. I will lead our Kingdom down the Path of Righteousness. I will help the other Kingdoms grow, and soon they will be just as Powerful!" The soldiers from both Kingdoms began to cheer and roar in agreement. Bulkest and Simone floated in the sky in silence.

Toni bent closer to Josh and whispered in his ear. "*Look at the King.*" Josh turned his head toward the Emerald King. King Absoulah's eyes were out of focus and he looked lifeless. Josh noticed a dark glow at the back of the King's neck.

Bulkum shouted again. "We shall hang the King, for he is a traitor!"

Chanting filled the air. "*Kill the King, Kill the King!*"

Thunder shook the sky and lightning struck above the soldiers. "SILENCE!" Jake's eyes were glowing, but they were narrowed in disgust. "You do not know the Truth. It was not the King at all!"

Simone gasped. "But he has admitted to the crime!"

Jake's eyebrows lowered. "Why would someone *admit* to a crime knowing that he would get away with it otherwise?" Jake shut his eyes and spoke sternly. "The King is being *controlled.*"

Chatters of conversation and sounds of disbelief were heard from the soldiers. Bulkum suddenly spoke. "Silence!—Where is your proof? This is all talk!"

"We were right about the wars!" yelled Mike. He was not quite sure if the others were right, but he knew he had to stand by them. "We were right about everything! How could you doubt us now?"

"YOU HAVE NO PROOF!" screamed Bulkum, voice raging. "THE KING HAS ADMITTED TO HIS WRONG DEEDS. HE SHALL BE HUNG AND I SHALL RULE—*YOU HAVE NO PROOF!*"

"You want proof?" yelled Josh. He jumped off Gladius and flew over to the King. He shot his arm out to the back of the king's neck and snatched off a black gem. King Absoulah screamed in pain and collapsed on the stone platform. Josh held up the gem so everybody could see it. "Here is your proof!"

Simone screamed. "It's a Zarrocken Gem! They are rare and powerful and only used among the most powerful sorcerers of Darkness—it has the Power to enter and control one's mind!"

Bulkum's eyes widened in fright. He looked down at the King who got slowly to his feet and looked warily around him. "Where—where am I?" asked King Absoulah, confused. "What is going on? I had just fallen asleep after a meeting with Bulkum, and now I am here! What's happening?"

"You have been a puppet to a horrible mind thief, your Majesty!" yelled Becca, flying down next to Josh.

"I WHAT? What about the race—is it over? Has someone won? Who took control of my mind?"

"We do not know who has been controlling you," said Misty. "But we are the Seven Chosen Protectors—we will show you!" She soared off Toni's shoulder and hovered next to the Zarrocken Gem Josh held in his hand. The other Fairies joined her, forming a circle around the Gem. They shut their eyes as they began to glow brightly. The Gem did the same.

Thor began to speak, "The Gem will next appear on the Dark Sorcerer's forehead." The Gem changed into a glowing black star and flew high into the air. It hovered there for several seconds then shot downwards and struck Bulkum's forehead.

Everyone gasped in fear and total shock. King Absoulah's jaw dropped, and his eyes grew wide. "*You* did this to me?" asked the King, through clenched teeth. "I have always known something wasn't right. Drake had to get his nasty mouth from someone!" Drake had been floating on his Nightmare the whole time, listening closely to every word. However, no expression crossed his face.

"Guards!" Simone called. "Seize him!" About ten soldiers flew over to Bulkum and grasped him tightly by the arms. He made no sign of resistance.

King Absoulah smiled and snapped his fingers, lighting the torches at each corner of the platform and the ones behind their chairs. "Now for the race! We must get prepared.

Toni giggled. "Your Majesty, the race is over."

"By golly!" gasped the King. "I have to wait another decade! Oh well—I'm sure I didn't miss anything. It's not like anybody won." Toni giggled again.

Mike came soaring down next to Becca, leaving Jake and Rachel high in the sky with the spirits of the Ancient Birds glowing around them. "Your Majesty," laughed Mike. "Someone *did* win."

The King howled, danced a jig, and fell into his chair next to Bulkum. "Someone won? Who!?"

Josh and Toni hopped on Gladius and flew over to the King. "We did!"

"I don't believe my ears." The King looked up and down at Josh and Toni. "You both look rather young, but very well—the prizes are yours!" He raised his glowing green hands. A golden light shone above his head as a boomerang appeared. It was made from a hard, polished brown oak, which was carved with many ancient symbols. The boomerang was the length of his entire arm, and on each of the three points was a large rectangular cut emerald. The King reached up and grabbed the Boomerang. "I hereby present this Ancient Boomerang of the Mythical Chosen Sage to the winner of the Emerald Kingdom race." He held it up for all to see and the cheers roared out once again. The teens could even hear cheers and applause all the way from the stands in the Emerald Kingdom.

A voice suddenly broke the moment. "I cannot allow that!" A glowing black light came from Bulkum as the soldiers restraining him flew into the air from a powerful exploding blast of energy. Simone waved her hand and the soldiers were stopped by a glowing red force field. Bulkum flew over to the King and shot a bolt of black lightning into his back. The King fell to the platform and dropped the Boomerang. Bulkum picked it up. "At last!" laughed Bulkum. "I will rule these Kingdoms, and I will get my reward from the Ancient!"

"NOO!" screamed Merlin. "You must get the Boomerang, Sages. He will destroy ALL with that Power!" Another loud blast echoed through the sky. The teens and soldiers looked over at the volcano. It was going through its final eruption. This time, lava began to pour down the cone.

"Our Kingdom!" yelled Bulkest in fear. "It will be destroyed!"

"Now to get rid of all of the rest of you!" screamed Bulkum, pointing at the soldiers. He held out the Boomerang and a glowing green beam shot from each of the emeralds.

Becca threw her hands out and a purple force field appeared around the soldiers. The green beams shot right through Becca's force field, sending the soldiers, Simone, Bulkest, and even Bulkum's son, Drake, tumbling over the edge, unconscious, down to the ocean far, far below.

Jake began to speak loudly. "Guys! Flare, Myth, and I will take care of Bulkum. Star and Quake have to stop the lava from reaching the Birandian Kingdom. Aquarius!" He pointed down to the unconscious, falling soldiers. "Save them!"

Josh jumped off Gladius and soared into the air. "Take Gladius with you. She will fly you down quicker." Misty hung tightly onto Toni's shoulder as Toni wrapped her fingers tightly into Gladius's mane. Gladius flew downwards as the wind blew strongly against them.

Mike and Becca were already at the Birandian Kingdom, thinking of a reasonable way to stop the lava from reaching the Kingdom. Strangely, all of the Phoenixes were resting, eyes closed, perched along the edge of the Kingdom, just like the Rainbonians were.

* * * * * * * *

Bulkum looked at Josh, Rachel, and Jake most disdainfully. He laughed at them. "Do you really think you can take me on? Do you even realize who you are dealing with?" Bulkum's eyes narrowed as they glowed black. "I am one of the Seven Lords of the Ancient!" His body began to glow a dark purplish black. So dark that the teens thought they were staring into an endless tunnel. He blended perfectly with the now darkened night sky. Suddenly, another pair of black feathered wings grew from his back below the pair he already had. A black flame appeared on the wings and burned all the feathers off, revealing two dark pairs of black leather wings. Black horns sprouted from each wingtip.

For the first time ever, the three teens were truly frightened. They felt as though they were going to feel pain beyond their imaginations. They did not know what kind of Power this Being had. "Do not be intimidated by his looks or Power!" said Thor. "We can defeat him, but we must have a strategy—you must think! We cannot afford any mistakes."

"He's right!" said Merlin firmly. "We can defeat him!"

"But he said he was a Lord!" said Rachel, as she looked at Jake. They were both still glowing with the Bird Spirits around them. "One of the Seven Chosen of the Ancient!"

"What does that mean?" asked Jake confused, and yet curious.

"We shall explain everything later!" said Flairen, resting on Rachel's shoulder, her face blank.

"Who *is* the Ancient?" asked Josh, flying up next to Jake and Rachel.

Bulkum laughed loudly. "Before I kill you, I guess you should know..." His eyes narrowed. "The Ancient is our God sent to finish what Satan started. To you, he is known as—*APOCALYPSE!"* He threw the Boomerang with great power and force. It glowed brightly as it hit the three teens. A green shield encircled them in the shape of a lion. It happened so quickly there was no time for them to react. They went soaring through the air, paralyzed with pain. The shield broke when they slammed into the ground only several feet down slope from the slowly moving lava.

Mike and Becca came soaring over to them. Mike laughed. "Hey guys... I thought the volcano was *our* job. *You're* supposed to be taking care of Bulkum."

Josh, Rachel, and Jake suddenly took flight, narrowly missing the tide of lava. "We're getting to it!" yelled Jake, annoyed. They soared off with their Fairies holding tightly to their shoulders.

"Well," said Granite, "we need to somehow stop the lava in its tracks, but then what are we going to do with it?"

"Let's just worry about stopping it for now," said Becca, soaring down the volcano and speeding past the lava. Mike followed her, pointing the palms of his hands toward the ground as yellow beams shot out. They traveled deep through the earth. The beams stopped and he raised his glowing yellow hands to his sides. With a flash of his eyes, a wide crack formed and quickly continued splitting around the volcano, creating a deep circular channel around the base.

Juhani took flight from Becca's shoulder and examined the gap Mike had created. "Quake, create a wall of earth all the way around the volcano or the lava will quickly fill up the crack and travel out of it."

Mike nodded as he took flight and made his away around the volcano. He raised earth in his tracks to create a thick barrier just outside the channel. The lava approached the gap and poured into it, filling it up rapidly.

* * * * * * * *

Toni was speeding straight down, holding tightly to Gladius. The ocean was in sight but the soldiers were still far from her reach. Simone easily stood out from the rest of them in her golden armor.

"I'm never going to reach them in time!" yelled Toni, her hope fading.

"Couldn't you control the ocean from here?" shouted Misty.

"I'm too far away! They'll hit the water before I can manipulate it. At that force and speed they'll die instantly!" Toni shook her head and kicked Gladius to go faster. "I'll never reach them in time."

Gladius' wings pulled in and her nose was pointing straight down like an arrow. They were gaining speed—but so were the soldiers. Circles of white light appeared on the ocean's surface right below the soldiers, and many blue objects began to come forth out of them.

"The Merains!" yelled Toni. "But what can they do?" The Merains raised their hands as they each began to whisper softly—chanting. Toni could hear them—there were hundreds of them whispering the same thing. Suddenly, a Merain shot out of the water, shooting like a rocket into the air. The Merains that rested in the water dived down. The Merain that was shooting high in the air was Whisper!

She spoke softly, but her voice echoed through the air as though amplified. Her Serenity enchanted the sea, sending chills through Toni and Misty. She stood still in the sky, floating in place. "*I call upon the Spirit of the Sea! It is I—Whisper, Princess of Meraintron—Horsaintion, I call upon thee!*"

The glowing light lit the waves below, making them a translucent green. The soldiers were about to hit the ocean—there wasn't enough time! A woman with blue skin and purple hair appeared above the glowing waves. She had glowing, blue-feathered wings that seemed to be made from water and light. She wore an emerald gown and carried a golden shield in the shape of a seahorse face. Her beauty lit up the sky and ocean for miles around. Horsaintion swung the shield above her and every single one of the soldiers stopped in midair, only ten feet above the ocean.

Gladius halted his downward plunge. "It can't be!" yelled Misty in disbelief.

"What is it?" asked Toni, eyes fixed upon Horsaintion.

"Whisper is a *Summoner*! There aren't many left on Earth, and she called upon the Ancient Spirit of the Sea, Horsaintion, the Guardian of the Atlantic."

"So they can call upon Spirits?" asked Toni. Misty nodded.

Horsaintion squinted her eyes. "*Reborn Aquarius, I shall lend you my strength.*" The golden shield started to glow as it shot a golden beam at Toni, lifting her and Misty off Gladius. Toni began to fly rapidly downwards, trying to reach the floating soldiers. Horsaintion shut her eyes. "*I cannot hold them much longer.*"

Toni waved her hand and a surge of water lifted from the ocean and traveled up under the soldiers. Toni's eyes flashed and the water transformed into a thick slab of ice. Horsaintion started to fade away, allowing the soldiers to drop smoothly down onto the giant ice floe that was now bobbing gently up and down on the surface. Whisper dove back under the waves as the light slowly died away.

Toni's hands began to glow gold as she used her strengthened Power to lift the patch of ice. She had the added strength of Horsaintion as part of her now. She soared upwards with clenched hands, as though pulling on an invisible rope. Misty soared off her shoulder and went below the slowly moving ice sheet, adding a blue beam under the bottom to help Toni push it upwards. Toni looked up at the small dark shapes far above her on the viewing platform. "This is going to be a *long* ride…"

* * * * * * * *

The Boomerang came soaring toward the three teens and spun viciously, cutting right through their wrist plates that were held up trying to protect them. Josh reached to grasp the Boomerang, but an electric green force shocked him and cut his hand. He cradled his injured hand with his other hand and screamed in pain. Night had completely fallen, making it difficult to see Bulkum—he blended perfectly with the surrounding Darkness. The only visible lights were the glowing embers of magma from the Birandian Kingdom and brightly glowing Fairies.

"I can't see him!" yelled Jake.

There was a rush of cool wind next to the teens, and they heard a dark voice echo in their heads. "*How about now?*" it bellowed.

"Look out!" warned Thor.

The teens turned quickly when Merlin shouted, "*RICOCHET!*" A protective green aura flashed like lightning in front of the teens, just as Bulkum's powerfully clenched dark fist hit it. Bulkum ricocheted back one hundred yards, as fast as a bullet.

Bulkum yelled in fury. "YOU BLOODY FAIRIES! ALWAYS MEDDLING WHERE YOU DON'T BELONG!"

"Thanks, guys," said Jake while smirking at Bulkum.

"This is our job," said Flairen grinning. "To protect you."

"I do not need Fairies!" yelled Bulkum. He held up the Boomerang and the emeralds started to glow. The teens felt a sharp pressure against their shoulders.

"*Thor*?" asked Jake, turning his head to the left where Thor was struggling to hold on. "What is it?"

Flairen screamed loudly as she was jolted forward; torn forcibly from Rachel's shoulder. Rachel snatched at Flairen's tiny hands and pulled with all her might as Flairen was being pulled toward Bulkum by some magnetic force.

Merlin and Thor lost their grip and went plummeting through the cool night sky. Josh and Jake dove after them, but they were too late. Thor was absorbed into the left emerald on the Boomerang and Merlin into the right. They could be seen punching and kicking against the inside of the emerald, struggling to get free.

Rachel still clung tightly to Flairen. They were both being pulled steadily and bodily forward by the force that had hold of Flairen. Rachel screamed as tears rolled down her face. "*I WILL NOT LOSE YOU!*"

"You won't Flare!" yelled Flairen, tears also rolling down her face. "You must fight him. Remember this—unleash more than one type of Being to aid you. You shall have the advantage with a loss of one of his senses. Magic will not defeat him, but Strength and Weapons shall—*I shall always be with you—guiding you.*"

The Boomerang started to glow brighter—so bright, it gave a greenish cast to Bulkum's face. His deep-set demonic eyes darkened and flickered like embers in a dying fire. He smiled, showing a set of

Vampire-like fangs. The force pulling Flairen became greater still, and Rachel finally lost her desperate grip, letting Flairen shoot away towards the Boomerang. She was absorbed into the center emerald. Rachel screamed again as Bulkum laughed madly. "I am one of the Lords of Darkness, Ruler of Hatred…You cannot defeat me!"

"You're wrong!" yelled Rachel, her eyes burning with fire. Rage had spread through her—her body slowly caught on fire.

"*That's right!*" Bulkum sneered, one fist held clenched in front of him. "Let your Hatred toward me grow!"

"This isn't *Hatred*!" yelled Josh, eyes closed. "We are compelled to fight by Love!" The grin was swept off Bulkum's face. His eyebrows lowered and his teeth clenched. Josh opened his eyes and smiled. "You are nothing more than a featureless shadow on the Path of Serenity that we are spreading."

Bulkum burst into black flame. "How dare you insult me, you little *brat*! I am tired of toying with you. You shall now suffer the kind of painful death you deserve as you burn in the flames of Hell, with the help of your own *worthless* Fairies!" Bulkum held the Boomerang and beams of red, white, and green shot from each of the stones. It formed into the shape of another Boomerang, which came whirling at the teens. Before it could reach them, it vanished.

Jake had a silver arrow pulled back in his shining ivory Bow. Rachel had her Spear of red flame pointing at Bulkum. Josh had six-inch long silver needles clenched tightly in both hands ready to be thrown like darts.

Bulkum screamed in fury. "That force should have blown you to pieces. How did you—"

"Our Weapons are equally as Powerful as the one that rests in your hand," said Rachel calmly, a grin tugging at the corners of her mouth.

"You don't seem to realize who *we* are," said Jake, his hair glowing like white flame. "We are the Chosen of the Ancient Sages, Protectors of the Heavens. We *shall* not and *will* not be defeated!"

Chapter 25— When Dark Warriors Battle

Toni was sweating profusely and Misty was moaning from the exhausting work of propelling the sheet of ice back up to the Kingdom. A slight groan from Drake worried Toni even more. If he woke up, there was no telling what he would do. Toni had to save these Beings! If Drake was the son of Bulkum, then what would stop him from helping his father try to destroy them all? She gazed ahead of her and swore loudly. They were only half way there, and Misty was about to pass out. If she did, then Toni had no chance of carrying the ice to the top on her own. "Hang in there, Misty!" she yelled.

"Are we almost there?" Misty grunted in misery.

"Nearly!" she lied. "*Misty has to hang in there,*" she told herself. "*Without her, all these people are done for!*" Toni heard another wailing moan from the ice floe beneath her. Drake was waking up and trying to push himself up with his arms. Fear swept through her. She couldn't battle him now, and she couldn't freeze him either. She was carrying an ice patch as big as many icebergs combined. If she lost focus, the thousands of soldiers she was carrying would perish.

Drake was now standing up and looking around in confusion. He fell to his knees beside the Nightmare. He let out a howl of rage and fury. The blast from Bulkum had killed his Nightmare! It was clearly dead, since its flames were extinguished. He looked sadly up at Toni who was gazing down at him. A tear rolled down his face and he sighed heavily, head down, looking at the ice beneath him. He began to glow black and gently touched the surface. A net of black force field circled the entire ice floe, including all the Beings on it, except for himself.

"*They're done for!*" Toni whispered. Drake flew into the air glowing an even darker black. He was holding a black rope that was tied around the ice. He flew next to Toni and grinned. Toni made a rude hand gesture in reply. "How could you hurt all these people?"

Drake laughed. "They're not people. They're Beings. And who said I was going to hurt them?" His eyes started to glow white as his hands glowed black. He was using his power to help pull the ice! It was traveling three times as fast as before, and it became a lot easier for Toni and Misty. "You know?" he said, his voice strained, sounding like he was talking from the other side of a wall. "You could find a better way to move this. I'm getting weaker by the second, and it looks like your friend down there won't last must longer either. She needs help."

Toni looked down through the ice sheet. Misty was vibrating and moaning loudly. She didn't seem to be aware of anything but pushing the ice. Toni's hands stopped glowing as she left and flew down quickly to help Misty. "Misty! Stop! It's okay! You can let go!"

"I will not stop! You need all the help you can get!" She suddenly stopped glowing, revealing her beautiful form in the darkness. She fainted and began to fall, but Toni caught her in the palms of her hands. She glanced back down to the ocean that was now barely visible far below.

She heard Drake yell loudly from above. "I can't keep this up much longer! Hurry up and do something or I'll just drop the whole load now!"

Toni rolled her eyes. "*I knew it was too good to be true!*" she whispered. She used her right hand to unsheathe the Trident while cradling Misty in her left. Toni dove straight down as the powerful, blue shimmering glow from her body transferred to the Trident of Glory. The crystal on the middle prong began to glow with an ethereal blue light, illuminating the entire sky as though it were daytime once again. Toni threw the Trident at great speed toward the ocean, leaving a trail of ice crystals in its wake as it plummeted downward. Waves began to form a circle and mist clouded the ocean's surface. The Trident struck the middle of the circle, sending a ring of waves like colossal ripples. Toni stopped in midair, twirled her hand in a circle and then lifted it upwards.

The Trident suddenly rocketed back up through the water. Behind it traveled a huge waterspout. The Trident swept past Toni and she grabbed it by the handle. She shot upwards as it made a flash of shimmering light. The vortex twisted and spun dangerously as it rose at great speed and hit the ice patch, Drake narrowly dodging it. Drake came soaring down next to Toni, eyes still focused on the ice overhead that was now shooting through the air like a missile. He was bewildered. He couldn't believe what he was seeing.

"Are you doing this?" he asked Toni.

Toni grinned, and then nodded.

"But how? I mean…how could someone…or should I say some Being like yourself, possess so much Power? I have never seen anything like it! Who are you really?"

Toni still focused her eyes upon the vortex, because she was controlling it with her mind. "I am one of the New Sages—The Sage of Water and Ice. I am one of the Seven Chosen of the Ancient Sages, Guardians of the Heavens."

Drake paused, and then said, "my father often spoke about the Ancient Sages and how they are his greatest enemy. He told stories of the unimaginable Power and Knowledge they possess. He also told me they were swept away to protect the Heavens from him and his Master. But by leaving the Worlds unprotected, it allowed him to find a way to reign with Evil and Hatred."

Toni slowly turned toward Drake, still holding one hand up toward the waterspout. "And what is your perception of us? We are the Chosen Beings, reborn to protect the Universe."

Drake sighed. "I loved my father once, before he gave himself completely to Evil."

Toni raised her eyebrows. "You're saying that your father was once Good?"

"He attacked the soldiers, not caring about me. He saw me as nothing more than a pawn to get things done for him," said Drake sadly.

"But why would he do that to his own son? Maybe he was possessed or brainwashed just like he did to the King of the Emerald Kingdom."

"He chose this path! It is his own wrongdoing that will bring him down. He had, I'm afraid, brainwashed me. However, seeing you helping so many Beings made me think differently. It made me think more about the true meaning of life. Therefore, I have to thank you. What is your true name?"

Toni smiled. "I'm Aquarius, but my close friends call me Toni. And right now, they need my help. We must go!" A neighing sound echoed as Gladius gracefully swooped near, her wings shimmering in the moonlight. Toni sheathed the Trident and grabbed her mane, letting Gladius pull her up to the Kingdoms far above. Drake laughed and sped up to stay close behind her.

* * * * * * * *

The glowing vortex and ice patch caught Mike and Becca's eyes, as they floated in the air, hoping their lava obstacle would work. They watched the ice patch jetting up ahead of the waterspout, making its way up to the Skytanian Kingdom. It still had a ways to go.

Mike laughed. "She is one powerful Queen of the Sea!"

"Well!" said Granite, annoyed. "She better come over here quickly before this lava breaks through your earth wall!" He was right. The lava was still spilling out of the cone and piling up behind the mounded walls of earth. A fine mesh of cracks was spreading across the face of the bank of earth. If any of the cracks burst open, the lava would pour out heavily like a waterfall. The ground vibrated as another shockwave caused by the eruption struck. A larger crack formed near the base of the wall. Mike's hands were glowing and vibrating with fury. The lava was only sixty feet away from the town! The cracks started to widen as lava continued to flow into the trench. It wasn't working.

Becca gestured wildly with her glowing hands as if throwing many balls. Huge pieces of lava merged together and flew through the air and back up toward the top of the volcano. It was no use. The lava just kept flowing, and the mass of it finally burst through Mike's earth dam. "Okay—Juhani—I'm going to need your help on this one."

Juhani soared off her shoulder and faced her. "What are you going to do?" Becca smiled, her arms still moving wildly. "Why do you ask questions if you already know the answers?" Juhani smiled and backed away as she glowed a bright purple. Becca jumped back to hover in the air next to Juhani. They both raised their hands. A silky purple substance, like a river of flowing, graceful purple water, surrounded the city and continued up and over it. A purple ribbon of translucent glass moved in an unbroken, unwavering line several hundred feet in the air until reaching the edge of the Kingdom, flowing over the side.

Mike and Granite moved off to safe distance and anxiously watched the lava. They were getting ready to help Becca and Juhani in any way. Becca's force field didn't work before, so there was no telling if it would hold this time. The glowing orange and red lava began to hit the undulating purple force field. Instead of stopping, the lava started to slide along the force field and move up over the top. It seemed to defy the laws of gravity as the large, burning, smoking mass picked up speed and was sent off through the air along the purple line toward the edge of the Kingdom. The force field was holding—for now. It was an incredible sight!

Becca's arms were still raised and her teeth were clenched. Juhani was standing on Becca's shoulder in the same pose, concentrating on the moving lava. Mike glanced over at the volcano. The flow seemed to be slowing, but there was still plenty of it traveling down to join the purple river. The leading edge of the lava, at last, reached the end of the purple river and began to pour down through the night sky on its way to the ocean far below. The Phoenixes opened their eyes to gaze at the lava flowing over their heads. They just sat there undisturbed for several brief moments and then went back to sleep.

Mike walked over to Becca and put his arm around her. "Keep it up!"

Becca laughed. "You know what's weird?"

"Huh?"

"How does a volcano in the sky erupt when it isn't even connected to the Earth's core?"

Mike laughed. "I never even thought about that. You are smart!"

"Well," said Granite, "since this is a Mythical land, lava can be magically transported from the Earth below into the volcano."

A deep sigh came from Juhani. She was getting stressed and annoyed. "Less talking! We're trying to concentrate, you two!"

"You're right, Juhani," laughed Granite. "I apologize. Young Quake and I will watch from a distance." He flew over to Mike and tugged on his cape, pulling him away.

Mike sighed as he followed Granite away. "I hope the others are okay."

* * * * * * * *

Josh, Rachel, and Jake were in awe as they watched from the King's floating platform at the finish line. The glowing, flaming magma glowed magnificently in the dark. Bulkum even seemed interested and was watching as intently as the others. Suddenly, the teens heard loud splashing from below. They looked down just in time to see a giant glowing sheet of ice heading directly for them at great speed. They leaped aside into the air, pulling the King's platform with them. The ice sheet was followed by a vortex of water spinning at great speed. A familiar voice shouted from below.

"Sorry guys!" Toni came soaring quickly past Jake, Josh, and Rachel, catching up with the ice platform with the help of Gladius. They stared up at her as they heard a crack, like very loud static. The teens looked ahead of them, almost losing track of time as three black beams headed toward them like arrows in a blast wave. Since the Fairies were not there to warn them, there was no time to protect themselves. They felt they were done for, until a translucent wave of darkness filled the air in front of them. Everything on the other side of the barrier was outlined in white, like someone had used a white colored pencil on a sheet of shiny black paper. Then three even blacker beams hit the dark wall violently, sending a loud, ear-splitting sound like a gunshot through the air. The black wall disintegrated as did the beams. They slowly lowered their arms, which they had put up to try to shield themselves from the blast. Floating in the air five feet in front of them was Drake. He was glowing white now, instead of black.

Josh gasped. "What are you doing?"

Drake laughed. "Saving your lives. I have unfinished business to take care of with my father."

Bulkum shouted in fury yet again. "You should have perished on the ocean floor! But still you are here and have stopped me from destroying these worthless brats!"

Drake flew over to where his father floated. Bulkum's devil-like, black leather wings were flapping slowly and his eyes glowed red-orange like coals on fire.

Drake shouted in rage. "You have never treated me like a son! I dreamed of reigning by your side, but this Darkness has turned you into something you are not. You are unimportant to me now, as I am to you."

Bulkum sneered at him. "You have always gotten in my way. You have been nothing but a failure to me. You are worthless and will burn in Hell with the rest of these imbeciles."

Drake shut his eyes. "I will give you one last chance, Father. Abandon this Evil-like form and turn away from the Darkness. You have chosen the wrong Path, but it is not too late. You still have a chance to recover from your Evil ways."

Bulkum laughed. "Are you threatening me? I was born into Darkness. I should have known better than to have tried to carry you along by my side, tainted as you are. It's in your blood after all."

Drake stopped in midair and squinted his eyes at his father. "In my blood? You said I was born into pure Darkness."

"Your mother was worthless! She was one of the angels who had turned from Good to Evil. We got along perfectly. But she tricked me into thinking that she was also born into pure Darkness. Then when you were born with black *feathers* on your wings, I knew she had betrayed me..."

A tear welled in Drake's eye. "My mother was an Angel of the Heavens?"

Bulkum gazed at his son with sparks of red dancing in his darkened eyes. "Why yes, and after you were born, I killed her, hoping to raise you to be like me, and reign by my side." He eyed Drake up and down. "But now, you are just a child that I am a father to no longer. A mere child tainted with Angel's blood. You are useless to me. I knew you would turn out to be a disappointment just like your mother. I shall get rid of you just as I did her!"

Drake clenched his teeth. Black-feathered wings began to grow from his back. They were enormous and far greater than his father's. A black ball appeared in his hand and mutated into a magnificent silver-bladed long sword. He swung it and pointed it at his father. "You have it wrong. It is I who shall destroy you."

All of a sudden, a mist of true Darkness rose up all around, the exact type that Josh and Toni were in at the end of the race. It circled around Drake and his father, completely hiding them and leaving a huge void in the air that blotted out the stars beyond. They heard Drake speak from inside. "Go now Sages. The others need you."

Josh shouted into the black cloud, "But what about Thor, Flairen, and Merlin!?"

"Do not worry," said Drake calmly. "I will set them free."

"Let us help!" yelled Jake.

"I'm sorry, but this Darkness would control you, making you weak and blind. This is now my fight. But please Sages, do me one favor?"

"We owe you our lives," said Josh. "What is it?"

Drake sighed. "Accept my apologies, and please forgive me for all of the sins that I may have committed while under the control of Darkness."

Rachel smiled and looked at her brother who looked brightly back at her. "We already have."

"Then," said Drake, "I thank you again—and please—give Toni my warmest thanks and let her know that in the end, Darkness did not prevail."

The teens heard the clash of steel from within the cloud of Darkness that consumed Bulkum and Drake. The duel had begun.

The three looked over at the Skytanian Kingdom where Toni had safely landed the huge piece of ice with the thousands of soldiers on it. They flew over the sleeping Rainbonians at the edge of the Kingdom and landed next to Toni, who was sitting cross-legged on the ground with her back to the ice sheet, holding the Trident upright in front of her. Gladius had laid down next to her, and Misty was lying across her lap glowing dimly, obviously asleep. Jake, Josh, and Rachel sat down on Toni's other side with their heads resting back against the ice. Sitting that way made it look as if it were about five stories high, which it probably was.

Toni squinted her eyes at them. She raised her eyebrows. "Where are Thor, Merlin, and Flairen?"

Jake sighed. "Bulkum has captured them and is using their Powers to help him fight Drake."

Toni's eyes went wide. She placed her palms on the sides of Misty's head, covering her ears. She whispered. "*How did he take them!? Weren't you supposed to defend them?*"

Jake and Rachel turned to look at Josh. He sighed. "The Boomerang. It has strong Power and can do many mystical things. It has absorbed Merlin, Flairen, and Thor."

"What?!" Toni screamed, waking up Misty who flew into the air, alarmed. Toni smiled at her, and then turned her head sharply to look at Jake. "Then what are you doing *here*? Go get them! Haven't you destroyed or captured Bulkum?"

"We can't fight Bulkum right now," said Rachel, gazing up at Misty. "Drake wants to deal with his father himself and he has forbidden us to help him fight."

They heard Misty sob. She obviously knew what was going on.

"Well, why didn't you fight with him anyway?" asked Toni, also watching Misty.

"Because," said Josh, "he put a Dark cloud around he and his father. They are where we have no chance of even putting a scratch on Bulkum. We're counting on Drake now."

"It's Dark Matter," said Misty.

"What?" asked Rachel, confused and taken aback by the sudden words.

"Dark Matter. The Dark Ones have the ability to manipulate matter so you see nothing but Darkness. And only they can see in it and live through their contact with it. We, for example, would go insane if we were in it too long. Luckily, we were able to get out of it okay. The only Sage that can withstand the Dark Matter is the one that can create it—Raven."

The others paused in thought. Toni looked over at the Dark Matter that surrounding Drake and Bulkum. She noticed for the first time the magnificent lava falling from the Birandian Kingdom. "Wow! Mike and Becca are doing that?"

Josh, Jake, and Rachel looked over to the spectacular sight. They smiled. "Pretty neat, huh?" laughed Jake.

Toni nodded, her eyes still gazing at it. "Let's go to them. They might need help and its better now if we all stay together as a team."

Misty flew to Toni's shoulder. "She is right. Alone we are strong, but together... we are Sages!"

"But what about Merlin, Thor, and Flairen?" asked Josh, now standing up with the others.

Misty turned her head toward the Dark Matter. "All we can do now is wait. We can do the same at the Birandian Kingdom, but we'll be by the side of Star and Quake."

"Agreed," said Jake.

Toni looked at Gladius. "Stay here and protect the soldiers until they wake up." Gladius stood up, shook herself and neighed as though she understood what Toni was saying. Toni smiled as she flew off into the night sky with the others, heading for the volcano on Skytania.

Chapter 26— A Phoenix From Within

Mike looked up to the sky and saw four glowing bright lights heading toward him.

A wave of calm spread over him. He waved at his friends who were smiling cheerfully. Becca and Juhani however, were still concentrating on holding the purple force field that was carrying the lava to the ocean. The four landed next to Mike, eyes focused on Becca and Juhani.

"Is she going to be alright?" asked Toni, walking over to Becca.

"I'll be okay," said Becca, turning her face toward Toni with her glowing bright eyes. She then turned her head back toward the volcano. "It's just that the lava keeps coming!"

Rachel walked over to Becca. "I'll take care of it, and then I'll get rid of it for you."

Becca nodded. "It's alright. Just stop more lava from coming and I can take care of the rest. But wait, why are you here? Shouldn't you be fighting Bulkum? And where are Merlin, Flairen, and Thor?"

Toni sighed and then explained everything. Mike had overheard what she said because he shouted, "why didn't you just help Drake fight him?"

"You didn't let me finish!" snapped Toni. "We can't survive in Dark Matter, but he can. We just have to wait to see what happens before we make our next move."

Rachel soared to the sky and flew like a bullet past Mike and Jake. She reached the peak of the volcano, stopped in midair, and gazed at the lava below that was pouring out of the volcano like a nonstop waterfall. Her body began to grow hot and liquid in her skin began to mutate into a thin layer of molten magma. Her hair became hair of fire. Her eyes grew a bright red like her smoking body. She raised her arms and all the lava on the volcano, not including that traveling over Becca's force field, soared rapidly into the air and back through the open gap at the top of the volcano.

Rachel looked down into the cone of the volcano and at the sizzling, crackling lava. The whole Birandian Kingdom began to shake violently. Rachel puckered her eyebrows in thought. "*Why is it doing this? I put the lava back into the volcano where it belongs—don't tell me its going to erupt again!*" The surface of the lava inside the cone burst into bubbles, like a bubbling cauldron, sending liquid embers up all around. Suddenly, the lava shot upwards as though in a cannon, hitting Rachel and going up like a jet of water. Luckily, it didn't affect her. She bent her knees then jumped up, soaring as fast as she could, trying to out-fly the spout of lava. She was now ten feet above it, but it was right on her tail. She stopped and shot her arms downward, creating her own jet of lava to power against the one shooting up. She then used all her might to push the jet of lava back down. The two beams of lava clashed together creating a sound like thunder, sending fiery sprays of lava everywhere. It lit up the darkened sky like fireworks. It was working! The force from her beam of lava overpowered the one shooting up out of the cone. The lava was finally traveling back down into the volcano.

Every single one of the teens at the base of the Birandian Kingdom gazed up at Rachel. It was extraordinary to witness her using so much Power to stop Mother Nature in action. Mike laughed in amazement. He then looked at the force field that was holding the rest of the large mass of magma. Once all the lava traveled to the ocean, Becca would be a great success. The teens waited anxiously. Toni was even jumping up and down, gazing back and forth at Rachel and Becca.

Suddenly, there was a loud scream. It was so loud and heart wrenching that it woke the Phoenixes from their slumber on the edge of the Birandian Kingdom. The screech came right from the Dark Matter. The Phoenixes then echoed the screeches sending their own ear-pitching screams through the night.

Rachel began to scream. Piteous cries were echoing through her head. She placed her fists on her head against her ears to block the sound. The lava burst upwards again at her as she screamed. Her screams blended and echoed with the shrieking of the Phoenixes.

Mike looked up at Rachel in horror. "Granite! What's the matter with her?" Granite said nothing. "Granite!"

Granite sighed. "I don't *know.*"

Mike gazed sympathetically up at Rachel. The ground shook below him as a mound of earth lifted him up as he soared to Rachel. Granite chased after him, but Mike yelled to Granite, "Make sure everyone else is okay! Don't come with me. I don't want you to get hurt!"

Toni ran to where Mike had been standing and called after him. "You must not go to her! It's too dangerous!" Mike simply ignored her and soared off. "No!" screamed Toni.

Jake and Josh ran over to Toni. A tear rolled down Toni's face. Granite flew over to Toni and rested on her shoulder, next to Misty. "He will be destroyed by the lava if something goes wrong," she said. Jake hugged her from behind as Josh put a hand on her shoulder. They watched Mike fly off toward Rachel, afraid of what was going to happen. "Why don't you go to her, Josh?"

Josh sighed. "I would, but Mike loves her as much as I do. It is between them now. I just hope they'll be alright." He closed his eyes as he listened to the screams of his sister and the Phoenixes. His eyes grew damp. "*Something isn't right.*"

"That scream," said Becca, "it was horrible. It sounded like someone was being torn apart. Not just the one from Rachel, but the one from the Dark Matter as well."

"We have to do something about the lava jet. If Rachel doesn't do something, this Kingdom is done for," said Jake.

"We are too late!" yelled Juhani. "Mike better get Rachel back to her senses or, like you said Jake, this kingdom *is* done for." This time, everyone turned their heads to look first at the Dark Matter and then towards Rachel.

* * * * * * * *

Mike reached Rachel who was hovering next to the jet of lava. It was burning hot for Mike but he didn't care. He approached Rachel without hesitation. He put his hands on her shoulders and yelled into her face. "Rachel! Rachel! What's wrong? Come on. Talk to me!"

Rachel continued screaming, but then she yelled, "*Something is inside of me—voices—more than one—several—something isn't right!*"

She opened her eyes but they were not glowing. Only the whites showed. Mike looked closely at Rachel and put his sweating, burning hand upon her lava face. He burned his hand but he didn't care. "Rachel you must save this kingdom. If you don't stop this lava… it will be destroyed!" Mike gazed into the whites of her eyes in confusion. Flames began to glow in them. Rachel began to shake, then spoke. "The Dark Matter!"

Mike turned his head toward the platform where the Dark Matter glimmered sickly in the torchlight. He squinted as a glowing black object shot out of the Dark Matter hitting Becca's force field and shattering it. The lava fell unchecked. "NO!" he screamed.

Becca screamed, then collapsed to the ground from all the Power that she was unleashing that had suddenly failed her. Juhani collapsed on her chest. Becca looked to her side and saw Drake lying on the ground in a puddle of blood, his own sword stabbed through his heart. Tears rolled down Becca's face as her eyes wearily shut.

The lava was falling quickly, and was about to hit the Kingdom when Jake ran over and shouted, "*WIND AURORA!*" A white magnificent beam shot out from Jake's arms and created a wall of white wind that held the lava up. But the force of the lava was too powerful and was pushing the aurora slowly down. Jake clenched his teeth. "It's too powerful! I don't know how you do it, Becca!" He looked over at Becca who lay on the ground, unconscious. "Becca!" He looked up at his own force field that now began to descend quickly under the tremendous weight of the lava. He then heard a frightening scream from Toni. He gazed up in the sky. The jet of lava that was shooting out from the volcano began to arc back to the ground, bridging the gap between the town's smaller Kingdoms and heading for the Birandian Kingdom. Jake began to shake in horror. The lava was falling quickly, and hit his force field with enormous strength. It was slowly cracking as more and more lava piled on it. Jake's arms began to bend as though lifting something many times his own weight. It was too powerful for him.

Toni ran over to him, shot her hands upwards and screamed. Ice beams shot out of her hands and created a wall of ice right below Jake's force field, helping him hold it up. Josh had run over and shouted, "*RICOCHET!*" The familiar green force field that had saved Becca, Jake, Toni, and Mike before, shot around the ice wall and wind aurora. It knit the two together making it as strong as it could be. The three stood by each other as they held up their glowing hands. Granite was flying high in the air and shooting beams of earth onto the force field where any little cracks appeared.

More and more lava began to pour onto the force field, making it more difficult to hold. Jake slowly turned his head toward Becca. Juhani was resting by her side. Misty had even flown over to her. She was looking into Drake's open black eyes. Becca was shaking and glowing. She kept chanting aloud as if possessed. "*We need you*! *Please Rachel, if you can hear me, help us!*" She said these words over and over, as Josh, Toni, and Jake kept holding on. The force field grew heavier and heavier. They were sweating and struggling to keep the force field together. Unfortunately, lava was collecting on it faster than it was hitting the ocean.

* * * * * * * *

Mike put his hands on Rachel's burning magma hands. His hands began to smoke but he held in the pain. "Rachel!"

Rachel stared back into Mike's glowing yellow eyes. "*The voices are strong—I can't think—the screams—eeh*!" Rachel began to scream again. "Flairen I need you!"

Mike looked into Rachel's eyes, his eyes now glowing purple rather than yellow. Mike began to chant in a whisper. "*We need you! Please, Rachel, if you can hear me, help us! We need you! Please, Rachel, if you can hear me, help us!*" Rachel's eyes flashed and went back to glowing red. "Becca, something is inside me. I can't control myself." Mike looked at Rachel, but instead of seeing Mike, Rachel saw Becca looking through his eyes. "I will show you the Way. Time will stop for us, but not for the others. I will come inside you and show you."

Rachel squinted at Mike in confusion. "How—are you doing this—how can—you help—me?" Mike smiled as he placed his hand upon Rachel's face.

Rachel was in darkness with a red mist glowing around her. She looked around in confusion and fear. A glowing purple object suddenly illuminated everything around her. She walked over to the glowing object, hearing her footsteps echo. Becca was smiling at her.

"Becca?" Rachel asked in disbelief. "What's happening?"

Becca smiled. "You are what is happening. You are evolving. My psychic powers have led us both here. Rachel, I am going to show you the Way."

"The way to what? I don't understand. Why am I evolving? I'm still just me."

"You are more than just you," said Becca, walking nearer. She took Rachel's hands. "There is more of who you are…deeper down." Rachel's hands, where Becca was touching them, glowed a faint red color from the inside as though there was fire burning in them. "Open your hands now."

Rachel let go of Becca's hands as she opened her palm. There was a small glowing red ball of flames. Rachel gazed at it in astonishment. "What—what is it?"

Becca smiled. "It's the Spirit of the Ancient Phoenix."

"The Ancient Phoenix?"

Becca held up her glowing hands. The Spirit soared up into the air, eye level with Becca. It was about the size and shape of an ostrich egg, but more like a many faceted gem that sparkled and glimmered. A fiery light illuminated the sky high above them. They looked up to find a fully-grown Phoenix hovering overhead. "When you were born," said Becca, "the Spirit in front of me was born inside of you. It has been sleeping until it was ready to finally grow, giving you time to evolve. The Birandian Phoenix above us has come to awaken your Phoenix. You're the only one who can save us. But first, you must let your Phoenix take time to grow, so you can have control when you unleash it."

The Birandian Phoenix screeched loudly as the Spirit began to grow, taking the form of a small Phoenix. Rachel walked over to the small Phoenix and began to stroke its back. "I have to wait until it grows to save the Kingdom?"

"Yes," said Becca.

"But it's so small. Won't it take time for it to grow?"

"Look," said Becca. The small Phoenix seemed to pulse then grow right before their eyes, quickly doubling in size.

Rachel looked into the eyes of Becca. "How do you know all this?" She walked closer to Becca. "You're not the same—who are you really?" Becca smiled as she began to glow a bright red. The glowing red began to expand high over Rachel. Then suddenly, the glowing was gone. What was now floating in front of Rachel made her put her hand over her mouth. A beautiful Angel, four times the size of any normal woman, was flapping her glorious, twenty-foot, red fiery wings. Her long, curly red hair was flowing down past her feet. Her dress was tight and long and swayed as she floated. The dress was bright red and had many unique designs on it. Her skin was reddish in color and it glimmered with a faint reddish light. Her lips were ruby red and her eyes, orange. Her ears were long like an Elf's. Embroidered in gold on the front of her gown were the two of the entwined diamond shapes that Rachel and the others had seen in the Temple of Destiny. They were filled in with rubies. The Angel looked almost like Flairen except for the feathery fiery wings.

"*I am who you are. I am the Sage of Fire and Magma.*"

Rachel was too stunned to speak.

"*Star was strong enough to bring you here for me and to stop time for us. Inside of you is where I continue to be. In your past, you were a Phinania: an Angel born as half Phoenix.*"

"In my past?" asked Rachel, gazing up at the Sage as though she were the most beautiful thing in the world.

"*We Ancient Sages have been reborn. You are us. You may think what I am trying to say is that you were simply chosen by Fate. You were not. You are us in every way. We created a Power that has let us be reborn in you. I am a Phinania. I am what you will soon look like in your future… because I am* you."

Rachel gasped, "That can't be true. I have no memory of being a Phinania. How can I be *you* if *you* are there in front of me?"

"*Because I am inside of you and you are inside of me. I am watching over you to make sure you succeed so we can be together again. Each one of the Ancient Sages are exactly who each of you are. Once you obtain your Final Power, you will slowly regain memory of your past, but still retain the same memory you have now. I know it is confusing, but you will soon understand."*

"So you are really me in my future form?"

"*Yes.*"

"But what if I don't choose this Path?"

"*Then that is your will.*"

"So you are relying on me—on all of us. You have created us to help you succeed. You have created us to end the Evil on Earth while you still protect the Heavens. When we obtain our Final Power from the Temple of Destiny, will you become a part of us again?"

"*Not right away. You will have to learn so much more. The Power we have created lets you be as one and lets us be as one. We both will live our own lives as we do now. But I will tell you this: I did not create you. I have been reborn—or I should say, you have been reborn. But remember, your Spirit is growing in its own direction while mine is growing in another. Now, it is time to save this Kingdom. When the Phoenix is full-grown, you will have the power to unleash it and control it. The Phoenix is also a part of you. Right now you are half Phoenix, half human, and soon to be half Phoenix, half Sage.*"

"If I am you and you are me, does that mean my parents aren't really my parents, and Rachel is not really *me?*"

"*Of course not. Your parents gave birth to you because they were the ones chosen by the stars to have you. They were the ones who showed so much love and caring toward you. They gave you the name Rachel, therefore my Spirit is not known as Rachel—but yours is. Your Spirit is moving in a different direction from where it once was with mine.*"

Rachel suddenly began to cry. "I am glad that I am still me. I love my parents more than anything and I want to get them back."

The Sage began to lower herself down to Rachel. "*You will always be who you are—you will save your parents. I must go now. Do not let the others know what has happened yet. You will know when the time is right. However, a friend I dearly miss, who you also must save, might want to be let in on the—how do I say this in your terms, on the* info!"

She winked at Rachel. Rachel laughed as she wiped the tears from her face. The Sage began to glow. "*Jasmine is the one guiding all of you right now, and watching over her Heaven at the same time. It is much closer to Earth than the other Heavens, which the rest of us Protect. Bring the other Jasmine into the Light."* The Sage was gone in a flash of light.

Rachel sighed. "Queen Jasmine? That means Raven is—" Suddenly, there was a light behind Rachel. She was still in darkness, but seeing what had to be a vision. Bulkum emerged from the Dark Matter and flew toward Josh, Jake, and Toni, who were still trying to stop the lava from destroying the Kingdom. Bulkum landed and approached the four on the ground...the view changed to the top of the volcano where Mike lay floating in the air, his hands still upon her face.

Rachel turned around and gazed at the growing Phoenix. It was one-third the size of the Birandian Phoenix. Rachel ran over to the Birandian Phoenix. "Time has started again and I'm still here. Please! You must hurry the growing process!" The Birandian Phoenix screeched. "I know you're trying your best." Rachel gazed back at the vision behind her. Jake, Josh, and Toni realized Bulkum was standing right below them. "Please, hurry. I have to help them!"

Bulkum suddenly looked down at Granite, Juhani, and Misty who lay on Becca. Bulkum smiled and began to speak. "Goodbye young ones and worthless Fairies!" He held his Boomerang up to Becca's face as it started to glow. Jake flew down and shot lightning at Bulkum, which sent Jake flying. The force field around the lava was cracking and it began to fall. Josh and Toni screamed in frustration. Bulkum was laughing as he flew away from the Birandian Kingdom.

"NOOOOO!" yelled Rachel. The Phoenixes began to screech. "She told me that I could save the Kingdom only if the Phoenix was full grown, but if it is not full grown, and if I unleash it now, will I still be able to succeed? I have to save my friends! *PHOENIX FROM WITHIN, IT IS TIME TO BE REBORN!!!"*

Rachel was now floating next to the volcano as her body turned to fire. She had become a giant Phoenix. Mike was pushed roughly backwards from the Power coming off Rachel's Phoenix. He crashed into one of the four pillars of earth that he had created. Rachel flew down at lightning speed above Toni and Josh, stopping the lava in midair only two feet above her head. Rachel soared off with the lava following. She flew straight and fast trying to get behind Bulkum before he noticed her. Bulkum turned around and swore loudly. Rachel stopped and gazed in his eyes.

"A Sage? A Phoenix—but how?"

"*Release the Fairies!*" yelled Rachel. Her voice was squeaky like a Phoenix.

"No!" yelled Bulkum, "I'll use them against you!" He held the Boomerang up and three green beams shot from it hitting Rachel. Rachel absorbed it into her fiery body. "But…how?" screamed Bulkum.

Rachel stretched out her fiery-clawed foot and snatched the Boomerang from Bulkum. She threw it up in the air where it began to glow with an intense green light. Flairen, Thor, and Merlin broke free! They each grabbed a hold of the Boomerang and headed over to the Birandian Kingdom.

Rachel blew fire from her beak. It hit Bulkum and he screamed in pain. She then flew over and sped all around him, slashing as hard and as fast as she could with her taloned feet. She raised her wing and the lava trailing behind her gathered up into a huge ball and struck Bulkum right in the chest. He gasped once, and then Bulkum's skin burned off, revealing a glowing black skeleton with black wings. It was consumed in Dark Matter and began to expand. Flairen flew up to Rachel. "You must save the others. Your Power has triggered his Darkness to use in its final attack before it is destroyed."

Josh, Toni, and Jake stood next to Becca with their Fairies. They gazed at Rachel in her Phoenix form, and were stunned at what she had just become. They were grabbed by a fiery light that shot past them and made everything they saw became blinding. Rachel held Becca, Jake, Toni, and Josh with their Fairies, including Granite, safely within the outline of her flaming body. She gazed around trying to find Mike. She looked behind her at Bulkum as the Darkness suddenly exploded outward into three beams, each heading for one of the Kingdoms. "Nooo!" yelled Rachel. She spread her wings trying to protect the Birandian Kingdom from the powerful beam. The black beam struck her and she screamed in pain. They were all knocked unconscious.

Chapter 27— After Shock

Rachel, Jake, Becca, Toni, Josh, and their Fairies woke suddenly, hearing a familiar voice. "Young Sages—you were able to save some, but I'm afraid—not all." Simone was hovering above them, her bright red wings leaving a trail of small red stars. The teens were outside lying on a grassy field. It was now light out—morning had come.

Josh had a pain in his stomach. He sat up and discovered that he had been laying on his mighty Boomerang. He picked it up and stared at it intently. "All of these terrible things happened—because of this..." His hand glowed and the Boomerang disappeared.

The rest of the teens stood up and looked to where the Birandian Kingdom should have been. There, in its place, were only large pieces of rubble and one tilted, broken pillar that Mike had created. They looked at the Emerald Kingdom but nothing was there. They stood there shocked, eyes watering.

"Was Mike able to survive?" asked Granite, staring at Simone, hoping the worst had not happened.

Simone sighed. "The blasts were aimed at all three Kingdoms. My soldiers and I regained consciousness in time to use the rest of our Power to save our Kingdom. With the help of the Rainbonians, we were able to succeed. Young Cyclone was able to restore our Power just in time, like he promised. The Phoenix, or I should say—young Flare, tried to take in the blast from Bulkum. It caused her much pain, and she accidentally deflected a more Powerful beam at the Birandian Kingdom, destroying it completely."

Rachel started to cry, collapsing to the ground, realizing that Mike was gone.

"I'll let you be alone for now. I must speak with Bulkest and the Emerald King." Simone flew off, leaving the others in a mist of pink stars from her exquisite wings as she headed off toward her palace.

"I should have been there to help Mike, but it was his wish that I didn't follow," sighed Granite. Thor flew over to comfort him.

Becca began to cry as she went over and hugged Jake. Tears ran non-stop down Toni's face. Her hand began to glow as a long lethal spear made of ice appeared in her hand. She walked over to Rachel and held it to her throat, her face soaked with tears. Rachel shut her eyes, tears rolling down her face, not bothering to defend herself. "*Give me one good reason why I shouldn't kill you*!""

"Toni, calm down!" yelled Misty.

Jake ran over to Toni filled with rage. He took the ice spear from her and broke it with his knee, snapping it in two. "Do you think she killed him on *purpose*? Do you think she destroyed the Kingdom on *purpose*? She was trying to save *us* and save the Kingdom at the same time. Without her, all of us would be *dead*."

Toni sobbed and put her hands over her face. "*I'm sorry Rachel. Mike's gone—why did he have to leave us?*"

Rachel stood up and hugged Toni and they rocked and cried together. "*I tried to save him—I was too late—I couldn't control myself.*"

Purple lights began to travel from the Skytanian Kingdom over to the Birandian Kingdom. The others stayed put as they watched Becca and Juhani fly off. Josh walked over to Jake, tears in his eyes. "I'm sorry, man," he said putting a hand on Jake's shoulder.

Jake sighed as tears rolled down his face. Dark clouds appeared in the sky and thunder echoed. "*Me too…*"

"You sense it too?" Becca asked Juhani excitedly, flying as fast as she could towards the broken pillar. Her face was red and damp beneath her smile.

"Of course," Juhani replied. "I just hope it's him." They flew past piles of jumbled boulders and earth and the sad remains of several houses as they descended to land on top of the leaning pillar. All of the rubble was mystically floating just like before. They landed and came face to face with Bulkest.

Becca stared at him. "What are you doing here, Bulkest? Queen Simone has been looking for you."

Bulkest sighed. "No, she hasn't. I told her I'd be here looking around. Why are you here?"

Becca frowned. "I sensed someone over here, and I was hoping to find a dear friend—it looks like it was just you."

Bulkest smiled. "*Just* me? And what would you consider me—a walking, talking lizard?"

Becca smiled, "I do have a question that's been on my mind for a while—the Phoenixes at the edge of the Kingdom—what were they doing?"

Bulkest sighed. "They were there to protect the Kingdom. But they can only do it if we are there to help them."

Becca raised her eyebrows. "Did they survive the blast?"

"Yes," sighed Bulkest. "They were able to make their way safely to Skytania."

Becca nodded, relieved. "I'm sorry about your Kingdom. I truly am—we did our best to save it."

Bulkum grinned. "Silly girl, you did save our Kingdom—or I should say the person you are looking for did."

Becca's eyebrows lowered. "What are you talking about? Can't you see that your Kingdom is in ruins and our friend is dead?"

Bulkest laughed. "Dear child, did you not look around you?"

Becca sadly gazed around her in all directions. "What is there to see but rubble?" she sighed.

"Look on the other side of the pillar. You must pay more attention to what is around you." Bulkest pointed to a large rock at the base of the column.

Becca looked confused but she and Juhani walked down the slanting column and over to the rock. Becca gasped. The rock was in the shape of Mike! He was lying on the ground with his arms up, holding a large seed. Becca went down on her knees and started to cry.

"Wait!" said Juhani to Becca. Juhani landed on the seed. "I sense life in this seed *and* in this rock!"

Becca quickly got up as Bulkest walked over. Bulkest walked to the stone figure of Mike and placed his wing upon Mike's head. "He is still alive. He has used his Power to turn himself to stone, saving himself. The only problem is—he has not gained enough Experience to know how to release himself from this stone form. Therefore, *he* can not turn himself back to normal."

"How does he get back to normal then?" asked Becca, running her hand along Mike's face.

Bulkest looked at Juhani. Juhani yelled in a magically amplified voice. "GRANITE! COME QUICKLY!"

Granite looked to the sky as he heard Juhani's voice. The others looked up too. "Was that Juhani?" asked Thor.

"Yes," said Granite. "I must go. The rest of you may follow if you wish." Granite soared off as fast as he could toward the stone pillar. Thor flew over and rested on Jake's shoulder.

"Should we follow?" asked Jake. "I mean, I want to be there if they need me."

"Whatever you believe, Cyclone. I will always follow," said Thor.

Jake looked toward the others, who were standing in a group watching him. Shadows flickered over them as gray thunderclouds passed overhead. "Let's go, guys."

* * * * * * * *

"Do you think Granite will be able to save him?" asked Becca, worriedly.

"I do not know the answer to that question," said Juhani, now sitting on the black seed in Mike's stone hands. "I just hope he can. He *is* the Ancient Fairy of Earth. I hope he will have the Power to revive him."

Becca felt something soft land on her shoulder. She looked over and saw Granite staring down at Mike. She looked behind her and saw the others land on the pillar. They walked over, stood next to Becca, and looked at Mike frozen in gray stone. Thunder shook the sky and lightning struck in the distance. It started to drizzle. "Are you doing that, Jake?" asked Becca sighing.

"Yeah," said Jake. "I can't control myself—this is my mood. Can you save him, Granite?"

"I will try." Granite flew off Becca's shoulder and landed on the black seed next to Juhani. Juhani flew away and hovered over Becca. Granite began to glow very brightly as he touched the stone hand of Mike. Mike glowed yellow as the stone slowly began to crack. Suddenly, the stone shattered, revealing a lighter grayish color underneath. Mike's body wasn't solid stone, just covered in a thick layer of granite.

"What is it, Granite?" asked Flairen, flying off Rachel's shoulder.

Granite stepped back and stopped glowing, revealing his true form without any glowing light around him. The rain came down harder, drenching him. He looked completely miserable—as though he had never been in more pain. "He has become granite—I cannot change stone into human flesh—I do not know why he chose granite to turn himself into." Granite fell to his knees and began to weep. The teens choked on their pain and sorrow. Tears ran down their faces. The Fairies flew off the teens' shoulders and circled around Granite.

Thor knelt down next to him. "You are strong, Granite—but your sorrow has overcome you. You still have Hope inside you—and the rest of us are going to help you magnify that Hope." Granite looked up at him. "Granite—it is time we used a Power from within that we have never tried using before."

Granite's eyes went wide. "But—we don't know if it will work. Ororo isn't here to help us—and if it doesn't—and something goes wrong, there is a possibility that we might d—"

"We have Hope though," smiled Juhani, tears in her eyes. "As long as we have Hope—we can *succeed*!"

Jake walked up to Granite. "*We* have Hope for all of you also—it will give you the additional strength you need." Granite stood up and shut his eyes. He was standing nobly again—mightier than ever.

Becca stepped forward. "Not only do we have Hope, but also *Faith* in all of you*!*" The Fairies stood up and stared at Jake, Becca, and the others.

"Please," said Toni, tears falling down her face. "*Save our friend...*"

Chapter 28— A Night's Knights to Remember

All the Fairies began to glow as they circled around Granite, shooting radiant beams of light from their hands into the sky. The beams merged together creating a single ball of blinding light. The beams stopped and the light dimmed. In its place were three rings banded together to form an unusual symbol with seven gaps.

The teens gasped and took a step back. Bulkest was even shocked. Becca stared at the symbol, her eyes glowing as if trying to gain more Knowledge. "Is that the Symbol of the Sages?—But I thought the fourteen diamond stars were?—why would the Symbol appear now?"

The Symbol of the Sages glowed brighter and brighter until it shot its own beam down to the Fairies, hitting Granite on top of the head. He began to scream and wail. The rest of the Fairies vibrated and shut their eyes, trying to hold the Power steady.

The teens had no idea what was going on—what were the Fairies doing? Granite's screams grew louder and the other Fairies started clenching their teeth and moaning. Jake shook in fear—he could feel their pain. Not only could he feel what the Fairies were feeling, but also the helplessness of standing there doing nothing—not knowing how to help. He suddenly got down on his knees and folded his hands in prayer. He looked to the right and realized that Rachel was praying right next to him—the Spirit of the Phoenix glowing around her. The Spirit of the Rainbonian began to glow around Jake and it hummed as though praying with him. The others, including Bulkest, also knelt alongside them and began to pray.

The teens were glowing brightly as a ray of light from each of them sprouted from their bodies and connected to each of their Fairies. The teens were linking their Spirits with their Fairies, giving them more strength. The teens did not know what they were doing or how they were doing it—all they knew was that they were somehow helping the best they could. The Fairies shot a beam of light at Granite supporting him, giving him more Power while draining their own strength.

All of the Fairies, except Granite, stopped glowing and fell to the ground, unconscious. However, Granite was still floating in the air, glowing brighter than ever. The teens' links of light were now focused on Granite—they were lending him their strength. The teens squinted their eyes shut as they felt the pain of their strength ebbing away. Granite's eyes burst open and his hands shot down to his sides—severing the links of light from the teens. The teens stopped glowing and collapsed to the ground, breathing heavily.

"*Enough!*" Granite yelled. His voice was deep and serious. "You have given me all the strength I need. Because of you young ones—you were able to keep the other Fairies from proceeding past the point where it would have cost them their lives."

The teens crawled over to the unconscious Fairies and cradled them in their hands. The glow from Granite now reached all the way to the ground, continuing to grow in brilliance and intensity. They shielded their eyes and turned away. When the light dimmed, the teens opened their eyes and gazed at a full-grown Granite. The teens stood up and stared. Granite was four times the size of a human and seemed stronger willed by his stance and facial expressions. His golden wings were now feathered—they lit up everything around. His powerful and stunning armor made him look even mightier.

"Granite!" shouted Becca, shocked, "you look amazing."

Granite smiled, but his eyes were still damp with sadness. "Thank you, Star." He turned around and faced the granite form of Mike. "Now I must save him." Granite raised his glowing hands, then placed them on Mike's forehead. The glowing stopped, and Granite stepped back. Upon Mike's stony granite forehead was the Three Golden Ring symbol, glowing a bright yellow. Granite got down on his knees, shut his eyes, and began to pray aloud. "*My seven Lords—my seven old friends, please hear me. This young Sage's soul has been trapped beneath the granite. He has not gained enough Experience to learn how to release himself. Forgive me, please, for borrowing a Gift of yours, the Knowledge of power to free him. But I must do what I must…*"

Granite's eyes opened again, but this time they were glowing. Beams of light struck Mike from Granite's eyes and Mike floated high into the air, still holding the seed in his hands. The symbol on his forehead shone, sending light rays all through the granite, cracking it. The granite burst apart revealing an unconscious Mike, floating in the air. Granite stood up and raised his hands. "Dear Quake—Awaken!"

Mike's eyes opened. He fell to the ground, the seed falling from his hands and rolling away. Granite helped Mike to his feet. Mike looked up at him in amazement. He didn't realize what had just happened. Tears rolled down his face. "Is everyone alright?"

Granite walked to Mike and looked down upon him nobly. "We are fine. We are just glad that you are okay. I almost lost you—I will never leave you again."

Mike stepped back from Granite and looked him straight in the eyes. "I'm sorry I had to put you and the others through this—I just didn't want you all to end up like me—then both of us would have been like this—*forever*." Mike looked over at Rachel whose face was very red from all her tears. "I know you saved the others—I am glad you didn't spend time looking for me—you and the rest would have been destroyed…"

Rachel ran over to Mike and hugged him, crying on his shoulder. "I am so sorry—I didn't know if you were dead or not—it was horrible!" Becca walked over to Mike and punched him on the shoulder. Toni then ran over and kicked him in the shin. They both yelled at him, in stereo, "don't ever do that to us again!"

Mike laughed hard. "For some reason, I'm glad to have the pain back—I'm just glad we're all together again." Toni and Becca hugged him and then Jake and Josh walked over and hugged him as well, happy that he was alive. Mike looked over at Granite. The other Fairies had regained consciousness and were hovering around him. "Granite?"

"Yes?"

Mike walked over and picked up the black seed. He hugged it tightly to his chest. "How long will you remain like this?"

Granite laughed. "I do not know. This is the first time I have been on Earth in this form."

"Well then!" laughed Mike. He held up the black seed and walked over to Bulkest. "You know what this is, don't you?"

Bulkest laughed. "It is our new beginning."

Mike looked over at Granite. "I guess it's time we gave you a final gift..." Mike and Granite soared off, high above the others, while the rest of the group climbed up on the tilted column to get a better view of the action. The Fairies flew to the teens' shoulders. Josh's eyes flashed green and his face lit up with amazement. He whispered into Merlin's ear, grabbed Toni's arm, and pulled her and Misty away from the others.

Mike held up his glowing hands and the black seed floated high above him. "Granite—I can't do this without you..."

Granite laughed. "Of course you can, young Quake. It would just be more difficult." Granite held up his glowing hands and shut his eyes. Mike did the same. The others were gazing up at Mike and Granite, unsure of what they were doing.

Bulkest's face lit up as the black seed began to glow a bright yellow. The light expanded more and more, faster and faster. The teens got just a glimpse of green vines spreading with the light.

"What is he doing?" asked Rachel.

Flairen smiled at her. "Because of you—he was able to give them a better home..." Rachel stared at Flairen but then her eyes widened. She understood.

A blinding flash lit up all around. Mike and Granite covered their eyes with their hands. Warmth and mist circled them. Even with their eyes closed, they could hear the sounds of running water: a waterfall and a running river. They breathed fresh air and could smell green growing things all around them. They opened their eyes and gazed in wonder at the new Kingdom. They were on the pillar that Mike had created, but it was now resting in an open field of long grass.

The teens gasped in awe as they gazed around them exploring every new detail. Instead of a volcano, there was a softly rounded mountain of green. An enormous lake was on the top of the mountain with a river running down through fields of grass, trees, and blooming fruit and flowers.

Mike looked at Granite and smiled. They were still hovering in the air. "A job well done again, Granite."

Granite laughed. "There would be nothing here, if it were not for you…but where did you get the seed?"

Mike shut his eyes as though thinking. "I—I don't know…I was unconscious and then, when I woke up, I realized I had it. I had to turn myself to granite to have the slightest bit of hope of surviving the devastation. But what I still don't get is—how the seed survived with me. How would you explain that?"

Granite sighed. "Inner power is far more exquisite and unexplainable than anything I know. Desperation often can tap previously unknown Powers. It is an endless journey…yet there is no beginning." Mike looked down at the others. They were staring up at him with smiles on their faces. Mike looked at Granite and laughed. They quickly descended to the others.

Bulkest walked forward to Mike and held out his wing. "You have given us a gift far more priceless than any other. My people can now get to work building new homes."

Mike shook the hand on Bulkest's wing. "It is the least I can do after all that has happened. But I couldn't have done it without *them*." Mike looked back at his friends. "Without them—none of this would have been possible."

Bulkest looked over to the others. "All of you have my thanks. I wish there was something I could do to show you how grateful I am for all that you have done."

Mike laughed. "What we've told everyone else is to have Faith in us—believe in us—we will always be here to bring Hope to this land. We may be new at this whole thing, but we're trying our best."

Bulkest laughed. "I have always had faith in the Sages, but you proved to me who you really are…" He looked at the teens and then at the Fairies. "And my Spirit has been raised." Bulkest looked out toward the Skytanian Kingdom and saw Simone and the Emerald King flying towards them on the stone viewing platform created for the race. They landed on the pillar, stood up from their chairs, and gazed around at the new face of the Birandian Kingdom.

"My word!" yelled the Emerald King. "The Heavens have given you another gift, Bulkest!"

Bulkest laughed and looked toward the teens. "They most certainly have."

Simone gasped. "Your people will no longer have to stay at my Kingdom! They will be able to rebuild and create a new beginning!" Simone laughed as her red wings sprouted from her back. "I am on my way to tell your people the fantastic news!" She took off quickly to the Skytanian Kingdom.

King Absoulah walked over to Bulkest and hugged him. "I am so happy for you..."

"Well..." said Bulkest. "Your people are welcome to come to my Kingdom anytime."

The Emerald King sighed, and his face went pale. "My people are gone..." Bulkest opened his beak but said nothing. King Absoulah sighed again. "This is all my fault...I trusted Bulkum—and he ended up taking over my life, my Kingdom, and my mind!" He clenched his fist. "Now because of me....the people who trusted me most are no more. No one will ever see the Moniques again. I have failed them," he said dejectedly.

Josh and Toni walked forward with their Fairies—they were both smiling brightly. The Emerald King noticed them and his face lit up. "Ahh...I almost forgot! Here are your one thousand gold pieces, useable in any Mythical land!" He reached into his robe, pulled out a bulging leather sack, and gave it to Josh.

Toni laughed. "Actually your Majesty...that's not why we have come to you."

The Emerald King lowered his eyebrows. "What do you mean, dear child?"

"Well," said Toni eyeing Josh, "you should never assume that something you love is truly ever gone."

Misty and Merlin flew off the teens' shoulders and hovered in front of the Emerald King. Misty sighed. "She is right...just because you can't see it...doesn't mean it isn't really there." The Emerald King didn't say anything but just stared at Misty and Merlin. The other teens were staring at them also...they didn't know what they were talking about—the Kingdom was obviously gone—what were they trying to accomplish?

Merlin laughed. "The Kingdom is there…It is like the wind…you can't see it—but you can feel it!"

Josh pointed to where the Emerald Kingdom should have been. "Your Majesty, look at your Kingdom."

The King turned his head and stared in the direction Josh was pointing. "I am seeing just an endless sky," he said sadly.

Toni stepped next to the King. "Your Majesty, a Promise made by a Mythical beast is always fulfilled. Myth made a Promise to a beast, setting all those free from Darkness if he succeeded in answering its riddle."

Josh closed his eyes. The King, along with everyone else was confused—and yet Toni, Josh, Merlin, and Misty were still smiling. Josh opened his eyes. "He is not sure whether it is safe to reveal what he is hiding. We have to let him know."

The King stared at Josh—he wasn't confused—but he looked as though he understood but couldn't believe it at the same time. "How can you be so *sure*?"

Josh grinned. "Your Majesty, I am the Sage of all Mythical Beings. I know what things happen and when they happen." Josh reached for the Emerald King's hand. He placed his own hand upon the King's hand and they both began to glow green. Josh let go as the King clenched something in both hands. "*Let him know that everything is safe…*" Josh whispered.

The King stared at Josh and the others, and then threw his hands up into the air releasing a white glowing dove. It flew high and banked gracefully. Suddenly—from where the Emerald Kingdom had been… appeared millions of glowing white stars. They circled like a tornado through the sky then collided in a blinding flash. The glare faded, revealing a beautiful Kingdom of green—the Emerald Kingdom!

Everyone gasped in awe. The King stood there shocked as tears rolled down his eyes. "But how?"

The others stepped forward and also looked at Toni and Josh, confused and yet excited. Jake placed his hand on Josh's shoulder. "Who saved it?"

Josh laughed. "A contestant in the race. He was the Light Elf—the beast that he flew was the white dragon. He was captured in the Dark

Matter, unable or unwilling to escape. I answered the riddle correctly—the beast showed all those in the Darkness the way out—including me. It freed us. Knowing that a powerful blast was coming his way—the Elf protected your Kingdom."

Merlin stared at the Emerald Kingdom. "Go to your Kingdom now—find the savior—and give him a thousand thanks." The King nodded as he began sobbing, and then suddenly jumped up and down with excitement. He ran to his platform and soared off, making his way back to his Kingdom. Josh stared back at everyone else. "This means that we haven't lost anything—except for *Drake*."

Toni hung her head down and shut her eyes. "At least he found out the Truth about his past—and he finally felt and *saw* the Good that was deep inside himself. Now he is on Peace's side. He is traveling this land in Spirit…helping the other Guardians guide us in every step we take." Toni looked over toward the Emerald Kingdom and focused on the Emerald Woods. "That reminds me…we have a debt to pay to a very special someone."

Toni looked at Josh who was holding up the leather sack, staring at it. He laughed. "You read my mind Toni." His eyes flashed green as he held his head up and stared at the Skytanian Kingdom. A small white object was flying quickly from the Kingdom heading their way.

Rachel pulled on Josh's arm. "Where are you going?"

Josh looked at his sister. "I promised a warlock that I would give him the prize money if I won. He was kind enough to give me Gladius free of charge." He looked at Toni. "Toni and I will meet the rest of you back at Skytania. We shouldn't be that long." Gladius came soaring over Toni's head and galloped down the stone pillar. She daintily stepped off onto the grass, snorting and sniffing. Toni followed and hopped up on Gladius, waiting for Josh.

Josh hugged Rachel. "I am glad you're alright. When you lost control…I thought I lost you."

Flairen smiled and ran her hand through Josh's hair. "You can't lose your sister. We are the same and I will always be by your side."

Josh grinned and walked down the column to get up on Gladius where she was grazing in the long grass. Josh and Toni waved to everyone as they made their way through the morning sky to the Emerald Kingdom.

Chapter 29— A Final Loss But A New Hope Gained

Toni and Josh arrived at the edge of the Emerald Woods and Gladius landed next to Jeeves's hut. Josh walked to the door and was about to ring the bell when he noticed that the door was open but not latched. Josh pushed the door the rest of the way open and walked inside closely followed by Toni. The hut was quite dark inside, since no fires burned and all the windows were shuttered. "Hello?" called Merlin from his shoulder. There was no reply.

"He must have gone into Emerald City," sighed Josh, disappointed. There was a loud crash and tinkling of glass from their left. Josh turned his head and saw Toni lying on the floor. "Are you okay?" he said hurrying over to help.

Toni laughed as she pushed herself up. "Yeah, I just tripped ove—" She and Misty screamed and put their hands over their mouths. In the glow of both Fairies, they could now see Jeeves lying on the floor, partly under the workbench, in a jumble of torn pages, broken crockery, and smashed bottles. His legs, with their striped stockings, angled out into the room.

Josh ran around to the other side of the pile to try and locate one of Jeeves' hands among the mess in order to feel for a pulse. He gently placed it back down on a nest of old quills and a tear fell from his eyes. Jeeves was pale and his eyes were wide open. Josh bent over him and looked closely at his neck. There seemed to be bloody scratches and bruises all the way around his neck—someone had strangled him.

"He's been *murdered*," whimpered Merlin.

Toni sobbed. "It can't be. He was such a kind man, with a heart full of gold. I don't think anyone ever appreciated him—but who would do *this*?"

"*Bulkum*!" yelled Misty, through gritted teeth. "Drake whispered in his ear and then he was off to do a quick *errand*."

Josh slowly walked over to the counter, righting a stool so that he could sit down. He slammed the leather pouch of gold coins hard on the table and then slammed his head down on top of it, tears running freely from his eyes. "It's all my fault—if I hadn't asked for Gladius, none of this would have happened!"

Merlin flew down and landed next to Josh's head on the counter. "Do not blame yourself, young Myth. Everything happens for a reason—it was his time to go—he has gone to a better place..." Josh said nothing. They all stood in silence for several minutes thinking of what had happened, and yet trying to forget at the same time.

Toni sighed deeply, wiping the tears from her face with her sleeve. "So what do we do now?"

Josh stood up and walked over to Jeeves. "We bury him."

After nearly thirty minutes of digging with the shovel that Toni and Josh had managed to find at the side of Jeeves's hut, the hole was finally deep enough for his body. They were burying him in the front of his home under a pine tree. Jeeves was wrapped from head to toe in a tattered blanket they found on a bed in a side room. Toni and Josh lifted Jeeves with difficulty and placed him in the hole. They piled the dirt back and packed it firmly. They stood up and looked at their little burial ground. Gladius walked over to them, laid down next to the grave, and closed her eyes—she could feel the other's sorrow. She knew that this had been her creator—in a sense, her father.

Toni bent her knees and touched the dirt with her index finger and it became frozen solid. The ice rose up, clear and perfectly smooth, into a rectangular prism. No one would ever dig in this sacred site again. "This ice will never melt," sighed Toni. "I figure it's the least I could do for him."

Josh tenderly smiled. "It's *beautiful*." His hands started to glow a bright green as he began to carve symbols into the ice—they were hieroglyphics. He recited aloud as he wrote: "*Here lies a Warlock with a will greater than any. His heart was pure gold and his words were rock steady. He had given the Sages hope, willing to sacrifice his own life for them. Here lies a Being far more different than any—a small and simple someone—but a large and unique Spirit. Here in this grave lies Jeeves. He has the Sages' blessing. May you rest in the Heavens and let your Spirit be free and happy...and let God guide you in every step you take.*" Josh raised his hands and large white and yellow roses bloomed all around the grave.

Josh grabbed Toni's hand and held it tightly. They both bowed their heads and shut their eyes—quietly praying. Misty and Merlin were doing the same, but mumbling softly. A gentle breeze filled the air—it made Josh and Toni raise their heads and listen to it whisper through the pine trees. Gladius stood up next to them and started down the dirt path that led toward a few huts and shops at the edge of the city. They all smiled as they ran after Gladius to catch up with her.

"Somebody wanted to go for a walk," Josh laughed. He talked calmly and quieter than usual. He had just suffered the loss of someone important to him; not someone he knew closely, but someone who had helped him to succeed. They walked on in silence. As the approached a turn in the road, they overheard a conversation coming from a hut that turned out to be an outside bar. There was a tall lanky man with long white hair standing at the counter. "This is all I have...Please say that it is enough—I'm really thirsty."

"I am sorry sir, that is not enough money."

The tall figure nodded and moved away from the counter to sit down at a table. He signed deeply. Josh and Toni walked over and sat down at the table across from him. They could hear him mumbling under his breath. "*Honestly, after all I did for this Kingdom; they could at least let me have some water.*"

Toni smiled. "Is that the Elf that was in the race?"

Josh beamed. "It sure it is! He's the one that saved this Kingdom without anyone realizing it."

Josh stood up and tapped the Elf on the shoulder. The Elf turned around and stood up, staring at Josh. "Is it really *you*?"

"Yeah..." said Josh. "And what you did for this Kingdom is far more spectacular than anyone realizes."

The Elf laughed. "It is good to hear some thanks from someone. I feel weaker than ever. Never before have I used so much power, and I wasn't even sure if I would succeed."

Toni came over and stood next to Josh. "By the way," said Josh, "I'm Josh and this is Toni, Misty, and Merlin."

"It is good to meet all of you. I am Moon." Moon held out his hand, and shook Toni and Josh's hands. "Congratulations on the race, Josh…you deserved to win, one hundred percent."

Josh grinned. "Thanks, and I'm glad you were able to survive through the Dark Matter."

Moon laughed. "Same here. I thought I was never going to escape. But then this weird three-headed beast showed me the way out. I followed it through the Darkness, and I ended up right here in the Kingdom. I looked out into the night sky near the finish line when I saw the dark beam blasting my way. That's when I used my power to alter the appearance of the kingdom, making it invisible and untouchable. I ended up fainting, and woke up early this morning. I saw a white dove and I heard you contact me through my thoughts. I felt your presence all around me. That's how I knew everyone was safe."

Josh looked questioningly at Moon. "Has the Emerald King contacted you yet?"

Moon sighed. "I am afraid not. Was he looking for me?"

"Yes," said Toni. "He is looking for you to thank you for all that you have done." Toni looked at the bar booth. "I see you're trying to get some water?"

Moon laughed. "I am a bit thirsty."

Toni twirled her hand and ice began to form and shape itself into a large crystal glass. Water magically began to fill it. She handed it to Moon who immediately drank it down without hesitation. He lowered the glass, breathing heavily. "Thank you so much. The truth is... I didn't have enough money. Where I come from you don't need money. But I travel a lot now, and it's hard to get around without some kind of currency."

Josh smiled and reached into his pocket to pull out the leather sack of coins. He held it out to Moon. "Please except this."

Moon stepped back, shocked. "Are you kidding? Is that your winnings? That's a thousand gold pieces! I could never accept that from you!"

"But we don't need it," said Toni sternly. "It's not going to do us any good, since we're not staying in the Kingdoms in the Sky."

"I cannot take it—it is not right. But I must thank you for your offer." Moon laughed as he looked over toward Emerald City.

Josh looked at Toni and winked. "Well Toni, I guess we can throw it in the ocean since nobody wants it."

Moon looked at Josh. "Are you kidding? Why would you do that?"

"Well, like I said," said Josh. "It's useless to us—you can either take it or let the ocean have it." Josh threw the sack at Moon's chest.

Moon stared at the sack, and smiled brightly. "I don't know what to say. This will really help me out. You do not realize how much I appreciate this."

Toni laughed. "What you're feeling right now? Multiply that by one thousand, and that's how much we appreciate what you have done."

Moon was humbled by their remarks. "I suppose so…I guess I better go find the King since he is looking for me." Moon noticed Gladius grazing in the field. His face lit up. "That Unisus is simply beautiful. I've never seen anything quite so spectacular." He looked back at the teens. "So, where are you off to?"

"Back to Skytania," said Misty. "Right now, the Young Ones have finished their tasks, and they need to get some much needed rest before departing on their next adventure.

"Very well," Moon nodded and raised his hands, bidding farewell. "I thank you for your gratitude, and I hope that I will see you again."

"You will!" said Merlin. "One of our adventures will lead back to you."

Moon laughed. "I can only Hope." He walked off toward the palace in the Emerald City, waving goodbye to Toni, Josh, Merlin and Misty.

"Do you think it was right to give the money to him?" asked Josh, glancing at Merlin.

"Most certainly," Merlin looked over at Misty. "He needed it. He may have lied about saying that everything where he came from was free, but that was only because he did not want to make himself look needy. But come, we must find the others and get some rest."

Josh nodded as he and Toni walked over to Gladius and hopped on her, soaring back into the afternoon sky. They glanced back at the glorious Kingdom of green, for they could feel that this was the last time that they would walk on it in a long time…

Chapter 30— Apocalypse and the Seven Lords

Becca, Rachel, Mike, and Jake were waiting at the edge of Skytania with their Fairies for Josh and Toni. Gladius came soaring gracefully through the air and landed lightly in front of the others. Toni and Josh slid down and turned to watch Gladius take off again for an evening jaunt on her own. They turned toward the others and smiled dimly. Granite was back in his original form and he lay proudly on Mike's shoulder.

"So," said Jake, "were you able to repay your debt?" Toni and Josh looked at each other and said nothing.

"What happened? Is something wrong?" asked Becca anxiously.

"It looked like Bulkum got there before us. He must have figured out that Jeeves was the only one who could create such a beast, and by the time we got there…it was too late," explained Toni sadly.

Becca put her hand over her mouth. "I am so sorry."

Josh smiled. "He's in a better place. We can't change the past…but for him a new future begins—but this time in the Heavens."

Rachel walked over and hugged her brother and then Toni. "We need to rest, guys. But first, we're going to obtain some Knowledge pertinent to the next part of our journey. We decided we should hear it all—right here—right *now*."

The grass beneath their feet quivered and then the teens were lifted up by a giant daisy-like flower that grew and expanded from one of the thousands of other flowers below. They stretched out and lay resting comfortably in the sun on its cushiony center with their backs against the arch of the petals. They had a marvelous view of the meadows spreading out from the new city of Birandia on the hill. Josh slid down so he could look up and watch Gladius gliding and swooping like an angel and chasing the occasional bird or butterfly.

The Fairies flew to the middle of the flower and circled around each other, stretching and yawning. They were *all* exhausted. They had gone for almost two days without sleep. The thought of acquiring more Knowledge was exciting, but at the moment, seemed exhausting. But, they knew there was more to learn for the Cause of Good, and the sooner the better. Thor sighed heavily as he watched the six teens resting calmly, eyes half-closed in the sun. He shook his head, irritably, knowing that what he needed to explain would be difficult, but the teens *had* to understand—they had gone through too much to have so little Knowledge about the importance of what was really happening in the grand scheme of things. There was more that they needed to learn about themselves and their abilities that was unique; like an exquisite work of art lying just beneath the surface that they had yet to study and understand. Now was the time.

Rachel opened her eyes and stared at Flairen. Rachel knew something the others didn't. She wanted to tell them, but she knew she should speak with Flairen first. She waited patiently for the Fairies to stop whispering and quietly arguing amongst themselves. She could tell that they were trying to decide how much information to give them and how, exactly, they were going to explain it. Rachel didn't know whether the Fairies were going to talk about what she had found out, or whether they were going to explain something different. She didn't know, but she was tired enough to wait.

Thor broke the silence with another deep sigh. The Fairies lined up opposite the teens, standing up on the petals. "Very well," he said when they were situated. "Do you wish to ask any questions before we begin?"

"Well," said Jake, "Bulkum said that he was one of the Seven Lords of the Ancient and that he was working for...Apocalypse. What are we really up against?"

Thor looked at the other Fairies and nodded. "The word 'apocalypse', as you know, means the end of the world through catastrophe and disaster caused by the ultimate battle between Good and Evil. It is also used as another name for any powerful Evil that threatens to bring an end to this Universe. The Apocalypse Bulkum is talking about was created by Satan to be his apprentice. He was the leader of the Dark forces and was the one that sent the Seven Lords to create havoc upon the Earth. Apocalypse hoped that in the process of spreading Hatred and terror, they would find a way to corrupt the Sages and take over the Heavens."

"He sent them from Hell?" questioned Becca. "So…Hell is real?"

"In a way it is—but like the Heavens, there are many Darkened worlds," said Juhani. "Hell is made up of many Evil sanctuaries, just as Heaven has sanctuaries set aside for different purposes. Satan created Hell to be the final resting place for all Evil Ones, and to be a source of soldiers for his army. Anyone who did Evil would be sent down to Hell, rather than enter the endless gray realm of Limbo. The Seven Lords were created on one of the Dark worlds."

Mike was playing with several flower seeds as he listened. One of the flowers was already full-grown and kept turning to face whoever was talking. Mike looked up at the Fairies before asking, "What is the main objective of the Seven Lords? What are they trying to accomplish?"

"Their goal is to disrupt and destroy everything they can and to sacrifice as many lives, innocent or otherwise, to free their master," sighed Granite. "The Lords are trying to reawaken Apocalypse because they need him in order to rule the Universe. The more sacrifices they give—the more important the sacrifices are—the better chance Apocalypse has of being freed. Each of the Seven Lords has their own Way of Evil that allows them to assist in setting Apocalypse free! That is why we must destroy them!"

"Free? Free from where, and how will he get free just by sacrifices?" asked Toni.

"Long ago, Satan was one of the Angels the Gods set to watch over the Heavens," said Merlin, flying around in circles, hands behind his back. "Satan turned on the Gods, using his Powers to incite rebellion and upheaval on Earth, so that he could try to take over the Heavens. The Gods decided that the destruction he had caused was so great that his punishment was to be cast down to the Darkened Lands to live for eternity. When Satan was banished, Apocalypse was banished with him because he was known to be Satan's apprentice. The Ancient Sages were created before Satan even existed, and were the ones who sealed the doors to the Darkened Lands because they were the only ones, at that time, who possessed enough Power."

"Apocalypse gains strength with every sacrifice his Lords make of the innocent. The more horrible and brutal the death, the greater the power. The Lords seek any means that will make them stronger, giving them the Power to win any battle or challenge that comes their way," said Misty. She shivered.

"Bulkum," said Flairen, "sent his final attack in hopes that he could take more lives before he was sent back by Satan. But he failed, and was sent to the Dark World where Apocalypse will punish him. The Dark World is like Hell for those in the Darkened Lands. None of the Evil Beings like going to the Dark World."

"So...is Satan more powerful than Apocalypse?" asked Josh.

"Yes," said Merlin.

"Then why aren't the Seven Lords trying to release Satan?" asked Josh, confused.

"Because they aren't loyal to Satan. Apocalypse was created by Satan, who in turn, created the Dark Lords," replied Merlin.

"So, essentially, Satan and Apocalypse have been down there for thousands of years, cast aside and forgotten by the other Gods, seething and plotting in the Darkness," said Mike, two flowers now nodding their heads along with his words.

"Yes," said Granite. "But, you Sages are still his greatest foe because you have more Knowledge."

"How can we have more Knowledge than him?" asked Jake. "We're all between fourteen and fifteen years old and we've only had this Power for about a month! How can we have *more* Knowledge?"

"You will know soon enough, young Cyclone," said Thor. "When your Destiny arrives."

Flairen looked questioningly at Rachel. "Young Flare, you haven't said a word!"

"Well," said Rachel, "I need to talk to you later, Flairen, in private. But I have to know...Cleopatra is one of the Seven Lords, isn't she?"

Flairen's eyes went wide since she didn't expect to hear this question. "She is, and that is why you must seek her and learn from within how to use your Power to defeat her! She captured your parents hoping to lure you to her to take control of you. Cleopatra means to use you to find more sources of Power so she can sacrifice more innocent lives to release Apocalypse. She will keep your parents healthy as long as she believes that you will come for them—that is a fact. But she doesn't know exactly who or what is coming for her! And, she doesn't know you have enough Power to defeat her."

Flairen sighed deeply and looked at the other Fairies, pausing to watch Thor while she spoke. "There is another truth I must tell you about her… Apocalypse has managed to create a break in the Seal on the Doors to the Darkened Lands, letting his Seven Lords escape. Once the Lords have killed enough and sacrificed enough souls, Apocalypse will gain enough strength to completely break the Seal and escape."

Thor floated high up above the other Fairies and looked down upon the teens. "Your objective is to obtain the Final Power from the Sages' Temple of Destiny. There, you will learn much and become more Powerful. But not only do you have to get the Final Power, but you must devise a way to Seal the Doors to the Darkened Lands forever so the Evil Ones can never break free again! You must destroy the Seven Lords and send them back to Hell. Do not let Apocalypse escape and bring Evil to our worlds. The only ones with the Power to do that are the New Sages. You are soon to be New Gods!"

The teens' mouths opened wide, in shock, but no words came out. Never had they even imagined that something like *this* would come their way! Never before had they thought that they would have to accomplish dangerous objectives in order to save the *Universe*! They had only known the Earth and its people…But now they had to consider the Good of all the peoples and Beings in the entire Universe! It made their task seem even more important, and more difficult, than ever.

"The Seven Sages were once the Fourteen Angels, right?" asked Josh, after several minutes of contemplation.

"Of course," said Merlin. "The Angels are the Sages—they are their own creation."

"So, at first they weren't Gods," said Josh. "But now, with their Power—their own Knowledge—they have become Gods."

"Correct, young Myth," Merlin beamed. Josh nodded then sat back again, deep in thought.

"So, we have to find these Seven Lords...and destroy them?" asked Rachel, disbelief in her voice.

"Yes," said Juhani.

"Why aren't the Ancients sealing the Doorway themselves?" protested Mike.

"Again," said Granite calmly, "the remaining Ancients are in the Heavens protecting and defending it against new Evil."

Mike laid down on his back on the cushy middle of the flower, crossing his arms under his head. He sighed and looked up at the sky, putting the three little flowers down on his chest where they waved in the breeze.

"And the Seven Lords are *all* on Earth?" asked Becca, looking for some assurance.

Juhani sighed deeply. "Actually…" she looked up at Thor. "No."

The teens all sat up, Mike's flowers falling in his lap.

Jake stood up and stared at the Fairies, his face growing more tense. "If they're not on Earth, then where are they? How are we supposed to destroy them if we can't find them?"

Thor smiled widely and lowered himself inches in front of Jake. "Young Cyclone—do you remember a certain promise that I made to you?"

Jake looked to the sky and thought, then his face suddenly lit up. He lowered his eyebrows and looked quizzically at Thor as though he didn't think it was really possible. "Yes… a couple of nights ago you said that you would take me beyond the stars. You really meant it!"

Thor beamed. "If I make a promise, I expect to keep it, and I expect you to do the same for me. So…yes, I shall take you beyond the stars. All of you. You possess great Knowledge now—you have learned so much in such a brief time—and yet—you still have *much* to learn." The teens were silent for several minutes

"How are we supposed to leave Earth?" asked Toni.

"You will find that out later," smiled Misty. "But what we really want you to concentrate on is getting all the Elements you need before you go to the Temple of Destiny. This is the most important thing. Not only are you doing this for others, but also for yourselves. Worry about learning more—training more—and helping more. The time will come when you will battle the Lords. The time will come where you will lose some battles, and yet, succeed in others. But we will always be by your side, guiding you—just like we requested."

Josh stared up at Misty. "You requested that the Ancients let you be the ones to guide us?"

Merlin laughed. "Of course! You could not go through this alone! We realize you have each other, but you need our help to get you through the maze when you get lost—to lead you in the right direction."

Thor's laugh boomed out. "Young ones, you have gained more Knowledge and still have more to gain. But for now, we have told you all we need to. Now you know why and what you have to do is so important to the Universe and to yourselves. Some things will change and some things will stay the same, but you must always have confidence and Faith in yourselves, so that those you are helping can have Hope. Only then can you be who you were born to be. *For the stars have definitely made you different from the Ancients.*"

The teens looked at the Fairies, confused, but knew some questions were best left unanswered. However, Rachel alone knew what Thor meant. The Sage of Magma and Fire herself had told Rachel, and she knew she had to discuss it with Flairen.

"Get some rest now, young ones," said Merlin. The teens laid back on their flower, thinking about the Knowledge that they had just received. They now knew their meaning and purpose for their lives—or at least they thought they knew...

Chapter 31— The End of an Adventure and the Beginning of a New Journey

The Fairies flew down to the teens and rested on their shoulders. Rachel nervously jiggled her foot, still unsure *what* she was going to tell Flairen or *how* she was going to tell her. "Flairen?"

"Yes?" asked Flairen, smiling.

Rachel sighed. "I need to talk to you—alone."

Flairen sighed. "I could tell something was bothering you."

Flairen and Rachel flew to the edge of the Kingdom and landed. Rachel sat down and hung her legs over the side. She looked to her left and saw that Flairen was doing the same. She laughed.

Rachel smiled brightly. "Flairen…I know who I really am."

Flairen smiled. "I thought maybe you knew, but I wasn't sure."

"When I was by the volcano and out of control, Becca used her power, not knowingly, to let the Sage of Magma and Fire into my mind to speak to me," Rachel sighed. "It was *so* real. I could feel everything."

Flairen beamed. "So what have you learned that the others do not know?"

Rachel took a deep breath. "I know that I am reborn as the actual Sage. I am exactly who she is."

Flairen said nothing and closed her eyes. "That is something I didn't want you to know yet. It is *far* too much to comprehend, much less understand. I can imagine that all kinds of questions are probably racing through your mind: not sure of who you really are or if you are even real."

Rachel smiled. "At first yes, but now...*I know*." Rachel looked at Flairen and laughed, again, at her expression. "Don't worry! My questions have been answered. I've learned that my Spirit is different from hers and so we can, and are, both growing in different directions." Rachel closed her eyes as though trying to remember. "She was so *beautiful*. I hope I turn out just like her. I almost cried thinking that I wasn't really *me*, and how my parents weren't really my parents."

Flairen suddenly flew into the air. "But that isn't true, your—"

Rachel cut her off by putting her finger up to Flairen's lip. "I know. My parents were chosen by the stars to have me. They gave me the name *Rachel* and my brother—*Josh*—and therefore, the Sages aren't known as that—but we are. She told me that we were born to protect the Earth and the lands beyond that, and in time we, and the Ancients, will come together as one again!"

Flairen laughed. "I am glad you know the Truth, but most of all—I am glad you *understand* it. You know, in a way, you are just like Flare—the Ancient one—and in another, you are far more unique and different in Spirit than she is."

Rachel smiled. "And I'm glad because of that difference. Knowing that I have my own mind and own Spirit to control, and yet, I am also a part of someone who cares just as much as I do." Rachel leaned back and looked up at the sky. "I know that I am a *Phinania*... half Phoenix and half Sage. That is why the Spirit of the Phoenix was unleashed—because it was always inside me—it was always...me."

Flairen flew up into the air above Rachel, looking down upon her. "To me, a Phinania is the most amazing of creatures. Phinanias are very rare, rarer than Unicorns or Pegasi. Something new and exciting always happens to them and those around them." She landed and laid down in the grass next to Rachel, looking up at the sky. "Even though I've only been with you for a short time, I feel so much closer to you now that you have shared this with me. Closer than I ever thought imaginable," she said softly.

Rachel smiled wide and her eyes grew damp. "I feel the same way towards you, Flairen. You have been like a sister to me—always there for me just like Josh." They fell silent. High above them they could see the Birandians and the Phoenixes returning to the Birandian Kingdom. They were all heading back to their homes, with new beginnings and new hopes. The Phoenixes called to each other, their voices harmonic and soothing to the soul. Rachel stood up. She felt warm flames spread around her as she gazed at the Birandians flying home. Flairen landed on Rachel's shoulder, even though she was still glowing with flames.

"Promise me something for now," whispered Flairen.

Rachel looked over into Flairen's red eyes. "Anything."

Flairen lowered her head. "Do not tell the others for a while. They will find out soon enough—when the time is right." Rachel nodded as she looked back up to the sky as her flames dimmed. They sat back down to watch the sun set. The sky was glowing orange and pink, but the sun was still a ball of bright yellow well above the horizon, but just dim enough to look at head on. Rachel laid back...

* * * * * * * *

A hand gently touched Rachel's shoulder. She woke and found that she was lying in her brother's arms. Flairen smiled at her. "I brought you back," she whispered. "You fell asleep." The teens all looked up, yawning and stretching, and watched the last few Birandians returning from Skytania and the Emerald Kingdom. They were all silent for about an hour, still sleepy, watching the sun sink into the horizon.

A breeze filled the air with the scents of grass and flowers and the singing of the Rainbonians echoed all around. Night had fallen and the stars came out of hiding. The moon was full and lighting up the darkened sky. The stars twinkled and danced as though feeling the rhythm of the song being sung by the Rainbonians. The teens were almost lulled to sleep once more, but their minds were too full for sleep now.

"Is it like this every night here?" asked Jake dreamily.

"It most certainly is," said Thor. "It is a remarkable place to be." Thor flew into the air, his body lighting up all around. He glowed like the moon as he pointed with his staff to a constellation in the sky. "This is Orion's Belt! He was a great God in the Ancient times, a protector of the innocent, and the key to unlocking secrets yet to be discovered."

Jake laughed. "You love the stars, don't you Thor?"

Thor looked down at Jake. "Of course, my young one."

"So much has happened to us," said Becca, looking at the others. "So many amazing things. It's almost impossible to believe, and yet, I want to let everyone know. Somehow, I want to bring my imagination and my thoughts to life and show them what we've been through."

"In time you will," said Juhani. "In time—*you will.*"

Becca's eyes narrowed as she turned to look at Juhani. Juhani stared intently back at Becca as though she knew that Becca was about to ask a question. Becca sighed and shook her head. Juhani shut her eyes and smiled. "You already know the answer."

Becca nodded. "The three rings—those are the symbols of the Seven Gods—the Seven Sages." Juhani nodded proudly as a grin swept her face. She put her arm around Becca's neck and fell silent with the others as they gazed to the sky.

Several minutes passed until Mike broke the silence once again. "I miss my parents—I miss them *so* much…"

Jake's eyes grew damp. "We all do Mike…but in a way they're always with us…we'll free them from her—I *swear it!*"

"We've completed an amazing adventure," stated Toni. "Each adventure we complete brings us one step closer to finding our parents. But there are more tasks and adventures to accomplish." She stood up and walked to the edge of the Kingdom. "I'm ready to begin another journey…A journey that will bring me one step closer to finding my mom and dad."

The others stood up next to her and joined her in staring at the forests of the Emerald Kingdom that reminded them so much of home. "Patience is a virtue, young Aquarius," said Misty. "But I have a feeling that it is one thing that will never change about you."

Toni smiled. "I have to agree with you, Misty."

"Don't worry guys," said Mike. "This adventure is over, but another one will soon begin. In time, we'll all learn more and experience enough to defeat the unthinkable."

"We were chosen to do this…" said Rachel. "Born to do this…"

"And in time…" said Jake, "there *will* be an end to all of this, but for now…" The teens and Fairies all looked up at the stars. "*We all know that a true adventure, a true journey—has only just begun!*"

* * * * * * * *

Jasmine was resting on a cloud high in the sky looking down upon the teens. She was smiling brightly and glowing as brightly as ever. Her voice whispered into the night. "*I am always watching over you, young ones. Your Destiny lies yet to unfold, and your Knowledge continues to expand. Young Flare, you have learned much, yet have much to learn. The Sage of Fire and Magma certainly loves you, as do I. To you all, I promise that your parents will be safe. My past Guardians—you have done well in protecting the young ones. Cyclone, you have done well leading your companions through difficult journeys. You are so right in saying that your adventure had just begun—but your journey still continues. Young Sages, you have been quietly evolving. A simple change has already taken place although you haven't even realized it yet, but soon you shall. Your Destiny lies far within you and more secrets shall soon be revealed. Aru Conoha Ra Nicto…you will soon learn the meaning of this. All of you have made me so proud. Remember that you must also bring one from the Darkness into the Light. Do not forget about her.*" Jasmine waved her hand and a luminous black ocarina appeared. She began to play in harmony with the song of the Rainbonians. The stars and moon were shining brighter than ever before and shadows were dancing with the light. The Light and Darkness were whole.

Jasmine closed her eyes as she looked to the stars and folded her hands together. "*Gods of the Heavens, hear my Blessing,*" *she prayed.* "*Watch over these young ones. As we all know, they are our key to the future. Help them when help is needed, guide them when they are lost, and listen to them when they pray to you. Give them the courage to start their new adventure and continue their journey. Give them the faith they need to get through the difficult times. For now that their parents are not with them, they need guardians to love them. But as we all know, Thor, Juhani, Misty, Flairen, Merlin, Granite, and lets not forget Ororo, are doing that very same thing for them. May all of us bless them throughout the Universe and beyond. Let them spread Peace and Harmony throughout the land. Let them fulfill their greatest desire, which is dearest to their hearts. Help them find their parents. Let us continue to guide them in the right direction…"*

A howl of rage filled the air. Jasmine raised her head. Bulkum's Spirit was staring at her through Evil red eyes. *"I had convinced my Lord that I could still succeed…succeed in leading the Chosen down the wrong path,"* he sneered. *"I may not be able to take over the Heavens with just you in my possession, but in time—I shall*!"

Jasmine's eyes went wide. She had realized that being away from the Heavens was risky, but she needed to bestow this special blessing upon the teens in person. "*You lie, Bulkum!"* she snarled. "*Your master didn't give you a second chance!"* An evil grin swept across Bulkum's face as he charged straight at her. "*You were not truly defeated!*" Jasmine suddenly looked down to the teens. She screamed loud enough so that they could hear her: *"Never forget, young ones—never forget the Prayer that I have given you once before—NEVER FORGET!!!"*

Bulkum's Spirit turned into a black fog as it shot into Jasmine's chest like a wide arrow, piercing her heart. Jasmine looked up at the stars through black eyes. "*She is mine now, Gods—and forever shall she be!*" Jasmine was gone in a flash of black light—for Bulkum was now her.

The teens woke up and looked all around them. Jake flew up, trying to find the source of the ear-splitting scream. It had seemed to come from nowhere and everywhere all at once. He looked down at the others. "What was that?"

Thor flew up to Jake and shut his eyes, as though he was feeling for the presence of someone. "There was only one life form here…for the voice.…the voice—it was *Queen Jasmine…*"

Printed in Great Britain
by Amazon.co.uk, Ltd.,
Marston Gate.